The Sol Empire
Volume 1
For the Want of Humanity

Vic Broquard

The Sol Empire Volume 1
For the Want of Humanity
First Edition
Copyrighted © 2018 by Vic Broquard
ISBN: 978-1-941415-82-5

What isn't fictional is the work that Humanity and Inclusion (formerly Handicapped International) is doing to help those who have suffered:
http://www.hi-us.org

Published by:
http://www.Broquard-ebooks.com
Broquard eBooks
103 Timberlane
East Peoria, IL 61611
author@Broquard-eBooks.com

For Morgan and L. Ron Hubbard

Table of Contents

Part 6

Part 1

Vic Broquard

Chapter 1 Confusions

Chicago, July 1, 2350

Fresh out of Galactic Defense Investigations, Molly "Cool Head" Parkinson followed her dream of helping people. She opened her company on the second floor of the Parker Skyscraper. As her phone chimed, the yellow touchpad on her desk vibrated from the distant roar of a spaceship lifting off from New O'Hare Spaceport.

"Molly Parkinson's Private Investigations and Security. Molly speaking. How can I help you?" She logged the call on her touchpad: 9 a.m.

"I'm with Galactic Medicine. Total Care Administration. DNA Section. I have a short assignment for you. Might take an hour or so. No danger. I'll transfer a hundred credits to you for your time. Just pay a visit to the medical examiner's office."

The voice sounds familiar, but I can't place her. A hundred for an hour? Great timing. Just paid my rent, and I'm broke again. Wait a minute. Visit the morgue? Oh heck, I really need the money.

"Okay. I'm interested. Who are you, and what am I supposed to do?"

Molly straightened and logged the address of the ME's office while the woman continued. "The victim is Sandy Ainsworth."

Never heard of her. It can't get any easier than this. "Okay, so what am I supposed to do?"

Wait, how do I help her by looking at a dead body? Maybe she doesn't know how Ainsworth died. "Look for cause of death? And who are you, anyway?" *Now I am curious.*

"All I'm asking is for you to view Sandy. She was murdered eighteen hours ago. Just look at her. That's all. And the hundred is yours. Then, if you want, call me on this number."

I love these new gadgets and this Whiz-ID unit—ah ha, she's using a burner phone. And no holographic video. She

3

mustn't be rich.

"Okay, lady. I'm game. Once I verify the money has been transferred, I'll head out."

"Hold on, Miss Parkinson. Sending it now. There. It's complete. Thank you for doing this."

This woman seems relieved, but why? Curious.

"Okay, I see the deposit. I'll leave now, but what do you really want me to do? How can I *help* you?"

"Just view the body. That's all. Then, if you want, call me back. Have to go. Bye and thanks."

Why did she hang up so quickly? She seemed worried or frustrated. Ah well, I don't know enough about her yet. Still, going to be an easy hundred.

Like most people, Molly owned an affordable-biometric-voice-activated-actualized-comm-device. Hence, everyone still called these devices "phones." While anyone could place a phone call on them, all other functions required a biometric match to its owner, which unlocked its advanced features including the personal details of its owner's life, such as bank account, credit-debit numbers, passwords, their ID number, and so on. Molly couldn't afford one of the costliest "phones," which also streamed a 3-d holographic video of the caller, though any phone could display such sent video. However, this woman used one of the cheap, limited-function, un-actualized comm devices—untraceable and still called "burner phones."

After stowing her touchpad in her backpack, Molly headed out of her office and stepped onto the MTES—the Mass Transit Eco-moving Sidewalk system—which had been installed throughout the world in all but the smallest villages and which connected all major buildings.

Free and environmentally green, these horizontal moving sidewalks transported millions of people around the city each day and mostly replaced city streets. One could ride the MTES from Chicago to St. Louis for free, switching MTES systems at Peoria. Many brought along portable seats for the longer trips. The MTES system spanned out much like blood vessels and capillaries, usually ending within a block or two of a residential street where one would have to walk to get to a home. Here and there, an unusually wide street might still have a single lane available for the tiny, obsolete electric cars. Furthermore, the MTES had a transparent plastic roof that kept off the weather. Molly joined a throng of others.

Towering concrete, steel, and glass-sided skyscrapers, each with flat roofs, dominated the horizon. She watched an Electro-Magnetic Air Car, or EMAC, landing on a skyscraper's roof. Molly spotted one departing the roof of the Galactic Defense building and smiled. *One day, I'm gonna have my own EMAC with my logo on it.*

On a smaller scale, tiny two-person shuttles darted like gnats about the skies of Chicago, the preferred rides of corporate executives. Like most people, she ignored these luxury vehicles, priced beyond what she could afford, though their presence reminded her that she couldn't afford them. She squelched such thoughts, having decided to save for a company EMAC.

A few minutes later and not far from the ME's office, Molly failed to ignore the louder roar of a spacecraft lifting off, bound for other worlds in the Sol Empire. She involuntarily covered her ears. Flying to moons, stations, and nearby stars with their Earth-like planets didn't interest her. Besides, for Molly, such a trip was prohibitively expensive—a year's salary from her sponsor, Galactic Defense.

The roar subsided once inside the ME's building. She flashed her PI badge and told the receptionist what she wanted. After notifying the medical examiner, the young woman directed Molly to the main operations room, where the medical examiner met her. He pulled out cooler drawer number nineteen. Molly double-checked the name she'd entered on her yellow touchpad against the name on the body's toe-tag. She pressed her lips together and nodded to him.

The medical examiner stared silently at Molly's face.
What's the matter with him?
He slid the sheet off the deceased woman. The ME spoke in a monotone, though his eyes darted from the deceased's face to Molly's. "Sandy Ainsworth. Teacher, first grade. I'll give you a few minutes alone." He stepped out of the

room.

Stainless steel equipment, tables, and cooler doors filled the white room. The intense overhead light forced her to squint.

"Shit!" Though her friends called her Cool Head, Molly gasped and stared at the corpse. She'd seen dead bodies before, particularly in PI class where she learned to notice details. Molly could see cause of death—a gunshot wound to the forehead, no hiding that grim detail—but this time was different. Her skin prickled. She swallowed hard, as her throat constricted. Her eyes focused on Sandy's bloodless face.

She stared at what seemed her own face.

For a surreal moment, she felt as though nothing existed. *Is that my dead body? Can't be.* Her heart pounded. *A sister? The same hair color. But Sandy's is a bit longer. Same round face. Same thick eyebrows and full lips.* Even in death, she had Molly's silly smile.

She forced her gaze off the body and onto the deceased's chart. Sandy was also twenty-two. Molly rubbed her eyes and looked at her again, hoping this was an hallucination. Ainsworth's appearance hadn't changed.

She cursed. *What the heck's going on? Do I have an identical twin? I never did find out why I was abandoned. And I want to help others so they don't abandon their babies.*

She took a deep breath and exhaled slowly, her hands pressed against her waist. A barrage of questions raced through her mind.

Just view the body? I've been duped. Okay, Molly, focus. I'm adopted, so it's possible I could have—er had—an identical sister. Maybe that's why she left me—too many babies to care for.

The ME returned.

"What happened to her? Who did this?" Molly swallowed but couldn't relieve the feeling of constriction in her throat.

"She was murdered," he said, glancing at his watch, "about nineteen hours ago. Was she a friend, a relative?" The ME's eyes bounced between her face and Sandy's.

Molly nodded. She snapped a photo of Sandy and

allowed him to cover the body. She mouthed a thank you, left the morgue, and stepped back onto the MTES.

God, my legs are butter. I feel sick. A sister? She had to be, and now I'll never know her. Damn. Well, I need a ton more info before I call this woman back. Molly, you sure made a rookie mistake this time. You should'a got the name of the mysterious caller. Well, first stop: the police.

As she traveled along the moving sidewalks, the Lake's pungent odor assaulted her nose, and she noticed the skyscrapers dotting the skyline. Many housed the fifteen galactic-wide corporations. Her sponsor, Galactic Defense, owned one of the taller buildings.

The Sol Empire's ruling corporations had a hierarchical arrangement. Local offices ran the affairs of their geographical area; here in Chicago, the local branches occupied the lower five floors of the corporate skyscrapers.

Next, each of the empire's two dozen inhabited "worlds"—though some were moons or outposts —had a set of worldwide corporations, which oversaw these smaller branches. The Earth-wide corporations were located in Moscow.

Finally, the highest corporation offices, also located in Chicago, ran the Sol Empire and its two dozen worldwide corporations.

Molly had received her PI license from the local Chicago Galactic Defense offices on the lower five floors of the hundred-story, empire-wide Galactic Defense skyscraper.

With her mind calmer, Molly walked into the Tenth Precinct. "Hey, is Frank around?"

The desk sergeant smiled and pointed toward the detective's office. Molly marched down the hall, knocked on Detective Frank Wells' open door, and stepped inside. Amid piles of folders surrounding his computer, Frank looked up, grinned, rose, and closed the door. Two years older than Molly, he had short brown hair, a square face, and dark eyebrows—handsome, she thought. They hugged, and he kissed her forehead.

"Hey, Cool Head. Reconsidered my proposal?"

She drew a deep, impatient breath. "You know how I

feel about marriage so soon." *Do I dare get married? How can I be a mother? I can't abandon my babies.*

Friends since high school, both had been sponsored by and were obligated to Galactic Defense, the corporation that paid for their education and now paid them a monthly stipend.

She wore a gray skirt, white blouse, and low black heels, and as they held each other, he touched her concealed 9mm Glock. Guns were still in widespread use despite being antiques because few could afford laser guns and deadly blasters.

He smiled wryly. "Ah, professional look, so it's business I see. What can I do for you?" He stepped back a few feet.

"Case—well, sort of. What do you have on the murder of Sandy Ainsworth? Teacher killed nineteen hours ago—9mm to the head, if I'm not mistaken."

"Not my case but let's see what's on file. We don't have many murders, though." He brought up the case and read from his 3-d holographic computer projection. "Not much, Molly. Found on Canal Street. Body dump. No ballistics match. No clues. Open case. As I said, not much at all. Why the interest?"

His eyes darted from Sandy's face to Molly's face and back again.

"Right now, I can't say." She shrugged her shoulders and sighed, swallowing hard.

Frank's eyebrows rose. He frowned. "Crap, Molly, I've seen some freaky things before, but this—she looks exactly like you, and I mean *exactly*. Have you been holding out on me? Or do you have a sister you've never mentioned?"

Molly exhaled sharply. "Precisely why I need your help, Frank. No sisters or brothers that I know of, but I'm going to check with Mom. So, can you take a look at this case? And call me?"

He nodded, still gaping at the image in the holographic projection.

Molly smiled, turned, flipped her hair over her shoulder, and strode out of the building. She paused on the sidewalk before the MTES.

I hate being so abrupt with him, but, hell, I don't know

what's going on, and I just can't show him that.

Molly inhaled and slowly let her breath out. *That was a damned waste of time. Ainsworth is murdered and no clues. I thought Galactic Defense had eliminated serious crime.*

Calmer, she glanced at her phone. *Does my mystery caller know that Ainsworth and I look identical? I'm going to ask her right now.*

Still standing outside the precinct, she dialed the number she'd logged on her touchpad. "Molly here. I saw the body. Did you know that—"

"Meet me at Luigi's Pizza on Canal Street. Six o'clock." The line went dead, but Molly heard other voices in the background.

Maybe she's at work. Shit, that didn't go so well.

Molly headed back to her home-office where she kept the adoption papers her mother had given her when she'd moved into her new office-home. Perhaps they'd give her a clue. Maybe Sandy was her sister.

Available homes or office buildings—empty or abandoned—were abundant in Chicago and on Earth because so many people left to colonize new worlds. But her monthly stipend from Galactic Defense wouldn't cover both housing and a PI office, so she'd doubled up. Like most people, Molly didn't worry about *what* she would be asked to give back to Galactic Defense. It was always "undefined future services."

Only the destitute didn't have a sponsoring corporation; they didn't live long or were shipped off to the Mercury penal colony, along with criminals. Given a choice between the penal colony and death, criminals often chose the latter, the main reason small-time crime was a thing of the past. Few ever returned from Mercury.

In her tiny kitchen, Molly sipped Earl Grey tea to calm her nerves. She found her electronic adoption and birth certificates. *What an idiot I've been. Should have questioned them or checked on their authenticity.* Comparing the papers against the many online databases, she discovered her birth certificate was false. The hospital had no record of her birth and neither did the records from online sources. Her face flushed; her legs felt weak. *This can't be happening.*

She took a deep breath and continued. Her adoption papers were in order and legal, but contained the same falsified birth data. Frustrated and confused, Molly decided to quiz her parents. *I've always thought of them as my parents, but...* When she was in high school, Molly learned she had been adopted. Neither parent ever mentioned she had siblings, but she had never asked them. *I'm a real fool.*

She headed out of her home-office, stepped onto the MTES, and stared at the sky through the clear plastic canopy that protected riders from rain and snow. Molly gazed at the cumulus clouds in the azure sky, as two-man shuttles darted across the skies. Likewise, she didn't pay too much attention to the EMACs zooming hither and thither. But she nodded and smiled to those she passed, though images of Sandy occupied her mind.

At street junctions, Molly had to pay attention, stepping off one conveyor belt and onto the next. There, giant signs indicated routes, while periodic kiosks held large-scale maps, allowing one to easily navigate from North Chicago down to St. Louis. Plus, there was a designated "fast lane" for those who wished to walk, jog, or run.

Her parents lived miles away on Bleaker Avenue, and the ride in the Chicago air cleared her mind. Her father's sponsor, Galactic Housing, had moved them into an assisted living facility four years ago and continued to pay their expenses. Before retiring, her father had remodeled homes for that corporation.

As she entered the carpeted foyer, the receptionist called out to her. "Molly. Molly Parkinson." She waved to Molly, who walked over to the polished desk. A long hallway led to the many tiny apartments. A large dining room lay beyond the reception desk, serving those who could no longer cook their own meals.

"I was just about to call you. It's your father. He's not doing so well..." She paused to soften the blow. "Galactic Housing has set his Termination-day for next Monday."

"What? But Dad is as strong as an ox!" Molly fought a surge of unexpected emotions. "He's only sixty-five!"

"I'm so, so sorry for you, Molly. No one lives much

beyond that age."

"Can't the doctors do something for him?" Molly slapped her palms onto the desktop in both protest and denial. This was the attitude that had caused Galactic Defense to take an interest in her when she was in eighth grade, the time of her first Career Choosing, though the one that counted occurred when she was a senior in high school.

The receptionist smiled in what Molly gauged as fake sympathy. "You should visit him."

Molly nodded and headed to her parents' room, her mind racing. Although she overheard the receptionist saying, "Yes, doctor. Molly Parkinson has just arrived," it didn't register in her mind. *Isn't there some clinic up in the Twin Cities? He can't die. I love him!* She walked in and found her parents in the small living room watching the Channel Nine news on their big screen comm set.

"Hi, Mom. Dad."

Her father grunted, but her mother said, "Oh hi, Molly." Then her eyes glazed over. "They made Henry retire at sixty, you know. But then they moved us into this nice home."

Her mother wore a simple cotton day dress with flower images. Her hair was still black but with a few streaks of gray. Her father wore a brown cardigan, corduroy pants, and slip-ons. His gray-streaked hair was cut short.

Molly sighed; she had heard those words hundreds of times. She gave her mother a hug that brought her mother more into the present. That distant look in her eyes vanished. "Watching the news?"

"Yes, but there's nothing new. Oh, your father's not doing so well. His T-day will be soon. They told me. Did they tell you?"

"Yes, Mom, but isn't there something they can do for Dad?"

Her mother sighed and looked toward her husband. "He's like this all the time—a ghost of his former self. Can't get him to say anything. It's best his T-day is near. I don't want him to suffer."

Molly sighed. "I don't want him to suffer either, Mom, but can't they do something? What's wrong with him? What did the doctor say?"

"They made Henry retire at sixty, you know. But then they moved us into this nice home."

"Yes." Molly's stomach knotted every time her mother repeated herself. "What's wrong with him? What did the doctor say?"

"Dementia. We all get it sooner or later. Everyone does."

Despite the awful knot in her stomach and her fight to keep her eyes from tearing up, Molly remembered what had brought her here. "Mom, tell me about how you and Dad adopted me. Did I have any sisters?"

"You mustn't blame your father. It isn't his fault he can't have children. Let's see. Back then, Dr. Ben Hall referred us to the adoption agency Kids on Call. Yes, that was its name. Only child, they said. Strange how I can remember twenty years ago but so little else."

Her father grunted again and pointed to the comm center monitor. Molly guessed he was asking them to be quiet. She tried giving him a hug, but he didn't recognize her, only continued to grunt and point to the big screen.

"They made Henry retire at sixty, you know—"

"I know, Mom." She looked at her parents and wiped her eyes. For a moment, childhood memories of the three of them gathered around a Christmas tree rushed into her mind. She wiped her eyes again and checked to see if they had groceries in their cabinets and refrigerator. Then, she gave them each a kiss on their cheeks and stepped out of their apartment.

Molly paused at the door. *Maybe I can call someone at Galactic Medicine about Dad. Or better yet, take him to a hospital or med center. Hold on. I should call someone at Galactic Housing; they sponsor Dad. Oh, wait, I forgot; they have doctors here at the center.*

Hastily, she turned around and visited their doctor. She stormed into his office; somehow he was expecting her, motioning her to sit. The doctor was in his forties, tall and thin. His face appeared emaciated, exaggerated by his loose-fitting suit. His bored expression instantly switched to a sympathetic one, though his monotone voice carried no emotion.

"I'm terribly sorry. His dementia has gotten so bad that he can't talk. We don't want him to suffer. Dementia is the number one killer of those over sixty years old. Thanks to Galactic Medicine's Padella doctors, who have pioneered silver nanoparticle healing, amputations are now easily handled with rapid healing and very short hospital stays. Based on that, I wouldn't be surprised if one day Galactic Medicine comes up with a cure for dementia. However, Miss Parkinson, all we can really do for your father is to keep him as comfortable as possible. Now that he can no longer communicate with us, it's best to let him go."

I don't want to let him go! "He's my Dad."

Fighting back tears, Molly thanked him and left. Once outside, the fishy odor of the Lake and the roar of another spaceship taking off brought her to the present.

She doubted she could do anything for her father. *I'll ask Frank about it tonight. I've got to focus on my birth situation.*

Back at her home office, Molly began to research the two clues her mother had given her. Minutes later, she pounded her fists on her desk, her coffee cup vaulting a half-inch into the air. Dr. Ben Hall was deceased, and the Kids on Call adoption agency had never existed. Molly screamed. "This can't be happening!"

She headed to the police shooting range and emptied many clips into targets, shredding the heads and hearts of the paper men. Only army soldiers were issued the modern blaster weapons because they were very expensive and considered far too dangerous to be in civilian hands; their destructive power was huge. More relaxed now, she returned to her office.

At 5:30, she took the MTES to meet with the mysterious woman who hired her. She arrived at Luigi's Pizza on Canal Street a little early, went inside, and took a seat facing the windows and door. The aroma of baking pizzas made her hungry, so she ordered a sausage and ham pizza. *If this mysterious woman doesn't like it, she can spend her own money.*

At 6:00 sharp, the door opened. Molly gasped. She saw herself as she walked into the restaurant.

The other Molly wasn't the least bit shocked to see herself sitting at the table. She moved across from Molly and sat. That answered Molly's question: this new woman knew Molly looked like Sandy and her.

"I'm Janine Le Clair. A temporary lab tech at Galactic Medicine's Total Care Administration. I do data entry of DNA samples. Have you ordered yet?"

"Molly. Molly Parkinson, but I guess you know that already. Yes, ordered sausage and ham. We can share it." She watched Janine changing shoes, stowing the five-inch stilettos in her purse. She now wore comfortable flats. Her raven hair was about six inches longer than Molly's.

"Company policy. We women must wear five-inch heels to work—look professional and all that. Unfortunately, my workstation doesn't have any drawers so I have to carry them in my purse. Anyway, I rushed over here after work. We have to talk."

"Are we sisters? Identical triplets?" Molly asked. She stared at every detail of Janine's face, but saw only her own, as though looking in a mirror—more than a little disconcerting.

Janine's face twisted, before relaxing into a frown. "I don't know if there's a word for us. Another of us was murdered a week ago—Beth Waterson. She was a receptionist for Snell's Robotics."

While twisting her hair, Molly asked, "So, four of us? Quadruplets?"

"Honestly, I'm not sure if I've found all of us yet. There's also Leslie Travers, Deanna Cartwright, Lynn Holmes, and Ami Ann Waters. I've found eight so far." She sighed.

"Unreal. Octuplets? Are we all this identical?"

The pizza arrived, and their conversation changed until the waitress departed.

Janine said, "I've printed everyone's bio for us. That's illegal, but considering..." She slid the papers across the table.

"About the only difference is how we style our hair. Leslie is a fetish fashion model; hers reaches the small of her back. Ami's a vet and keeps hers shoulder length, much

14

shorter than yours or mine. Lynn is a biologist. What's so fascinating is Deanna is an engineer, married to Peter Cartwright. Heard of them?"

Molly shook her head.

"Those two build the EMACs. They're billionaires. I heard Peter inherited the business from his grandfather."

Electro-Magnetic Air Cars were both green and revolutionary in design, replacing most other vehicles. Nearly silent, EMACs flew through the air and didn't need roads. Corporation executives often parked them on their buildings' roof. As a result, maintenance of highways and bridges ceased centuries ago. However, Molly had inherited her grandfather's tiny electric car, though she seldom used it.

"Anyway, our DNA is the same down to the last detail. I'm told identical twins have very similar DNA, but their DNA isn't totally identical. Ours is—amazingly so. If I enter my DNA, any one of us eight could show up as the match. Maybe our fingerprints might be different. But those aren't in the database."

Molly's eyebrows rose, and lines creased her forehead. "So what does it mean?"

Janine grimaced. "It means we're clones—lab rats. Someone *made* us. And that's illegal! Besides, it's supposed to be impossible to do with humans, although it's been done with sheep and other animals. I've read up on it a little."

"Made us?" Molly asked. Janine nodded. "Lab rats?" Again, Janine nodded, but also sighed. "Are we still sisters then?" Molly breathed deeply and rubbed her forehead.

"I suppose so. I don't know what else we could be."

"Honestly," Molly said, "I never wondered much about who my birth parents were or if they had other children." She ran her hands across her face. "When I learned I was adopted, I guess I should have wondered if I had other brothers and sisters—maybe tried to find out if I had any."

"Well, I always wondered who my birth parents were. If I had any siblings. But never expected this. In my opinion, sisters would be okay. There isn't terminology for us. As far as I can tell, we were orphans and adopted by different families. Probably shortly after birth. We shouldn't exist. Yet, here we are. And someone is murdering us."

Molly said, "By the way, the police don't have any leads in Sandy's murder. I checked, and based on what I've seen, I doubt they ever will."

"Not surprising, I guess. I've tried contacting some of the others. Most are ignoring me. I'm not sure why anyone would want to murder us. Unless someone is getting rid of the evidence of their illegal cloning. Except for Deanna, none of us is an important person. I'm certainly not."

"Hey, we're all important in our own ways. Just because we don't make millions and have our own EMAC doesn't make us any less important."

"True, I suppose. Anyway, I've got an idea for you to consider. Ami works at First Choice Vets. Lynn works in a secure lab downtown. Leslie, you, and I are likely the most vulnerable. But I think I'm safe in my office building—at least when I'm at work. Leslie's fashion work takes her all over town, especially nightclubs—"

"Crap. She's probably just asking to get shot if she's clubbing."

Janine nodded. "Yeah, I've tried talking to her. She isn't taking this seriously. Her parents own a costume shop, and Leslie helps out there. Could you to keep watch over her? I suppose you have a gun. I heard PI's do. Perhaps you can stop whoever is killing us."

Molly's face broke into a broad smile. "You got that right. Okay, I'll do it. Need all you have on her."

Janine handed her a more detailed printout. "I'll give you expense money. I'm not rich, but my parents left me a little. Galactic Medicine pays us data entry people just enough to get by. Does Galactic Defense pay you well?"

"Thanks for the credits. No, my GD stipend is just enough to cover my home-office. This'll help me pay expenses. We should meet with the others. For me, seeing my double is believing."

"Okay. But there's danger in having us all in one place—"

"Right. If the murderer gets wind of it, he could kill us. I'll keep you updated about Leslie and whatever the police

16

discover about the murders. Stay in touch with you on your burner phone?"

"Yes, please. It's safer to use a burner. I think."

The two finished their pizza and then departed, each going their own way, but not without repeatedly looking over their shoulders.

Chapter 2 The Model

"I've like stayed too long!" Leslie Travers said, as pandemonium broke out on the dance floor of the Lariat Club, the hottest fetish nightclub in Old Chicago, the place to be seen, the place to be whatever you chose to be. Of course, your look had to be fetish (latex or rubber) to get past the bouncers at the door.

Leslie's photographer had departed hours ago but had gotten all the candid shots needed for the next article, "Leslie's After-hours Haunt" in *Shiny Magazine*. She'd already banked their check, a tidy sum for one night's work—for her, one night's play. Leslie was a fetish fashion model, an up and coming star, or so everyone claimed.

Tonight, she looked the part. Her oiled, bright blue, floor-length, latex gown tightly fit her curves, reflecting the strobe lights as if she was a shiny blue mirror. Here, latex and rubber of every imaginable color saturated the eye. Very high heels predominated. Determining gender: often problematical. The music was loud.

True, it had taken her a half-hour to melt herself into the gown, but the striking look it gave her form made that worthwhile. A contrasting blue and white striped outer corset added to her image, as did the black stockings and matching blue, six-inch, oxford-style stilettos. Her sponsor was Galactic Entertainment or GEnt; they took eighty percent of the money she made.

A minute before, she'd seen *that* man again, the man with the gun. He wore old jeans and a hoodie and definitely wasn't fetish-looking. For a moment, Leslie wondered how he'd gotten past the beefy bouncers. Had he shot them?

From across the densely packed floor, his eyes met hers, instant recognition yet again. The man raised his gun and fired at her. Leslie knew she'd stayed too long.

As she expected, the slug missed her, shattering a nearby strobe light, whose beams danced wildly around this section of the room, adding to the chaos. She saw several men trying to tackle the shooter, amid screams of terror and fright. More shots rang out.

Frantic fetish-clad patrons fled in all directions, making for one of the four emergency exits. Unworried, but slightly fearful, Leslie allowed herself to be pushed along by the wave of terrified patrons until at last, she found herself in the back alleyway where the frightened men and women headed off in all directions. None waited for the police to arrive. The slight knot in her stomach subsided as she breathed in the humid night air. She'd been lucky again.

Leslie followed along with several others, who, like her, were unable to move swiftly. Her steel-tipped spikes echoed as she tried to keep up. When she reached the street, a woman wearing blue jeans and a bluish jacket with its hood pulled up stepped out in front of her, forcing her to stop. The woman pulled her hood back. Leslie gasped. She stared at her own face.

Leslie was twenty-two with raven hair, lush, thick, and wavy, falling to her lower back. She had blue eyes and a round face, accentuated by thick eyebrows. Her lips were full, inviting with tonight's choice of lipstick, and even in tense situations such as this, retained their characteristic smile. Galactic Entertainment had genetically enlarged her bosom from B to that of a DD size, as fitting for a fetish model. The woman spoke, but it was Leslie's voice that Leslie heard barking.

"No time. Get in!" The woman pointed to the tiny electro-car parked at the curb. Leslie froze. "Get in, Leslie, if you want to live. The gunman'll be here soon. Move it. I couldn't get this car any closer."

Leslie saw the woman drawing her own gun and decided to obey, struggling to get herself into the tiny, cramped passenger seat. Such efficiency cars were not conducive to the fetish-corset clad. The woman slipped into the driver's seat, and the silent car sped off into Chicago's night.

"I'm Molly, by the way. Molly Parkinson, PI. I'm the owner of Molly Parkinson's Private Investigations and Security." She cracked a smile.

"Leslie, Leslie Travers. Like, crazy. You look like me. Like, where're we going? Are you like trying to kill me too? Like, why do you look like me? I should be like going home."

"Some place safer for the moment, but I'll let Janine explain. Keep watch. Make sure no one's following us. Glad you aren't panicking too badly." While Leslie watched out the rear window, Molly drove in silence.

***

The MTES occupied what had once been roads, making navigating around Chicago in an obsolete car challenging. Molly had to take round-about residential streets and alleyways, turning what should have been a five-minute trip into a half-hour nightmare. She pulled into a ramshackle motel, where Janine had already rented a room for emergencies such as this. After parking, she got out and lent Leslie a hand, whose constrictive outfit made exiting the car challenging.

Molly's car looked out of place in the motel's lot, where two EMACs were parked. Those vehicles had western designs on their sides, suggestive of New Mexico origins. Out west, public EMAC trains and shuttle EMACs covered the vast empty distances.

A raised vegetable garden occupied half the parking lot. Molly suspected most guests arrived on foot via the MTES.

Janine met them at the door, her eyes scanning the parking lot. Once inside, Janine introduced herself.

Leslie said, "So you like weren't joking with me. We're like identical. Sisters? I like thought I was like an orphan."

After more explanations of the clone situation, Leslie admitted something that gave both Molly and Janine pause. "He's like tried to shoot me three times now, but I like always have phenomenal luck on my side. Always have. So I'm like not too worried. He'll like miss me just like he always does. Do you like have super luck too?"

"Not that I know of," Molly said. Her eyebrows rose. "What's with all the 'likes?'" "All fetish people like talk this way. We're like supposed to put a like in front of or behind each verb. Right? You two like sound very strange to me."

Janine and Molly laughed. Later, Leslie agreed with

their advice. "Okay, I'll like be extremely careful. We like shot my final scenes tonight. GEnt doesn't have me like scheduled for more fashion shoots for a while."

Leslie sat on the bed, tossed her hair to one side, and changed the topic. "So like we're not like orphans but clones? Weird. Mom and Dad are like going out of business, GEnt's orders. They're sixty-four, so I'm like closing the store after this coming Halloween."

She sighed. "I'm like running their store until then. That's why I've like taken so many fetish fashion shoots these past two years. I've like salted away enough money to survive for a while. Molly, are your folks kinda like zombies? Mine are now. Like really strange. They like don't recognize me anymore. I like don't want to be like them. And GEnt has like set their T-days for early November. I like don't understand it. When they like made them retire and move into the assisted living complex, both were like alert and healthy."

Molly sighed. "Yes, my Dad is really bad. It's as if he's on another planet or something. His T-day is Monday. I can't get him to talk about anything; he just grunts. Mom's mind is going, too. Boy, this is strange—both our parents losing their minds at the same time. Smells fishy to me. But I did talk to Dad's doctor, who said dementia was common. Still—"

"Yeah, that like sounds like my parents," Leslie said with a sharp exhale. "I like love them, but they like don't even know me when I like visit them in their new place."

She paused before continuing. "It's like taken me a year to sell their home in the suburbs, and I like had to cut the price in half—too few people and too many available buildings, what with so many like moving off-world. Galactic Entertainment like took ninety percent of that money." She giggled and added, "Okay, like count me in on whatever plans you two have. We like have to stick together and survive, but we like will, 'cause we're like lucky."

The three shook hands and made further plans. Janine said, "If they find out about us clones, I'll bet anything they'll put us in a lab somewhere and study us. Or they'll terminate us. That's why someone's trying to kill us—to get rid of the evidence."

Molly grimaced, nodding her agreement. Before she could comment, Janine lowered her voice.

"I shouldn't be telling you this—just learned this yesterday. Someone left a classified document on my desk. I couldn't resist looking at it. It explained how the corporations are *killing* all older people. They force people to retire. Then move them into the assisted living complexes. They give them a drug. It causes the dementia. That allows the corporations to legally set a termination day. It's been going on for centuries. They say it's used to control the world's population. I think it's positively criminal."

Molly and Leslie gasped. Molly said, "So there's nothing wrong with my Dad? The corporations are murdering all older people! Wow, so darn much of what I've seen makes sense."

"That's about the size of it. They create dementia in older people. So it's only humane to terminate them," Janine said. She lowered her voice again and looked intently at both women. "Suzie, who used to be a friend of mine—she didn't do what Galactic Medicine ordered her to do. They wanted her to write an illegal drug prescription for some guy. She refused and told me about it. Two days later, she was dead—an EMAC accident. Very suspicious."

"That's like not right," said Leslie. "So they're like murdering my folks. Well, I like didn't have any choice either. They like ordered me to get my boobs enlarged. What else can we do?"

"Nothing," said Janine. "I don't see how we can do anything about it. My old boss at Toys for Tots refused to repackage and resell damaged toys. He got fired. So I lost my temp job there. Fortunately, I got another temp job at Total Care. Last I heard, he's starving. No sponsor. No income. So we have to be careful. We'll be in deep trouble if someone finds out about us."

Leslie frowned and changed the topic. "But I'm like a real person, aren't I? We like all are." She put her hands on her hips. "Well, I'm like not going to worry about that. I've like always had super luck, ever since I like was a little girl."

"Yeah," Molly said, "you're a real person, Leslie. We all are. Plus, I'm not about to become someone's lab rat. We have to stick together. And I'm going to call you my sisters, not clones."

After exchanging contact info, dropping Leslie off at the costume store, and giving her a hug, Molly began to wonder about Leslie's comments about always being lucky. *Was it luck that I was adopted? Was it luck that GD I accepted me as a PI? Not a soldier or cop?* She had no answers. But that they were systematically killing her parents bothered her more than she cared to admit.

Hence, Molly stopped by a convenience store and picked up a six-pack of Brown Ale. She then phoned Frank and dropped by his place, a small apartment on the south side. With the six-pack in hand, she knocked on his door.

"I come bearing gifts."

He welcomed her into his place, though he dashed about, tossing dirty clothes off the couch so they could sit.

"Thanks, Molly. I've got us tickets for the Hot Rock's concert on Saturday." Frank helped himself to a brew, but not before raising a bottle towards her.

Molly frowned. "Darn it, Frank. You know how much I dislike that group."

"Hey, you'll go with me and like it," Frank growled, before smiling. "Thanks for the beer. Come sit." He patted the couch next to him.

A bit reluctantly, she did so, helping herself to an ale. Frank jested, "We should take up home brewing." Both chuckled.

Then, her smile vanished. "Did you check into that other murder I phoned you about? Beth Waterson—that receptionist?"

"Yeah, incredible. You must have had two identical sisters you didn't know existed. I checked. No suspects yet. I've no idea why someone is killing your sisters. Make sure you've always got your Glock on you. I'm starting to worry about you."

Molly couldn't bear to tell him she wasn't a normal person, but a lab rat clone. Besides, he was a cop and thus obligated to report her to—well, she didn't know to whom. So it was safer to let Frank and the world believe in identical sisters. For now, anyway.

"Always do, dear." Molly changed the subject to her pressing topic. "Frank, they told me that Dad's T-day is Monday."

Frank sobered and sat his beer on an end table. "Gosh, Molly, so soon? I'm so sorry. He was going downhill last time we talked, right? So it's probably for the best. Want me to come with you? I can take some personal time."

"Will you? Thanks. But that's not all, Frank. I just heard something we're not supposed to know, and it's horrid—but I believe the source. It makes sense. The corporations are *killing* anyone who reaches sixty-five. Yeah, when they move into the assisted living complexes, they give them a drug that gives them dementia. Frank, they're killing Dad and probably Mom too."

Frank looked wide-eyed at her, his mouth ajar. Then, he took a long drink. "Wow! I had no idea. No one I know of has lived beyond around sixty-five. I just figured my parents' bodies wore out. Why didn't I see this pattern years ago? Remember, honey? I kept telling you my folks were developing a degenerative brain disease, but Molly, I bet every last person in that assisted living home had it—just before they were sixty-five. Damn, this is a conspiracy. The corporations can't do this." He fumed and his face reddened, but that quickly gave way to watering eyes.

"Yes, they can," Molly barked. She clenched her fists around the beer bottle. "They must have been doing this for centuries. Hell, they'll likely do it to us in another forty years." She took another long swill before she lowered her voice and leaned towards him on the couch. "Do you think I could sneak my parents out of the home and keep them at my place? If I do, will their dementia go away?" *If he says yes, I'll get them out of there tonight.*

Frank downed the ale, popped another cap, and took a long gulp before replying with a deep sigh. "We're both orphans and lucky to have been adopted by fine parents. We both belong to the Galactic Defense corporation." He grimaced. "So admit it, Molly. We know nothing about medicine or doctoring. Now if Galactic Medicine sponsored us, we might have an idea about the disease, but they aren't. So it's all for the best."

Molly frowned. Frank took another long swill. "If you remember, it almost killed Dad when he had to close his towing business. No electric cars, no tows, no money. Other than you, I don't know anyone who even has one of those cars. Heck, no place to drive them."

He asked, "Remember how I helped support Mom and Dad for a couple years? Remember how grateful I was that Galactic Supplies took them into their assisted living facility when he turned sixty? We both thought was wonderful. They got good care, at least until their minds went. Now you're telling me they were poisoned. Well, I suppose that was for the best for Dad. So while we could sneak your parents out of their facility, I've no idea what we could do for them after that."

Molly sighed deeply before replying. *That's true. We cheered when they got in. But the best for his dad? Hardly.* "You're right. I don't know a thing about medicine. Still, I could kill the corporate executives who authorize the murder of older people."

Frank took another long gulp. "Problem is, honey, we've no idea who those people are. Probably it's the CEOs; they run everything. They're untouchable. They pay our salaries, for heaven's sake." The detective fidgeted on the couch, and his hand gripping the bottle turned white.

He exhaled and changed the subject. "It's a crime—shooting that first grade teacher. Given how corrupt the system is, we'll probably never find out who did it. Until these shootings, only been two murders all year. Getting sent off to that hell-hole prison on Mercury is enough to make anyone think twice about committing a violent crime. Anyway, what time on Monday? I'll drop by your place. We'll say goodbye to your Dad together."

"Nine. Thanks. I'm a little afraid."

"I know. You'll be alone, too. Been there. Remember, you'll always have me, Cool Head."

Molly grinned and hugged him. While she desperately needed and wanted his support, she still had reservations about marrying him. More so now than ever before.

***

Early Monday morning, Molly and Frank said their farewells to Molly's parents. Her mother insisted on having her T-day with her husband, a double and shocking loss for Molly.

"Mom, you *can't*. You're not as bad off as Dad is. Please, I still *need* you. I love you. I can't lose you too." Molly pleaded with her mother, but she could see her mother's firm resolve.

"I can't go on without him. You have Frank. I can't live like this, dear. It's awful. Let me have one last hug."

"But I heard those pills they give you—they cause the dementia," Molly said.

The monotone voiced doctor said, "Molly, on Earth, our bodies wear out around age sixty. The pills postpone the onset of dementia a few years at most. Galactic Medicine has been working on a cure, but no luck so far. There isn't anything anyone of us can do, except be with them and allow them the dignity to pass way."

Stunned, Molly could only hug her mother and then hold tightly onto Frank. *Maybe this is for the best. Why don't I believe him? Damn whoever poisoned them!*

She said, "Maybe they could have lived many more years. Well, maybe not Dad. He went downhill when he quit his business, kind of like his life stopped for him."

"Yes, yes. It is that way for us all," the doctor said, his hands folded at his waist.

"Frank," she whispered. Then, she sobbed.

He nodded, holding her close, but Molly sensed Frank struggled to keep his emotions under control. Neither said anything further. After the brief funeral and cremation, Frank headed back to work.

Molly stopped to pick up a six-pack of Brown Ale on her way home, her mind swirling with conflicting thoughts. Several beers and a good cry later, Molly recovered some control of her emotions. *I just can't sit here and feel sorry for myself. I need to do something—anything.*

Low on groceries, especially chocolate ice cream, she decided to do her weekly shopping. Wiping her eyes, she powered up her comm center and logged into her favorite grocery store. In fact, other than a few convenience stores, all grocery stores were online stores. The last brick and mortar grocery store had closed over a century ago.

Food. One had two choices: synth food and actual food. The former was cheap, but only the very wealthy could afford the latter. Synth food contained everything needed for a healthy diet. In its base form, it appeared as bluish-green goo and was often used on long space voyages. However, various flavorings and dyes turned it into synth chicken, ham, roast, vegetables, synth chocolate ice cream, and so on. Thus, one appeared to have a wide variety of food choices and tastes. Automated food production facilities harvested crops and made the base form. Galactic Manufacturing then converted the goo into marketable synth products. One merely needed to warm the product; no real cooking required.

Molly filled her shopping cart, checked out, and received a message to expect delivery of her order within an hour. For a moment, Molly imagined a young worker pushing a cart with her order along the MTES. She wasn't wrong.

She tidied up her home-office, carrying two trash bags and empty beer bottles down to the recycle machine next to the building. Every block in the city had one of these machines. Anything to be disposed of was tossed into the metal hopper, about six feet square. An auger in the bottom activated, forcing the trash along underground passages, where they merged into larger and larger tunnels until at last the garbage reached the recycling operation's heart. Here, some was turned into compost, while plastics, metal, and glass were recycled.

Molly also saw a decrepit couch sitting next to the machine, but from experience, she knew once a week, a garbage crew with their EMAC came by to pick up the larger items. As she watched the auger churning and crunching her bags and bottles, she wondered if criminals could dispose of bodies this way. After all, it was mostly an automated system.

Finally in control of her emotions, she headed back to the assisted living home to clean out her parents' small apartment, donating most to Goodwill, while recycling the rest. As she packed a photograph of her Mom and Dad into a box, she remembered what her father had often told her: "Do the right thing." Her father's voice echoed in her mind. She agreed with him that it was right to donate to others what she couldn't use.

But hell, it isn't right to poison and murder everyone when they reach sixty-five! I hate these corporations, but I can't survive without them. Damn it. If the world wasn't so utterly dependent upon these big corporations...

***

Meanwhile, across town and after lunch, a delivery EMAC driver entered First Choice Vets. Miss Ami Ann Atwaters said, "It's my signature. But we didn't order a hundred thousand rabies vaccines. There must be some mistake."

He showed her his shipping order and insisted she come around to the rear to accept delivery. Still protesting, she agreed and unlocked the back door. As she stood in the doorway baffled by this order mix-up, the driver pulled out a 9mm and fired twice.

***

Late Monday afternoon, Frank phoned Molly. "It's me. There's been another murder. She's a dead ringer for you. A veterinarian named Ami Ann Atwaters, murdered over at First Choice Vets. We found the delivery driver in the back of the EMAC, also shot to death, I'm guessing from the same gun. Also, I have the ballistics report back on the two earlier shootings. The same gun was used to murder the schoolteacher and the receptionist. I've put a rush on the ballistics on this current shooting. I think we're looking for one perp, a serial killer. My guess is you had three identical sisters you didn't know about. So what's going on, Molly? I don't want you going anyplace without me. It's not safe."

Chapter 3 Counter Moves

At this same time in Chicago, Ace Bok reported to Dr. Nelson Padella, a homely man in his late fifties.

"Boss, what's going on? Somebody's killed three of the women I'm supposed ta put a scare into."

"You've got a good start. Leslie's showing great promise. We should have tried this years ago. Anyway, I don't know who's killing the others. Makes no sense. Keep trying to find out. Here's your next grand."

"Thanks. I will. Any leads on the locations of the others you want scared? And what about the men you wanted frightened?"

"I've been looking into the men. I think you can scare two men at one time. If you'll start a small fire in District Five, two of them should respond. Step up your efforts. This whole affair must be handled by August 1. Is that clear?"

Counting the stack of credits, Ace grinned. "Easy. Long as your leads are good. Say, what do I do if I run into whoever's killing them?"

"Kill him. You'll get ten grand extra if you terminate him."

Nodding, Ace turned and left.

As soon as Ace departed, Nelson's wife, Dr. Janet Padella, stepped into the room. With short brown hair, she was a year younger than her husband but just as homely. "Do you think we'll make it? Less than thirty days before they get all the DNA samples entered. After that, anyone could discover the clones."

"I've no idea if we'll get the Lucky Gene expressed before then or not. But the clones can't be traced back to us—not as long as General Fuller keeps his mouth shut. And even if someone discovers them, it's ancient history. Thanks to Ace, our Lucky Gene is finally showing great promise in Leslie, don't you think? Perhaps we haven't waited long enough for the gene to express itself, though you'd think it would have done so long before these twenty-plus years."

"Nelson, you can't rush science, even if it's obsolete experiments. These days, everything is nanoparticles and genetic mutations, not cloning. In fact, if we're being honest, we completely forgot all about those clone tests we made over two decades ago. It's the corporation rush to get everyone put into that massive DNA database that's the real culprit. Who could have foreseen that coming? Anyway, what bothers me is who is killing off our specimens? And why?"

"True, we've spent some twenty years developing the gold nano spot technology. And if I say so myself, it shows far greater potential than our original genetic engineering mutation methods with cloning. Nine months before we could really see what the results were. Those were the dark ages." He rubbed the stubble on his chin.

"Contingency plan. Nelson, it's time we worked out a contingency plan. We may have to disappear. Go underground. We can use our atoll in the South Pacific."

"Janet, I'm getting too old for such hide and seek games, but I see your point. If the corporations find out about our older clone research, they may want to terminate us. Do you suppose the corporations are behind the murders?"

"Hardly, Nelson. If they were, then we would have been terminated."

He nodded, rubbing his hands over his face. "But I still believe the clones hold great potential, if only we could get their Lucky Gene to express itself."

"Are you getting senile on me, Nelson?" She spat on the floor. "The corporations only want us to work on their specific gold nanoparticle experiments. If we want to continue our *real* research free and unencumbered, we'll have to disappear. Our atoll isn't registered with any corporation, so we can work from there in complete freedom."

"I don't know, dear. The South Pacific—that's going a long way. Still, you're right. We need a contingency plan." He sighed. "Okay, you make plans to get the supplies we might need shipped there. We must be ready to take action soon."

Janet smiled. She looked at the female names on his list, three of which were crossed off. "Such a shame, Nelson. But back then, we did prove humans can be cloned without apparent defects and with perfect copies. Unfortunately, we showed each clone's personality was completely different. While the cloned bodies were identical, their minds weren't. Who could ever have guessed that would happen? So much for Galactic Defense's super-soldier program."

Nelson nodded. "And our funding. Yes, they sure didn't like that discovery, did they?" Both laughed heartily.

***

Molly's keen eyes took in the entire situation.

"Look, we like should be safe here," Leslie said. "When I like was a little girl, my folks like had these back apartments added on behind their storefront. Extra income for a while, but they've been like empty for years. Besides, we can like don disguises from the costume shop. I like can fix up some apartments for Janine, Lynn, and you, if you like think we'll be safe enough here."

The long but skinny, two-story, gray brick building stretched for a half block. A narrow sub-alley lay behind it, and the row of small apartments opened onto it. Molly guessed this area had once been a parking lot for the store before Leslie's parents had the apartments built. The real alley stretched behind these new buildings, lined with the usual automatic dump recycling facilities. There was just enough room to park her tiny car.

"Okay, I agree. The apartments aren't visible from the street. I've got a hunch we'll be safe here for a while. The problem'll be coming and going. Lynn and Janine travel the MTES to and from work each day. Not so good. They work on different sides of Chicago, so I can't watch over both of them at the same time."

"Lynn like did say she'll have her boyfriend escort her back and forth." Leslie chewed on her lip before asking, "Say, Molly, like have you noticed we always have great luck on our side? That same man has like tried to shoot me three times, but each time I like saw it coming. Somehow, he like messed up the shots. Missed my head by an inch last time—shattered a strobe light above my head."

Molly merely smiled and helped Leslie carry racks of her fetish outfits from the storefront to her new back apartment.

Leslie frowned and said, "I like looked up cloning on the Internet last night. Did you know it's illegal? And yet someone like cloned eight of us that we know of some twenty-two years ago. I like remember being five years old and going to kindergarten, so we like must have been babies—at the start, I mean."

"Don't know about the luck thing, but I've always done well for myself. Then again, luck ran out for Ami, Beth, and Sandy. I'm only getting started in the PI business; I haven't had time to provoke anyone. So I'm with Janine. Someone is trying to wipe out all traces of their illegal experiments."

Leslie's brows creased sharply, as she accepted Molly's conclusion.

Janine arrived carrying a duffle bag of her things, likely overhearing Leslie. "We're closer to twenty-three years old. You're forgetting nine months in Mother's womb. Wait a minute. Who was our birth mother?"

"I like never thought much about that," Leslie admitted.

Janine asked, "Another thing. Did we all have the same biological mother and father? I would guess we must have since we're so alike. But then I know nothing about cloning."

"How would we like even find out?" asked Leslie.

"If my records weren't falsified, I might have been able to find out who our biological parents were," Molly said.

Janine said, "Well, we must have been babies, because I can remember when I was four years old and got my favorite doll. Say, which apartment is going to be mine?"

Leslie pointed to the one next to hers, and Janine dropped her bag there. She sat on the bed, took off her heels, and massaged her feet.

"This is the only drawback of my temp job at Total Care. Of course, this job only lasts for another month. All the DNA is supposed to be entered by the end of July. Then I'll have to find another receptionist job. I shouldn't complain though. The pay is double what I was making."

Molly teased both her sisters. "I don't know how either of you manage to walk in those heels. Janine, I've been thinking about what you said. I agree with you. I'll bet the people who made us are worried somebody will discover someone's been cloning human beings, and they're trying to get rid of the evidence. Us."

Janine brightened up. "I'm a data entry person, not a geneticist. I don't think there's any way to find out who made us—just from our DNA. But if I can find us in the database, so can others. Besides, donor parents aren't important to me. All I care about are the ones who raised me. And they're dead now."

Molly wiped a wet eye. "Same with me. What we need is a DNA expert. They might figure out who our parent donors are. But you're right. Who cares about them? I want to know who made us. They're the criminals. How'd they do it?"

"More importantly, Molly, *why* did they make us?" Janine said.

"How many more sets of clones have they made?" Molly said.

"Are they like still making more clones?" Leslie said.

"We need justice." Molly stomped her foot, vibrating the water in a flower vase on the tiny desk next to her.

Janine nodded. "I'll keep searching the DNA database for more of us. Hope I don't get caught. It's almost funny. I entered my own DNA and up came Leslie's ID. That's how I've been uncovering us. Meanwhile, Lynn's looking into some of that fancy stuff for us—like maybe a way to find our birth parents. She's a biologist. So it's not too far afield for her. I always thought a clone would be a duplicate of the original. But only our bodies look alike. Our minds are different. I'm a receptionist. Molly's a PI. Sandy was a teacher."

Leslie laughed. "What about me? I'm like a fetish fashion model. I like always did like to dress up in the fancy costumes Mom and Dad like have here in the store. So I like guess that's why I like turned out as I did."

Molly chuckled. "Leslie, I can see why you loved to play dress up. I've never seen so many costumes before. Still, you'll never get me wearing heels like you and Janine wear, though maybe you could get me into one of those fancy ball gowns."

The three women grinned. Leslie added, "I like to wear fancy clothes and look pretty. Like Miss Galaxy for a day. My sponsor, Galactic Entertainment, first like wanted me to become one of those new Super-Sexy Galactic Dolls for the corporate executives. The ones with the gigantic bosoms and curvy forms. I like said no. But they like did enlarge my breasts for the photos. Of course, I like did have a Galactic Doll when I was little, but then, what girl like didn't? So I can like see why some men might want their wives to look gorgeous."

She gabbed on. "I like know about magazines, editors, and photographers, too, though I was like kinda hoping I like could run the costume store and still model, but GEnt like vetoed it. No like getting around what our sponsors tell us to do. But now, I'm like becoming afraid of our world. I like wanted to meet a handsome man, get married, and have a family, a nice house, fancy clothes, and run the costume store."

With a wry grin, Janine said, "I think Molly's found her handsome man. She showed me his holo image yesterday."

Molly blushed. "Frank. Well, he's handsome and all I could want. Plus, he's proposed, but I said no—well, actually I said not yet—let's wait."

"Oh no! Like why?" Leslie said.

"I'm not ready for it. Got my PI business to get going. I enjoy helping others, and I can't see me settling down, becoming pregnant, having the allowed two children, and then being a housewife until the kids grow up. At least, not yet."

Not entirely true. There's something else, but I can't put my finger on it. I'm so stupid about such things. I want to be loved and to have love like my parents shared. But what kind of a mother would I be? Maybe my babies would be defective. I best not marry. Help others; avoid marriage. That way I can't have babies that are weird or something. Then I don't have to worry about myself.

Leslie's cringed expression faded. "Oh, well then, that like makes sense. I suppose I'd like have to give up modeling if I like got married and pregnant. Got a pic of him? Can I like see what he looks like?"

Molly pulled up a couple photos of Frank on her phone, using the hologram projection app to display him in a rotating 3-d image. Leslie ogled at him, causing Janine to break into a laugh.

34

Just then, Janine's phone rang. "Excuse me. Have to take this." She left the room, but returned minutes later. "Well, perhaps we're making headway. That was Deanna Cartwright—you know, the billionaire CEO of Cartwright Enterprises, makers of the EMACs. She's agreed to meet with us. Deanna wants to meet tonight. I've texted Lynn, but she's not answering."

Over the past centuries, incredible inventions had sprung up in many arenas, some due to the necessity of getting a handle on global warming. Peter Cartwright Sr. invented the EMAC. Today, his grandson, Peter III, and his engineer wife, Deanna, made modifications to it, making the EMAC the most successful transportation invention ever, with the possible exception of the MTES, spaceships, and shuttle crafts. Subsequently, Adolph Michaelson of London redesigned it to become the replacement for airplanes: the Airliner. Adolph's grandson's wife, Jena, who worked closely with Deanna, modified it, creating the EMAC train. Both families were billionaires.

Molly suggested, "Let's take my electric car. If we cram in, we can make it. I have a strong feeling we should drop by Lynn's place on our way. Where's Deanna live?"

"Can't miss it. Cartwright Enterprise is down on Lake Shore Drive, corporation row. Okay. Let's drop by Lynn's. Now you mention it, I have a funny feeling too."

"Me too," Leslie added. "Like how come we all have a funny feeling?"

No one answered her.

"I'm glad we're all on the small side. Otherwise, we'd not fit in this electro-car of yours," Janine said.

Molly laughed and headed off on one-way, side streets and alleys, where the makers of the MTES occasionally left just enough space for maintenance EMACs to land, but which these mini-cars could navigate. They drove to within a block of Lynn's apartment. An ambulance EMAC was parked in front of her place, but Molly counted six police vehicles cordoning off the block.

"I suppose we should check," Molly said. Two solemn faces nodded, and she parked the car. Molly walked as close as she could until a police officer cut her off. Molly returned to her car. From the tearful look on Molly's face, the two knew what was going on.

"She's been murdered; her boyfriend, too. Double homicide. We best get to Deanna's place. Damn it. I've only known I have sisters for a few days and already half of them have been murdered. I swear I'm going to kill whoever's doing this." Molly swiped at her tears.

Janine laid a hand on Molly's shoulder. "Calm down. We should get going. The killer might still be around here."

A half-hour later, three sober-faced women walked through the spacious doors of Cartwright Enterprise's main headquarters on the edge of Lake Michigan. A security guard stopped them, but before he could do anything, they saw their sister coming their way.

"It's all right, Jones. They're with me," Deanna said. As the trio moved past Jones and up to her, Deanna's jaw dropped, and Jones rubbed his eyes. "It's true then. My goodness, you three look just like me—well, except for your hair." Hers was a short, easy-care bob style, but she looked identical to the other three: raven hair, round face, thick eyebrows, full lips, and the angelic smile.

Janine took charge and introduced everyone to Deanna, who insisted on hugging each of her new sisters. Deanna commented, "Until this moment, I believed I was an orphan. Recently, I had to say my farewells to my parents. It was their T-days. A really sad day for me. Let's go up to my office on the top floor."

They rode the elevator up fifty floors. "This used to be my husband's office. Peter Cartwright III. He was injured in an industrial accident a week ago. At least, he's getting the best gold and silver nanoparticle healing care available. I have to be hopeful for his recovery."

"What happened to him? It sounds awful," Janine asked.

"A crane cable hit his head; he wasn't wearing his hard hat. His mind is rather scrambled, but the Galactic Medicine doctors are hopeful this new nanotechnology will cure him. Time will tell."

The view from the many windows was breathtaking. On one side, Lake Michigan stretched into the horizon. Three sides gave spectacular views of the city and skyscrapers. Many rooms divided the central space, and all were richly decorated. A thick, rust colored carpet covered the hallway floor. Paintings illuminated by their own lamps adorned the hallways. Several offices abutted the halls, but the spacious living room held only top quality furniture. Deanna led them here, where several brown leather couches faced the lakeside windows.

After a sigh, Deanna went on talking rapidly. "I've had to take over control of our company—there are always new modifications that must be designed and built. Jena Michaelson's husband also had a bad accident. So Jena and I are working together. Her company makes Airliners and now Air Trains, based on our EMAC technology. This is the most important thing happening in our world today. We simply have to end global warming. If not, Chicago will become as hot as the Sahara Desert, like it was two hundred years ago. Canada will return to being the next breadbasket of the world. The US will once more lose an enormous amount of coastal lands. Florida might be totally underwater."

She continued, "Worse, the Earth could well end up being uninhabitable by humans, rather like Venus, and we'll all have to migrate to the other planets in our Sol Empire. Well, maybe that's a bit of an exaggeration, but I'm serious. The warming began centuries ago, and our history books tell us how terrible things got before they were able to reduce the warming effects. It's still not completely handled. So EMAC technology offers the only real hope Earth and the other habitable worlds have right now. Jena and I aim to see this done to a completion."

Molly studied the face of her newest sister as she talked. She thought Deanna was a highly educated woman quite used to getting her own way.

"As you can probably guess," Deanna said, "she and I are sponsored by the Galactic Transport corporation—GPort as we commonly call it—though we also have many contracts with Galactic Defense, especially with this Sixth Invader War that's being fought on the edge of our Sol Empire. Today, however, I got a high-pressure call from some man in Galactic Entertainment; he wanted to buy out my contract with GPort and have me undergo gold nanodot therapy to become a corporate Super-Sexy Galactic Doll. Can you believe that? I assured them in no uncertain words that I wasn't a sex doll or toy. When I told him I was pregnant with my daughter, he hastily backed down. Apparently, being pregnant interferes with their Doll image."

All four women laughed. Leslie said, "I'm like a model for GEnt. They like wanted me to become one, too, but I like turned them down. I like want to be more than some man's sex toy."

"Congratulations, Deanna," Janine said. "When are you due?"

Deanna smiled. "Next April. Going to call her Jana. Anyway, please tell me about yourselves, your lives. It's incredible discovering you have sisters—er, identical clones—when you always thought you were an orphan. Are clones sisters?"

"I like think of you as my sisters," Leslie declared.

"Clone sounds so institutional—medical-like," Janine said. "Besides, we can't mention we're clones. We think that's why someone is killing us—to get rid of the evidence before the DNA database is completed."

"Okay, sisters it is. I believe that's wise," Deanna said. "I thought there were five of us. Are we missing one?"

Molly provided the grim news. "Lynn and her boyfriend were murdered tonight, just before we came here. I've sworn to kill this fiend who's murdered four of us."

Hours passed as each of the three took turns relating their life stories. Molly kept a sharp eye on Deanna all the while, for here was a CEO—a real corporate executive and powerful person. She'd never seen one before. And yet, Deanna was personable and did want to hear about the lives of each of her new-found sisters. She wasn't the beast that Molly presumed all corporate execs were.

With the introductions done, Deanna said, "So, Molly, tell me what you know about the murders of our sisters and what the police are doing about it."

Molly did so, ending with, "I'm hoping by tomorrow Frank will have ballistics back, confirming it was the same shooter. The police are calling the shooter a serial killer."

Deanna ran her hands through her short hair. "Okay, sisters. I want you three to move into this building with me. I know you just moved into Leslie's apartments, but the murderer can't get at us in here. This headquarters is secure. Plus, I'll send along a security squad with you, Janine, to make sure nothing happens to you when you go to and from work."

Just then, Molly's phone beeped. "Excuse me. I have to take this. It's from Frank."

Leslie giggled, while Molly stepped away from the others and answered his call. His voice wavered; he sounded terrible.

"Molly. Thanks for picking up right away. Something's come up. Something awful. It'll be on the news at ten. Two men were just murdered. One was a fireman and the other a reporter. There was a small fire at a warehouse, and each was called there. Same MO, single shot to the head. Molly, these two men—I swear they look just like me! They could be my double. How can this be?"

Molly swallowed hard. She hadn't told him she and her sisters were clones. He had been accepting of the fact that perhaps she had sisters, separated at birth. But now, two who looked identical to him? Were there male clones too? Ought she tell him? No, she decided. *Not until I'm certain he's a clone too. But if he's a clone, then maybe his life is in danger like us. But if he's not, then—god, let's not go there. Not yet.*

She said, "Take a deep breath. Perhaps you had brothers. Remember, we fantasized about having unknown siblings when were in high school right after we learned we were adopted. But let's not get ahead of things. Get DNA samples from the corpses and from yourself. Send them to me, and I'll get them analyzed for you. I've some connections."

"Oh, thank you, Molly. It takes our lab a week to process DNA, so I owe you big time for this. I suppose it's possible we were triplets. Few will adopt three babies at one time. Okay, I'll have the samples for you tomorrow. I'll text you when to drop by the precinct." They talked a bit more before Molly returned to the others.

"Janine, tomorrow, can you analyze three DNA samples? Looks as if we aren't the only clones in Chicago." She told them about the two dead men who looked identical to Frank. The news surprised them as well.

Since it was getting late, Deanna took them down a floor to her private quarters. She and Peter occupied one whole floor—their personal space. They met Peter, but his head was bandaged, and he couldn't talk.

Twelve personal living suites opened off a long, carpeted hallway. Peter and Deanna occupied one suite. Except for the views, each suite was identical, large and with all the convenient features money could buy, including a dry cleaning machine, a dishwasher, a washer, and a dryer. Molly felt as though they were queens in a fairyland castle.

The next day, Deanna did as promised. A security squad of four men accompanied Janine to work, promising to return at five to escort her back to the skyscraper on Lake Shore Drive. She also sent a squad with Molly and Leslie, who returned to their apartments to pack some of their things and Janine's. By early afternoon, they finished moving into the skyscraper.

Late that morning, Molly received the expected text message from Frank. The protection squad accompanied her to the police precinct to pick up the three samples, on over to Total Care, and then back to the skyscraper. For the first time in days, Molly felt safe.

Later the same afternoon, Janine called her. "Crap. More clones. The two dead men and your Detective Frank Wells are clones, too. Identical DNA. It's weird. I entered the deceased Tony's DNA but got back the ID of Frank. Frank's DNA came back as belonging to the dead reporter, Fred. I'm running a program overnight to identify how many more of them there are. And I'm checking to see if there are more of us. Anyway, you can tell Frank."

"Thanks, Janine. I'll wait until you get your results back in the morning. Best be armed with all the info." Molly knew he had already gone home early, and she promised herself that she'd catch him first thing in the morning and tell him everything. If this killer tried something, she was certain Frank would terminate him.

They didn't see Deanna until dinnertime, when they met the pair in Deanna's suite to share the meal prepared by the Cartwrights' personal chef. Deanna ignored Peter, who ignored everyone. Molly thought Peter looked worse than her father had on his T-day. A nurse fed him. Grim, she thought.

Deanna said, "Well, I made some calls today and did some investigation of my own. It seems as CEO, I'm supposed to sponsor some of these new Galactic Dolls. Apparently, they're encouraging all CEOs and other key leaders to sponsor these women. Hence, GEnt is expecting me to sponsor one or more Dolls or even hire them as regular Cartwright employees. She's supposed to entertain my many executives. If Peter was well, he'd probably accept one, but I've turned them down. I hope that's the end of it."

She continued the conversation. "Leslie, I've given some thought to what you were saying about us being lucky. Sisters, she might have a valid point. I had incredible luck getting pregnant just before Peter had his accident. A week later, he couldn't have done it. The doctors still don't know if he'll recover. Also, I've had incredible luck in getting the chance to run this company and to work on the EMACs. So I think there might be something to what Leslie's been suggesting."

Leslie giggled. "See, I like told you. We like have incredible luck. The murderer has like missed me three times."

Molly's right cheek rose, while her eyebrows arched. She said, "Do you suppose the clone makers could *really* have bred incredible luck into our DNA?"

Everyone laughed, but Janine said she wasn't so sure this was far-fetched.

***

On July 21, the three women moved the rest of their personal possessions into the Cartwright Building. Also, Leslie arranged to unload the costume stock and then sell her parent's store after Halloween. Deanna made a Cartwright Corporation EMAC available to them, along with four security guards.

When the EMAC landed beside Costumes R Us and its

doors opened, Leslie yelled, "There! There, that's him! That's the man who has been like trying to shoot me."

As Leslie became visible in the vehicle, the gunman opened fire. Closest to the door, Molly reacted far faster than the four security guards did. She rolled out, landed prone, her 9mm Glock drawn. The gunman's slugs ricocheted off an electrical wire just above the EMAC doors, knocking out one of the EMAC's headlights and shattering one of the vehicle's windows, but luck was again with Leslie, who was unharmed. Molly fired her gun, tap-tap-tap. Her three slugs struck the man in a tight pattern centered on his heart, killing him instantly—so the ME later concluded. Seeing the man go down, the security guards swarmed out and rushed across the street to deal with the gunman.

A guard dropped back to report. "Three shots to his chest and heart. Damn good shooting, Miss Parkinson. It's safe to enter the store. We'll wait here for the police and handle their paperwork."

"See, Molly," Leslie said. "Lucky shots. I like swear our makers bred luck into our genes."

Molly frowned and felt sick. She'd just killed a man. True, he was trying to kill them. Self-defense. Still... However, Molly knew nothing she could say would persuade Leslie to change her opinion despite the many hours spent on the shooting range with Frank. The security men handled the police for her, for which she was grateful.

Chapter 4 More Problems

Meanwhile, Detective Frank Wells had his own problems. "No, detective," his captain said, "I'm not about to let you work on the dual murders at the arson scene. The dead men must have been your unknown twin brothers. Not a chance you're working on that case. I want you to solve the murder of Lynn and her boyfriend, even though Lynn could well have been an unknown sister of Miss Parkinson. That's an order."

Molly found him sitting in his office going over the initial reports from the on-scene officers. "Hi, Frank."

"Molly. Grim business. What brings you by?"

"We got the DNA results back. I'm not sure how to tell you this, dear."

Frank leaned back and ran his hands across his face and then through his hair. "Out with it. It can't be any worse than my day is going."

"You're a clone. You and those two men killed at the arson fire have identical DNA. Identical. I'm a clone, too. There are eight of us that we know of, including the dead women."

She saw that he didn't, or wouldn't, accept it. "No chance we're identical triplets?"

"I'm so sorry. No." She paused; her eyes met his. "Worse, this morning, Janine told me there's a maker's marker stored in an unused DNA sequence. She said there are bits of DNA sequences, which aren't used to make or control our bodies. That's where the clone makers stored their manufacturing ID in a binary code rather like computers use. I don't understand any of that. Anyway, today, she's looking into my DNA to see if there's a marker in it. I've got someone searching the DNA database to see if there are more of you out there. Shit, that sounds so freaky, but you know what I mean."

"Yeah, I do, Molly," he sighed and rocked back in his chair, hands behind his head. "I'll be honest with you. Human cloning is illegal; I looked it up. Ever since I looked into the murders of your sisters, I've wondered about this. I can see identical twins, but not this many. I felt sick when I saw the two dead men who looked like me. Clones.

"Molly, we *have* to keep quiet about this. I don't trust the corporations any longer. Hell, they might be sanctioning this serial killer. But I also thought about us. I mean, can clones marry? If clones can't, then I'll withdraw my marriage proposal. I don't want to hurt you because of this."

Molly smiled but didn't break eye contact. "We've been talking about what we sisters are. We've decided we're just people, too. None of us can carry on if we don't think of ourselves as people. So who's to know if we marry? Deanna is married and even expecting a daughter.

"It's just—I'm not ready to make such a strong commitment, not when there's someone out there murdering us and you fellows."

Molly took a deep breath. She didn't like how he always had to have his way, sometimes even making her do things she didn't wish to do, such as attending that awful concert. But these killings convinced her how short life could be.

She reached a decision. Her eyes drilled into his. "Frank, once we get this serial killer behind bars or dead, let's get married. Okay? We have to continue thinking of ourselves as ordinary people."

A huge grin spread across Frank's face. "Honey, you got it! I've been assigned to the Lynn and Tom case. Ballistics came back. Same gun was used in all four crimes, so we're looking for one serial killer who's murdered your sisters, one boyfriend, and a delivery man."

"That simplifies it. Also, a few hours ago, I killed the man who was trying to kill Leslie. Cartwright security guards are handling the details with the CP. If you can get hold of the man's gun, see if it matches our serial killer's gun."

"Damn, Molly, why didn't you tell me right away? Are you hurt? Others okay?"

"We're fine. The man missed, but he killed one of the EMAC's headlights. I still feel nauseous about having killed someone, even if the CP on the scene said it was a clear case of self-defense."

"You wait here. I'm all over it. If we're lucky, we have

our serial killer." Frank grabbed his phone and made calls. "You're sure? Okay." He hung up, his face sour.

"Well, crap. Naturally, they called for ballistics right away, but your shooter's gun isn't a match for the killer of your sisters nor is it a match for the murderer of my clones at the arson fire. Man, that sounds weird saying it that way—my clones. Anyway, the slugs from my two dead 'brothers' match the slugs from your sisters. So, Molly, whoever was shooting at Leslie isn't the same man who's been murdering our clones."

He forced a grin. "Okay, Cool Head. I'm holding you to your promise to get married after we get this murderer. Let's catch this serial killer soon."

They shared a kiss, and Molly departed.

***

Frank returned to his examination of Lynn's murder. He logged onto their computer system and studied the 3-d holographic arson scene reconstruction—the case he wasn't supposed to be working on. The fire had done little physical damage to the abandoned building. With no clues to follow in the Lynn case, he decided to check out that warehouse. Maybe those working that case missed something. Ballistics proved the men's murder connected to his case—the justification he intended to use if his boss questioned him.

Detective Wells flashed his badge to the officer guarding the scene and crossed the yellow crime scene tape, entering the building. After pausing to double-check his gun and flashlight, he stepped over the waterlogged debris at the entrance. The building's power was off, so he clicked on his light and began his search. The second floor held many side rooms off one long hallway. Broken out windows lined the street side. Vandals, he concluded, after spotting numerous small stones littering the floor among bits of glass.

Frank wasn't sure what he was looking for—just something, anything. He came upon what appeared to be a squatter's den. A mattress and some discarded clothes lay against one wall while a clutter of food wrappers littered the floor nearby. Dim light entered from a broken window across the hall. He knelt, inspecting the scene.

Just then, a shadow blocked the light. Frank turned.

Bang. Bang. Bang. Darkness surrounded him.

***

Molly would always remember the call that came from Frank's captain at 4:00 p.m. "Miss Parkinson, I'm sorry to have to inform you that Detective Frank Wells was murdered this afternoon. Someone shot him while he inspected the arson scene. Ballistics has confirmed we're looking for the same serial killer. You two were close, so I wanted you to hear it from me first, not on the news."

Molly's voice squeaked, "Thank you." She couldn't say anything further. Her mind reeled. Her legs turned to butter. She grabbed the back of a chair to keep upright. *We were going to be married. Oh god, no. This can't be happening. Not now. Not after I said yes.*

Since she didn't say anything further, the police captain hung up. Clinging to the chair, she stood beside Leslie in the Cartwright Skyscraper, tears streaming down her cheeks.

"What's happened?" Leslie whispered. "Janine? Deanna?"

Molly swallowed hard and sniffed. "Frank. He's murdered Frank."

Leslie opened both arms up wide, and Molly fell into them. Her sister hugged her tightly while Molly's tears flowed. Neither said a word for several minutes, not until Deanna walked into the room to check on them. Leslie mouthed, "Frank," and Deanna understood. She, too, joined them in their silent hug.

"I said yes. Just today, I said yes. We were going to be married once this serial killer was terminated. Now he's dead. I'll never get that chance, not ever again. He waited on me so patiently. Oh god, what have I done?"

Deanna said, "Nothing, dear. You've done nothing. It's that murderer—that psychopath—who's guilty. Where did it happen? When? Any clues?" She ushered the pair over to a couch.

Molly sat down, just as her legs gave out. After wiping her eyes on her blouse, she related what little she knew, wishing she'd not been so shocked when the captain had called. "He's got no one left. Both his parents are dead. I suppose I should volunteer to help with the arrangements."

Deanna said, "Yes, that's a positive thing you can do. Call up the captain and volunteer. I suspect the CP will want to hold a memorial for him." Molly did so.

"Yes," the captain said, "we plan to hold a memorial service for him. Frank had just told us that you two were engaged, so we'd like you to be there. Also, he has an uncle and aunt coming in from Kansas City. They would like to coordinate his funeral service with you. Perhaps, you could help them clean out his apartment."

"Yes, I'd be glad to help them. I'll be there. Thank you." Molly hung up.

When Janine arrived shortly before dinner, Leslie met her near the front doors, relaying the news so she wouldn't be taken by surprise.

"Will it never end?" Janine said. She, too, hugged Molly when she and Leslie joined the others for the evening meal. The somber group dined on a meal based on several Chinese chicken dishes, including one with snow peas, made from real ingredients, and quite expensive. For the sisters, this was a real treat.

"Well, I've some news," Janine said. "Positive this time. There are more of us clones." Several gasps interrupted her. "Yes, there are at least three more of us. They're two years younger. Randi Tucker, Eve Burkey, and Celeste Sawyers. I think the makers changed the cloning process. These sisters have different hair and eye colors from us. Also, a Ted Billings is another clone of Frank and the other two men. There could be more men. My search is still running.

"So far, I've been lucky." Janine sighed and her arm trembled. "No one's discovered my tinkering. Not sure if I can continue running these searches. Eventually, someone's going to catch on. Plus, I was thinking. What will happen to us when the corporations discover we have identical DNA?"

"I've got some connections," Deanna said. "I think I can get us some warning if trouble is coming. As long as we're all staying here where I can provide security, we'll be all right. But I think you shouldn't run any more searches."

Janine breathed a sigh of relief and nodded.

Molly said, "Incredible discoveries, Janine. We need to contact them before this madman gets to them."

Deanna agreed. "Absolutely. We'll bring them here. I've plenty of room. Where are they located? By the way, stellar job, Janine."

She flashed a big smile, before her face sobered. "That's just it. I found an ancient email address for Ted and sent him a query. He said they're on some remote atoll in the South Pacific. He and Celeste, Randi, and Eve are being held prisoner by some mad doctors. They only have a vague idea where the island is. They've no way to escape to the mainland. Anyway, Ted said they were in no danger, but not to use that email address again. He claims it's too risky for them."

***

No danger. Days later, Molly claimed that when she decided to do her own investigation of Frank's death. She had helped clean out his apartment, made all the more poignant because she found the wedding rings he'd purchased. She kept them but was now fired up to find the killer.

Leslie used parts of various costumes to disguise Molly.

"I don't look like myself."

Leslie giggled.

"I admit you don't," Deanna said, "but be careful. I wish you'd take the security men with you."

"Can't. That would give me away. No, I've got a hunch Frank was onto something, and it got him killed."

With that, and looking like an older washerwoman, she exited the skyscraper using the janitor's exit. Twenty minutes later via the MTES, she arrived outside the warehouse. The police tape was gone, so it was a simple matter to enter. Once inside, she drew her 9mm Glock and her powerful flashlight. Molly began a methodical search.

By noon she found the location where Frank had been killed. Dried blood was on the wooden plank flooring. Molly spotted evidence bag wrappers here and there, a sign the CSI personnel had taken samples. *Bet Frank thought our serial killer stayed here.* Even though she figured the technicians had done a thorough job of it, she searched the room before moving on to the next room.

Rodent droppings and bird excrement inhabited many other rooms. Plaster had fallen off walls, and windows were broken out. Like so many other abandoned buildings in most cities, this one was on the lengthy waiting list to be demolished. Molly persisted in her search, primarily because of logic. "Look," she said to herself, "if someone was sleeping in here and shot Frank, it's likely he's still using this building. If not, I'll try other abandoned buildings around here. I'm not giving up, Frank. I know you were onto something." She wiped her damp eyes and moved on down the hall to the next room.

When she reached the last room on this floor, the outside hall door was so damaged that only the frame remained. She could see the rusting fire escape stairs through the opening. Upon closer inspection, Molly noticed some of the rust had been wiped off the rungs, suggesting recent use. She turned to better inspect this room. "Ah ha."

Someone lived here. An old mattress lay on the floor, and a sleeping bag rested on top. Some dirty clothes belonging to a male had been tossed in a pile in one corner. A gas lantern rested on the floor. It felt cold to her touch, and she relaxed a little.

The outer wall of this end room had six windows; most were cracked or broken out. The opposite wall had gaping holes in its plaster. A barrel of plaster bits rested near the door as though someone had begun demolitions some time ago. Bird droppings covered the plaster pieces near the top of the barrel.

As Molly looked over the setup, she pretended to be its inhabitant. "So where would I hide something valuable?" Her eyes moved to the mattress first. She raised it up but found nothing beneath it. She went through the pile of dirty clothes, half-expecting to find something hidden beneath them. When she stood back up, her eyes rested on the holes in the plaster and lath wall. One such hole was low to the floor. On a hunch, she leaned over and shone her flashlight into it.

"Bingo," Molly whispered, pulling out a gray touchpad, the same model as her own yellow pad. She turned it on. Unlike her own, this one had almost no icons on its screen. She tapped the lone briefcase icon.

Molly gasped. She stared at her own face, her high school senior picture. Next to the image, a document outlined her recent history, her parents, and their address before they moved into the assisted living complex—the facts needed for someone to locate her. Hastily, she paged through the other documents. She stuffed the touchpad beneath her blouse and raced out of the building, heading back to the Cartwright Corporation skyscraper as fast as she could, running down the fast lane of the MTES.

"Everyone. Come see what I found!" Molly's eyes glowed with excitement. She had answers at long last.

"Look here. Twenty-five years ago, the Galactic Defense Department of Defense authorized a secret program called Operation Lucky Strike—a kind of a joke it says, but I sure don't get it. The two doctors behind this operation attempted to make two breakthroughs. First, they hoped to genetically engineer 'lucky' soldiers. Second, they wanted to perfect cloning, proving they could create untold superman-fighting machines, replacing normal grunts.

"Here's a photo of the baby boys. One must be Frank." She passed around the touchpad displaying a collage of twelve young male faces, identical except for their haircuts. "I'll bet there's someone out there who doesn't want superman soldiers or even lucky men around. That's why they're killing us, but way too many of us aren't lucky. They're dead.

"And listen to this. Doctors Nelson and Janet Padella were in charge of the cloning operation. According to these records, they cloned us, genetically enhancing us with what they called the 'Lucky Gene.'"

"See, we like *are* lucky," Leslie said. A huge grin illuminated her face.

Molly brought up another document. "As proof of concept, they split up the boys and got them different adoptive parents. But this more recent paper says Ted Billings was abducted years ago, while two others have vanished.

"This one documents us. They cloned a dozen women, calling us Test Two of the Lucky Gene." Molly smiled at Leslie. "Okay, Leslie, I'll concede your point about being lucky, but Sandy and the others weren't so lucky."

Leslie frowned, but Molly finally duplicated what else she'd just read. "Wait! There must be four more of us."

"I'll check into it, tomorrow," Janine said. "With these records, I can see how the assassin tracked us down."

The four sisters pored over the documents, but little else of value appeared. No one understood the many genetic modification notes, but the clinical notes meant little: height and weight at birth and periodic checkups. Other documents recorded their adoptive parents' jobs and addresses, though no data was more recent than five years ago.

Unfortunately, the old records cast no light on who the assassin might be. Molly dusted the touchpad for fingerprints, but found none but her own.

Taking no chances, Deanna kept a security squad escorting Janine to work each day and escorting Molly and Leslie whenever they went out, often to visit Leslie's parents or to make more arrangements since Leslie had to sell her parents' costume store. Further, Deanna sent an anonymous tip to the police, suggesting where the assassin had been staying. Later, they learned nothing came from the tip; the assassin had abandoned that location, leading Molly to speculate she'd spooked the assassin either by her appearance there or by snatching his touchpad.

Next, Molly decided to see if she could discover anything more about these two doctors since that was the only real clue she had. A day later, her frustration crescendoed because these doctors weren't evil bastards. World-famous for having achieved major breakthroughs in biological nanotechnology, they often worked with Chicago's Galactic Medicine.

Downing a beer, Molly reflected on what she'd learned to date. Then, it struck her. Ted Billings. His name sounded familiar. She dug out her high school yearbook, leafing through the pages. And there he was, a twin of Frank, but with very short hair—a buzz cut. Ted was in Science Club and Computer Club, groups that Molly and Frank had completely avoided. "So he was a geek."

She did an Internet lookup on him and found only a single, old newspaper article.

Sixteen-year-old   Ted   Billings   was
arrested ... reputedly heavily into computers
and   hacking   ...   was   caught   breaking   into
Galactic   Defense   systems.   GD   officials
arrested him and took him away. His parents
claimed they had no idea what he was up to in
his   bedroom   at   night.   GD   officials   refused   to
comment   on   what   damage   Ted   did   or   might   have
done   to   their   systems   or   even   how   a   young   high
school   student   could   get   access   to   their
secure   servers.   A   GD   official   hinted   that   the
young   man   would   shortly   have   his   T-day.

"So, he isn't dead, but on some isolated South Pacific
atoll. Interesting."

Then, she saw Frank's photo and the short message
he'd left in her yearbook. Tears flowed freely.

***

The next day around noon, a special courier wearing the blue
and gold uniform of Galactic Defense arrived at the Cartwright
Skyscraper looking for Molly.

"Ah, here you are, Miss Parkinson. You're a hard one to
find. Special Delivery Orders from GD. Sign here."

Molly signed for the sealed package and watched the
young man leave. The last time she saw a uniformed GD
courier was when she graduated Private Investigation training;
he presented her with her PI license and her first monthly
stipend. Molly opened it and read the document. She had
received her first obligatory assignment from GD. She gasped.

Miss   Parkinson,   you   are   ordered   to
undertake   an   investigation   of   retired   General
Clay   Fuller.   During   June   and   July,   he   has
withdrawn   an   unusually   large   amount   of   his
life's   savings   and   in   cash.   GD   must   know   where
that   cash   has   gone,   particularly   if   it   has
aided   our   Sol   Empire   enemy,   the   Sixth
Invaders,   or   possibly   our   ongoing   war   with
them.   If   you   find   he   has   been   aiding   our
adversaries,   you   are   authorized   to   terminate
him   and   any   others   connected   to   his   nefarious

52

`dealings ...`

Current information on the general followed, including a photograph, bank account numbers, and a host of relevant papers. The package included a burner phone along with specific orders about when and how to report her progress.

When Molly finished reading the documents, Leslie walked up.

"So like what's this all about? Like a corporate assignment?"

"Astute observation, Leslie. Yes, my first one. They're ordering me to investigate some retired general. This couldn't come at a worse time."

Leslie chuckled. "No kidding. We've like got a serial killer like gunning for us. Your fiancé was like murdered, and it's not like safe for us to be on the streets. So what are you like going to do?"

Molly sighed. "Well, it's not as though I have any damn choice. Everyone's obligated to their sponsoring corporation. We have to do what they want and when they want."

"But like couldn't you explain you've got like a serial killer gunning for you? Maybe they'd like ask someone else."

"Fat chance. You know corporations as well as I do, Leslie. No, I have'ta see this through. Can you fix me up with a disguise?"

"Like, wouldn't let you out of here without one. Follow me. Remember; call like every day so we know you're safe. Promise me."

"I will, Leslie. Thanks for disguising me."

***

The general's home was in the far north side, close to Rockford. Molly couldn't take her electric car and so had to use the MTES. She packed some of her surveillance gear into a small backpack, along with food and water. After hugging Leslie goodbye, she headed out the back janitor entrance, disguised as an older, plain-looking woman, perhaps a maid or janitor.

By late afternoon, she arrived in the northern suburb of Rockford, regretting not having brought a portable chair for the long trip. Chicago stretched from the northern edge of the state down to just north of Peoria. The MTES ran the length of the city though Molly did have to follow directions. She navigated the last block on foot, looking for a good surveillance point.

Luck was with her. The home across the street from the general's house was vacant and scheduled for demolition. Perfect. She sneaked inside and took up a position in a window of a second-floor bedroom that had once been a boy's room; faded posters of girls and video games covered the walls. From here, she could see the entire front of the general's white, clapboard home. She set up her spy binoculars and her eavesdropping dish, plugging in the earbuds. Molly unwrapped her sandwiches and prepared for a long night.

Around ten, movement against a street light caught her attention. A man dressed in dark clothing slipped up to the front door. He didn't knock; rather, the general opened the door as the man arrived. Whoever this was, he had been expected, and Molly pointed her dish towards them while listening to the pair and making a recording of what she heard.

"General, they're holed up in the Cartwright Skyscraper. I can't get to them. Ideas?"

The bass voice of the general barked. "We'll have to get more creative." After a pause, he said, "Okay, we need them outside and together. So we'll arrange a bomb threat. Blame it on the Sixth Invaders. Have the police handle the threat. Make it official and believable. But do it in the morning when they're just getting up—before the place is swamped with workers. Have someone block the back doors—a delivery EMAC. Make them come out the front doors. You be in position, and they'll be sitting ducks."

"Brilliant, general. One more day and you can finally rest easy. All the clones will be terminated. Nothing to trace back to you."

"Precisely. Here's your next advance payment. Come back for the rest when it's done."

"Aye, sir."

Molly stifled a gasp. Not only had the general run the cloning project, but worse, he was behind the assassinations. Her hands nearly crushed the binoculars as she watched the man salute General Fuller. She cursed, unable to get a good view of the assassin's face.

He must be the assassin. Probably a former soldier and closely tied to the general. Damn, I'm too far away to terminate the fiend when he leaves that front porch.

While she could follow him, she knew where he'd be tomorrow morning. No, her orders were to handle the general.

Thus, she made two phone calls, the first to GD using the burner phone. "Yes, I believe the general is paying this hitman to murder men and women, who were made around twenty-three years ago by the two Padella doctors who worked for General Fuller." She reported what she'd heard about the latest assassination setup, but didn't feel comfortable using the word "clone" to whoever was on the phone. "We should warn those living in the Cartwright Skyscraper."

From the various grunts or sighs, she concluded this wasn't what the corporate executive at the other end of the phone expected to hear. She felt vindicated in not mentioning the word "clones." *Does GD already know about General Fuller and the clone project?* Her stomach knotted. If they didn't, then the GD officials wouldn't know the real motive behind the murders. But if they knew, then why had they sent her on this assignment? Her mind raced down many lines of thought while her stomach twisted tighter and tighter.

"No, we'll handle the warning. Here's what you're to do. It's too late to follow the assassin, right?"

"Yes, too late, but he'll be outside the front of the building in the early morning."

"Okay. Then, you're ordered to break into the general's home and under extreme prejudice, terminate him and anyone else living there. Once he's dead, search his place thoroughly, and wait there until we can send a team for you. Together, we'll trap and terminate the assassin in the morning. Understood?"

"Yes, terminate the general and everyone else inside. Search and wait for backup. Got it. Are you sure we don't just want to arrest him? Put him on trial?"

"Terminate everyone in that house, search it, and wait there for backup, who'll be there in about an hour. Those are your orders. Follow them!" The line went dead.

Molly's stomach knotted. *I'll become a murderer, too. He should be arrested and given a trial. What should I do? I'm obligated to follow orders or they'll arrest me. Shit. I want to help others get justice, not be an assassin for hire.*

She called Leslie. "I found the man who's paying the assassin to murder us and the men." She outlined what she'd heard and her new orders.

"Oh my god! Let me like get Deanna and Janine on the line. Maybe they'll like have some ideas." Leslie did just that, bringing both women up to date on what Molly discovered and what her orders were.

Molly said, "I have to at least confront this man. Trust no one now, not even GD people. They may not warn you three and let the assassin kill you before they step in."

Deanna said, "Thanks for the alert. I have some ideas we can pursue here to avoid the mess. I don't like them sending in backup for you. What's backup going to do that you aren't supposed to already have done? I think you're right. It sounds fishy. You be damn careful, Molly. I'll make sure we're safe here."

"Thanks, Deanna. I'll call you back around midnight no matter what. If I don't call back, then you know something has happened, so forget about me and get out of Chicago if you can."

"Okay. Midnight then."

Leslie said, "Remember, you like have luck on your side."

Molly chuckled. "But sometimes we can't see where luck might lead us. Bye. Until midnight." She hung up.

As fast as possible, she packed up her spy gear and headed out of the building into the deserted street. Molly slipped across to the general's home, still uncertain what she would do. She paused before his door. *Damn, I'm not a murderer.*

She knocked. General Clay Fuller opened the door, a surprised look on his face. Molly flashed her Glock. "Let me in. We have to talk."

He opened the door, glanced up and down the street,

and motioned for her to enter. Gun in hand, Molly entered. She saw no others present. The man was three inches taller than she was, somewhat overweight. She estimated his age at around sixty. Streaks of gray ran up the sides of his short-cropped hair. His face was squarish. He led her into his living room, turning on one small light. He wore pajamas and slippers.

"Misses is upstairs in bed. Keep it down. What do you want? Cash, jewelry? You—you're one of those clones! Damn."

"Yeah, true. I'm from GD. I heard all you said to the assassin who's murdered many men and women. Clones, you call us. Hah, we're people, too."

He mumbled something, probably a curse, and slumped into a chair, trembling, obviously shaken. "So—so what now?"

"Is it true? You and the two doctors illegally cloned men and women?"

"No sense hiding it any longer. Yes, we did. Empire security and all that. Now that the Sixth Invaders are attacking us, I only wish we'd been successful."

"Why? Why kill them now?"

He sighed and buried his face in his hands for a moment. "I'm retired. If the current GD execs find out about this, I'm dead. Word can't come out that GD sponsored illegal human cloning. So when the project failed, I tried to destroy all traces of it. I had hoped the current CEOs didn't know a thing about it. I expect that's what you're here for, right? They found out and told you to terminate me."

"Well, yes. I argued that you should be arrested and tried. No go. But I'm not a murderer. I'm supposed to murder everyone in the house. That'll make me no better than your hired assassin."

The general slumped forward, rubbing his head in his hands. He sighed again. "Those clones I had terminated—it's been for nothing. I'm a dead man, but can we make a deal?"

"Go on."

"Let my wife go. She's innocent. She had no role in any of this and knows nothing about it. Once she's gone, I'll borrow your gun. Look. I'd do it all again—make the clones. What folks here on Earth don't understand is that these Sixth

Invaders are making great gains in our Sol Empire. Before long, they'll be invading Earth, but by then it'll be too late to stop them. Our civilization is doomed. Let my wife flee, and I'll do it for you. Deal?"

Molly didn't have to think twice. "Deal. Get her out of here fast. GD's sending in some kind of backup, so make it quick. I'll step outside, so when I enter next, I can say honestly there's no one else in the house."

In spite of the dire situation, the general cracked a fleeting smile. Molly stepped outside, hiding in the shadows. Within a few minutes, she heard the back door shut, followed by running footsteps. She could tell they were heading towards the MTES. For a moment, she wondered if that could be the general fleeing for his life. She shook her head, flinging away that notion. She knocked on the door. The pale face of the general appeared. He motioned her inside.

"Look beneath the main bed. You might find it interesting. Now, put your gun to my head."

Molly hesitated. "I'm not a murderer."

He grabbed her gun and put it up to his head. Bang. He slumped to the floor beside the couch, dropping her gun.

"Shit!" Molly realized General Clay Fuller had made sure she wasn't guilty of his murder. In that moment, her opinion of the man changed. While he'd ordered the murder of her sisters and Frank Wells, he took an honorable way out. She stood motionless for a minute.

Then, she recalled he'd said to look under his bed. She raced room-to-room, looking for the bedroom. Beneath the bed, she found a package and pulled it out. A top-secret band held it shut. She opened it; he had preserved the details of the entire cloning project, including the roles played by the Padella doctors. As she leafed through the papers, one stuck out.

It mentioned the Padellas had constructed a research laboratory on a South Pacific atoll. Some numbers were written beside that entry. She had a hunch. She brought up the navigator app on her phone and entered the numbers. Sure enough, an image of an atoll appeared. Zooming out, she saw it was in the South Pacific.

Hoping she had time, she dashed out of the house and ran across the street into the derelict home. She hid the packet in the basement beneath some discarded refuse, along with her backpack of spy gear. Then, Molly ran back to the general's home. She spotted a man on the street, but thought nothing of it.

Once inside, she tossed things about, making it appear as though she'd searched his place. She uncovered a pile of cash, probably the assassin's final payment. Satisfied nothing was missed, Molly sat down to wait for the GD backup. She texted Leslie, saying the deed was done and where she'd stowed the top secret papers and her gear. Further, she confirmed that she would call at midnight, but before she could elaborate, six black-clad men barged in the front door. They wore the GD blue and gold armbands.

One said, "Molly Parkinson?"

She nodded. "There's the general. He's dead. House is empty. Found some cash. It's there on the table." She pointed to the money.

A man walked over to the body. He verified he was dead and then put the man's fingers onto an electronic device. Meanwhile, the leader said, "Well done, Miss Parkinson, but let's make sure we've got General Clay Fuller."

After an awkward silence while they waited on the fingerprint identification, the other man nodded. "Excellent. One traitor terminated. Okay, boys. Carry him out to the EMAC. Molly, come with us. We'll give you a ride back to Chicago."

Molly didn't trust the man—something intangible about his attitude. True, there wasn't one particular thing, just a gut feeling. "I can walk home."

"Come with us. The boss will have some more questions for you."

Since her orders hadn't mentioned that, Molly felt more ill at ease, but there were six of them—well armed. Sensing she had no choice, Molly followed them to their EMAC. At least they stowed the dead body in the cargo hold and not in the passenger area. Molly took the indicated seat and busied herself with the seatbelt. The other men took seats, and one of them moved up behind her. She felt a pinprick on her neck. "What?" she mumbled before the world turned black.

***

It was two o'clock and still Molly hadn't called as promised. Leslie's texts went unanswered.

"Something's like gone wrong. I just know it," Leslie said.

Since Molly hadn't called, Deanna acted. "Okay, ladies. Time to evacuate." Already, she'd left notes for her domestic staff. A nurse would watch over Peter since she couldn't bring him with her.

Each woman carried a large duffle bag with some of their clothes and necessities. They headed to the roof, where the corporate EMACs were parked.

A sleepy-eyed security guard saw his boss and said, "All warmed up and ready for you, ma'am."

"Thanks, John. Send someone to New O'Hare in the morning to pick it up. I hate these rush meetings."

He smiled at Deanna and stared curiously at the three women as they walk up the ramp and disappeared inside the vehicle. After watching the vehicle lift off into the star-filled skies, he went back to his post by the elevator doors and pressed the Resume button on his movie player app.

Part 2

Vic Broquard

Chapter 5 Corporate Arrival

The year was 2330, twenty years before Molly's abduction. A message from Karla's corporate sponsor appeared on her touchpad. She brushed a long, honey-colored lock of hair from her light blue eyes, tucking it behind her ear. An assignment—a corporate assignment—one she couldn't ignore.

A month ago, Dr. Karla Ziegler received her doctorate in anthropology and xenology from an Earth university, and Galactic University now sponsored the tall, thin young woman. Her orders read in part:

A discovery ship has found a new planet rich in rare earth ores but inhabited by human-like people who use stone tools. You are ordered to join the crew of the mining ship, Flammender Stern. The discovery crew left many notes on the people's basic language. During the week-long trip, you are to add this world's primitive speech to the ship's many Language Translator devices. Then, you are to act as the liaison between the miners and the local inhabitants, so study the native population in depth ...

Karla jumped about, waving the letter in front of her roommate. "I can't believe it! Me! Study this new culture. Stone tools even."

Her friend said, "Oh Karla, this is a career maker! Lucky you." The two danced around the tiny living room before Karla packed.

***

The Flammender Stern, a giant mining spaceship of the Sol Empire's Galactic Mining corporation, arrived in orbit above the newly discovered planet in the habitable zone of the type M6 red star known as Ross 248, about eleven light years from Earth.

Modifying the Language Translators occupied Karla's full attention during most of the journey. The original exploration ship's first-contact personnel had recorded around five hundred basic words of the language spoken by these people, as yet unnamed. Karla entered them in the various Language Translator or LT boxes. Via them, she hoped to carry on conversations with the natives. Also, she'd gone over all her new equipment, verifying the many types of recording devices were ready, along with their rechargeable power supplies. By the end of the voyage, she had developed a reputation as an intellectual recluse, having spent most of her time in her quarters.

She looked up rare earth ores and found they contained many critical elements used in most electronic devices, view screens, metal alloys of spaceships skins, filters, superconductors, solar panels, and so many more things that she grasped just how much civilization depended on these ores. While rare earth elements were plentiful in the Earth's crust, they were typically dispersed and rarely found concentrated enough to mine. Thus, she understood how vital this mission was to Earth and the Sol Empire.

"Orbit is achieved. Prepare for landing." The voice of Major Dirk Von Rahn, commander of the huge ship, echoed through the ship's intercom system. A tall man with a square jaw that gave him an imposing appearance, Major Von Rahn made her feel as though she was an outsider. While the others wanted the valuable rare earth ore, Karla longed to study these unusual, alien people.

Karla moved over to the port window to get her first glimpse of this new world, while her mind replayed the major's initial, but boring, briefing to her and the crew when they departed Earth.

"We'll be landing on the planet tentatively named Bahira. It orbits about half an Astronomical Unit from its sun, Ross 248. This is a dim red star, so its habitable zone lies close to the sun. The discovery ship listed Bahira's year as 182 Earth days, while its day is thirty Earth hours long. Unfortunately for our mining operations, stone-age primitives inhabit this world.

"As you've heard, Dr. Karla Ziegler is charged by her sponsor, Galactic University, to study these primitives. She'll be updating our Language Translators with these primitives' language and will be our interface to the natives."

Many crew members cast resentful glances at Karla as though her presence was an annoyance.

"Captain Franz Specht and his company of soldiers are ready for any eventuality, but I'm sure these primitives can't harm us with their stone weapons. I must remind you we're here to mine rare earth ore. We are authorized to use deadly force if necessary."

After hearing that phrase, Karla felt a knot in her gut.

"What are we going up against? Stone-age people and a world where visibility is near zero. Rare earth deposits lie in the central plains of the north continent, and the locals call this region Kaseeb. The exploration ship reported clouds covered the area, and it rained every day. Visibility is always zero down there. Thus, night vision goggles will be issued to everyone. We'll land in the highlands—called Kadar by the natives who inhabit the rocky hills—where we may expect better, but limited, visibility. Once we land, Captain Specht will secure our perimeter. Then, our mineralogist, Hobart Engel, will verify the precise locations where we need to mine for the rare earths."

Karla noted he didn't mention what her duties might be. He continued, "The exploration ship reported this world is safe for us. No poisonous plants, vicious animals, and warlike cannibals or unpleasant alien life forms. Just make sure you decontaminate when you re-enter. Let them keep their bugs.

"Now listen up, everyone. This is vital. If we can fill our hold with high-quality rare earth ore and return to Earth in thirty days or less, we each get a twenty percent bonus on our stipends. Need I say more? Let's make this one darn fast trip." Amid loud cheering, Major Von Rahn finished his briefing.

A week later, the ship touched down on the planet, buckling Karla's knees. She stowed her equipment, including a flashlight and night vision goggles in her backpack, and then made her way to the bay doors. Already Captain Specht and his men had scrambled out to secure the perimeter. Indicators beside the open bay doors showed gravity was almost that of Earth, while the oxygen levels were higher, making breathing easier. She stepped through the UV-light disinfectant station, which prevented the transmittal of germs to and from these people. She stood on the ramp and looked at this new world while awaiting the captain's all-clear signal.

Even though Karla had seen images of Bahira, she stared, eyes wide, mouth open.

Red. Everywhere, nothing but shades of deep red. Karla had no idea there could be this many ruddy hues. Near the sun that seemed as large as Earth's sun, brighter reds predominated, approaching a dingy cherry red; yet a short distance away, the sky darkened into a sinister blood red. What would sunset or sunrise be like?

Used to Earth's yellow sun, deep blue sky, and billowing white clouds, here, she felt she wore a pair of dark red sunglasses. Karla waited, hoping her eyes would dark-adapt. They did, but the sky wasn't blue. She remembered reading that air molecules scattered blue light, making Earth's sky look bluish. Trouble was, Ross 248 emitted almost no blue light or green or yellow. The sky appeared as a color wheel stuck on the reds, gradually going deeper and darker as her eyes moved away from the sun. Not blue, but black. The sky was coal black, and she saw stars in the daytime.

The rocks and ground also appeared ruddy. Karla wore blue jeans, a blue blouse, and sturdy brown hiking boots. But they appeared blackish or darkish like the Chianti wine she used to drink on college weekends. Her stomach knotted, so she turned on a tiny penlight for a moment. Relief. Her jeans were blue, and surprisingly, the rocks now looked like ordinary Earth rocks—blacks, browns, grays, whites, and greens, but the gabbro and olivine from Karla's geology lab classes vanished from her mind like undrunk wine swirling down her sink.

Still waiting for the all-clear signal, Karla breathed deeply and tried to analyze the odors in the air. It smelled musty and humid with a hint of rotting wood. Yet, it was clean and somehow fresh, devoid of all the "civilized" odors found around the giant cities of Earth. She glanced at her multi-function wristband-sensor, noticing the humidity at ninety percent.

Beep. Beep. The all-clear signal sounded, but she blinked furiously when the ship's outside lights flooded a small circle around the mining spaceship. After turning on her various recording devices stowed in her backpack, Karla stepped down onto the new world, thankful for the bright lights. The ship had landed on a level ridge; small rocks littered the ground. Along the ridge-line, she spotted a well-worn path, lined with rocks, giving the impression someone had moved the stones aside. The original reports stated the local people had been friendly to the discovery crew members. After checking her nav system on her wristband, she decided to follow the path or trail because she suspected people had constructed it.

After going a half mile from the ship—a distance given by the nav device—Karla noticed the illumination had become dim. Yet according to the sun's zenith position in the red sky, it was local noon or thereabouts, again confirmed by her wristband device. Behind her, she saw the white lights around the ship and the shirtless miners scurrying about.

She had grown up on a farm in Illinois where she could see her neighbor's house over a mile away. Here, was she even seeing a hundred feet ahead? To her, space had suddenly and irrevocably collapsed, threatening to squash her into a reddish oblivion. She tried to discount her growing sense of claustrophobia, but couldn't.

Trickles of sweat ran down her back. Although facing away from the sun, her back felt as though she stood in front of several red-hot stove burners, though her skin didn't feel itchy as it would from such dry heat.

Infrared. Karla's scientific mind finally made the connection. Ross 248 emitted much of its radiation in the red and infrared spectral regions, and she rather wished she could go topless, like the miners swarming around the outside of the ship. She'd seen them plastering their bodies with heavy sunscreens, but were they any cooler?

Would it snow on this world? If it did, would the snow be crimson, Dracula's heaven? Karla shook her head as if she could discard such thoughts, but her mind didn't cooperate. It was like being slow-cooked in that red microwave they had bought in their third year of college. She longed for a wind, any wind, or even better, rain. The exploration ship reported it rained every day. Would the rain be red, too? And the water? Surely not. She wondered how the people living on this world could ever get used to the constant infrared heating, the interminable sweating. She drained her first water bottle after just five minutes.

As she dabbed the salty perspiration from her face with a handkerchief, Karla noticed a tiny bird embroidered in one corner. Were there birds on this world? Couldn't hawks and birds of prey see in the infrared? A whirlwind of unrelated images flooded her mind. A shrill cawing cry from overhead pulled her into the present. She saw only a black form against the black sky, motion marked by fading and reappearing stars.

Off to her right, pale reddish, spindly plants starved for life-giving light. Ferns. For the first time, Karla smiled. She had a passion for tall ferns, which as a child she had raised on the north side of their farmhouse, but these ferns riveted her attention. The fronds rose upwards almost six feet, thick and broad, hiding her face from the sun. She couldn't resist shining the penlight on them, for surely, they weren't a sickly pale red. No, a washed-out, light green reflected back to her eyes. However, the fronds curled up as though stunned from the brilliant light. Karla relaxed; plants were still green. Photosynthesis still worked, but she swore she could hear the plants begging her to give them more light, just not as strong as her penlight.

Still, she had a job to do: interface with and study the inhabitants. Karla continued slowly along the path, refusing to take out her powerful flashlight or use night vision goggles, because when she met those who lived here, she wanted to appear as normal and human-like as possible.

"Oh!" Two feet in front of her, two men carrying spears blocked the trail. Humans, yes, but... They towered over her. She was five feet eight inches. The men were dark skinned, thin, and spindly with long, matted hair. While their faces broke into broad smiles, their eyes caused her to gasp. At first glance, their eyes seemed twice the size of hers, and their pupils were even more startling, covering much of the eye and with only a thin ring of iris surrounding it. Almost no white was visible.

"Hello. I am Dr. Karla Ziegler." The LT box on her waist translated her speech into theirs. When they responded, it also translated theirs into hers. She felt confident because her video and audio recorders were already on and recording. Karla heard them speak. Having programmed the LT boxes during the voyage, she found their vocal sounds familiar, though they still reminded her of the ancient Australian Aborigines' language recordings she'd once studied as a grad student. She depended on her LT box.

"Ah, you sky people come again. We see your blinding lights. I, Malik of Kadar. He, Tarik of Kadar."

Both wore a loincloth made from a soft, brown fur. Sandals of the same material covered their feet. Malik was the taller of the two while Tarik had a bushy beard. If not for their unusual height and large eyes, they might pass for tall, skinny Earth humans.

After this first exchange, Karla took heart. "Do you live nearby? I would like to visit your village or town. Are there many of your people here in Kadar?" She hoped she could get a conversation started. This was so fabulous.

"Kadar, not far; we look for stone blanks," Malik said.

"Flint blanks? Oh, I get it. You're looking for flint to use in making spear points and arrowheads."

"What arrowhead mean? Spear points, yes. We make spear points to trade with the Kaseeb for food and hides." He pointed off to his right—the lowlands, which were always cloud-covered.

"May I watch you? I've never seen anyone making spear points before."

Thus began an interesting afternoon for Karla. She learned that in the highlands, there was little or no food—neither plants nor animals. The people lived in caves, so they had to trade with the Kaseeb for their sustenance.

"No rocks down in the Kaseeb valley, only ferns, animals, and tall plants," Malik said. "Our ancestors came from valley—many generations ago. Today, if we go down to Kaseeb, we cannot see. Always nighttime for us."

"I see. You depend on trade with the Kaseeb, and they must depend on you for their spear points and scrapers."

"They do." Malik continued flaking off more chips, and she watched the spear point taking shape. "Tomorrow, Tarik and I take a bag of points and scrapers to the Meeting Rock, part way down the valley path—a compromise. There, we barely see, and they squint, so fair to all. We meet with the Kaseeb and trade. You want to come with us?"

"Yes, that would be wonderful. Thank you for asking me." Karla was infatuated with these people.

"So, do sky people need spear points or scrapers?"

"Er, no. Our people work with metals." She wondered if they knew what metals were.

"Ah, so that why sky people have returned. You dig up metals. We watch other sky people digging. They say want metals."

"Yes, that's right. Say, do you have gods and goddesses here, like a Fertility Goddess or a Hunting God? Religious ceremonies?" So caught up in the moment, she forgot her training.

Both men laughed. Malik said, "Silly sky people. Each of us *is* a god. You be like the sky people who came before. None of them was a god."

Tarik chuckled, adding, "And they had no faith. They believe in Creator God, but one who is never seen or felt. They did give one god a name, but it sounded strange to our ears. Sky people truly primitives, eh Malik?"

"We should be polite and ask her, before jumping to conclusions, Tarik. So, Karla, are you a goddess or do you believe in that invisible Creator God? Perhaps we should use simpler words again. Sky people might not understand us if we speak properly."

"Good point. We must talk simpler for her."

Karla flushed. This wasn't going at all the way she had imagined it would. Maybe they didn't know what she meant by a god. "I'm not a goddess. Someone had to have made the universe—all this." She swept her arms about, encompassing all the land about them.

"See, Malik. Sky people really primitives," Tarik

pronounced, indicating the matter was definitively settled. "Flying machines do not make them gods."

Malik sighed. "So it must be. It is as the Kaseeb woman, Ulima Al Atia, has said. Technology doesn't make sky people gods."

Tarik smiled and suggested, "Perhaps they just need time to evolve into gods."

Karla didn't understand what they were suggesting, but it was close to dinnertime.

"I have to head back to our ship for supper. Where do I meet you tomorrow and when? And please, you can talk the way you normally do. I'll ask if I don't understand something."

***

Over dinner, Hobart discussed his mineralogical findings, verifying the accuracy of the preliminary scans done by the exploration ship that had discovered this world.

"Vast quantities of rare earths are down in the Kaseeb valley. Tomorrow, I'll establish the precise location of the densest deposits. We're going to be rich, fellows, rich," Hobart said.

"Excellent. I can see big paychecks for us all," Major Von Rahn said.

Karla listened to the table discussions, but ate rapidly, returning to her cabin to analyze the day's recordings, still confused over the primitives' talk about gods. The video recording was abysmal; she couldn't make out anything beyond the bright lights of the ship. Hence, she abandoned further attempts to capture video streams, focusing on sound recordings. Today, she had doubled the number of known words in their language, adding them to her LT box.

***

At noon, she saw Malik and Tarik coming towards her, but her first glimpse of them put them ten feet away, though she heard them long before she saw the pair. Even on the hilly land above the dense clouds, for her, visibility was severely limited. She still refused to don the night vision goggles that the crew members wore because it made them look like strange aliens.

Both native men carried a fur bag bulging with spear points.

"Hi Tarik. Malik."

Nodding to her, Malik said, "This way. We go down the path halfway to Table Rock. We trade there. Come on."

The two men walked rapidly down the path.

"Er, I can't see well enough to keep up with you."

The two men halted and looked at each other.

Malik said, "I walk slow for you. Tarik walk normal and be at Table Rock on time."

"Sorry. I didn't mean to delay you. I don't see well in this dim light." She worried that if she used her flashlight, she might blind them.

He laughed. "The Kaseeb complain the light here far too bright; they cannot see. That why we meet halfway."

Karla estimated they'd walked about two miles downhill. The path was rocky and well-worn, but not too steep. Yet, as soon as they entered the top layer of the red clouds, visibility grew steadily worse. She knew they were close to their destination, not because she could see the rock and people, but because she heard many voices, some female, discussing trading for spear points. She almost bumped into several before she saw the rock and group of traders.

"Ah, here Malik and sky person, Karla. This, Table Rock, and these Kaseeb who trade with us: Rasha, Hana, and Aleser."

Karla squinted and spotted the giant rock, perhaps twenty feet across. Food bags, hides, and other items covered its top. Aleser held a spear and stood guard over the two women, who had been handling the trading before Karla arrived, temporarily halting it. He wore a loincloth much like Malik and Tarik. The women were even taller than the two highlands men—at least six-six—and just as thin and wiry as the men. Since everything appeared reddish to her, she presumed their exceptionally long hair, which was thick and shiny in the pale red light, was likely black, almost touching the ground. They wore fur boots and a loincloth, but their ample breasts were bare.

"Welcome, sky woman," Rasha said. She ceased her bargaining with Tarik. "We heard your flying machines yesterday. We saw you coming down the path. Strange that sky people see as poorly as the Kadar. Tarik said sky people come to dig metals from the ground."

"Hello, Rasha, Hana, Aleser. Yes, we're here to dig for the metals we need."

Hana giggled. "What good be metals? You can't eat them."

"Our people make all kinds of useful things from the metals, like bowls, plates, silverware, wash basins, and our flying ships—things we need to stay alive. Metals are important to us." Karla tried to use nouns she thought these people might understand, but she didn't want to mention weapons.

Rasha nodded to the others. "See, I told you they make more flying ships. We Kaseeb need no flying ships. We walk well. Karla, please come to our village and share our dinner."

"Sure. I'd like that, but I should let you continue your trading. I'll watch."

For another hour, the four haggled over boots, sandals, bags of vegetables, bags of dried meat, and various bone tools. Karla wished she could have photographed the tools, but in the dim light, she could barely see their probable outlines.

Finally, Tarik said, "Done. We return in seven days to trade again."

"We be here," Rasha said. She and Hana picked up the items that hadn't sold.

They watched the two highlands men head off up the trail, lugging several bags each. Aleser examined the spear points. "You bargained well, Rasha. These be good points and make fine new spears." He picked up several of the heavier bags while the women grabbed the rest.

He said, "Sky woman. Stay on the path. I lead the way. We might see a wild boar. If so, don't move. Let me chase it away or spear it for dinner. It not harm you, but good food."

"Okay. Are there other dangers I should be aware of? Also, I don't see too well, so please don't go too fast for me."

"No dangers." He chuckled. "We already know that. No Kadar can enter the valley of the Kaseeb, for they cannot see at all. And we be blinded by the brilliant light up in the highlands."

Karla noticed their eyes. The lowlanders' eyes seemed enormous compared to hers, perhaps double that of the highlanders. She thought, evolution and adaption. She could barely make out things, so it was no wonder the Kadar didn't want to come down into the valley. Ouch. She stumbled into something wooden, but she couldn't see what it was.

Before long, the trail ceased descending, opening onto a vast valley system. Each footstep sank into the very soft, moist ground. On either side, giant ferns wavered as they brushed against some of the fronds. The earthy scent of decaying plant matter hung in the humid air. A light drizzle fell, soaking Karla's clothes, though the Kaseeb didn't seem to mind.

Aleser stopped, raising his hand. Off to the right, Karla heard a grunting sound. Only now did she wish she'd brought along a gun for protection. "It be there, wild boar. No harm you," he said, pointing to it, but she couldn't see anything beyond about two feet from her face. Karla suspected these people might be seeing in the infrared—that is, body heat. When the noise moved off, they continued on the path.

She heard sounds of a village long, long before she could see any part of it. Domed huts dotted the land with fern fronds acting as thatch, held up by what must be branches from a tree. The strong pungent odor of cooking fires announced dinnertime was near. Karla wondered how difficult it was to keep fires going in such a wet, humid valley. They stopped before a sunken cooking fire in front of Rasha's hut.

Many four-legged, furry animals roamed around the fringes of the village. These looked and acted much like llamas that Karla had once seen in a petting zoo, here called bacas. Over dinner, she learned these were their pack, milk, and fur animals.

While her hosts prepared their evening meal, many children and other women came over to see the sky woman, some touching her wet clothes and giggling.

"Will rot," one older woman remarked upon seeing her clothes up close.

"I expect so. They'll dry out when I return to the sky ship. Rasha, can I do anything to help?"

"No. You my guest tonight. Soon, we eat and then talk."

Karla thought the meal was interesting, filled with exotic tastes and textures. By Earth standards, the meal was balanced, with meat, vegetables, and fruits, according to Rasha's descriptions. The meat was stringy with a gamey taste. The tubers appeared whitish to her eyes, but so did nearly all the food items. Saltiness disrupted the otherwise bland taste of the various vegetables. The fruits tasted somewhat like apples and dates, if first dusted with salt.

After the dishes were cleared, they served a dessert that had a light, nutty taste, washed down with warm mead, which tasted good. Soon, she felt the buzz of its alcohol. Karla logged each item that was served, including its name, the basic food group it belonged to, and what it tasted like. Her recorder was running, so capturing this data involved nothing more than normal conversation around the dinner table, except, in this case, it was around the sunken fire pit. She listened to the surrounding conversations.

Rasha said to another woman, "Yes, we made a good trade today. Good spear points for your sandals. Make two more pairs for next trade trip. Oh, and Malik says 'hi.'"

The woman giggled. She and Rasha talked until Aleser joined them. Since Karla wasn't spending the night, she thanked them for everything and had him point her to the return path.

"Don't worry. I'll use my flashlight so I can see."

That brought many chuckles, but Karla was careful not to turn it on until she was well clear of the village. In silence, she hiked back up the trail, only now noticing what must be trees in the distance, fifty feet to her right or south, their trunk and branches a stark white. With her bright light, she felt safe walking back alone. From her wrist sensor, she determined the path was four miles long and climbed a thousand feet. After two hours of brisk hiking, she saw the bright lights of the giant ship illuminating the rocky highlands around it. Two sentries marched about, nodding to her when she approached.

Chapter 6 Corporate Action

After taking a long shower, Karla sat down to work up her day's field notes. Classified as in a stone-age civilization, these people she'd found intelligent. They made use of the natural resources available on this peculiar world. Other than the Table Rock, she'd not seen one pebble in the lowlands. Hence, the need for people in the highlands to make the spear points necessary for survival. She logged the precise location of this village on the ship's main planetary map as her last action.

As she did so, she noticed Hobart and his people had been active. They'd filled in many details on this original map made by those who first found this planet. The village lay inside one large red oval that Hobart had drawn. From his notation legend, the red lines enclosed the highest concentrations of rare earth ores. The yellow lines showed the locations of secondary deposits, while the blue lines represented lesser deposits, likely to be mined in cleanup operations, perhaps years from now.

Even though he'd only surveyed half the valley, Karla fretted. They'd go after the richest deposits first. Unless the map changed, they would wipe out this village and the land many miles around it. Worried, Karla wrote a lengthy note to Major Dirk Von Rahn, explaining the village location and the ecosystem she'd uncovered. She begged him to avoid damaging the village and its surrounding fields. As the hour was late, she turned in.

The next morning over breakfast, she purposely sat next to the major. "Sir, did you see my field notes from last night?"

He chuckled. "Yes, I could hardly miss them. Pinned to my door." He laughed again.

"So what allowances can we make? Their village and lands lie smack in the middle of Hobart's red oval."

"Nothing. Hobart expects to have his initial mapping done late today. Tomorrow, we must begin ground prep work and hopefully start filling our cargo hold with the rare earths."

"But sir, what about these people?"

"You can tell them they have a day to move elsewhere."

"But we can't just wipe out their homes and fields. It's not humane. These are people."

"Weird ones. Stone-age. No one will miss them. Besides, you've seen the orders we've been given." He repeated them for her benefit, including the use of deadly force. "The Galactic Mining corporation will arrest and hang us out to dry if we don't follow their orders."

"But it's not right. It's not ethical."

"Who cares? They're stone-age primitives. That's the end of it. Go tell them they have to move today, doctor. You *are* our liaison officer."

"Sir, I'm going to send word of this up to my boss at Galactic University. Dr. Hilda Eichhorn has a lot of pull. I bet she'll get Galactic Mining to give you different orders."

She rose and left her half-eaten breakfast on the table. Besides, her stomach had just knotted. She ran back to her room, composed a dispatch, went to the radio room, and fired it off to Earth.

Ross 248 was about eleven light years from Earth, meaning that light or radio waves sent now would reach Earth in about eleven years. In fact, this was the most formidable barrier the Sol Empire faced centuries ago. Back then, a brilliant Indian physicist named Hyber developed his theory of four-dimensional space. Some very short straight lines in 4-d space translated to extremely long distances in 3-d space. By proper line segments, vast spatial distances could be traversed by stepping into 4-d space, traveling that short distance, and stepping back into 3-d space. His name became integral with its name, hyperspace.

One hundred nine stars and eight brown dwarfs that never achieved nuclear fusion lay within twenty light years of Sol. About two thousand stars were within fifty light years of Sol, and most hadn't been visited or explored.

The Sol Empire spaceships traveled these vast distances by using hyperspace. Communications were possible via hyperspace relay, which is how Karla's message was sent back to Earth, received later that day. She didn't wait around to hear the reply since the round trip might take hours. She packed her things and headed off to the village. She had to warn them.

***

"Yes, Rasha, they will dig up the ground all around here. I'm not sure how it works, but I'm sure the machines will strip the earth down several feet to lay bare the ore. It's monstrous that my people would destroy your village, your people. If you stay, everyone and everything will be killed.

"I've begged our leader, and I begged my boss back on Earth to stop this madness, but they aren't listening. Well, I've not heard from my boss yet, but I'm not hopeful. Honestly, we are the barbarians—the uncivilized monsters. I beg you, flee while you have the chance."

Rasha cursed, as did Aleser, who left to tell others the sky people had become their enemy. "So can't we fight back? Our men have spears." She gnashed her teeth and stomped one foot on the soft ground.

"Your spears will be useless. Our fighters have guns, which kill from a long distance. Your fighters will be dead before they can even get close enough to toss a spear. Besides, spears won't harm our metal flying machines."

"So we cannot stop your people from destroying our world?" Her head sunk and rested on her hands.

"Rasha, your people and world have nothing that could stop my insane people from doing this."

Loud yelling and cursing distracted both. They stepped out of her hut and saw the entire village was protesting this terrible news. Karla didn't need her degree to sense these people felt betrayed and that her people had become treacherous.

Aleser stomped over to her. His face tightened, muscles rippling. He thrust his spear into the soft ground. "Sky woman. Our people will not stand for this. We march on your flying machine tonight when the bright sunlight will not blind us. You be spared since you came to warn us." He turned and left, joining another group of men.

Hana joined the two women. "Is this true, sky woman? Your people will destroy our village and lands?"

Tears streaming down her cheeks, Karla could only nod

78

yes.

Rasha said, "Come. We must visit Ulima Al Atia. She be the oldest and wisest woman in the Kaseeb." She pulled Karla along with her. Hana followed them into the old woman's hut.

Ulima was ancient. Her face was extremely wrinkled. On Earth, Karla knew no one lived beyond sixty-five, and dementia took everyone before they were terminated. Ulima must be far older than any Earth person.

Rasha relayed Karla's awful news. "She says we cannot fight the sky people—that we must move. We have nowhere to move to. What can we do?"

In her raspy voice, Ulima said, "Children, have I not always told you the answer is always knowledge? It is not facts or data, but true knowledge, which is certainty. Remember always we are spirits, not bodies. Yes, the sky people have flying machines and many fancy devices that we do not, but that does not make them powerful or wise. Wisdom comes from knowledge of both the physical universe *and* the universe of spiritual beings."

Rasha said, "But tomorrow the sky people will destroy us and our village."

"And the rains may come and wash out our crops and drown our huts. Tomorrow, our sun may explode, as we know suns sometimes do. Remember our history, Rasha, Hana. We are gods and goddesses and came to this world seeking more knowledge of the physical world. We have become complacent, believing we know all there is to know, but the sky people show us our misbelief.

"They know far more about the physical universe than we do, so the answer is clear. We should return with them and learn their superior knowledge of the physical universe. But remember in your quest for knowledge and technology, do not lose your knowledge of spiritual beings, for the sky people are showing us, reminding us, of what happens if we do. When people forget their true natures or have never found it, they commit atrocities; they become criminals."

"Thank you, Ulima," Rasha said. "In the rush of the awful news, we forgot the duality."

"Because we have become complacent, it is a blessing

the sky people have come to show us how much we have misjudged the universe."

Hana said, "Aleser and many other men have already forgotten. They are angry and may act out of anger."

"An angry man always misses the true target," Ulima said. "Anger attempts to stop motion. Only more communication and more understanding resolve a conflict. Remember that, Hana, but do not give up on Aleser just yet."

Karla listened to what Ulima said, but didn't grasp everything the old woman said. She knew she had to try harder to prevent this disaster. After promising to return later, she headed back up the trail using her flashlight. She needed speed.

Upon her return, she found her boss had answered her detailed message.

```
Dr. Karla Ziegler,
    Yes, ordinarily, the situation on Bahira
should be handled differently. However, at
this time, acquisition of rare earths in as
pure a form as possible is the top-most
priority of Galactic Manufacturing. Because of
the ongoing war with the Sixth Invaders, this
has also become the highest priority with
Galactic Expansion, which oversees the Sol
Empire and all other galactic corporations.
    I queried this on up the lines. It's been
seen by Galactic Manufacturing, Galactic
Expansion, and even the Galactic Defense
corporations. Your best option is to convince
the many primitives living in the affected
areas to move elsewhere.
    Sincerely,
    Dr. Hilda Eichhorn
```

Karla cursed, took a deep breath, and headed off to find Major Von Rahn.

"Ah, Karla. I take it you received your query reply."

She nodded. "Sir, I've told those in the lowlands what is supposed to happen tomorrow. Some are threatening to attack the ship, but I've explained such would be futile. They'd just be killed."

"Primitive stone spears are hardly a weapon." He smirked.

"Sir, you're asking a whole village to move. Can't we give them more time to do that? I don't think it's physically possible for them to do that in just a few hours."

Major Von Rahn glared at her. "Look, Hobart is finishing his last exploratory run in an hour. After that, he's submitting his final report. Thus far, we've seen no other deposit of rare earths that is as concentrated as this one is. I'm certain he'll want to excavate this site first. As for giving them more time, I've gone over the mining details: clearing the topsoil, excavating the ore, filling our cargo holds, and making the return trip.

"Everyone on this ship, except you, is counting on being able to pocket that twenty percent bonus for bringing in a full load of high-quality ore before the thirty days are up. My calculations show that if we work two shifts each day, we can make the deadline, but only barely. Are you willing to explain to everyone else on this ship that they will lose their huge bonus because you want to give these primitives another week to move?"

Put that way, Karla knew she'd be kicked off the ship, if not worse. She tried one last point of view. "Sir, I've only been able to study this civilization for two days, but one thing is clear. The people living in the highlands depend on those in the lowlands for their food and cloth. There are no plants or animals in the high country, but there's lots of flint. So they make spear points and trade them with those in the lowlands for food and other essentials. If we destroy the lowlands, because of their dependency, we'll be committing genocide of a people. Are we really going to do that?"

Major Von Rahn frowned. "Can't be helped, Karla. I've my orders. Years ago, when my boss didn't follow orders, they shot him and promoted me to major. So if I don't bring back this ore, Galactic Mining will terminate me, and I've no death wish. You best get your primitives to move and move quickly."

"Yes, sir," she replied with a deep sigh. She knew how wonderful it had been to get her university education at no cost to her, but she hated being obligated to a corporation and having to carry out their whims, especially this one.

She waited until Hobart turned in his final report late that afternoon. It hadn't changed. After a silent curse, she stole a comm set and headed back down the village. She had to get them moved out of the area. Failing that, she decided she'd place herself in the middle of the village and use the comm set to report to the major that she would not move. She'd be a human shield. Surely, he would then listen to reason and a compromise found.

"Hi, Rasha. I'm back. Is everyone moving away from here?"

"Hardly. Some are joining the Kadar in attacking your flying ship tonight. Most of us will follow Ulima Al Atia's advice. We will come to your sky people's world and learn much that we do not know."

Karla's face grimaced. "But I'm sure the major won't accept any passengers, not when he wants the cargo holds filled with the ores."

Rasha smiled. "You do not yet understand. Perhaps in time, you will. We will see. Come. Hana and I made warm mushroom ale. We only have this on special occasions, but since we may be gone tomorrow, no sense in letting it go to waste."

All three women got drunk and fell asleep.

***

Meanwhile, several hundred men rushed the spaceship, brandishing their spears, intent upon stopping the sky people. Captain Franz and his battalion dispatched them long before they got within fifty feet of the ship. By using brilliant lights so the soldiers could see, they blinded the local men, making the assault even more one-sided.

***

"My mind feels like mush," Karla lamented early the next morning.

Rasha said, "Time to rise. Here, sip this. It replenishes what the ale depleted out of your body last night."

She handed her a gourd of a reddish liquid. Karla downed it in one long gulp, trying not to taste it. Soon, she felt better. While the village women stoked their peat fires outside their huts, Karla made use of the comm device.

"Karla calling Major Von Rahn. Come in, please."

She didn't bother following protocol. Only the major could alter the planned destruction of the local lands.

After a couple minutes, his voice replied. "Karla, where the devil are you? We're about to begin mining operations."

"I'm standing in the middle of the Kaseeb village, sir. They haven't had time to move everything. They need more days. I'm not moving until we reach a compromise that avoids genocide of these people." She couldn't make it any plainer. He'd have to give a little now.

Onboard the Flammender Stern, several junior officers looked over at the major. He turned off the comm, not even deigning to reply. In his mind, she'd made her decision and so had he.

"Lift off. Commence mining operations." He rattled off the coordinates, which put the ship about two miles south of the village, but their path ran through the village and beyond.

Momentum lay behind the latest in strip mining operations. The giant mining ship circled the planet, accelerating rapidly. Then as it passed over the designated high concentration area, it dropped a generated force field constructed in a V shape, reminiscent of ancient plows. The momentum of the ship was converted into a plowing force that eventually slowed the ship down to a low cruising speed. On the ground and based on the depth of topsoil to be pushed aside, the "plow" removed all matter down to the indicated depth, mounding it up high on either side of the cut, laying bare the rare earth deposits.

On the next path and with the force field now shaped like a giant scoop, the ship excavated the ore, mounding the dirt in one of the cargo holds. Many such passes extracted the ore, though in this case, the significant depth of the ore required many passes.

In the village, Karla heard the mining plow coming. Its forward lights blinded her. When it was a few feet away and the ground beneath her feet shook, she screamed a curse. She felt her body being violently shoved up and to the side while a great pressure crushed the air out of her lungs. Pain. Excruciating pain gave way to blackness.

Chapter 7 Recovery

The realization that man consists of several distinct parts thrust itself upon Karla. Until now, she thought of herself as a female human being—that is, a flesh and blood female body but with a bright mind. Now, her body was dead, compressed into the giant mound to the southeast of the strip mine.

Some religions of ancient Earth suggested man was composed of a material body made of physical universe matter, a mind composed of mental images or pictures or videos, and the person, the personality, the "you," the spirit or spiritual being—immortal in terms of the physical universe.

When one's body died, the being, the person, moved on and picked up a new baby body, creating an ongoing cycle of birth-growth-decay-death.

Karla found herself floating above the red clouds of Bahira. She could see the dim M6 red sun and stars—vast numbers of stars. Ross 248 wasn't bright enough to wash out the Milky Way. Unlike perception via her eyes, Karla perceived everything within a sphere around her, greatly confusing her.

What's happening? Shit. They killed me along with everyone else. Oh, god, I'm dead!

***

Rasha and Hana, lifelong friends, rose upward from the cloud-covered lowlands and viewed the heavens and stars. Via telepathy, Rasha sent to her friend, 'Wow. So this is what we have been missing all these centuries. I had forgotten what it looked like. Incredibly beautiful.'

Hana sent, 'Indeed. Oh, there's Karla. Is she ever confused!'

'She's not a goddess. She doesn't even know what she is. Since she sacrificed her body to prevent her sky people from doing this to us, we should help her.'

Hana sent, 'She made the ultimate sacrifice on our behalf, so yes, we should.'

Hana moved over to the confused Karla, who appeared as a yellow ball of energy, and placed concepts into Karla's mind.

'Hi, Karla. You're a spiritual being, just like us. We're going to your sky people's world to learn much about the physical universe. We'll hitch a ride on your flying ship, along with hundreds of others.'

'You're in my mind. How is this possible? You're dead, too. What's happening to me? Hana? Is that you? How? I'm dead, aren't I? How can this be?'

Hana sent, 'Silly sky people. You know so much about the material world around you, but almost nothing about your own selves. Since you tried to help us, we'll help you. Karla, like all sky people, you are immortal; you cannot die. You aren't made of physical universe matter and energy. Your mind of mental images is the interface between you and your human body. You think a thought, and your mind makes your body respond to that thought.'

'I don't understand. This can't be happening. They killed me, but I'm not dead. I keep hearing you in my mind.'

Hana sent, 'With much practice, you can manipulate the material universe directly. You won't need a body's force to move things around.'

'I keep hearing you in my head, only I don't have a head. We're all dead.'

Hana sent to Rasha, 'She's in bad shape. We'll have to work with her a great deal.'

Rasha agreed.

Hana sent, 'Karla, we'll bring you with us, unless you know how to get home.'

'I'm lost! I don't know which way is up or down.'

***

Karla felt a gentle tug as though someone pulled on her arm. Without a body to resist it, she floated along. Karla strained to see who was doing this and thought she saw two whitish energy spheres. Then, she spotted the Flammender Stern ahead. Trying to avoid smashing into the solid spaceship, she flinched but found herself pulled through the hull of the ship as though it was as thin as air. Bright lights invoked her reflex to blink, but she had no physical eyelids to dampen it.

Hana placed reassuring thoughts into Karla's mind.

'Here we are. We'll park ourselves along the ceiling so we're out of the way of your sky people. If you look, you can see hundreds more of us resting on the ceiling. We're going to go to your world, get new bodies, and learn about the physical universe from you sky people, who know so much more about it than we do. Don't worry. Rasha and I will take care of you and see you get a new body, too.'

Karla looked around. *I don't understand. This is our ship. Am I on the ceiling? But I'm dead. No, somehow I didn't die. What's happening? Is this a really bad hallucination? Where is Heaven?*

Hana tried a different approach. 'Karla, look at that floor.' When she did, Hana sent, 'Okay, look at that ceiling. Good.' She had Karla doing that for several minutes until Karla brightened up and some of her confusion lessened.

'See, you're a spiritual being, but right now you aren't in a human body. You can still perceive even if it's rather confusing to you. Before your body died, you probably only used your eyes to see. We'll help you get a new baby body back on your world. Then, we'll help you discover your true nature. In return, we want to learn from your people all about the physical universe. Okay?'

'I don't know what I'm doing or supposed to do or even how. So yes, I need your help. Thank you, Hana.'

Hana sent, 'Well, it's simple. We enjoy inhabiting human bodies because of the wonderful sensations we get from them. When those bodies die, we find another baby body and take it over as it's being born or shortly after its birth. This cycle has been going on for eons.'

'Long ago, our people used to have bodies that weren't alive as these bodies are. We called them plastic-like doll bodies. They were indestructible, more or less. If something broke, you installed a replacement part, but those bodies provided us little sensation or feelings. These bodies have fabulous sensations—especially sex—and we've become addicted to them. Anyway, once we reach your world, Rasha and I will help you get a new one and learn more about yourself.'

For a time, Karla watched as the crew members moved

up and down the hallway, like ants around their hole. Her sense of time vanished, but she didn't dare move from her spot on the ceiling. For one thing, she didn't know how to move, and for another, she was too afraid to even try. Everything was so strange without a physical body.

***

Rasha sent to Hana, 'Look down there. It's their world. That island looks incredibly beautiful.'

Hana sent back, 'Fantastic. Hey, I see three baby bodies down there. Let's grab them. I love that island. So picturesque.'

The South Pacific atoll was crescent shaped, two miles along its curve. A landing pad and several concrete buildings lay at one end while a spacious villa house rested on the opposite end of the island. The babies they saw or sensed were inside a concrete building, the secret research laboratory of a pair of geneticists, Doctors Nelson and Janet Padella. In their early thirties, this competent pair had ended their cloning projects and were now experimenting with the latest biological nanotechnologies. Each held several advanced degrees, but both were homely. Intelligence and shared interests formed their marriage bond, not physical attraction.

***

In 2324 or six years before the returning mining spaceship passed over the atoll, the two doctors worked on a secret Galactic Defense Department of Defense (DOD) project to develop human cloning technology. Cloning humans was illegal—hence their secret research laboratory on this atoll. During their research, the doctors believed they had discovered the lucky gene, a slight mutation on one chromosome that supposedly resulted in phenomenal luck.

Four years ago, the DOD wanted identical, lucky superman soldiers, so the pair created a series of clone males and two years later, a series of clone females, introducing the lucky gene into the DNA. As the years passed, the experiment proved that while the cloned bodies were identical, each had their own unique personality, completely not what either the Padellas or the DOD had expected. Further, after four years, the lucky gene hadn't yet expressed itself in the males or in the two-year-old girls.

Then, around nine months ago, the two discussed their research projects. "We're losing our funding for clones," said Nelson. "Still, we've got to thank that Kane fellow; we used his research on cloning technology before he vanished. I wonder whatever happened to him."

Janet clenched her lips. "Nelson, don't knock Kane. Serendipity is our benefactor. His subsequent nanotechnology hints allowed us to create the Fetal Regeneration Stimulus. Because of that, we've been able to begin to genetically modify humans, just as Galactic Medicine wished."

Nelson frowned. "Point taken. Besides, we also stole his ideas on silver compound nanoparticles and the silver nano mesh to speed healing. Those show incredible promise. Also, I don't see why GMed refuses to let us research cures for genetic defects and diseases, but instead work on their beauty modification for women."

"Hey, they're paying for our research, not Galactic Defense. We've proven humans can be cloned successfully. We won't win any awards for that incredible breakthrough, but you're right about the funding. Honestly, who'd have thought the clones would end up with totally different personalities? Cloning is utterly useless."

"Except to get us terminated if they find out," Nelson said. He bit his lip while drumming his fingers on the desk.

She nodded but raised her eyebrows. "What I can't fathom is why we haven't seen their lucky gene expressing itself. Theoretically, it should have become apparent by now."

"Well, I don't get it either, but we must do something fast or drop this entire line of research. I'm being pestered to join the nanotechnology research group. They're hounding me to further explore the nanoparticle healing processes we published last month."

Janet waved their cloning document in the air. "Well, we need to provide a real reason for their lucky gene to manifest itself, and I've an idea that may work."

"Another round of clones?"

"Yes, three should be enough. We'll house them here on the atoll where we can watch them. Besides, I wanted to tinker to see if I can change hair and eye colors. We can use our new genetic mutation gold nanoparticles and find out if they work. If they do, GMed will pay handsomely for our work. We can use the various nanoparticle approaches to continue our funding."

She cast a sly glance at her husband. "Good thing that Kane fellow disappeared, allowing us to use his breakthrough research. I wonder whatever happened to him. He was a strange fellow. Reminds me a little of CEO Hardy. You know, his gesture—the way he puts his hand forward, palm down, and sticks his little finger toward the ground. Kinda weird."

"Hum, I like the sound of those tinkerings. I'm convinced nanoparticle research is the way to go both for healing and for genetic mutations. What did you have in mind this time?" Nelson asked.

"Give them a challenge. No parents, no interactions with society. This might make ordinary life more of a problem, forcing their lucky gene to manifest itself. We'll provide a nurse to watch over them until they're around five years old. They'll never be allowed to leave this atoll. Yes, I know it's simpler to find adoptive parents. Perhaps here in a controlled environment that gene will express itself. We'll try the new beauty genetic mutation on them, proving it works. I was also thinking of making life more challenging for them by removing their hands. What do you think?"

Nelson ran his hands over his face and hair before sticking both hands nervously into his pockets. "How will having no hands help activation of the gene? We'll need to provide for them their whole lives. They'll be helpless unless we give them prosthetic hands, which are expensive and not too workable or so I've heard."

"Of course we aren't giving them prosthetics, Nelson. Every day, babies are born without hands or arms somewhere in the world, often birth defects, to say nothing of other accidents that occur resulting in limb loss. I've been collecting many Internet holographic video postings from such people. They show how they use their feet and toes as hands and feet. We'll provide them with laptops loaded up with all these 'how to do it' holographic videos. Come on, Nelson. We have work to do to save our funding. Besides, we'll not only get to test our new Fetal Regeneration Stimulus loaded onto the gold nanodot mutation technology but also our new silver compound nanoparticles and the silver nano graphene mesh. We want very rapid healing after surgeries."

"Are you sure, Janet? If nothing happens, then what? We can't very well release them into some city if the gene doesn't show itself. Too many questions would be asked, especially since they'll look identical."

Janet bit her lip. "You're right. If the gene doesn't manifest itself, we'll have to provide prosthetic hands before we dump them on the mainland. Our job is to create and enhance life, not terminate it. Let's see what hair and eye colors we can engineer."

Nine months passed. Shortly after their birth, Janet brought the new babies to the atoll.

***

As the mining ship flew over the atoll on its descent, Hana pulled Karla out through the hull and into the building with the three newborns.

Via telepathy, Hana sent, 'I've had enough red to last a lifetime. Dibs on the blonde-haired baby.'

'Ditto,' sent Rasha. 'I'll take the brown-haired baby. Karla can have the red-haired baby.'

Whoosh. Hana pushed Karla close to the baby body's head, and the tiny body pulled Karla inside its head as though it was a suction pump. Karla's confusing spherical vision collapsed down to the forward tunnel vision coming from the baby's eyes. And she felt her new body's hunger. She cried out.

Hana sent, 'Karla, once our new bodies get older, we'll help you become a goddess. For now, just relax and be a baby for a while.'

A plump but jovial woman in a white smock entered the nursery, where the three cribs lay side by side. She picked up the blonde girl, smoothing her hair. "Let's see who you are. Ah, you're Eve Burkey." After putting her back in the crib, she wiggled the baby's toes. Hana/Eve focused on remembering her new name.

The nurse walked over to the next crib and bent over

the brown-haired baby. "Oh, aren't you a sweetie." She picked up the chart at the side of the crib and said, "Ah, you, my darling, are called Randi Tucker." She gave the baby a kiss. Hana noticed Rasha/Randi mentally repeating it to herself several times.

Then, the nurse picked up the redhead, kissing her cheek. "Let's see. Celeste Sawyers. My, you're going to have gorgeous red hair."

A man entered. "We're ready for them, Nurse Leslie."

She nodded and carried Karla/Celeste out of the room, returning later for the other two. Hana/Eve heard this. Curious, she slipped out of her baby's body and followed Karla/Celeste.

She observed the doctors discussing the operation and putting a mask over Karla/Celeste's mouth. She watched Karla/Celeste try to wiggle out of it before drifting unconscious. Based on what Hana/Eve had heard, once the baby body was under, she acted. Later, Hana/Eve took the same action with her own new baby body and that of Rasha's.

Hana/Eve observed Karla/Celeste waking up to pain in her wrists. The baby screamed loudly, but Nurse Leslie put a bottle in her mouth. A few minutes later, Karla/Celeste's stomach was full, and the pain had gone away, thanks to the drug in the milk.

No one knew that Hana/Eve had discovered what the doctor intended to do to these babies' hands and that she had taken an action of her own. Years passed before Hana/Eve revealed what she'd done.

Days blurred before they moved the three babies into the fancy mansion where Nurse Leslie acted as their surrogate mother.

After several years, the two doctors gave up all expectations of seeing the lucky gene manifesting itself early. They forgot about the three, focusing on their successful gold and silver nanoparticle research, while the girls' programmed lives continued more or less on automatic.

***

When they were two years old, Nurse Leslie sat them before a big monitor. For several hours each day, she played and replayed a host of 3-d holographic videos made by various women and men who had no arms. Their videos showed how they did everything from eating to dressing to bathing to cooking. One video showed how one woman could fly an antique airplane, but that video was made over two hundred years ago; these days, such crude flying vehicles no longer existed outside the Moscow and Chicago museums. Why the girls were seeing such ancient vehicles eluded them until they saw videos of others flying a glider and an EMAC.

Eve said, "So when get hands? When they grow?"

Randi added, "Yes, when we get'em? Be like you."

"Silly girls. Your bodies were born without hands. That's why the doctors want you to learn how to do everything for yourselves using your feet and toes as hands and fingers."

Celeste was quiet. Intuitively, she knew if her body didn't have hands now, it would not get them later on. If asked how she could know that, she couldn't say. She was only two—or was she? In her mind, she kept seeing a reddish world, strange looking people with huge eyes, and a large spaceship—so confusing.

The trio had little choice but to continue watching the videos and to practice the movements with their feet and toes. Why? As the months went by, Nurse Leslie did fewer and fewer things for the girls, forcing them to become independent. When the girls turned five, their lives changed significantly in two major ways.

First, Nurse Leslie provided them with fancy satin dresses and tall, matching shiny, little pumps with matching bows, and took away all their other clothing and shoes.

"It's time you learn to be darling princesses. When you grow up, that's what you'll be—Galactic Dolls. So you must always look your best."

For a few days, she helped them get dressed, before she insisted they learn to do it themselves while she watched. Soon, the girls complained they had no choice in the colors of their gowns or heels; all were cherry red. After enduring their complaints, especially from Eve and Randi, Nurse Leslie brought them other colored gowns and heels, but only for a few years. The mansion had a dry cleaning machine along with a washer, dryer, and dishwasher, so they could clean their clothing and dishes.

Second, Nurse Leslie gave each girl her own laptop computer, loaded with grade school education courses. "It's time for you girls to go to school and learn to read and write, and to do many other things. These are the latest computers. They project a 3-d holographic image that can be manipulated by hands or voice commands. There is no screen or glass to break. I've taped a list of the basic commands on top of each laptop. Notice, each computer has its own name. Eve's is called Psyche. Watch. Psyche, show a menu of how-to videos."

Eve's laptop powered up, displaying a colorful holographic screen in front of her. The display listed many videos, showing their initial scene. "Psyche, start Grade One."

The display shifted to what looked like a full classroom. A teacher addressed the students. "Welcome to First Grade, Eve Burkey."

"Psyche, pause." The video halted.

"Oh wow. This is what I've been waiting for," said Eve.

"But we need hands," Celeste protested.

"Wonderful. We get to learn new things, Eve," Randi said.

"Thanks, Nurse Leslie," Eve said. "Psyche, continue."

Both ignored Celeste's protests and watched as the nurse showed them how to get their computers going and how to recharge them by using the wireless solar recharge units.

"Come on, Celeste," Randi said. "There's so much to learn. Isn't there, Nurse Leslie?"

She said with a smile, "Yes, there most certainly is."

"But we need our hands," Celeste continued to protest. As her computer booted up and the first lesson appeared, her attention drifted onto the virtual screen. She soon forgot about her complaint.

From this point onward, Nurse Leslie only came to the mansion in the morning and at suppertime to prepare their breakfast and dinner. The girls were responsible for cleaning up and for making their own lunches. Two years later, the girls had to cook their own meals while Nurse Leslie looked on.

One day while the trio struggled to make bacon and

eggs, Celeste complained, "So when will we get our hands? I want my hands."

Previously, the doctors briefed Nurse Leslie about this eventuality. "Look, girls, your bodies have been genetically altered. This is the way they'll always be. Well, that's not exactly true. Soon, your breasts will begin developing. The doctors told me that your bosoms will be very large, making you three stunningly beautiful princesses. When you're older and have your own children, they'll look exactly like you do. You'll learn about that in the biology classes you're studying."

"Stunningly beautiful" resonated with the three young girls, who giggled for several minutes, effectively ending that discussion. They were just at that age where they had begun to pay close attention to how they looked, especially their long hair, which fell to the small of their backs, rich and full.

***

When they reached Grade Five, all three knew their lives were wrong. Celeste, who periodically continued to ask about getting hands, led their protests. "This isn't right. Where's our moms and dads? Where's our families? We're not like the other kids in the class. They have hands; we don't. We should, you know. Besides, the ends of my arms are always throbbing. Sometimes, I feel like my bed sheet is crushing me, and I can't breathe. We take forever to do anything. Where are the trees and parks and stores? How can we be princesses if there's no one around this island? Okay, I like the feel of these satin dresses, but the heels keep getting higher, which only makes everything ten times harder for us. What's going on?"

Eve sighed. "She's got a point. It's time to help her and us. Remember, Celeste, ten years ago, I promised we'd help you. Now we're old enough to do it."

"Not really. What kind of help? Get us hands? Make my arms stop hurting?" Celeste asked.

"Let's start with the throbbing arms. Close your eyes," Eve said. "Okay. Now, let's find the last time your arms were throbbing?"

"Well, they hurt a lot yesterday morning."

"All right. Now go to the beginning of that time. Move on through it and tell me what you're seeing, what you're

95

feeling, what you're smelling."

"I'm getting up. We're helping each other get dressed. The ends of my arms are hurting. It's hard to do things when they hurt. Oh, I smell breakfast cooking. That's all."

"Good. Let's go back to the beginning and run through it again. See if you can discover more details," Eve said.

After three passes, Celeste said, "Something is really wrong. My arms—they're really, really hurting, Eve. Maybe this isn't a good thing to do. Maybe we should call the nurse."

"I understand what you're saying. Trust me a little longer. Is there some trauma that happened earlier that is similar? Like another day your arms throbbed?"

Celeste quickly found another particularly bad morning and ran through that a couple times, telling Eve all about it. Eve then asked if there was another one that was earlier.

"I see the Janet doctor looming over me. She's putting a mask over my face. I don't like it. Can't breathe. I'm struggling to get it off me. I can't. Everything goes black. I wake up." Celeste screamed loudly. "My hands are gone, vanished. Must be magic. My arms throb horribly. I'm screaming. I'm hungry, too—no starving. The nurse puts a bottle in my mouth. Ah, the pain goes away, and I go to sleep."

"Good going. Now, go back to its beginning and go through it again. Tell me what you are seeing, smelling, and tasting."

This time, parts of the operation appeared. "She's cutting off my hands!"

After six more passes through the operation, the arm pain had lessened but wasn't gone. Also, an element of confusion swept over Celeste. Hence, Eve asked if there was a similar trauma that happened even earlier.

"I see a blackish thing."

"Good. Go to its beginning. Now move through it and tell me what's happening as you go along," Eve ordered.

"Oh, I'm on a roller coaster ride. Some kind of park. Way high up. We're flying down. I'm screaming. We twist and turn, and my stomach nearly heaves. So confusing. Then, I heard something break. I'm flying through the air. Falling. Spinning. I hit the ground with my hands." Celeste screamed.

"My hands—shattered—broken. The pain. I tried so hard to not move anything, but the pain. I pass out. I wake up. I'm feeling dopey. My arms are bandaged below my elbows. I've no hands. Someone—mom—wipes my forehead. She says, 'Don't worry, Pumpkin. When you heal up, you'll get new hands. Mommy promises.'"

Eve said, "Very good. Let's go back to the beginning and go through it again."

After another two passes, the actual trip to the Med Center and surgery appeared. Then, Celeste opened her eyes. "Wow! The pain—it's gone! So's that spinning confusion. I feel great. No wonder I kept expecting our nurse to give us new hands." She started laughing. "Not likely on this island."

"Okay. We'll stop here for today," Eve said.

Still laughing, Celeste said, "Okay. Wait! I've lived before. That must have happened at least a hundred years ago. Wow. Thank you. I feel so much better, and they don't hurt anymore."

The next day, Eve continued with Celeste's therapy. "Today, let's see if you can find a time when you felt your sheets were crushing you."

Celeste did so, running through several nights when she had nightmares in which her sheets threatened to crush the breath and life out of her. Eve kept asking for an earlier time, and at last, Celeste ran into the trauma on Bahira, where the sky people destroyed the native village while mining for rare earth ore.

After ten passes through that trauma, Celeste laughed. "Wow, I feel fabulous. I really thought that by my being in your village, I could get the major to compromise. I was incredibly naive. Oh, my god! All my university education in anthropology just reappeared in my mind. This therapy of yours is just incredible. Can I have more?"

Eve said, "That's all for today. Yes, you can have as much as you want, but let me help Randi deal with the amputation of her hands. Then, she can do me."

"How does it work—this therapy thing?"

"It's very simple, as long as you grasp that there are three parts to a person. The being—the personality—is immortal and isn't made of universe stuff. We each have a mind that we use to think with and which stores everything that happens to us, rather like a 3-d holographic video. Finally, we have these physical bodies. When we experience trauma, loss, and pain and unconsciousness, our minds are still recording all that happens. Only since we're unconscious or dopey, we can't later review those recordings on our own. It takes another person to help us get enough power to see those recordings."

"Why is that?" Celeste asked.

"Because when those incidents are active, they impress their content onto our bodies, just like your arms throbbed and how you felt so confused."

"Oh, I see. The pain came from when that doctor cut them off. Oh yeah, and when I was spinning and flying through the air. Those traumas were active and influencing me then. No way could I have seen what was going on without you guiding and coaching me through them. Heck, I didn't even know they were there—that they'd even happened to me."

"Precisely."

"That was incredible. I could smell your world again— the red heat and the musty humus. And the pain and pressure. So real. I had no idea this was stored in my mind."

"Yes, but these are only the first baby steps," Eve said. "Back on Bahira, I said I would help you, and I meant it. First, we'll erase the mind's video images that are filled with pain and unconsciousness and severe loss. Then, we'll work on helping you discover what you are and how to operate as we do."

"Well, this is fantastic," Celeste said. "I want more— that's for sure. But first, you've got to help Randi and then yourself. Those phantom pains are very real. I'll watch you."

"Ayieee!" Randi later cried out. A bolt of pain shot through her right wrist and then her left wrist. "God, that doctor—she's cutting off my hands."

"I see. Okay. Continue re-experiencing that trauma," Eve said. "What do you smell?"

After several more passes, Randi started laughing. "The pain—it's gone. My, what you and I have done just to discover and learn what the sky people know about the physical universe." She roared. "Well, we'll learn everything they know! Give me a few minutes to calm down, and then I'll do you, Eve."

The girls now knew what had happened to their bodies, though the reason for their mutilations eluded them, as well as why they were still alive and on this isolated island. None believed the "genetic defect" reason given to them.

What Celeste found interesting was that after handling the amputation of their hands, both Eve and Randi had no further problems, aches, or pains. Yet, from time to time, she still did.

In fact, the next day, Celeste noticed that she had a vague head pressure and a slight headache. Eve asked for the last time Celeste had felt them and ran Celeste through that light headache incident, which didn't erase or discharge. Eve asked Celeste for an even earlier time, and Celeste uncovered a birth, filled with pressure and head pains.

"My nose feels crushed or squashed," Celeste said. "Oh, and my head aches, too. Someone keeps saying push, but I don't know what to push."

"Thanks for telling me. Let's go back to the beginning and run through it again. Tell me what's happening as you go along," Eve said.

After running through her birth a dozen times, the pressures hadn't vanished; she wasn't cheerful either. So Eve asked for something earlier. This time, Celeste found her birth as Karla Ziegler and re-experienced that birth incident many times. Still the pressures and aches didn't fully vanish but did ease up, so Eve continued to look for an earlier trauma that was similar.

Celeste said, "Okay, I see something whitish here, but I don't know what it is."

"Okay. Let's go to its beginning. Go through it and tell me what you are seeing as you go along."

Celeste did so. After a few times through this one, she discovered her new baby body died during a bloody surgery shortly after birth. Having her hands cut off so soon after this lifetime's birth had triggered the activation of this chain of birth incidents.

Laughing, Celeste said, "Well, no wonder I was so spooked when I landed on Bahira. Everything was so red! It reminded me of this botched surgery. They were trying to fix my heart and instead, blood flooded over everything. No wonder I felt so uneasy when I got to your red world. Incredible. I didn't know this was there or even why I felt so claustrophobic when I first set foot on your world. Wow."

"Okay. That's all for today," Eve said, smiling.

"Say, does this mean there could be trauma incidents behind all my feelings of frustration, annoyance, anger, fear, and helplessness? And all kinds of other weird aches and sensations? Like drowning while I'm lying in bed?"

"Absolutely," Eve said. "We have the time to work on all them. Besides dealing with the traumatic things that have happened to you, Celeste, we also need to handle the times you did those very things to another person. We also need to erase times you did those things to yourself, which will handle any suicidal tendencies you might have. Lots to work on, but I want to keep on studying. Randi and I came here to learn everything your people know. There seems to be so much to learn."

"Funny thing," Randi said, "these people know nothing about spiritual beings or their own minds. That's so weird."

"True, but they know so much about the physical universe that we don't," Eve countered. Both girls laughed.

Each morning, Eve gave Celeste another therapy session. Soon, Celeste often found herself outside her head when each ended.

Months passed. When Eve judged Celeste was ready for advanced work, she asked, "Celeste, can you make or mock up a small gold ball in your mind?"

"Yes, why?"

Eve didn't answer her, but said, "Okay, make eight of them. Position them at the corners of a box and position the box so it surrounds your body. Can you do that?"

"Sure. It's kind of hard, but okay. Sort of feels like I'm in a coffin or something."

"Good. Now make the balls vanish. Blow them up—

anything so they're gone."

"Two didn't want to go away." Celeste giggled. "Okay, they're gone now."

"Good. Now close your eyes. Have Randi put up eight gold balls in a box around my body."

After more giggles, Celeste said she had. "Good. Now make the eight balls disappear anyway you can."

"Okay. Now have Randi put up eight gold balls around your body and then make them vanish."

"That's hard. I don't want her to do that to me, but okay."

"Good. Now you put up eight gold balls around Randi's body and then make them disappear."

Around and around they went for several hours. Suddenly, Celeste sat up straight. "Oh, my god! I'm right here. I'm really *not* my body. Those gold balls—they mark the framework of my body. Hundreds of them. But I'm quite different, something separate from it. I'm behind its head right now. Is that okay?"

"Well done, Celeste. Yes, that's great. We'll stop for a while. We'd best get on with our school work."

Celeste had a hunch that the therapy Eve was giving her was critical, but as a young girl, she couldn't put it into proper perspective.

The lure of learning drove Randi and Eve forward, and they brought Celeste along with them. A year and hundreds of hours of therapy later, Eve hinted, "Girls, I can get our hands back, but we better not do it right now. Minutes before the doctor amputated your hands, I manipulated the gold balls that form the framework of our bodies, specifically, our hands. So I'm pretty sure I can force our bodies to regenerate hands."

"Wow. Cool. Why not now? We take forever to do things," Celeste said.

"Because those evil doctors are probably watching us. Remember last year when we vocally pretended to be ill and the nurse didn't come? We proved they aren't listening to us. But the nurse did come when we got the flu. They're watching us. If we get hands back, then they're likely to want to study us more or maybe cut them off again. For some unknown reason, they want us without hands. We'd best play along for now. If we can ever get away from here, I'll get our hands back. Trust me."

Celeste sighed. "Okay, Eve. Following corporate orders isn't an excuse for all those evil acts. Why do those doctors want us maimed for life? That makes no sense. None of this makes any sense. Why keep us here, isolated on this island?"

The months rolled along while the trio moved from First Grade through Eighth Grade. All three were straight A students, though they had to spend long hours at it. Just as they were completing Eighth Grade, something unexpected happened.

Chapter 8 Unexpected Company

In 2342—or eight years before Molly's abduction—Ted Billings was sixteen and in love. Unfortunately for him, his affections weren't reciprocated. In fact, Molly Parkinson ignored him, while she hung out with another classmate, Frank Wells. The object of Ted's admiration had raven hair, a round face, thick eyebrows, full lips, and an angelic smile that he loved.

Both Ted and Frank had brown hair and eyes, along with a square face and thick brow ridges. Frank knew he was handsome, combing his long hair in the latest style. Frank wore the latest fashions, the "tank-jeans," but Ted wore only patched faded jeans. Thus, the two boys looked different, more so than one would have expected of identical clones. Ted saw girls looking Frank's way when Frank passed by them in the halls of Eastland High School. Though Ted smiled at the girls, the girls never looked his way, perhaps due to his buzz haircut.

Ted participated in Science Club and Computer Club, but Frank and Molly joined the Soccer Club and the Basketball Club, though neither made the high school sports team. Still, Ted dreamed of one day having a relationship with her, if only he wasn't a geek.

One day at the lunch tables, he overheard those two discussing their hopes for the future.

Molly said, "I want to be a private investigator, Frank. It's the only thing in the world that truly interests me, except you, naturally. I like to help people, and I think I'd make a great PI."

Frank chuckled. "Molly, I can see you as a hot PI—your own office, gun, and everything. Heck, everyone knows how you uncovered what happened to the school's mascot. You'd make a great investigator, if only Galactic Defense will sponsor you."

She smiled, "And if they'll sponsor you. I know how much you want to be a policeman. I hope we both get in."

In his enthusiasm to do something nice for her, Ted acted. He was a computer whiz. Whereas Frank spent his funds on the latest fashions, Ted spent his on fancy computer equipment. Sophisticated gear filled his upstairs bedroom. After several nights of trying, Ted broke into and got access to GD's computer system. He zeroed in on the Choosing Day system.

Each year, when a student reached the end of his or her senior year, one corporation, or more if one was exceptionally lucky, would make an offer to sponsor them. (They also did a preliminary selection when one was in Eighth Grade, but that Choosing wasn't always binding.)

With a few keystrokes, Ted changed the database entry for Molly. Someone had already entered her name and a profession of Army Soldier. He gasped and changed her sponsored profession to Private Investigator. After saving the change, he smiled and logged out of GD's system. True, that entry wouldn't activate until Molly was a senior, but it served as a good guarantee that GD would sponsor her as a PI.

The next day at school, Ted had a huge smile on his face and a bounce in his step. He even nodded to Molly when he passed her though she didn't return it.

A week later, Ted saw how desperate Frank was to become a Chicago Policeman. Over lunch, Frank showed Molly a stack of Chicago Police literature. Again, Ted acted. It was obvious Molly would never look at him, but he wanted her to be happy. That night, he hacked into GD's system again and had GD sponsor Frank as a Chicago Policeman, changing the proposed entry of Army Soldier. Why GD would want these two to be grunt soldiers eluded him. Again, he smiled and logged off. Now Molly would have her heart's desire and Frank, too. He didn't try to find his own entry because GD wasn't likely to sponsor geeks.

The next evening after supper, without warning, GD guards burst down his parent's front door. One yelled at the shocked parents, "Where's Ted Billings?"

Dumbfounded, his father pointed to the stairs. While two heavily-armed men stood before the two, the others charged up the stairs. A minute later, one soldier carried the young, screaming and kicking teen down the stairs, tossed over his shoulder as though Ted was a sack of potatoes.

The original speaker said, "Ted is being arrested for hacking into the secure computer network of Galactic Defense. We don't know what he did while he was in our system, but we'll soon find out. Did you know what he was doing up there in his room?"

Stuttering, his father blurted, "No, no sir. We thought he was doing his homework. He's always gotten good grades. Surely, there's been a mistake."

"If there has, Ted will be returned to you. If not..." His hand moved across his neck as though cutting his throat. His meaning was clear; Ted would be terminated.

As the man carrying the still struggling Ted reached the front door, another man stepped up and injected something into Ted's neck. In seconds, all resistance ended. Ted's world went black. He never got a chance to "explain." He never knew the controversy he'd caused, at least not for many years. On the other hand, no one discovered what he'd done while he was inside their system.

Ted remained unconscious for several days while men transported him to a South Pacific atoll.

***

Nelson reread the written orders that came with the unconscious Ted.

Use Ted Billings as a guinea pig in your beauty enhancement experiments. The only requirement is that Ted must never be able to hack into our systems again or ever return to civilization.

Dr. Padella smiled. He always needed test subjects, so of course he'd use him. Since three other test subjects were housed on the island, Ted would join them. Simple. The husband and wife doctor team had long since forgotten about their initial cloning program. That was sixteen years ago. Besides, the babies were now teens and still showed no signs of being lucky. He'd not seen the three girls for years.

Nelson took a blood sample to study and found some strange defects in Ted's DNA, though he figured they wouldn't affect the genetic modifications. Today, everything involved using the latest gold and silver compound nano dot processes.

105

He asked, "Dear, what if I alter his genes and make him lucky too? Hold on! I just realized those genetic defects *are* our Lucky Gene. He must be one of our male clones. Well, he's not been very lucky. Maybe we can enhance his lucky genes. What will happen if those three young women we've been keeping breed? Will we get doubly lucky offspring? Interesting long-term test, don't you think?"

Janet replied, "Heavens, Nelson, those girls haven't shown the slightest inclination of being lucky. But on the positive side, with no hands, they haven't been able to interfere with our work, escape the island, or trouble us. We don't need any long-term test subjects, but we could use another test of the silver compound healing nanoparticles and the nano graphene healing mesh. Besides, neither of us has the time to spend working up a new set of genetic male beauty modifications for use on this single male subject. We aren't being paid to make male beauty modifications, only the proposed female modifications."

"Quite true. It'll take months to concoct a male genetic modification formula of some kind, assuming we even know what changes could or should be made." He brightened up. "Wait. We still have that original beauty enhancement formula we used on the three girls. Let's use that on him. It's obsolete, but it shouldn't matter since he's never leaving the atoll. I'll deal with modifying his body using our new gold, genetic mutation nanoparticles, while you handle the amputations and the tests of the healing nanoparticles and the silver nano graphene mesh. Take photos to document how well the mesh holds."

"Oh, you are brilliant." A wry grin creased her lips. "Transgendered, he'll never even want to leave this island. And like the girls, he'll not be able to bother us. If they should breed, then we'll have a new test."

The pair set to work. After waiting the requisite hours for the gold nanoparticles to disperse into Ted's body tissues, Nelson fired up the infrared gun, passing the beam across Ted's entire body. The gold nano dots absorbed the infrared radiation which then activated the tiny mutating particles attached to the dots. Shortly, the unconscious Ted slipped into a genetic mutation coma, driven by the Fetal Regeneration Stimulus. His body's cells mutated into their new DNA format. The accelerated and amplified process took over a week to work its miracles.

***

Eve spotted an Airliner landing and two men carrying an unconscious boy into the lab. Ever curious, she slipped out of her body, floated down to the lab, and spied on the proceedings. When the mutation process finished, she observed Dr. Janet Padella preparing for surgery, so she acted just as she had years ago. As before, nothing Eve did was visible to the doctors.

Janet used her scalpel on him, removing his hands. After applying the nano graphene mesh coated with silver healing compounds to his wrists, she marveled at just how well this new technology worked, carefully documenting the results. His wrists healed in mere days. In a month, the mesh and nanoparticles would be dissolved and flushed from his body. Thus in her mind, medicine had made giant steps forward.

Satisfied that Ted's mutations were finished and his wrists fully healed, she disconnected the IVs and tubes. Still unconscious, assistants carried Ted to the mansion at the isolated far end of the island where the three young women lived. They laid the naked Ted in a bed and covered him with a sheet. One assistant also placed a note on top of him for the women. After they left, Randi read the note for the other two.

Here's a new person for you to train in your special ways. Give him the works. Spare no effort. Dr. Padella

As babies, the three girls had been subjected to this same gold nano dot mutation as Ted had been, but with slight differences in hair and eye color, proving that the new nanoparticle process yielded far better control over the mutation process. Janet had proven that these young women adapted to their physical limitations quite well, even if they didn't display "luck." These independent young women felt they were "grown up" princesses.

***

Ted stirred, woke from the coma and anesthetic, and felt awful. Noticing his missing hands, he shrieked, but then screamed even louder because his tenor voice had become a soprano. A heavy weight threatened to crush his lungs, but no—his breasts were huge, nearly the size of his head. He screamed again and tried to get up. His hair fell to the small of his back, further shocking him. Something was also wrong with his feet. They wouldn't lie flat on the floor. He shrieked again, falling back onto the bed. He was still male, however, and managed to cover his lower body with the sheet.

His screams brought his three housemates into his bedroom. Each was fourteen, each was handless, and each had been cloned from the same genetic material as Molly and the others had been two years earlier. They wore fancy, cherry red satin gowns with matching pumps with the highest spiked heels Ted had ever seen. They looked like younger Mollys, except one had brown hair, one was blonde, and one was a redhead.

Ignoring his screams, Randi took charge. "Hello. What's your name? I'm Randi. She's Eve. And she's Celeste." She indicated each with a point of her arm.

His twisted stomach threatened to cut him in half, but he uttered, "Ted. Ted Billings. Where am I? What's happened to me?" His voice and body shook wildly beneath the sheet.

Randi said, "We believe we're on an atoll in the middle of the ocean, but we're not sure where. Don't worry. We'll show you how to do everything. You'll catch on in no time. Gosh, you don't look like a man, though we've not seen many men. We're completely isolated."

Eve said, "You didn't fully answer him, Randi. Ted, they mutated your genetic makeup—altered your DNA. That accounts for the impressive breasts, your hair, voice, and feet. In spite of what they might later tell you, they cut off your hands."

Celeste added, "Hey, they sent along a computer for him. Ted, they've probably put hundreds of 3-d holographic videos on it showing how other people adapt to having no hands or no arms. Some videos show how we brush our teeth, take showers, and many other normal things. We're

108

independent, just like you'll be—once you learn ways to do everything." She giggled and added, "But I didn't think men had breasts like us."

"They did this to me! I didn't have breasts before or hair this long. I'm as helpless as you are. My stomach's a knot. I think I'm going to faint or vomit."

Randi said, "Take a deep breath and let it out slowly. You've been in a genetic mutation coma for days. That's what they do on this research station—genetic mutations. Breathe slowly. Let's start again. I'm Randi Tucker. She's Eve Burkey. She's Celeste Sawyers." Randi indicated each with a nod of her head.

They had lush hair that fell just below the small of their backs. Each woman was about five-six, but in their heels, they seemed taller, though they were still shorter than his six-foot frame. The Padellas had long ago stopped providing other colors of dresses—"too expensive" they'd said in a message to the girls.

"I'm Ted Billings," he repeated himself. "Am I still a man? Oh, guess so. We're totally helpless. Who dresses us? God, I'm thirsty."

The three women giggled. Randi said, "We're independent. We live alone and do everything ourselves. We're supposed to teach you how. Celeste, get him a glass of water. So, you looked like other men and boys before they did this to you?"

Ted nodded.

"Well then, I can see why you are terrified. Don't worry. We'll get you fixed up."

"How? I'm helpless. My stomach is cutting me in half. I'm going to throw up."

Celeste returned, carrying a glass of water clenched between her arms. She sat down, slipped off her heels, and retrieved the glass, holding it up for Ted to sip, which he could do. The water helped, but only briefly.

"Oh god, I can't live like this." He panicked again.

Randi countered, "I suppose it'll take a while for you to learn how we do everything. Let's get him dressed. I'm afraid there isn't any male clothing, only gowns like these. There isn't even a color choice anymore."

Celeste giggled when Randi used her teeth to help pull the sheet off Ted, whose face reddened. Randi ignored his embarrassment, and all three women worked together to get Ted dressed, using a combination of stumps, toes, and teeth.

Randi then showed him how to slip on the pumps. "We're constantly taking them off when we need to use our toes for something."

Once they had him dressed, they worked together to get his long hair brushed out. As they did so, Randi said, "Getting dressed is the hardest part. So we help each other. Working together, as you can see, allows us to do what one of us can't quite do on our own, at least not easily. There, you see, we did it."

Eve said, "Right. We use our toes as other people use their fingers and hands. Now stand up and see how good you look in the mirror."

"Thanks. I feel better being dressed, but I look like a woman."

All three giggled. Eve said, "You do, but we know differently." He flushed again.

Celeste said, "First, we'll have you practice walking. Take small steps. You're doing fine. Let's tour our house. Are you any good at cooking? None of us is much of a cook."

She chatted, as she led Ted on a tour of their atoll home, whose windows were both large and nearly always open except during storms, allowing the sea breeze to pass through the home. There were five bedrooms, each with a queen-sized bed in them; one was still unoccupied. Their kitchen was small, as was their dining room, but their living room was spacious, with two couches along two walls, a large table, and six chairs centrally located. Four laptops sat on the table.

Celeste said, "Each of us has our own laptop. This new one is yours. You have hours and hours of 3-d holographic video to watch. They've scoured the Internet for videos made by others showing us how they do things. Anytime we get stumped, we go back and look at all the videos to get new ideas. But we almost never have to watch them anymore."

"So where do you come from?" asked Randi. "We were

born on this atoll. What's it like out there?"

"Chicago, Illinois. Wait a minute. You three look like my girlfriend, Molly. Well, I wanted her to be my girlfriend. She doesn't even see me. But the resemblance is amazing."

Celeste giggled. "We know. For some reason, we three look quite similar, except for our eyes and hair. We aren't sure why since we have different last names. I wonder if our breasts will get as big as yours are. We're almost fourteen." Ted flushed again.

Eve said, "I hope not, Celeste. Ours are big enough already. We have to keep getting bigger dresses. Let's go outside. It's harder walking on the roadway. That's the main village down there, where they have their offices, their genetics lab, and the general store. We walk down to the store to get our groceries, clothing, and stuff. Now that he's seen the atoll, let's go back inside and get lunch. Whose turn is it to make lunch?"

"Mine," Celeste said, "but you show Ted the videos on how to dine."

Back inside, Randi booted up Ted's new laptop for him. "Yours is named Alpha. You can give it vocal commands or manipulate the 3-d holo images with your nose, arms or toes. Alpha, show us videos on Methods of Eating." While the computer displayed that menu, Randi said, "I know—such a crude, weird description. We didn't make them up. Some idiot probably did. Okay, see how they are using their toes? See how they lift their cups?"

Another wave of panic flooded over Ted. "I don't think I can do any of that!"

"Practice. That's all you need," Eve said. "Give yourself time to learn these ways."

Thus began a terrifying new way of life for Ted. However, beginning the next day, Eve and Randi took turns running their special therapy on Ted, while the others continued their high school studies.

The therapy was tough going at first because his pain and unconsciousness lay buried beneath a wall of fear and terror. As the frightening aspects diminished, the pain-ridden part crescendoed before it too subsided, as Ted confronted what had happened to him while he was unconscious. When he faced the images of the female doctor standing over him and cutting off his hands, he screamed and swore to one day cut off hers. Four days later, Ted laughed over the whole adventure. The trauma had blown off, and he felt alive but so helpless.

While the pair continued to work their therapeutic magic on him, days stretched into weeks. Then one day he roared with laughter.

"Eve, I'm me. I'm not this body. I have a body. Wow! What a distinction—*am* versus *have*. Wow. It's incredible how the mind records everything, even when you're unconscious. I feel like someone's lifted a ton off my chest. No, that's my monster boobs." He continued laughing and so did Eve as she ended his therapy session.

Eve said, "I might have a way to restore our hands, but we best not try it until we can leave this place. If they see us with hands, they might just cut them off again."

"Nothing will surprise me now. You and Randi are amazing. How did you ever learn how to do this therapy thing?"

Both women shrugged. Eve said, "It's the natural thing to do, as normal as using a fork and spoon to eat with."

Ted shook his head in utter disbelief. These two young women had to be goddesses. He wanted to do something in return for the precious gift Eve had given him with her therapy sessions.

***

Weeks later, Eve complained, "Oh darn. We've finished all the courses in this High School Program. I want to learn so much more."

Ted grinned. He had been looking for ways to repay the girls for their kindness and therapy. In a flash, he saw how.

"I know a way. Let me tinker with your computer, Eve. The Earth's universities have online curriculums so anyone can study from home. In fact, most corporations prefer their sponsored students to study from home rather than going to the real university campus; it costs much less money that way."

Ted hacked into the Padellas' computer system, setting up direct lines to the outside universities but making sure the doctors didn't know this happened. With a slight tweak, each of the four had access to every course offered by every Earth university, all paid for by Galactic Defense, who'd done this to him. This time, GD didn't detect they'd been hacked. Ted learned from his mistakes.

Six months after Ted's arrival on the atoll, the four became official university students. Even lab courses were online, and some were done in real time, especially exams. Sophisticated programs allowed chemistry experiments to be done without dealing with the chemicals in a real lab. Other programs simulated the construction and testing of complex electronic circuitry. However, those wishing to become medical doctors had to spend their last three years working in real hospital and lab settings as did those studying dentistry and a few other fields.

Randi studied math, astrophysics, and hyperspace theory and applications. She had a head for complex mathematics. Eve studied anything having to do with genetics and biological nanotechnology. Celeste became fascinated with the behavior of chaos systems and the ability to predict future events. That accurate predictions could be made via mathematical formulae was her goal—that and learning all she could about how the two did their therapy.

***

Eight years passed for the four. Ted found these women's thirst for knowledge unbelievable and unquenchable. By the time the girls turned twenty-one, they had earned two doctorate degrees and were working on their third. At first, Ted continued studying complex computer systems and networks but soon became enchanted with the field of robotics.

However, Ted's favorite time of the day was the evening just after supper, when the gentle sea breeze blew through all the open windows. The four sat around the table brushing each other's long hair while sharing what new knowledge they'd learned this day. In his eyes, each of the young women was beautiful. Although they looked more and more like

Molly—only with long hair and dolled up—they weren't Molly.

Chapter 9 More Unexpected Company

The GD men kept Molly unconscious while they transferred her into an Airliner bound for the South Pacific. The giant ship landed on a tiny atoll. A security man carried her into the research laboratory, where Dr. Nelson Padella met them, a his body trembling.

The guard said, "Here's another guinea pig for you. Do what you want with her; the only requirement is she can never leave this island. Why we didn't just terminate her is beyond me. Gotta follow orders. Guess you must really need them." He placed her on a worktable, turned, and marched out of the building.

Nelson exhaled deeply; his shoulders slumped.

Janet entered the room, glancing at Nelson and then the young woman on the table. "What do we have here? Who was here?"

"A GD guard. He gave us another test subject. I was worried for a minute. I don't trust GD. Anyway, it's the same orders as that young lad we did some years back."

"Well, we don't have time to mess with her, Nelson. Wait, she looks like one of our clones."

"Search her," he said. "See if there is any ID on her. If not, I'll email GD about her. We don't have time to deal with her, so I'll use what's left of our obsolete nanoparticle genetic mutation serum. You can do whatever surgery you wish when I finish modifying her. Let's spend as little time with this one as we can. We've got much more important things to do—a deadline to meet with these female beauty modifications."

"Wait," Janet said. "This says her name is Molly Parkinson. Ah ha. I remember now. She was supposed to have the lucky gene, but it sure doesn't show, especially if she's here with us. Okay, I agree we don't want to mess with her. Use up the last of the obsolete serum. What I don't understand is why our lucky gene hasn't produced far better results because I just know we were on to something with Leslie. I'll amputate more this time. Maybe that will help force her lucky gene to manifest itself."

"Personally, dear, I think the lucky gene is a dead issue, but I guess it won't hurt to give it one last try. Still, I don't see how amputating body parts will force the lucky gene to express itself. Never did."

"It gives them a challenge to overcome. We've just not yet found a big enough challenge for them, except perhaps that fetish model. She showed signs of being lucky when Ace was shooting at her. Oh wait! I just remembered. Molly was the person who killed Ace and ended our attempts to get the lucky gene to manifest itself. Well, Miss Parkinson, payback is going to be a bitch!" A sadistic smile spread across her lips.

***

Eve saw the Airliner landing. As she had done with Ted, she slipped out of her body and floated over the complex to observe. Later, she acted on Molly's body, just as she'd done four times before. She didn't know this time her action with the golden balls wouldn't be enough.

***

Ten days later and using a small electric cart, an orderly drove the unconscious Molly down the long road to the manor house.

"Kids, here's another one for you," he said, depositing her naked body on the spare bed and covering her with a sheet. "Here." He tried to hand a note to Randi, but flushed. She had no hands to take it from him, so he laid it over Molly's body and departed.

Randi opened the attached note and read it for the others.

```
Here's a new woman for you to train in
your special ways. Give her the works. Spare
no effort. Dr. Padella
```

"So we have someone else living with us," Eve said. "I wonder what her DNA looks like. I'm going to find out because I think she's like us."

Ted joined the three girls. "The guy left a computer for her. Wow, she looks just like you three."

The three young women giggled.

Celeste said, "She must be a sister clone. Our clothes

116

should fit her. Her breasts are as big as ours and yours, Ted."

By now, the three women's breasts had filled out and were the same giant size as Ted's were.

Eve said, "They always take a DNA sample before they do any work. I'll sneak a peek with my computer." She pulled the sheet back to better see Molly. "Oh no! They cut off her arms, not just her hands."

All four gasped.

Ted said, "She's *really* gonna need to watch those videos. The damned butchers!"

Molly didn't regain consciousness for another hour, during which Eve hacked into the Padellas' network and discovered Molly's DNA matched theirs, confirming what she suspected.

***

Molly awoke lying in a strange bed. A gentle, balmy breeze filled with the salty smell of the ocean drifted across her body covered only by a thin sheet. As she tried to get up, she discovered her arms had mysteriously vanished, and her breasts were more like small soccer balls. Molly screamed. A terror knot balled up her stomach.

Four similar-looking women responded to her screams, entering her bedroom, their heels clicking on the hardwood floor.

"Hello. What's your name? Welcome to our home. I'm Randi Tucker. She's Eve Burkey. She's Celeste Sawyers. He's Ted Billings. I know. He looks like us, but trust us; he's a man. You'll soon see."

Molly gasped, her attention bouncing among the four. "Ted? High school Ted? Dear god, what have they done to me? To you? Where am I? I'm hallucinating. Wake up, Molly. Focus. Gotta be a hideous nightmare. Wake up! I feel sick. I'm going to puke."

"Sorry. The vicious Padella doctors did this to you. It's not a dream. I wish it was. Take deep breaths and slowly let it out. I'm Ted Billings. I know—I don't look like a man anymore. They did this to me. You look much like a high school girl I was in love with. Who are you?"

Gasping and trying to control her panic, she said,

"Molly. Molly Parkinson. Is it really you, Ted? They've mutilated you too. And these three as well? Oh!" She realized where she must be and who these four people were—that they were on an isolated Pacific atoll. "You're our three younger sister clones. Ted, the paper said you were terminated."

"I might as well have been. I've been stuck here for eight years and look like a freak."

Talking helped Molly fight to keep from vomiting and from shaking. Her mind raced to sort out what she was seeing. One moment she was fastening her seatbelt in the EMAC and now here she was with her body terribly mutilated. The two didn't connect. Then and now refused to join. Instead, she talked, hoping to wake up from this awful nightmare.

"We're helpless. So who takes care of us? I can't do anything. But your email said you weren't in danger. We certainly are. We need help. God, I'm going to throw up."

Eve said, "Waking up like this must be shocking for you, Molly. Take a deep breath and slowly let it out, like Ted said. You'll be all right. We four are fine. In time, you'll be okay, too."

"I'll never be okay!" *Breathe, Molly, breathe!* Her body shook nervously as she fought for control. She wanted to scream, to run away, to wake up from this hallucination. Instead, she focused on one breath and then the next.

"We're independent, but we help each other," Celeste said. "They sent along a laptop that has hundreds of hours of 3-d holographic videos of others who lack arms or hands showing how they do everything. First, we should get you dressed. Ted, why don't you go get her computer going? She needs to watch a lot of those videos."

"Er, right," he said.

Molly saw his face flush. His voice tone sounded so unlike Frank's voice, higher in pitch, a woman's voice. He left, and the three young women gathered around Molly.

Celeste asked, "So are you the Molly that went to high school with Ted?"

Fighting to keep from fainting or vomiting, Molly continued to talk, praying this was an awful dream. "Well, yes. He was there, too."

118

"You don't know, do you?"

"Huh? Know what?" *Is she trying to get me to think about something else? Keep breathing. Don't panic. God, I am panicking.*

"Ted's still madly in love with you," Celeste burst out. "He's here with us and transgendered because of what he did for you and that other boy, Frank."

Of all the things these hallucinations could have said, this wasn't one of them. Molly replied, "Huh? What did he do? I saw an article that said he was terminated because he broke into the Galactic Defense computer systems." As she talked, her panic subsided a little.

"He was sent here. They genetically modified him and cut off his hands like they did to us when we were tiny babies," Celeste said. "But you don't know why he hacked into their computers, do you?"

What Celeste was saying made some sort of sense, more so than much else had. So Molly played along. "Er, no. Why? Is it important? How can we live like this? I'm helpless! I think I might throw up." As she tried to move her arms to adjust her position on the bed, the panic returned again.

Eve said, "Keep on taking deep, slow, relaxing breaths. Celeste, I think you had better tell her the whole story because this has to be embarrassing for Ted. Meanwhile, we'll get her some clothes. Molly, just focus on breathing."

Yes, focus, Molly, focus. "Tell me what?" Molly's attention vacillated between curiosity over Ted and her mutated, helpless body, whose stomach raged out of control. But even now, her Cool Head attitude asserted itself, reclaiming what was left of her body.

"He was in love with you. Over lunch, he heard you wanted to become a Private Investigator more than anything else. So he hacked into GD's computer systems and found they had chosen you to become an Army Soldier. He changed it to Private Investigator. After seeing how much the Frank boy meant to you and how much he wanted to become a Policeman, he hacked in a second time and changed Frank's entry from Army Soldier to Policeman. But they found out and sent him here. He's paid an awful price for you."

Hearing this story helped Molly get her attention off herself. She clenched her jaw tightly. "I—I had no idea. I thought they chose to sponsor me as a PI. My god, both of us as soldiers? I must make it right with Ted, somehow."

A wave of guilt swept over her before reality flooded in again. "How can we live like this? I can't even get up."

Eve and Randi returned to the bedroom with clothes draped over their arms. Randi said, "One good thing is that we're all the same size, so one dress fits all. Things are much easier for us than they will be for you since we still have arms left. But trust me when I say that the men and women in the many videos found ways and means to do nearly everything without arms, but it won't be easy."

While Eve spread out the clothes, Randi continued chatting as though this situation was normal. Molly realized the chatting helped calm her terror.

"With Ted, he took a long time to adjust, but he does quite well today, and you will, too. Trust us. Even so, we have to assist each other. None of us can do everything alone, at least not easily. We need help. So, let's get you up."

Randi used her arms to pull the sheet off Molly.

"I'm naked. I feel sick and helpless. I can't even get up. My arms don't work."

Eve giggled. "Of course, they don't work. They're not there. Ted had similar issues with his hands for a couple of years, but he told us it does eventually go away. I'll take his word for that, since Dr. Padella cut off our hands when we were newborns. Don't worry. We'll help you. First, you should see exactly what they've done to your body."

She slipped an arm under Molly's neck and helped her sit up. The three got Molly onto her feet. But she wobbled, wildly moving her non-existent arms about to keep her balance.

"Something's wrong with my feet and legs!"

"No, they modified your legs and feet so your feet won't lie flat on the floor. You must wear the tall heels like we do. That's one of the mutations they did to your body. Your hair is a gorgeous black, but I suspect they've lengthened it."

"It's so long. Yes, it was just down to my shoulders. Can

120

someone cut it?" Molly stared at her hair, which fell below her waist. Only now did she notice that the three women's hair almost reached their ankles. That sight caused her stomach to knot tighter.

Eve added, "And they enlarged your breasts. None of us can figure why they did that. Ted claims they look like small soccer balls, but we're grateful they aren't drooping, sagging breasts. Still, they're annoying. Now, let's get you dressed."

"Don't you have any jeans or t-shirts?"

Eve laughed. "They took those away from us when we were very little. Since then, we've only had these fancy gowns to wear, along with matching pumps, which we put on and take off a zillion times a day. We have to use our toes as fingers. You must learn to do that, too. Ted said keeping his balance was the hardest thing he had to learn. But we three have been wearing them since childhood. Because you have no arms to help you, I think you'll have a more difficult time. The women in the videos did just fine, though they weren't wearing such heels."

Randi added, "Lots of practice. When they first gave us these fancy gowns to wear, they told us we were princesses and that we needed to look elegant all the time. Now, we know better. They even gave us a dry cleaning machine for the satin gowns. Sorry, but they only provide the gowns in cherry red. Are we ever tired of wearing red—but we've not been able to get them to do anything about that. Come on. Let's join Ted in the living room."

"This is frightening."

Molly took her first steps in the heels, though being dressed helped calm her nervous stomach.

"We won't let anything happen to you." Eve encouraged her.

They joined Ted in the spacious living room. He had Molly's new computer up, displaying its menu of video choices. He had "How to Feed Yourself" highlighted.

"Wow, Molly, you look fabulous. Your computer's name is Apollo."

"I look positively terrified, Ted, and completely helpless."

She watched the three women tossing their hair to one side, before setting down, so she emulated them, managing to avoid sitting on her own hair or falling down.

"I suppose we should have better introductions," Randi said.

"Please, keep me talking. I'm starting to regain control over my nerves. Talking is helping," Molly said. "A lot."

Randi smiled. "Thanks to Ted, we're attending online universities. We three have two doctorates already, but we're working on our third. I'm Randi Tucker." She had wavy brown hair. "My doctorates are in math and astrophysics. Now, I'm working on hyperspace theory and applications."

"I'm Eve Burkey." Her light blonde hair was also wavy. "My doctorates are in genetics and biology. Currently, I'm working on another in biological nanotechnology. Believe it or not, those Padella doctors on the other end of this atoll are the leading figures in this field. So my theory is that we're their guinea pigs."

The flaming redhead said, "I'm Celeste Sawyers. My doctorates are in the Behavior of Chaos Systems and Probability Theory."

"I've got my computer science doctorate," Ted said, "but now I'm studying robotics. Okay, this is your computer. Apollo. You can control it by giving it commands. A list of the basic commands is taped to the computer. Or you can control it by touching the hologram with your nose or by using your toes. Apollo has the Main Video Menu up. As you can see, they've organized the hundreds of 3-d holographic videos into action categories. Feeding yourself is more critical than any of the others, such as brushing your hair or getting dressed. Heck, we have to help each other with those. It's too hard to do those alone."

Molly nodded, and he continued. "It's okay to be terrified. I was at first, but this has to be even worse for you. Trust us. We'll be with you always. It takes emulating the ways these three girls found for doing things and lots of practice. You can do it. If anyone I ever knew could survive what they've done to you, Molly, it's you."

He went on, "One thing is certain. We're *not* helpless.

In fact, we're quite independent. We do *everything* ourselves. Those three are the masters. We've found nothing we can't do, but many things take longer to do than before. However, unlike us, you must learn all the new ways to do things that the people in the videos use."

Randi added, "Before you start watching videos, we should give you a tour of our mansion. It's picturesque. Ted just loves the balmy sea breezes that blow through our house each evening. I wonder if you'll love the same thing. Anyway, come on. Up and at it."

"Damn, I never expected just getting up would be terrifying, but it is."

Celeste volunteered, "We'll have you practice walking. Ted had a tough time learning to walk in the heels. I don't know why, but he did. Take small steps."

Molly said, "Probably because men don't normally wear heels. These must be as tall as Leslie's are. Crap."

Celeste chatted on as Molly teetered; a new wave of terror swept over her. "This is so scary. I keep trying to use my arms to keep my balance."

Ted encouraged her, "I did too—with my hands. But that'll pass in time. It did for me."

Celeste said, "You're doing well. Let's tour our house. Are you any good at cooking? We're always looking for someone who can cook better than we can. Ted's dismal at it."

She chatted away, further calming Molly, while she led Molly on a tour of their atoll home, whose windows were both large and nearly always open.

"So where do you come from?" asked Randi. "We were born on this atoll. What's it like out there? Ted's talked about Chicago lots, but we want to hear it from you."

"Chicago, Illinois, but if I don't focus on what I'm doing, I'll fall down."

Eve said, "Come on outside. That's the main village down there, where they have their offices, their genetics lab, and the general store. We walk down to the store once a week."

"You walk all that way? No MTES? This is impossible." Molly felt more hopeless than ever.

Eve giggled. "We've only seen pictures of that. Don't

worry, Molly. We'll show you how. Let's go back and get lunch. Whose turn is it to make lunch?"

"Mine," Randi said, "but you show her the videos on how to eat."

Back inside and safely seated, Molly watched the first of the many videos various women and men had made showing how they handled their meals by using their feet and toes as arms and hands. Watching the videos, another flood of panic swept over Molly. "I can't do any of that."

Randi brought in the sandwiches and drinks. Molly watched how effortlessly the three women used their feet to manipulate their sandwiches. She observed Ted wasn't quite as effortless in his movements. Near tears, Molly said, "I can't do this."

"Practice. That's all you need," Ted spoke up. "I was awful at it for the longest time, wasn't I, girls?" Three giggled. "Give yourself time to learn all these new ways. I had to learn a new way for darn near everything. It was horrible. One day, I was a man, and the next day I woke up like this, some kind of freak. At least you're still a woman."

Eve said, "Once you can eat well so you're getting good, balanced nutrition in your body, Randi and I will run our therapy sessions on you. That alone will make a big difference."

"Golly, Molly," Ted said, "that's an understatement. Their therapy thing is priceless."

Celeste said, "He's right. Their therapy is beyond incredible." She changed the subject. "We were thirteen when they brought Ted to our house. We're twenty-one now. After we helped Ted learn to do things, he fixed up our laptops so we can get access to all the learning courses on the Internet. We owe Ted everything for getting us the ability to learn such things. What are you studying, Molly?"

Randi interrupted. "Wait. She should tell us about herself while she's practicing. Come on. Let's go for a walk around the island. Molly can tell us all about herself. It will keep her mind off things."

"Yes, I'd love to see your island," Molly replied without thinking about it. Had she thought, she would have panicked again.

As they walked, Randi kept prodding Molly to continue telling them the story of her life, including all the details about discovering the clones and that Ted was also a clone, a detail that shocked him.

After dealing with supper, which Molly found even more challenging to handle, they adjourned to the living room. While they took turns brushing out each other's hair, the sea breeze brought a tropical freshness into the room. As they worked one person's hair, she or he told the others what new and exciting things he or she had learned in the day's studies. This impressed Molly, who had ceased her education when she graduated from high school, though she'd taken a few occupational PI courses.

***

Days passed. Each dawn brought more challenges for Molly to face. The four were relentless, forcing her to do more and more.

"Okay, today, it's time Molly learned to hop around on one leg," Randi said.

"But I can only just barely walk."

"We must wear these heels, and we have to stand on one foot while we use the other foot's toes to manipulate things. You've got to maintain your balance. Plus, Molly, you don't have arms to help you like we four do."

The four tied up Molly's right leg and forced her to stand up. Wiggling and wobbling on her spike, she again flailed her arms about, but nothing happened. Randi had the others tie up her leg, and she hopped about showing Molly how to do it. Then, they pushed and shoved Molly, forcing her to hop or fall down. Molly hopped and wobbled, terrified once more.

Celeste observed her panic and explained why she needed to learn to hop. "When we go shopping, we stand on one foot, slip our other foot out of its heel, swing the leg up, grab whatever we're after with our toes—a box of cereal, a bottle, a can, or a dress—lower it down into our basket, and then slip our heel back on. Yes, we know that all the food is the same goo, just flavored differently. This is probably the hardest thing any of us has to do. At least food and clothes don't cost us anything."

Ted admitted, "It took me months to be only halfway confident at it."

***

After a week, Molly was eating well enough to handle the energy and vitamin drain the therapy sessions would have on her. Thus, Eve began to work her magic on Molly.

Eve said, "Okay, close your eyes. Good. I want you to go back to the first moment when you suspected something wasn't right just before you were abducted and brought here."

"I think it was when I got the orders from GD telling me about General Fuller."

And so the first of many therapy sessions began. After two days, Molly had unburied, re-experienced, and erased all the pain and unconsciousness that stemmed from her body's genetic mutations and from Dr. Janet Patella's brutal surgery.

She shed buckets of tears, grief over the horrible loss of her arms. She wasn't cheerful, though, and a further session ran into all the losses she'd recently suffered: the death of her parents, the deaths of her sister clones, and the death of Frank.

"I blew it. He proposed, and stupid me, I turned him down, saying I wasn't ready for marriage yet. Later on, I relented, saying we'd get hitched when the murderer of our clones was arrested or killed, but Frank was murdered before we could. I blew it."

"Okay. Let's go back to the start of that time. Run through it and tell me what you are seeing, smelling, and feeling."

After another couple more times re-experiencing that heavy loss, Molly brightened up. "Wait a minute. That's the wrong reason. I gave Frank the wrong reason. He had a controlling, dominating personality. He wanted to always control me. For example, once he made me go to a concert by a music group I hated. Sometimes, I wanted to control our relationship and what we did. Oh, it's cause and effect. He always wanted to be the cause, to dominate me, but sometimes I wanted to be cause, too. That's why I felt it wasn't quite right

126

between us. Wow. Good thing we didn't get married. Ted is just as handsome as Frank, but he has a different personality. Oops, *was* just as handsome as Frank was. He's not always demanding that he be in control of things, is he? Incredible."

"We'll end off here today," Eve said. Her grin was as big as Molly's was.

That evening when everyone retired to their bedrooms, Molly walked over to Ted's room.

"Hi, Ted. May I come in?" she asked.

"Of course, Molly. Please. Sit by me on the bed. Do you want me to cover up or cover you up?"

Both wore only panties and their tall heels so they could walk. He flushed, but there wasn't anything he could do to not appear as a freak to her.

Molly shook her head no. She tossed her hair to one side and sat down beside him. She sighed.

"Ted, I've got to say this to you. I had no idea you were in love with me in high school, and I didn't have the faintest notion of what you did for me and for Frank. Our lives would have been ruined if we'd been chosen to be Army Soldiers. Thanks to you, I was able to become a PI, even if it was only for a short while. Frank was a good cop for several years—all thanks to you. I can't begin to ever thank you enough for what you did for me, especially after what they did to you for helping us."

Ted let out a huge sigh. His eyes watered.

"I think I'm going to cry. You've no idea how much hearing this means to me. Finally, I've closure on that whole thing. But if I had to do it again, I wouldn't hesitate. Your happiness meant and means everything to me. I'm just glad I can be here for you today when you are in desperate need."

Molly smiled. "Ted, we were kids then. There was so little difference between how you and Frank looked—a haircut and clothes if I remember right. You both were and are handsome, but there was a reason I never married Frank. Eve helped me see what it was today, and I figured I should tell you." She explained about the control aspect.

Ted smiled. "I could see that back then, but I can see that neither Frank nor you could see it. We were young and blind."

"Ted, I made one mistake. I won't do that again."

She leaned over and gave him a passionate kiss. Ted flushed, but his arms encircled her, holding her to him.

"What's that for?" he asked when their lips parted. "Surely, you can't love me. Not like this. I'm a freak. I look like a woman." He attempted a jest. "It has one advantage: I don't need to shave. Molly, you deserve a handsome, whole man, not a freak."

"Shut up and kiss me."

He did so, but soon tears trickled down her cheeks.

"What's wrong?"

Molly rose and stood before the full-length mirror. Ted got up and moved behind her. He watched her as she twisted her body from side to side.

Looking at her armless shoulders, she winced. "I feel as though something's been taken away from me... Forever. I'm not whole, just a helpless cripple." Again, more tears seeped downward with an occasional salty drip onto her chest. "I can't ever hug or hold you. They've taken that away from me forever... And so many other things."

Ted gazed into her reflection. Her empty shoulders were a constant reminder of the magnitude of her loss. "Yes, Molly, they took your arms from you. They're trying to take away your independence, to make you dependent upon others like some helpless cripple. They're trying to make you into someone who can only receive help and who can never help others. It's like they're trying to distance you from being able to live life."

His words resonated with her. She nodded and allowed her pent-up tears to flow, as they desired, but Ted wasn't finished.

"Molly, that's just how I felt when they did this to me." He raised his handless arms up, again reflected in the mirror. "But we fought back. Those hundreds of videos of all those other men and women who don't have hands or arms—they hold the key to regaining your dignity and life."

He smiled. "I fell in love with you back in high school because you were the most independent and brightest girl in our school. I'll never forget how you found the lost school mascot."

A smile flashed on Molly's face. "Well, even as a little girl, I didn't want to play with dolls. I was always solving puzzles. Now, I can't even write my name." Tears returned.

"I promise you, Molly, I won't stop working with you until you've regained your lost independence and your ability to help others. Those videos show us we can do most everything, only we use different ways, and it often takes more time. Like any skill, it requires lots of practice. I needed years to master these new ways, but with those girls' help, I made it. Now, I'll help you recover your life. I swear, Molly."

"Ted, you mean well, but I don't think I can do it, not like this. I feel so helpless, so afraid. I won't be able to help anyone, let alone get them justice. There's nothing left to live for. And I can't even kill myself." Molly sobbed, allowing suppressed tears to flood down her cheeks.

Ted sat down beside her, slipping an arm around her. She leaned her head into his shoulder. "Cool Head, if anyone can bounce back from what they've done to you, it's you. That's what I so admired about you. You didn't take no for an answer. Not the few years I knew you in high school. There's hours and hours of holo videos to watch. Other men and women have managed to find ways to do nearly everything. It's hard, damned frustrating, and annoying, but if they can do it, Cool Head can, too."

"But how can I be a PI? I can't even help myself."

"At the moment, no, you can't. That's because you, like the rest of us, have to learn entirely new ways to do everything. That's going to take time and a hell of a lot of practice. Look, if backwards me can manage to learn how to get by and survive this, you certainly can, too."

"You aren't backwards or stupid, Ted. You're brilliant. You've already got ten times more education than I ever will." She paused and looked into his eyes. "You really think I can overcome this? Be a PI again, even if I can't hold my own gun?"

"If anyone can, Cool Head, it's you. I'll bet anything on that. Besides, I'll be right here with you and help you master everything. Lord knows, I need the practice, too. Come on. You've a lot to learn before we can put our heads together and find a way to escape this island. If we're ever going to get back to Chicago, you're going to find a way to do it. I've given up trying and so have the girls."

"Okay, I'll try." She flushed, as a sheepish grin formed. "Oops. There is no try, only do." Both chuckled.

"Remember, you aren't alone. You have me. I'll never leave you. Your motto must be: Stop. Instead, think: 'How am I going to do this?' Every time you say 'I can't,' I'm gonna say 'Stop; think how.' You must find some new way to do it."

"Easy for you to say." She flushed. "Sorry, that's not true."

After a pause, she asked what she'd wondered about since waking up and seeing her three sisters here with him. "Have you been sleeping with the others? Eve, Randi, or Celeste? They look much like I used to look before they mutilated me."

Ted chuckled. "Molly, I won't deny they're as gorgeous as you. But while they're beautiful people in their own ways, they aren't Molly Parkinson, PI. I've only had one love in my life. Now that my body is so freakish looking, I don't expect anyone to love me back. How could they? I look like a woman, but with monstrous boobs."

They rose and gazed into the mirror at their reflections.

Molly chuckled. "Well, they are big, Ted, but you can't really call them soccer balls; they aren't quite that big. I feel so funny without my arms there. Sometimes, my stomach knots when I sense they're gone and will never be back."

"I know. Hey, how about this?" Using his arms, Ted gently draped her long raven hair over her shoulders, hiding them. "There, now you look normal, as though your hair is merely hiding your arms."

Molly cracked a smile. She twisted her body from side to side.

"You're right. My hair hides what I'm missing. I keep expecting to pull my arms out from behind my hair. Weird feeling. Actually, I rather like this look. Okay, from now on, I'll keep my hair like this, hiding my empty shoulders—at least when my hair won't get tangled up in whatever I'm trying to do."

"I love your smile, Molly. Say, how about putting your detective mind to work? Why did they want to remove our hands? Why did they want to remove your arms? What's the point of all this? Why these giant boobs? And why did they want to make me into this freakish form?"

Molly chuckled. "You're trying to get me to put my attention outward and not inward." Ted flushed. "But those are key questions. We can only speculate. Since GD dumped me here, I think they wanted to make sure you and I can never leave this island. Hell, I killed one man who was shooting at us and helped to bring down the DOD general who created the clone projects and who hired the assassin that killed many of us. Probably GD views us as dangerous. GD knows if I had my arms and hands, I'd find a way to escape and rescue you four."

"Makes sense. Still, the girls are content to stay and learn all they can. They're learning fanatics. But why not just terminate you and me?"

Molly had no answer for that. Even she thought they should have been killed, not mutilated and stuck on this remote atoll. She decided to change the topic.

"What's with your interest in robotics? A way to make prosthetic hands for everyone?"

Ted flushed. "Well, I examined that aspect, but since Randi has been working on hyperspace theory, I want to see if robots could help with the mundane work of exploring hyperspace and the coordinates.

"Randi says the way they do it is to move their spaceship one second through hyperspace and stop. Wherever you reappear, you pinpoint your location and any dangerous objects around, such as black holes, dead stars, and the like. She says it takes years to extend our knowledge of hyperspace coordinates on out another light year. Maybe robots could do it for us."

"Wow. So those three—they must be geniuses."

Ted chuckled. "You can say that again. Anyway, while they study during the day, you and I will practice doing everything shown in the many videos. Soon, you'll be writing your name with your feet, just as we do. There is hope for the future, Molly, but it won't be easy. I won't pretend differently or lie to you."

"Thanks. I know it'll be hard. I wish I didn't always have these funny feelings all the time. We best get some sleep."

She turned and gave Ted another kiss.

The next day, Eve began the next phase of Molly's therapy. She expected Molly would experience many worries, frights, aches, and perhaps phantom pains, which she did. Eve was determined to track each back to their source.

"I feel so hopeless," Molly said.

"Okay. Let's return to the last time you felt hopeless," Eve said. After running Molly through several recent times here on the atoll, she asked for something earlier.

"I see something here," Molly said. "I'm having a baby. We're in a hospital." After confronting the pain and unconsciousness, Molly discovered what happened after that. "I got sick while I was there. I'm running a fever, so delirious. Got some kind of infection. Oh god! They're cutting off my hands and feet." She shrieked from the re-experienced pain and trauma.

After more passes over the incident, Molly saw the aftermath. "I'm being wheeled home. I'm helpless now. My husband has to take care of me and our son. It's all so helpless. Oh no! He's cracked up. He's got a gun. He shoots us all. I am floating above my dead body, thinking how hopeless this all is. Eve, that's exactly how I was feeling this morning, so hopeless." Molly laughed long and hard.

Another day, Molly felt withdrawn, morose, so Eve had her re-experiencing that. Before long, she asked for an earlier incident. "Oh, I see something. I'm sick. I live alone. A neighbor takes me to the medical facility. My fingers look blackish or grayish. The doctor says I have something. Diabetes or something like that. They have to come off." Molly blacked out.

Eve was patient. When Molly woke up, she explained what had happened. "Operation. They put something over me. I blacked out. Pain, excruciating pain. Twice. They cut off both hands. I'm awake now, sitting up in a bed. I feel so morose. I don't want anyone to see me like this, so dependent on others."

After Molly went through the incident a few more times, more became visible. "I'm home now with a live-in nurse's aide. I never go out after that. I don't want anyone to see how I look. I mostly stay in my bedroom. Oh, I gave up on life!" Once more, Molly laughed. "I gave up. Well, I'm not giving up now, Eve." She continued to laugh over her decision.

During the following days and weeks, Eve took up every one of Molly's complaints, including feelings of embarrassment, loneliness, helplessness, worthlessness, nervousness, no self-confidence, and many more. Each one traced back to one or more painful incidents that had happened to her, usually in previous lifetimes.

At last, Molly declared, "Eve, I really have lived before, many lifetimes. I'm not this body, right?"

After that, Eve had Molly mock up eight golden balls, forming them into a rectangular box surrounding Molly's body.

"I feel like I'm in a coffin," Molly responded. Both chuckled, and Eve continued.

A week later, Molly was sitting comfortably behind her head, observing her body and the world. Then, she exclaimed, "Eve, I see a host of small golden ball things around my body."

Eve ended the session there. "Yes, those are the points that your body uses to anchor its physical form. When we escape this prison, we'll work on this further. We're all gods and goddesses, but so many have forgotten entirely who and what they are—an immortal spiritual being who has immense powers."

Molly knew she wasn't a body, but she also knew she didn't have immense powers. But there were now many times when she wished she did.

***

As the days progressed, the four continued to press Molly hard, forcing her to do more and more on her own and to get better at it. They made her do the grocery shopping. Molly complained, "But in Chicago, it's all automated, and they deliver your groceries."

They rigged a rope loop around a wagon tongue. Using it around her waist, she pulled a wagon down the road the two miles to the grocery and apparel store. Upon entering the store, she had to practice all the moves she'd been learning. It was scary and anything but fun. On the positive side, she enjoyed not having to pay for the groceries. Then, she pulled the heavy wagon back to their home.

Randi was relentless. Once back with the groceries, she insisted Molly stack them in their proper places in their kitchen.

Exhausted, Molly slumped onto the couch. "I'm certain of one thing, Randi. It takes me *much* longer to do everything now than it used to do."

Randi commented, "There you have me. I've no idea how long you took to do things before. Sorry. I've always been as I am. Let's go swimming."

At least once a week, the group headed off to the beach to swim. Long ago, the Padellas gave them explicit permission to go once a week, but they had to wear heels and swimming trunks to the beach. They swam topless. The first time she went, Molly felt a wave of panic sweeping over her. "I can't swim without my arms."

"Sure you can. We've done it ever since we learned to walk to the beach when we were little girls," Randi countered. "Without hands, our arms are pretty useless. Float on your back and kick with your legs."

***

Six months passed. It was late February and Molly's turn to do the grocery shopping. As she arrived at the store, she saw an Airliner landing just at the edge of the main office and lab, but behind the tall fence that prevented her access to them. Her heart raced as her mind grasped what the Cartwright logo on it might represent.

Part 3

Vic Broquard

Chapter 10 If You Want to Live

"So like where are we going?" asked a sleepy Leslie. The trio of young women had just fled the Cartwright Skyscraper, taking a company EMAC over to New O'Hare. "It's like two in the morning."

Deanna said, "This way. We keep our company Airliner parked in Stall Twenty-nine. I'm worried. Molly's not called in. So I'm being overly cautious with this bomb threat and the assassin waiting for us to leave the building. We'll take the ship to our plant in Singapore. It'll take twelve hours to get there."

Janine said, "I see your point. When we get there, we should know what happened in Chicago. Good thinking. But I can't wrap my head around why they want us dead just because we're clones. I'm no threat to anyone." Worry lines creased her forehead.

"Precisely. While I have good security, I'm sure someone could smuggle a bomb inside. With what's been happening, I don't trust GD any longer. Molly should have checked in long ago. Your phones are still on, aren't they? We don't want to miss her call if she can still make it."

"Yes, mine is," Leslie replied, "but like would they really blow up your company headquarters? Why?"

"Damned if I know. There are always difficulties between corporations. Jockeying for more power and influence over each other. Until now, Peter and I have kept Cartwright Enterprises out of those squabbles. Ah, there it is. Come on."

The Airliner seemed gigantic to Leslie and Janine, who had never been in one. Further, until recently, they'd not been in an EMAC. Both gawked at it while Deanna met with the nighttime technician.

"He'll roll it out for us. Over here," Deanna said. She led them off to one side. They watched the man use an electric tow machine to pull the liner out of its hangar as the roar of a spaceship lifting off forced them to cover their ears.

Deanna entered a code, and the side door lowered, steps unfolding until they reached the ground.

"A larger door is on the other side, but it requires a ramp. At the rear is a driving ramp where large containers can be loaded. Come on up. I'm qualified to fly it, but the autopilot mostly flies it. We enter the destination, and the computers handle the rest."

"Wow, luxury," Janine exclaimed, taking a seat in a soft, leather sofa. A table swung out, allowing one to work during the flight. That new leather smell filled the air.

"I'll get us airborne and then give you a tour of this ship. It's darn impressive."

Shortly after liftoff and the tour, Leslie and Janine dozed. Around five in the morning, Deanna turned on Channel Nine news. At six, the news trickled in.

"We've just received word of an explosion in the Cartwright Skyscraper located off Lake Shore Drive. Reporters are on their way."

She roused her sisters. "Something bad is happening."

Two hours after sunrise and via Channel Nine EMAC airborne coverage, the trio saw the damage. An explosion on the second to the top floor had blown out all the windows and caused a large fire that swept upwards to the top floor. Later on, casualty reports appeared. The blast killed Peter Cartwright, along with a nurse and four security guards.

The reporter commented, "Far more lives would have been lost had the explosion occurred during working hours."

Janine cursed. "We were supposed to be inside and evacuated, according to what Molly said the GD man told her." Then, tears trickled down her cheeks. "Peter... I'm so sorry, Deanna. I'm thankful only four lost their lives. Perhaps, it was a blessing for Peter, but *not* for his nurse and the others. I hope the police catch the bomber."

Leslie agreed and tried to cheer her up. "See, Deanna. We're like really lucky. It's like in our genes. I'm like *sure* of it."

For a time, Janine and Leslie hugged Deanna, consoling her.

Sniffing, Deanna said, "Yes, honestly, the doctors didn't

hold out much hope that he'd ever recover more than he already had. But the others... They didn't deserve to die. I'll make it right with their families when I get back. I can do that much. Maybe I should head back. Someone has to arrange his funeral."

"Maybe you can have your next in charge handle the arrangements," Janine suggested.

"Yes, perhaps you're right. But what's happened to Molly?" Deanna's face felt ice cold. She ran her fingers through her short hair. "What do we do now? It's obvious to me that GD wants us dead. Lord knows why. I've always done quality engineering design work on the EMACs."

"Could the assassin have had time to plant a bomb?" asked Janine. "Was it GD? After all, they're supposed to protect everything."

Deanna said, "Unless the man had access to explosives, I doubt it. I'll calculate how big the charge would have been to have caused the amount of damage we're seeing on the comm display."

This gave her a chance to focus on something other than her grief. A few minutes later, she looked up; her face felt frostbitten. "Fifty pounds. Good god. I highly doubt anyone could get a hold of that much in such a short time, except for GD men. Ladies, I'm scared. This is escalating all out of proportion."

Her voice trembling, Janine asked, "Could we go into hiding once we land in Singapore?"

"Yes, I suppose so. I have millions in my account. We'll stop at a bank, withdraw a lot of credits, and see if we can find a place to hold up for a while."

She headed up to the pilot's seat so she could grieve in private. The thought that her unborn daughter would never know her father brought on another round of tears. Now more than ever, she wished Molly were here with her. She'd know what to do. "I'm only an engineer," she whispered to the control panel.

Around three that afternoon, they landed at Changi Airport. Deanna requested the Airliner be towed to her corporation's hangar. Thirty minutes after landing, the towing vehicle parked the huge ship and scooted off. Deanna lowered the side door, and the three headed down the steps.

When they reached the concrete, two men with guns drawn stepped out of the shadows from deeper inside the hangar. "Mrs. Cartwright?" one said, glancing from woman to woman, surprised to see three almost identical young women, differing only in their hair length, its style, and their clothing.

"Yes? What's the meaning of this?" Deanna said. She attempted to use her commanding tone of voice, but under the circumstances, her tone wavered. At least, it didn't squeak. *If only Molly was here...*

The first man wore a military uniform though Deanna didn't recognize to which corporation it belonged. The second man wore an expensive business suit. He responded to her query.

"I'm VP Russell Godwyn of Galactic Entertainment, Chicago Office. This is Captain Felix Baker, my new chief of security."

Russell was a big man, slightly overweight, with a pudgy face. He had a look that demanded respect. Felix was handsome; he had short brown hair, a square face, and thick brow ridges. A small mustache added to his attractiveness. His uniform was green with red stripes, a bit flashy.

Russell glanced at his watch and continued. "If you want to live, follow us. We're only about two minutes ahead of a GD hit squad. So move it. This way."

He turned and headed out of the hangar. Felix waved his gun as though ushering or urging them on.

Deanna wasn't Molly. She suspected Molly would have fought these men. "Do we have a choice?"

Russell pivoted. "Yes. Live or die."

He turned back and continued his brisk walk. Deanna saw no practical alternative and scampered along after him, followed by Janine and Leslie. Each carried their stuffed duffle bag.

An official GEnt Airliner sat outside the next hangar. Its gaudy green and red logo emblazoned along its sides reminded Deanna of a rose. Upon seeing the ship's emblem, Deanna relaxed a little. He wasn't lying about his affiliation. She followed him up the side steps while Captain Baker turned around and pointed his gun towards the world behind.

As Deanna reached the top step, she spotted another Airliner landing not far from her hangar. She recognized its blue and gold colors—a GD ship. Felix also saw it and backed up the steps as fast as Leslie climbed up. Once inside, Felix closed the door, but already the three women had taken plush seats. He joined them. Russell had them airborne in seconds.

Deanna looked out the window as the ship lifted off. She saw a dozen well-armed GD security men in their blue and gold uniforms running into the Cartwright hangar. Russell hadn't lied. She swallowed hard; her stomach clenched.

Only Leslie seemed unfazed by their narrow escape. She smiled at Captain Baker.

"We're like lucky, you know."

"You're like that fetish fashion model, right?" he asked.

"Yes, that's me."

Felix grinned. "I've like got your May Shiny Mag photo on my bunk's wall."

She returned his smile. "Terrific. Too bad you like don't have it here. I like could autograph it for you." Both chuckled.

Once they were out over the ocean, Vice-President Russell Godwyn joined them. "We're on autopilot," he said. "Now then, ladies, we need to talk."

"Do you know who I am?" asked Deanna. She attempted to play her CEO card.

"Mrs. Deanna Cartwright of Cartwright Enterprises and their top design engineer. Your husband was murdered this morning. On behalf of GEnt, please accept our condolences. Peter Cartwright was a brilliant, young man."

She wiped away another tear and kept a stern face. She had to since she was now responsible for her sisters. "Yes, we heard about the explosion on our way here. A friend of ours warned us that something was going to happen. We chose to evacuate. I don't trust Galactic Defense any longer."

"You're wise in that regard. They've been gunning for you three for some time now. But before I go on, please check your bank account."

"Why? I have millions in it. So has Peter, but I guess I'll

inherit his."

"Log on and check it, please, Mrs. Cartwright."

Deanna felt sick, but nervously, she retrieved her phone and activated her banking app. She swallowed hard.

"You've been wiped out. GD has confiscated your funds as well as Peter's. We discovered that had happened about three hours after the explosion. Now, do I have your full attention?"

Her dry mouth forced her to gag. Felix retrieved a bottle of water, handing it to her. She gulped some down before answering.

"Okay. What's going on?"

"We aren't entirely sure, but it's big. We know you three are clones, made by a secret GD DOD program about twenty-three or twenty-five years ago. That became known only after Captain Baker here retrieved the package a Miss Molly Parkinson took from General Fuller. He's dead, but he used to run that illegal cloning project. Miss Parkinson supposedly terminated him. Maybe she did and maybe she didn't. We don't know for sure."

Leslie blurted, "No, she didn't. He like killed himself after she like let his wife flee."

"I see. Things are becoming clearer, but not entirely. GEnt has contacts within GD headquarters, but whatever this is about, it isn't broadly known within that corporation. Captain Baker followed Miss Parkinson to the general's home, but he arrived much too late. He saw her carrying a package into a derelict home across the street from the general's home. She left without it. Then, he hid from the GD squad who arrived and took Miss Parkinson away, along with the deceased General Fuller. It took a while, but Captain Baker found the package she left along with Miss Parkinson's spy gear.

"Since then, we've been going over everything in it. In truth, I haven't; my boss has. He's kept us informed. We knew something was up with this clone business. Miss Le Clair isn't the only one with access to the DNA database. All corporations have complete access to it. We've studied the data. It seems there are twelve female clones, but someone has killed four in the last couple of weeks, and the status of another four isn't known. Plus, there's a batch of older male clones."

Felix sighed. "Yeah, I'm like one of them, Goddamn it. Can you like imagine—well, I guess you can. I like saw my own face on the news—those two men like murdered at the fire and then that policeman, Frank Wells."

Russell dabbed his brow and resumed. "That's why I have Captain Baker here with me. An ounce of prevention as they say. Miss Parkinson uncovered the complete details of those two cloning projects. Doctors Nelson and Janet Padella cloned twelve men and twelve women—the men, two years older than the women. Eight women are accounted for now. We suspect four are dead and likely Miss Parkinson is as well."

Leslie interrupted him. "No, she's not. We're like lucky. She's like alive somewhere. I like know it."

Felix smiled at her.

Russell continued. "My boss has done a thorough DNA search, just as you have been doing, Miss Le Clair. Only eight of the twelve are in the database. In going over the packet of documents Miss Parkinson snatched, we have the names of the other four. We've tracked down one of them. Three remain at large, but my boss is using all his resources to find them.

"We've had worse luck with the male clones. You know about three of them. Now we've added Captain Baker to the list. Plus, newspaper accounts suggest they terminated a Ted Billings when he was sixteen for hacking into GD's computer system."

Leslie interrupted him again. "He's like not terminated. He's like with three others, a prisoner on some island. Molly like sent us the coordinates before she was abducted. We like have to rescue them."

"Interesting, Miss Travers. You are a fountain of information."

"Just because I like enjoy dressing up in fancy outfits doesn't like mean I'm a dummy."

Felix grinned. From the annoyed look on Russell's face, Deanna suspected no one had ever bandied with him before.

"So we know of five of the twelve male clones. We believe two others are dead, leaving five unaccounted for.

Captain Baker here has only recently returned from extensive training on Pylon, Epsilon Eridani. Thus, his DNA hasn't yet entered Earth's new system."

"I like aim to keep it that way," Felix added.

"So my boss is searching for the other five male clones. In the meantime, I'm under orders to keep you three safe. GD is hunting you. They've stolen your funds. As soon as you use your electronic devices, they'll know your precise location and route that hit squad after you. So hand over all your electronic devices. Captain Baker will drop them in the ocean. I have replacements for you."

Leslie protested. "But I'm like trying to sell my parents' costume store. And like what about the people who want to contact me about my next photo shoot? Oh... That's you."

"Yes, that's us, Miss Travers. We'll see the store is sold. When we saw them confiscating Mrs. Cartwright's money, my boss did the same to your account and to Miss Le Clair's. Your new burner phones can't be traced to you but will have access to the new accounts, thanks to a special GEnt software patch. When your store sells, we'll deposit your share of the funds into your new account, Miss Travers. So I need your devices, including computers."

They handed over their phones, and Felix copied their contacts to their new phones. Only Deanna had a computer with her.

"I can recreate my latest design. But what's happening to my corporation?"

Russell answered, "As I understand it, GD put your uncle, Charles, in charge of it for now."

"He's a fool."

"Hey, Deanna, we're like alive," Leslie countered.

Russell added, "If you'll look at your new account, Mrs. Cartwright, you'll see that GEnt has put ten thousand credits in it as seed money for now. You aren't totally broke."

"Thanks. Thanks for everything," she replied. "You've saved our lives, but what do we do now?"

"While Captain Baker disposes of the electronics into the Pacific, I'll explain. My boss has decided that the highest priority action right now is to extricate this other female clone,

144

Miss Beverly Blossom Blythe. Her DNA isn't in the new database, though the army likely has it. She is a senior captain in the GD Army and is fighting the Sixth Invaders on Brussels, Tau Ceti. She is leading Company D of Battalion I of the Forty-second Regiment of First Division. So to answer your question, Mrs. Cartwright, we're heading for the spaceport in Buenos Aires. There, we have a light cruiser waiting for us. You three will be off-world and safe for the time being."

Deanna grimaced. "As safe as we can be in a war zone. There's a war going on out there if I recall the last news reports."

Chapter 11 A Losing Battle

Brussels was the third planet from the type G8 yellow star called Tau Ceti. While its gravity was slightly less than Earth's, its oxygen content was five percent larger, making breathing easier, especially at higher altitudes. Four large continents held three billion people. Brussels was the third major world colonized by the expanding Sol Empire, and now it was the focus of the ground war against the Sixth Invaders.

No one knew where the name Sixth Invaders came from, but their ships were spotted on fringes of Sol Empire space thirty years ago. Back then in 2320, a long cigar-shaped scout ship penetrated the commercial lanes populated by transport ships hauling goods between the dozen-plus worlds of the empire. Not long after that first sighting, many of their warships appeared and attacked random ships. Galactic Entertainment recorded these events and later interactions. Space battles made exciting entertainment. So VP Russell Godwyn's trip to the major war zone was not unusual. Only a month ago, the Sixth Invaders landed a ground force. Why they invaded Brussels was unknown.

As they flew through hyperspace, taking six days to cover the twelve light years, Russell replayed some of the news highlights for the three women, educating them on how the war was progressing. They saw six space battles, resulting in the loss of five Sol Empire ships and two enemy ships.

Deanna said, "Okay, so GEnt has been covering the war with the Sixth Invaders. But why hasn't anyone seen what these people look like?"

Russell said, "They're always wearing those gray battle armor suits. Some speculate that's because they can't breathe our atmosphere. Others suggest they look hideous to us, but I can't see that as a reason to stay in those suits."

"But haven't you killed one of them? You could then peel that suit thing off it and see. Besides, we could have our engineers studying their armor for weaknesses and such."

"Yes," Russell said, "we've killed some of the invaders,

but due to the severe combat results, we haven't been able to retrieve one of their dead. I believe that's about to change. They've brought the battle to the ground, invading North Continent, Brussels, Tau Ceti. That's our destination. The Brussels GEnt corporation is filming a documentary on the ground-based war. I'm using that as a justification for this visit. I'll return with key footage for Earth."

Leslie asked, "Where's like our sister in all this? You like said she's a soldier."

"Captain Beverly Blossom Blythe is leading Company D of Battalion I. According to the answer I received this morning, she's likely to be in the thick of the battle. They told me she's called Kick Ass BB or Bebe or Be Be. I didn't quite follow. Apparently as their senior captain, she's on track to becoming a major, one day leading a whole battalion. She's got quite a reputation."

Janine said, "Gosh, I hope she doesn't get hurt."

Leslie piped up, "She won't. She's like got our lucky gene, too."

Deanna rolled her eyes, but Russell just smiled.

***

Mountains, valleys, hills, rivers, towns, large cities—Earth civilizations looked much the same throughout the empire, except for those that inhabited moons, icy worlds, or those whose suns were the reddish stars. Brussels appeared Earth-like, at least from above when their light cruiser skimmed the planet before landing at the sprawling spaceport of Grant City in the far northern part of North Continent.

A wiry man with dark glasses met them. "Welcome to Grant City and Brussels, Mr. Godwyn. I'm your host, VP Bill Short; just call me Bill. I have ten film crews embedded with First Division. We've been recording the battles. I trust you'll take this footage back to Earth and see that key corporation officials see it. We need backup if we're to defeat these Sixth Invaders."

"Glad to be here, Bill. Just call me Russell. You have my promise to do that. As I said in my message, we're here to follow the exploits of one of these women's sisters, Captain Beverly Blossom Blythe, though I believe you called her Kick

147

Ass BB. I didn't quite follow that. Anyway, this is Mrs. Deanna Cartwright, the designer of the troop transport EMACs the division is using. She's interested in seeing if the various majors need blasters larger than the fifty-caliber in the transport's turret. If so, she'll get right on the modifications. In part, that's why she's here."

Deanna flushed. She expected to remain incognito or even given a new name. Instead, he thrust her into the limelight.

"Wow! Mrs. Cartwright, this *is* an honor. I'll make sure we get you captured on film and will inform the GD general you're here. He'll let you know about the gun situation right away."

He waved to a digital camera crew, motioning for them to film her and the group that had arrived.

Two hours later, Russell and Deanna faced a wall of cameras. They were inside the temporary, bombproof communications bunker of the First Division, North Continent. In an exaggerated motion, First Division General Spitzer shook hands with Mrs. Cartwright, while several men of lesser rank looked on. Then, he asked her to make a short speech.

Deanna was a corporate executive and a top design engineer. As soon as Russell revealed her identity to Bill, she guessed his ulterior motive. He gave her a way to counter GD's attacks on her. By thrusting her into the political limelight as a major contributor to the war effort, GD execs had to back down on their attempts to blackball or terminate her. Perhaps, they'd restore her wealth; thus, she played her new role well.

"I'm honored to be here today. As you know, I run Cartwright Enterprises back on Earth. I'm here today to see just how well our transport EMACs perform and whether our soldiers need a larger caliber gun in the transport's turret. If so, I'll see the changes are made as fast as possible. Nothing is too good for our brave soldiers who are our last line of defense against these vicious Sixth Invaders."

She lowered her voice. "On a personal note, I've learned that shortly after I left Earth on this trip, terrorists attempted to blow up Cartwright Headquarters and that my husband,

Peter, was one of those killed in the blast and fire. I can't help thinking the attack was meant to prevent me from being here today and helping with the needed redesign of our army's transportation EMACs. If so, it has failed. I'm here, and I will see any needed changes are done swiftly. Then, I'll head home and bury my husband. Thank you."

"Damn, Deanna, you're really good," Janine whispered as Deanna stepped back joining her small group.

Deanna and Russell exchanged a slight head nod. Each acknowledged what the other had done, though Deanna sensed Russell was doing this with something else in mind, likely far larger. She suspected it involved Galactic Defense.

Hours later, the group moved closer to the front lines. They joined the Forty-second Regimental Headquarters unit, led by Colonel Hamilton, and he gave them a guided tour of his facilities, filmed by the GEnt crew.

He explained, "Each of my platoon lieutenants and company captains wears a body camera, providing sound and video. Those wireless signals are sent back to HQ. As you can see, those dozen monitoring stations show what the captains of each of the twelve companies of the regiment see, while that larger group there shows the feed from the thirty-six platoon leaders. Thus, my battalion majors and I have real-time feeds and can issue necessary orders. Technology has greatly aided the army."

With his crop, he pointed out the troop location on a large map. "I have two battalions or eight companies deploying along the south bank of the Rios River. Satellite feeds have shown us where the Sixth Invaders landed their transports on the north side. The feeds show only a small group of enemy ground forces. We have them blocked in here at the river crossing and have a three to one combat advantage, more than enough."

He turned to Russell. "You're interested in Battalion I Company D. Captain Blythe is our senior battalion captain. Since her company has seen recent combat, I'm holding her company in reserve on the bluff there. As you can see, I've arranged the companies in an east-west line along the river bluff. We expect the enemy will move towards that line. You can watch the action as it unfolds. Just don't talk or interfere with operations. Keep your film crew back. I'll see they have a live video feed so they don't have to zoom in on the monitors. Now, if you'll excuse me, I've got a battle to win."

The colonel left and returned to his group of HQ personnel while Russell and the three women took seats behind the big screen displays of Company D's video feeds. All around them, GEnt film crews were busy "ants" setting up their equipment.

"What are we here for?" whispered Deanna.

Russell replied, "Between us, I've heard things haven't been going at all well. We're here to document what's happening. If rumors are correct, it promises to be something of a revelation. Some of us believe GD has been hiding something about this war from everyone. We'll see."

Around one o'clock, they watched as soldiers disembarked from EMACs parked in a cornfield. The troops marched to the trees lining the three hundred foot slope that led down to the flat Rios River valley. The Sixth Invader troops were on the other side of the shallow water.

***

"Okay, we deploy here," said Captain Kick Ass BB. "Platoon leaders on me." Three lieutenants rushed to her side. Although she wore a thick vest on top of her blue and gold uniform, her arm muscles were twice the size of Leslie's, as were her legs. She carried her helmet. Her raven hair was closely cropped, even shorter than Deanna's bob cut. Even so, the three sisters saw how identical she looked to them, a fact not lost on Russell either.

"All right. This time, our job is to be back up for the other seven companies. We get a well-deserved break. The companies are forming a long line here on the river bluff. Got a good growth of trees on the hillside that will make a mess of mortar disruptor shells. The Sixth Invaders have to cross the shallow river down there, probably three hundred feet below us. The companies are deploying in alphabetical order, A to F. We're the rear guard this time, so we'll stay back here closer to the line of EMACs. But stay damned alert for those dog whistles."

150

"Hey, Kick Ass, no need to warn us about those nasty things," one lieutenant said.

Russell's group didn't know what the dog whistles were, but Captain Blythe and her soldiers had encountered them before. These electronic devices swept up in sound frequencies beyond the audible range. Those within a three hundred foot radius were rendered unconscious for at least an hour. Her latest orders from Colonel Hamilton requested she capture one. In fact, Captain Kick Ass had seen a note from GD offering a hefty reward for one of these Sixth Invader devices.

"Hey, I don't like the way the other company captains are setting up." Captain Kick Ass BB pointed off to their left and right. "Too low on the riverbank. Colonel—Colonel Hamilton, you seeing this? Companies C and E to our immediate left and right are setting up halfway down the riverbank. They should be on the high ridge line like A, B, and F."

"Ah, they're fine, Kick Ass," the voice of the colonel entered her ears.

She shrugged and reached a snap decision on where to place the three platoons of Company D. "Okay, I want Third Platoon to flank left behind Company C, but stay up on the ridge line. Hell, if we have to retreat, there's nothing but cornfields behind us for miles. Second Platoon, you flank right of us and get behind Company E but stay up here on the ridge line. First Platoon, you're with me. We'll stay centered between them. Our weak link will be Companies C and E's positions. Mark my words."

Farther off to their left, Company A and B positioned their soldiers on the ridge line, but Company C had gone about halfway down the hill towards the river where they could get a better shot on the enemy as they crossed the river. To their right, Company E deployed the same way as C had, while Company F on the far right was at the ridge line. Captain Kick Ass shook her head as men and women scurried about.

"Engineers, to me," she barked. Coming out of the three platoons, the equivalent of an Engineering Platoon, each wearing large backpacks, rushed over to her. "Okay. It will go south damned fast. I want you to plant explosives about twenty-five feet from the riverbank's hilltop behind C and E. If they lose their position down there on the hillside, we have to buy time for them to retreat."

Several saluted her, and all dashed off to carry out her orders.

"Mortars, set up here, here, and here." She pointed to three widely spaced locations about fifty feet back from the ridge line. The riverbank sloped downward three hundred feet to the shallow Rios River. "Set up so you can blanket the entire slope behind C and E with disruptor shells. It's going to go south down there by C and E, so I need you to buy time for the survivors to retreat up here."

The three crews nodded and headed off to set up.

"Okay, corporal, set up our monitor here. Let's get satellite imagery online. We need to see these fiends coming. They'll hit Companies C and E hard. If Colonel Hamilton is wise, he'll have Companies A and F flank right and left after they hit C and E."

"How can you tell all this, Kick Ass?" her communications man asked. "We haven't even seen the enemy."

"Unless they're dummies, the weak link is there. Companies A and B are set up in a solid defense at the ridge line, making the enemy have to fight their way up the entire riverbank. C and E are halfway down, making them sitting ducks. F also has it right. No, they'll come at us through those two. As backup, we have to be behind C and E."

He laughed. "I'll hold you to that one, Kick Ass."

She flashed a smile.

"Here they come," her communications man yelled. He'd gotten the sat images up. Everyone could see the dark, manlike images moving towards the opposite riverbank.

Thump! Thump! The distinctive sounds of artillery shells broke the stillness, followed by the explosion of smoke shells just on their side of the river. Within a few minutes, the smoke hid the enemy while they sloshed their way across the shallow river. Here and there, one poked its head out of the smoke screen, which had already begun to dissipate. The soldiers held their fire. Because of the dense smoke, they didn't have a target to shoot.

Kick Ass yelled, "Okay, here they come! For god's sake, stay alert for the dog whistles. Anybody spotting one is free to concentrate all their fire on it. Don't let them set up a dog whistle—not if you want to live. Second and Third Platoons—get your covering fire ready."

"Shit! You're right, Kick Ass," her communications man cried out. "They're hitting our lines spear-point fashion, centered on Company C just like you said."

She ordered, "Third Platoon, get your covering fire ready. Company C is in deep shit. If you see them setting up a dog whistle, take it out if you can. Damn, they're being butchered!"

Now images of the enemy were clear on the monitors. They appeared human-like, walking on legs and using their arms to fire their weapons. A suit of armor encased each fighter, head to toe, and they carried small breathing tanks on their backs. Thus, they were immune to any form of gas attack. Some blaster shots ripped through their armor, wounding them. Kick Ass's thoughts echoed others. *These Sixth Invaders aren't immune to our weaponry.* However, they walked both clumsily and slowly, perhaps weighed down by their massive armor.

Each enemy soldier carried a rifle-gun, a blaster amazingly similar to those that the GD soldiers were using. They also had the same blinding mortar disrupter shells, which often stunned the soldiers, and the invaders effectively used them to weaken pockets of resistance on the slopes. The invader's mortars were positioned back across the river.

Those who took up a position back of the top of the ridge line fared better because too many of the enemy mortar disruptor shells landed long off target. Soon, the invaders ceased firing up there, focusing instead on decimating the two lower companies, just as Captain Kick Ass had predicted.

No one mentioned the obvious: why wasn't either side using air power or heavy artillery or armored vehicles or even drones or missiles?

When about half of Company C's men were out of action, Kick Ass saw it. Three enemy soldiers pushed a strange device across the lower ground towards the slope on which the battle was raging. With everyone's attention on the advancing soldiers, few saw the three enemy soldiers bringing it across the river. It looked much like a giant loudspeaker on wheels or a cart. She screamed, "Dog whistle! Dog whistle!"

The platoons of Company C had already lost their mortar personnel along with several engineers. Two other engineers fired off RPGs but missed.

"Third Platoon: take out that dog whistle!"

In fact, they didn't need her orders. Their lieutenant had seen the three enemy men and ordered their mortars and RPGs to attack them. Three hit. When the dust cleared, there was no sign of the three enemy men, and Kick Ass breathed a little easier.

She could see the enemy's plan now. Punching through Company C, they would clear the ridge line and cause the rest to rout. It could just as easily have been Company E that was hit so hard.

Colonel Hamilton also saw this and ordered Company F to pivot left to flank the enemy who now rushed towards the left side and Company E. Stuck halfway down the bank, Company E was too out of position to be of any real use. Instead, they executed a fighting withdrawal up the slope, a wise move.

Then, it happened. Company C's morale and line broke. Men ceased fighting and ran back up the hill. Many were shot in the back as they fled. Two more enemy groups pushed their dreaded dog whistle machines up towards the battle line, but with the company retreating, there wasn't anyone free to take them out.

Kick Ass watched one engineer in her Company D Third Platoon fire his RPG, eliminating one of the dog whistle units, but there was nothing stopping the second unit from activating. It was a hundred feet below the fleeing Company C men. Soon, everyone heard a low-pitched sound that rapidly rose in frequency until it wasn't audible any longer. At that point, the remaining soldiers of Company C who were clawing their way up the hillside collapsed, unconscious. Even their wounded men passed out. Over a hundred men and women lay motionless on the hillside. Kick Ass knew what the eventual outcome for these victims would be: a horror beyond all horrors. She'd seen it twice now, but at least they weren't dead, though they might have wished they were.

Nothing stood between the enemy and the cornfields but the hillside, and the enemy continued their slow march upwards. Once they reached the top, the entire regiment would be in dire trouble.

"Shit!" Kick Ass barked. She ordered her Company D platoons. "Okay, all platoons on me. We'll throw up a defensive line here behind where C should have been. Plug that hole or no one's getting out of this alive!"

Over her comm device, she heard Colonel Hamilton order a retreat, but she smiled when he asked, "Kick Ass, can Company D hold them while the other companies evacuate?"

"Aye, sir. We're ready. Okay, you heard him. We're covering everyone's retreat. Move it. Engineers, ready your charges. On my mark. Wait 'til the enemy moves past Company C. Wait. Wait. Now!"

A long line of enemy soldiers stepped over the last of the fallen men, heading up the final yards of the riverbank's slope. The only thing standing in their way was Kick Ass's Company D. Behind them, soldiers raced towards their waiting EMACs and safety, but if the enemy reached the hilltop too soon, they could cut off everyone's retreat and destroy far more personnel and transports.

Her engineers had done as she'd ordered, laying a long line of charges. She timed it perfectly. The bombs detonated. When the dust cleared, most of that enemy group was down, temporarily at least.

The enemy's reaction: pepper the ridge line with mortar disrupter shells. As far as Kick Ass was concerned, this was fine. She was delaying the enemy, giving the other soldiers time to reach their EMACs and lift off. If the Sixth Invaders used artillery shells or drones or AFVs, far more people would have been killed. The delay also gave them time to manhandle another of their dog whistles on up the slope towards her position. Pinned down by the blinding and deafening mortar fire, no one saw it until it was almost too late.

"Company A is off. B is off." Colonel Hamilton's voice called the news. "F is off."

From her position, she could see Company E would not make it, for they also had to run halfway up the hill to get to the top. She had a choice to make. If she kept her company in place, the dog whistle would get them before they could evacuate. If her company left now, most of Company E wouldn't make it.

"Engineers, to me. Mortars, to me. Everyone else, retreat to the EMACs. Now! Retreat fast, you goddamn fools! Run!"

"Drop them beside me," she ordered when the others reached her position squarely in the middle of the ridge line on which Company C should have deployed. No one argued with her, but dropped their RPGs beside her and dashed off. At least, the mortar crews set up their mortars for her. Kick Ass became a flurry of action.

She fired mortar shell after shell just as fast as she could drop them in, alternating between the three tubes and the ridge lines where Company C and E should have been. It didn't matter she wasn't aiming. With disrupter shells landing across the slope below her, only a fool would dash through such a random volley. A minute later, she fired the last of her shells. Then she rolled over, grabbed an RPG and fired at the nearest enemy.

Ducking under the cover of the hilltop, she rolled over, grabbed another one, rolled up to a firing position, and shot at another. Rolling again, she saw she'd bought enough time for the retreating companies to evacuate. Their shiny transports took to the air. On the next roll, her platoons raced up their respective ramps. After firing off another round, Kick Ass got up and raced towards the nearest EMAC of Company D. She saw three of them lifting off, but the fourth waited for her.

Several men leaned out of the bay ramp, firing their giant guns at the enemy rushing after her. Then, she heard that awful noise, that low pitch sound of the dog whistle. Though she ran quite fast, as the sound rose in pitch, she found her legs refusing to obey her. She stumbled. Then everything went black.

***

Back in the HQ area, three young women screamed. They saw her transport lifting off, but their sister was down. The camera on her vest continued to relay images. They saw two enemy soldiers pick her up and carry her down the slope to the riverbank.

"Can't you do something?" asked Janine, her voice more of a squeal. A dazed look covered her pale face while she watched her sister taken captive.

"She's not dead. Watch. But I warn you, it's not good," Colonel Hamilton said. He turned back to his personnel, engaging in private communications with his divisional leaders.

What happened next, recorded by GEnt's film crew, was beyond ghastly. Several in the HQ area vomited before it was finished. Someone propped Kick Ass's body up against a tree. Her camera's position was such that the sisters could see everything else that was going on. Later, Deanna suspected that was the enemy's intention.

A transport arrived, and the enemy soldiers unloaded three large machines, each big enough to surround a human body. Then, they attached cables from a large power generator, bringing all three devices online. In the meantime, enemy soldiers dragged all GD soldiers, whether dead, wounded, or unconscious, down before the machines, arranging them in lines. Two other soldiers dug a long trench while more enemy soldiers brought out dozens of barbecue pits and stoked them. Soon the streaming videos showed red-hot coals, heat waves rising. During this time, the wounded or dead enemy vanished across the river, presumably carried to their own medical facilities.

What happened next shocked those who hadn't seen this previously. Via the streaming video cameras still attached to some of the officers' chests, everyone had a ringside seat, as horrific as it became. The enemy soldiers, still hidden from view by their body armor, dragged GD's unconscious but unwounded male soldiers up to the three machines. They stripped them down to their underwear and sat them on seats, closing the machines around their bodies leaving only their heads outside the devices. Then, someone waved something under their noses, rousing them.

When interrogated, they said they felt pinpricks, numbness, and then intense pressure. Later, the device opened, revealing the machine had removed the soldier's right leg and left arm at their hip and shoulder. What many found amazing was that their bodies appeared healed from the amputations.

The four women gasped, and a compassionate soldier around the group explained. "You're seeing silver compound nanoparticle and graphene mesh healing."

"But isn't that our latest healing technology?" asked Deanna. "That's what the Med Center used on Peter."

The soldier nodded. Deanna noticed Russell paid close attention to her exchange.

The enemy forced the shocked men to stand up on their remaining leg and gave them a crutch for their arm. They pushed each forward, making them walk far out on the flat ground by the river. The machine operators tossed the amputated leg and arm on down an assembly line of workers.

Aghast, they watched as the Sixth Invaders barbecued the appendages and apparently ate them—though no one saw that—later tossing the bones, hands, and feet into the trench. The ghastly scene caused many to gag and vomit, and soldiers handed out bottles of water.

The Sixth Invaders were cannibals, and the film crews captured the entire scene, but many turned away, unable to watch the horrid scene.

In the midst of this, one victim screamed and yelled. While hopping about on his single leg, he tried to kill an enemy soldier using his crutch as a club. He was Private Ernest Torelli. Enemy soldiers grabbed him and put the man back into the machine. A few minutes later, only his head and torso remained. He was still alive, but they tossed him into the garbage pit face up so he could continue to observe before he was buried alive. Months later, Deanna learned the repercussions of Ernest Torelli's death; it almost cost the Sol Empire the entire war.

The four watched in disbelief as over a hundred men

were mutilated and left crutching their way down the river valley, deep in shock.

Leslie said, "They like haven't done this to any of the female soldiers, not yet anyway. Bev just has to be lucky." Her face was wet with tears. She glanced around her and saw everyone had wet faces.

Someone picked up Kick Ass and carried her across the stream, up the other side, and into the tree line. Her streaming video still functioned, and everyone saw a large encampment of the enemy with their own transport pool parked nearby, along with many tables, though they only saw the backs of those who were apparently dining on the barbeque. A soldier carried her into a huge tent where people, who looked humanoid but who wore white surgical gowns and masks over their body armor, waited beside a huge machine. Enormous wires came out of its top, disappearing out the back of the tent. They stripped Bev and placed her body into the machine. The video feed ended with the destruction of her clothes and camera.

Colonel Hamilton walked over to the group, his pale face taut. "We don't dare bomb them into oblivion, because so many of our people are there—mutilated yes, but alive. Don't worry about your sister. They'll return the women to us in a few days, as long as we don't bomb them. At least, that's what will happen if they stick to their earlier methods. They'll tell us when we can recover the crippled soldiers, probably in a few more hours. We've lost fifteen women this time, so it might be longer before they return our female soldiers."

He turned to glare at Russell and Bill. "I hope you've captured all this on film and show it to other corporation executives back on Earth. This is what we're dealing with here on Brussels. If we don't get real help soon, we're going to lose the war."

"Excuse me, but what happens with those men?" asked Janine. She wiped her wet face on her blouse.

His voice replied as though all hope had left him. "Assisted living. We move them into assisted living homes scattered around our world. We've never been able to recover very many of the head-torso soldiers since they're usually killed or buried alive along with all the bones, hands, and feet. These Sixth Invaders are murderous cannibals."

He turned and left them. Seeing how green Russell looked, Deanna was certain he would show the dramatic video to the powers back on Earth.

"Why? Why would they like do this? They like have to know we're seeing all this," Leslie asked. She tried hard not to vomit, cupping her hands over her mouth and lips, while grabbing for a bottle of water.

Deanna sighed, wiped her wet eyes, and answered, "Fear. Something like this puts fear and terror into the mind of any soldier. Soon, we may not be able to get any soldiers to fight against these invaders. Good plan. Hideous, though. Sorry, I don't think bigger guns on the transports will make any difference."

Russell turned around and rushed out of HQ. He upchucked just outside the tent. When he rejoined them, Leslie handed him a bottle of water.

Deanna said, "Notice one thing. We didn't see anyone *actually* eating our people. We saw their appendages being prepared, but we didn't see anyone eating them. Someone inside a tent could be scraping the flesh off the bones. What I find curious is that we haven't yet seen the bodies and faces of these Sixth Invaders. What do they look like?"

"I think they're like barbarians," Leslie said. "Probably, they look like demons or something. Too hideous to show their faces."

***

Around suppertime, a sign held in front of one of the remaining operational streaming cameras notified the colonel that his people could recover their wounded and dead. He dispatched several transports to pick up the men, who were still in deep shock, struggling to walk using their crutch. They took the wounded men to the field hospital for a complete examination.

At dark, the four listened in on one of the field doctors' reports to Colonel Hamilton. "Sir, same as before. Silver compound nanoparticle and graphene mesh healing. No scarring, just severe shock. We're dividing them up among the usual assisted living homes across Brussels. You'll receive three lists so you can notify the next of kin of the deceased, notify them where they can find their wounded men, and later on, notify them where they can find their women. We'll be using DNA, where possible, to sort out the other remains, when we can get to the burial pits."

He thanked the doctor. Turning to Russell, he said, "These Sixth Invaders are using our own latest and most advanced healing methods on our soldiers." He exhaled deeply. "I guess it could be far worse. Excuse me." He left the HQ tent.

***

Eight days later, a transport landed near the First Division headquarters, ferrying the fifteen women back from where the enemy dumped them, again on the same riverbank. The three sisters rushed to see their missing sister, Beverly Blossom Blythe. What they found shocked them.

Chapter 12 Dealing with a Mess

Bev no longer looked like a soldier. Gone were her thick arm and powerful leg muscles that had so impressed the three women when they first saw her image. Now her arms and legs looked much like Janine's and Leslie's—well formed, but not overly muscled. No longer was her hair shorter than Deanna's was. In fact, its waves fell to her lower back, rich and shiny, a fact that pleased Leslie, since she kept hers this long. What shocked the trio of sisters was Bev's gigantic bosom. This gave Bev a striking figure.

She wore a red satin gown that fit her curvaceous form. Her six-inch heels matched her gown, giving her a fetish look, which also pleased Leslie. In short, Bev appeared to be a perfect Super-Sexy Galactic Doll, a look and form that had become very popular with the corporations and wealthier men. A close comparison with the children's toy, which was still popular so many centuries from its invention, showed that someone had grossly exaggerated the shape of these Galactic Doll bodies.

But her physical transformation wasn't the problem. They had done something to her mind. When the trio met the fifteen women arriving at the headquarters, Bev and the other female soldiers acted wildly.

Bev muttered to herself. "I have to look pretty. Am I pretty? How's my hair?" She adjusted her hair with her hands, revealing her inch-long nails, painted to match her heels and dress.

She saw Russell and teetered over to him. "Please, I need you in me now. Do I look good for you? Do me now. I have to have sex right away. I need it badly. Please, please. Do it now. Stop torturing me. Stick it in me right now. Kiss me. Kiss me. Hold me." She ranted on and on, pawing her talons on Russell's face while trying desperately to kiss him. It was all the man could do to keep her off him. Meanwhile, other soldiers had to fight off the other returning Galactic Doll women, who were ranting and begging with identical words.

A group of female soldiers rushed in, relieving their male counterparts, who ran out of the building. Likewise, Russell departed as fast as he could.

Janine got Bev calmed down. "Hi, Bev. We're your long lost sisters. I'm Janine Le Clair."

"I have to look pretty all the time. Am I pretty? How's my hair? I have to please men. Where did they go? I have to find them. I need them in me now. I have to have sex right away. Please, take me to the men. I need it now, please, I beg you. I can't stand going without it much longer. You have to help me. Please. I have to have it now."

Janine didn't know how long Bev would continue to rant, but the female soldiers had seen this before. One called out to her and her sisters.

"Push them along. Ignore them. Guide them into the EMACs."

Janine had no choice and did as asked.

"Oh, you're taking me to the men. Do I look pretty? How's my hair?" She rattled on, but the heartsick trio ignored her, focusing on getting her to the waiting vehicles.

While Deanna headed off to find Russell, Colonel Hamilton, and answers, Janine and Leslie went with Bev.

In the cramped EMAC, one soldier explained, "We've seen this before. Those dog whistles somehow stun our people. You've seen what they do to our male soldiers. This is what they do to our female soldiers. In a way, they are luckier than the men are, except their minds are gone. I'm sorry for you two. Your sister isn't ever going to recover. But she'll get psychiatric care at the assisted living home."

"Will that help her?" asked Janine.

She shrugged her shoulders. "They can keep them quiet with drugs. Makes them walking zombies. No, it won't help her. No one knows what the Sixth Invaders have done to their minds, but they haven't raped them or cut them up like they did our men."

Janine and Leslie helped guide Bev into the facility on the edge of Grant City, the largest city of the far North Continent. Ten single-story wings fanned out from a central hub and main entrance. While checking each insane woman into the facility, the doctors allowed the victims to see only female workers. Bev and the others continued their non-stop ranting, begging, and pleading.

A doctor came to examine Bev. She checked her over, ignoring Bev's constant chatter, but politely agreeing with her. "Yes, you look pretty. Hair is fine. Do you hurt anywhere? How about here? No? Okay."

When the doctor rose, Janine asked, "Is she all right?"

She turned and looked at Janine and Leslie. "Ah, your sister, right?" Both nodded. "Well, she's undergone the typical new Galactic Doll genetic mutations—big breasts, for example. As far as I can tell, she's in perfect health. Her virginity is still intact, which I find remarkable, considering. So physically, she's just fine. It's her mind that's a mess."

"Will she recover? I mean, in time?" Janine asked, her face creased, a tremble in her voice.

The doctor sighed. "I'm not a psychiatrist, but we've had these cases from the battlefield before. So far, none of the victims has recovered, but they can give her drugs that will quiet her down so she stops attacking every male in her vicinity. I'm so sorry." With that, she headed off to examine the next patient.

A nurse entered. "We're putting her in Room J101. If you'll follow me, I'll take her there now."

An hour later, a sedated Bev lay resting in her new room. Janine and Leslie had helped her get settled in. Then, a social worker arrived to talk to them.

"I'm Agnes. I'll be blunt. There's no sense in hiding the situation from you. The army will come by in a few days to give her a medal for her heroic actions. After that, GD will void their contract with her, transferring it to Galactic Medicine. They'll see she has seven fancy outfits because we've discovered if these women don't wear these elegant outfits, they become wildly upset, and then even sedatives have little effect on them. For a few days, we'll keep her sedated. In time, the psychiatrists have no workable alternative but to heavily dose them on the best anti-psychotic drugs. Unfortunately, the women then have a very limited ability to function. We'll keep them here in this home until they die, compliments of Galactic

Medicine."

"Wait a second. Can't we take her home with us?" Janine asked. The future this woman was describing for Bev sounded awful.

"Well, if that is your choice. That can be done after she's been here a few months during which our staff will do everything they can to get her and the other victims to control their insanity. After that point, yes, you can take her with you, but you must sign papers taking full responsibility for her."

"We want to do that," Janine declared.

"I'll log that on her chart. Let's hope by the time she's able to be released, her mind will be back to normal." From the covert tone of her voice, Janine realized the social worker was only being polite. Bev wouldn't be back to normal, far from it.

She left the two. Bev dozed, and the pair headed off to find something to eat. Just as they were leaving the room, Captain Baker came walking up to them.

"Hi there. Found you. Russell like sent me to guard you, Leslie. I guess I'm like your personal security man now."

Leslie smiled. "Thanks. I like feel safer already. We're like going to find something to eat. Care to join us?"

"Absolutely." He grinned.

As they ate in the small visitor's cafeteria, Felix said, "Miss Leslie, there's like a big dance tonight. Like would you care to come with me?"

She giggled. "Are you like asking me out on a date?"

He flushed. "Well, yes, I suppose so. Like would you?"

"Sure. I've like not had any fun at all since my last photo shoot night out when I stayed too long. Gosh, so much like has happened since then."

"Great. You'll like have to tell me all about it. I'll like pick you up around seven."

When they returned to Bev's room, she was asleep. There was activity in the next room, J102. Several soldiers in parade uniforms marched into the room. Curious, Janine stepped out of Bev's room to see what was going on. Besides, she wanted to give Leslie some private time to chat with Felix.

"Please join us. We're honoring Sergeant Hank West. He's getting his medals," one soldier said.

"He's certainly earned that," Janine said. She stepped into the room.

"On behalf of the First Division, we hereby present the Medal of Valor to you, Sergeant Hank West." He saluted the man sitting on the edge of his bed and handed him the purple ribbon medal. "Galactic Defense thanks you for your brave service to your world. May we win this terrible war."

He said a few more remarks and then departed, heading for the next medal delivery. The honor guard had thirty-five medals to deliver in this facility. That left Janine alone with Hank.

"Hi. I guess I'm their witness. I'm Janine Le Clair."

"Hank. Hank West. I heard they have Kick Ass BB in the next room."

"Yes, she's my sister."

"I owe her my life, as pathetic as it now is. Why didn't they just kill us? How am I supposed to live like this?"

"Don't you have any family? Brothers, sisters?"

"No, my folks retired and got put in one of these assisted living places. They were dead in just a few years. I swear these places somehow create degenerative brain disease. Now here I am, too."

"But you can still get around on your own, can't you? Are they going to give you some artificial limbs or something?"

Janine wished she'd kept her mouth shut. She watched huge tears well up in his eyes. Like a dam bursting, they flooded down his cheeks, embarrassing him. Janine sat down beside him and gave him a solid hug. "There, there. At least, you're alive. That's what's important."

"But I'm helpless now. I can't get a job. No corporation will sponsor me. I'm doomed to live in this miserable place until my mind goes bonkers."

"I saw you walking away from those Sixth Invaders so I know you can move around. Probably not easily, but you can move. And you've still got a good arm, and most importantly, Hank, you've still got your mind. My sister's mind is scrambled. They're calling her insane. I think she's been brainwashed or something. Is there anything like brainwashing?"

He sniffled. "Yes, well, we can move about slowly. At first, they said I was in shock. Then, I bawled my head off. Now, I'm angry about it all. I'm useless to everyone. And these damned pants and shirt—the missing leg and arm sleeve keep getting in my way."

"I'd be angry too, Hank. So no corporation is sponsoring you now, but Galactic Medicine is taking care of you? Is that how it works?"

"Damned if I know, but I think it's something like that. No one will sponsor me because I can't do anything any longer."

"Did you always want to be a soldier?" Janine asked. She wanted to steer the conversation elsewhere.

He chuckled. "Now you mention it, hell no! In high school, I wanted to study history. I had hoped I could become a history teacher, but no. GD chose me to become a soldier. Now here I am—a broken half-man, of no use to anybody. Hell, Janine, they can't give us artificial arms or legs. They say the way our limbs were removed, there's nothing left on which to mount the prosthesis, and if they did, the thing would be mostly useless, just cosmetic. So you are looking at a half-man until I die."

"Well, for a half-man, you are a handsome fellow." Hank's face was round, with blue eyes that seemed to penetrate to her soul. His black hair would definitely look better after it outgrew the army-cut, while his black mustache made his face look quite appealing. As her eyes looked further down his body, his left arm was gone at his shoulder socket, as was his right leg at his hip, destroying any such illusion.

"Oh get real, Janine," he griped.

"Well, I can do something about your pants and shirt. I sew a little. Let me see what I can do. I'll bring a needle and thread with me tomorrow. Anyway, I think you should keep on with your history studies. The world always needs more teachers. I have to go. They're signaling me. I'll see you tomorrow. Bye."

***

Over supper, Deanna relayed what she'd learned. "This situation with the male and female victims has happened twice before now. According to the colonel, each time the outcome has been the same. The men have a leg and arm removed while the enemy turns female soldiers into Galactic Dolls but with their minds scrambled. What I find most curious—and so does Russell after I pointed it out to him—is that these Sixth Invaders are likely using our own biogenetic nanotechnology to turn our women into Galactic Dolls, just as our medical people are doing. Also, Russell told me that in the last ten years, there has been an explosion in the number of high school graduating girls who plead to become Galactic Dolls. If I didn't know better, I'd say these Sixth Invaders are using our own genetics technology on our female soldiers."

"Like sending us a message?" asked Leslie. Her brows arched while her eyes had a blank look in them.

"That females shouldn't be soldiers, but should be sex Dolls—at least, that's the message as I see it. I think I've convinced Russell, too. But the scrambled mind thing is beyond our medical people. No one knows what they've done to the women, but they all act the same way, spout the same words, and act similarly around men. It's as though they've had their brains identically rewired. Conclusion: our doctors don't know how their minds were altered and have no way to undo it."

"So it's like hopeless for Bev?" asked Leslie. Her trembling hands grasped her stomach.

"Not exactly. Russell researched it for me. It seems once the doctors get them somewhat stabilized so they aren't so frantic about demanding sex, some corporate executives are planning to hire them as official Galactic Sex Dolls. They're making a new category for them. What I didn't know about the Galactic Doll program is that they *prohibit* the Dolls from having sex with their clients. It's verboten. But with these new victims, they can't avoid sex, so they're making this new category. I think that's despicable."

"So do I!" Leslie agreed.

"Me too. Taking advantage of the poor woman's situation. Awful," Janine said.

"We like can't let that happen to our sister," Leslie said.

Janine said, "Got that covered. I've already told them

we'll take Bev with us when they release her. Not sure when that will be, though."

"Good thinking," Deanna replied. "But there are more fishy things. These ground attacks. They're just toying with the GD army. If these invaders were serious, they should follow up their successful attacks. We saw them crossing the river and taking the riverbank hillside from our forces. Yet, they've not advanced from there. Nor have they advanced from any of the other locations where they've won the battle. It makes no sense. Their army should sweep down towards Grant City as we speak, but they're stationary."

She continued. "One idea now being put forward is that they're trying to demoralize our soldiers. The videos that GEnt shot the other day are going viral on this world. In time, no one will offer any resistance to the enemy out of fear of losing an arm and leg."

Janine asked, "Does that hold credence with the generals?"

"Maybe yes, maybe no. Another theory is that the invaders have only a small ground army. Still, others think they're waiting for the bulk of their army to arrive around Tau Ceti."

Janine chuckled. "I'm glad I'm not a general. Those sound reasonable, too."

Deanna added, "Looks as though we're stuck here for several weeks. You both look after our sister. I'm going to see what I can do to help the army win this war."

"Okay. I've like got a date tonight," Leslie said. "With Felix. He's like darn cute."

Deanna smiled. "He is. You have fun."

***

The next day, Janine dropped by Hank's room. "Hi, Hank. I'm here to fix up that dangling leg on your pants and the sleeve on your shirt."

"Hey, Janine. You don't have to do that."

"True, but I want to. It's something I can contribute. I can't do anything about your missing leg and arm, but I can do something about the fit of your clothes. So have you given any more thought about what I was saying about becoming a history teacher?"

He laughed. "Sure. I'd love to do that, but let's get real, Janine. I'm a half-man, stuck in this assisted living home. We both know what will become of me in just a couple of years in here. My T-day will come."

Janine sighed. "I shouldn't be telling you this. Not after all that you've done for the empire. But you deserve to know the truth. You're right about everyone dying in these places. I worked at the Galactic Medicine's Total Care Administration as a DNA data entry person. I learned the corporations force everyone to retire at sixty. When people move into these places, they're given a drug that destroys their brains in about five years. That way, their T-days can be predicted. Yes, the corporations are murdering everyone over sixty. So you're right, Hank. If you stay here, they'll drug you until your mind goes and then terminate you."

"Damn! I thought so, but, Janine, I want to live. I've been giving what you said some serious thought. I'm only twenty-five and want to live another forty years. And I want to study history. The problem is money. No sponsor, so no income. No way to pay for my keep, let alone pay for my schooling, even if I do it all online. I'm so screwed."

The doctor entered. "No, miss, you don't have to leave. Good news, Hank. The silver compound nanoparticles and the graphene mesh are holding nicely. A month from now, they'll have dissolved and be flushed out of your body. You should expect no lingering aftereffects. I want you to relax for another couple of weeks and give your body time to complete the healing process."

Janine asked, "Doctor, isn't there some prosthesis that can be fitted for his missing leg or his arm?"

"I'm sorry, miss. We'd like nothing more than to do just that, but he has nothing left of either on which to fit one. We could hang a useless arm on his left side, but he'd have virtually no function with it. As far as the leg goes, we could fit something on his rear, but most people find it's so uncomfortable that they'd much rather not use it. With practice, Hank should be able to navigate around fairly well. Hank, I'll check on you in the morning." He nodded and departed.

Janine frowned. "Well, I had to ask. Deanna checked on that yesterday, but I had to satisfy myself. What he said is encouraging, Hank. You should be able to move about okay. So we should practice like he said. First, let me finish fixing up your pants and shirt."

"You're cutting off the leg?" Hank asked, growing curious.

"Yeah, you don't need it. Besides, any dangling material in the empty leg will only cause you more trouble. Same thing with your sleeve. Off it comes. I'll sew up the hole. Look, Hank, you might as well show off your streamlined body form."

Hank looked at Janine for a moment and then broke into the first laugh he had since the battle. "Streamlined body form? You have to be joking."

"No, I'm serious. Bev now has these giant breasts, which give her tremendous body curves. While I'm sure that's not what Bev ever wanted, she has them, and she might as well be proud of them and that she's still alive. Same with you, big man. You should proudly show the world that your body is missing an arm and leg and that you aren't trying to hide that from everyone—what you've given to protect your world."

"Oh brother," Hank said. "But at least Kick Ass is whole, not a half-man as I am."

"You're not quite right. If you are a half-man, then she's a half-woman. Her mind is gone. Isn't one's mind far more important than a mere arm or leg?"

"Point taken. I can't dissuade you from helping me, can I?"

"No, you can't, Hank. Besides, I'm stuck here for weeks, too, and I enjoy your company."

***

Days turned into weeks for the sisters. After weeks of rest, Bev ceased ranting and raving continuously, though the moment a man entered her vicinity, Bev couldn't help herself. And she still could not carry on a significant conversation with anyone though Leslie was hopeful that one day soon she would be able to at least do that.

Captain Felix Baker and Leslie continued to go out each

evening, and their relationship became serious.

"I like think I'm in love," she whispered to Janine, who grinned. Felix looked like Molly's Frank Wells, only with a mustache.

For her part, Janine spent much of each day with Hank, since she could do very little for Bev, other than brush her hair for her and help her dress. She made him get up and practice walking, insisting he go farther each day, much to his annoyance.

"See, you're getting stronger and more adept at walking. Good job, Hank."

"I have to admit, Janine, I can see I'm better at it. I'm incredibly slow and awkward, but more confident getting around."

"Well, you did say that you wanted to live and that means getting up off your bottom." She grinned.

"Yes, Nurse Nancy."

***

Knowing she couldn't do anything for Bev because she wasn't a doctor, but an engineer, Deanna took a different approach. She was furious with what GD had done to her and to Peter. She explained to Janine, "If I can design something highly beneficial to the war effort, then GD will have no choice but to restore my company and give me back my money."

First, she observed GD's military on Tau Ceti. Then, she watched all the stored video of previous Sixth Invader attacks. Finally, she examined all spaceship battles and the current disposition of the enemy forces, as best GD knew. She found many strange aspects, such as how the enemy was able to use Galactic Doll technology against them, or their inability to ever see what an enemy soldier looked like, or why they didn't swarm over Brussels. These, she had to ignore, since as far as she could tell, engineering played no role in them. But there had to be something she could work on. If only she could get a hold of one of those dog whistle machines and see how it worked and why it knocked everyone unconscious.

For days, she studied the videos taken by the body cameras of the many victims and those just out of range. She concluded its range was no more than three hundred feet.

Further, the sound generator had to warm up, sweeping in frequencies from very low on up out of human hearing. Conclusion: the knockout sound must be an ultra high frequency, which also meant the device drew significant power.

Then she had a bright idea. A controlled electromagnetic or EM pulse might knock out the device, but it was certain to knock out its power generator parked somewhere behind their lines. She set to work. The device had to be small and portable and yet pack the necessary punch. For days, she worked on her drawings and design, often forgetting to eat lunch. Once she finished, she took her design to Colonel Hamilton.

Why him? He continued to act as their liaison with the GD army. Corporate headquarters on Earth hadn't told Brussels GD executives to arrest her or stop her, so she continued to deal with Colonel Hamilton.

"Sir, I believe I have a way to stop those dog whistles."

Colonel Hamilton gave her his full attention. "Yes, cancel all calls. All appointments are to be rescheduled. No one is to interrupt Mrs. Cartwright and me. There, that should do it. You have my undivided attention."

"Well." She unrolled her plans and explained her device. She finished up with, "Since we've never captured one of those dog whistles, there's no guarantee my device will stop it. I've no idea what its circuitry is like, but this EM pulse stands a good chance of working. If it doesn't stop the whistle, it will certainly knock out its power generator. I suspect the whistle device draws a hefty amount of power."

He replied, "You understand I have to take this on up the lines for official okays and trials."

"Of course. Just keep me in the loop as you would any other GD corporation affiliate."

As Deanna expected, within a few days, she received notification that a GD corporation representative from Earth desired a meeting with her and her sisters, along with Russell, representing Galactic Entertainment.

Chapter 13 The Return

The meeting was held on neutral ground in Grant City in GEnt's local headquarters. Russell, Deanna, Janine, and Leslie walked into the fifty-ninth floor conference room, where the GD representative from Earth waited. The room looked like any other meeting room, sterile and white, with lots of stainless steel on the chairs and table. As they entered, Deanna guessed they were meeting with a junior executive, perhaps a VP, but not top leaders. She sighed and took a seat. Her group sat on the opposite side of the table from him.

"I'm Sam Deckerson, legal representative of Galactic Defense, Earth Division, Moscow, but temporarily stationed in Chicago. For the record, Mrs. Deanna Cartwright is present. Will you please introduce the others?"

From his formal tone, Deanna knew he was making a video recording of the meeting. Probably his bosses back on Earth were watching via streaming video sent via hyperspace relay. Still, she had their attention, so perhaps there was hope.

She said, "Misses Janine Le Clair of GMed and Leslie Travers of GEnt, both of Earth. With us is our host, VP Russell Godwyn of GEnt, Earth."

"Ladies, sir," Sam acknowledged. "Now then, GD is interested in the EM pulse generator of your recent design."

"*Portable* EM generator." She corrected him. "The whole point is that it's portable enough that one soldier can carry it on his back."

"Yes, portable EM generator. Now then, Mrs. Cartwright, what are your terms?"

Right to the point. Well, he is a lawyer. "Okay. I want my company returned along with all the money you stole from my account and from my late husband's account. Stop all further attempts to kill or harm my clone sisters and the other male clones. All must have appropriate corporate sponsors. We want our lives back. In return, I'll sign all rights to the portable EM generator over to GD Earth."

"Is that all?" he asked with a sneer.

"That's enough. I'm not asking someone to take the blame for blowing up Cartwright Enterprise and murdering Peter and the others. You can't bring Peter back, but you can stop trying to hurt us."

"So you aren't demanding any form of justice for those who were involved in the explosion and deaths of Peter and the others?"

"No. You heard me. What's the point? GD would just find patsy to take the fall, instead of those who *are* responsible. I *am* a CEO, if you recall."

"And you aren't seeking damages for what has happened to your company, your personnel, your clone sisters, and the male clones?"

"No. You heard my demands."

"Just so we're perfectly clear in this matter. You're waving all rights to any form of retaliation against those who may have perpetrated harm or threatened harm to you, your company, your clone sisters, and the group of male clones?"

"Correct."

He looked over a paper in front of him, checking off several lines while going mechanically down the page. At last, he looked up, his eyes meeting hers. "Okay then. You've asked a lot. It's only fair that GD asks something of you and your sisters in return."

Deanna wanted to protest this point. She hadn't asked a lot, only what was fair and just, but she kept quiet and waited to hear what he said.

"If GD agrees to all your stated requests, then GD needs you to agree to its few requests made here today. First, any settlement between us requires that you and all your clone sisters become genetically mutated into the current Galactic Doll format. You don't have to become Galactic Dolls for other corporations and executives, just that your bodies will be changed. Second, since all Galactic Dolls are sponsored by GEnt and not GD, GD and the other corporations will cancel sponsorships of said women, transferring them over to GEnt, but only if GEnt will accept the transfer."

"Wait, are you suggesting that Cartwright Enterprises becomes a subsidiary of GEnt? We're sponsored by Galactic

Transport and as a subsidiary of GD."

"That detail is open to negotiations. GD would prefer to retain Cartwright Enterprises as its subsidiary, but as I said, this is negotiable. Your company remains Galactic Transport, but you become GEnt."

"Is that all?" Deanna barked. Her eyes narrowed, and she frowned. This made no sense.

"Third, you agree to work with anyone GD asks you to in terms of this war effort. Things are going badly for the Sol Empire. In the future, GD might request you work with others you might not desire to work with. We need your agreement to put aside personal feelings for this war effort."

Deanna chuckled. "Any sentient person would agree with that. If we don't all work together, these Sixth Invaders will conquer our empire."

Sam checked off additional boxes before looking up once more. "In that case, Mrs. Cartwright, I believe we have a deal, subject to acceptance by GEnt of their small part. I will prepare the formal documents. Mr. Godwyn, will you please consult your corporation? We will need your signature on the final documents. Oh, one final detail. GD would appreciate it if you remain here on Brussels until the device is tested and is ready for production. That should only be a few months at most."

"How soon will we be required to be genetically modified? I'm pregnant, you know. And how soon will our funds be returned? We'll need new clothing."

"Just as soon as the doctors tell us it's safe for them to perform it. Each woman might have a different time scale. Your funds will be returned when the document is signed by all parties and is thus official."

That ended the meeting. Russell didn't think there would be any problem with getting GEnt acceptance, but he and Sam had to place secure calls back to Earth. So the women left. Deanna remained at her temporary workspace while Felix escorted Janine and Leslie to visit Bev and Hank.

"Well, it looks like I'm going to be like genetically mutated into a Galactic Doll, Felix. It's like part of the settlement with GD so they stop trying to kill you and us. Are you like still going to like me if I look like that?"

"You look like fabulous always, Leslie. Don't like worry about it. You'll like have curves that are more impressive. If only Bev could like recover her mind..."

***

While Leslie sat with Bev brushing her hair, Janine paid Hank a visit. "Sorry, I'm late today. Had a meeting. I'm going to have to have my body genetically made into one of those Galactic Dolls."

"Oh no. What's going on?" Hank said. He struggled to get up onto his foot.

"I've got a long story to tell you while we walk. Mind you, handsome, you might have to walk farther than normal."

He chuckled and crutched his way out of his room.

Janine began, "I'm not what I appear to be..."

Much later, Hank said, "Janine, you are more a real person than anyone I have ever known." This time, he hugged her. That led to a passionate kiss.

"If this all happens," Janine whispered, "when we're able to leave for Earth in a couple months, I'm taking you with me, Hank."

He laughed. "Isn't the man supposed to do the proposing?"

"Sorry buster. I'm not waiting on this man." They kissed again before continuing his practice walk.

***

The following morning, the group met once more with the GD representative. This time, Sam had a mountain of legal forms for everyone to sign. Everyone involved had a copy. Also, there were copies for all those not present, including Bev, Molly, and many others. This way, the other clones couldn't act independently of this agreement.

Once signed, Deanna verified they had restored her old accounts. She was again a very wealthy woman since they also deposited Peter's funds into her account. That done, two GD guards escorted the trio to Bayview Gardens Hospital for the pre-mutation checkup.

After a thorough exam, the doctor said, "Well, Mrs. Cartwright, I assure you the modification process will not

177

harm your unborn girl in the slightest. It's a perfectly safe procedure to have now. If you wait until the third trimester, then I would recommend putting it off until after you have the baby."

No one yet knew that future children would inherit the genetic changes made to the mother. Although Deanna tried to have hers delayed until after the portable EM pulse generator was operational, GD refused the delay. The device required several weeks to build, plenty of time for Deanna to get the operation completed.

Hours later, doctors injected the three women. After the doctors passed the infrared activation beams over their bodies, they slipped into genetic mutation comas. The three women were unconscious for around eight days before the doctors removed the various tubes and roused them. Deanna's first comment upon awakening and sitting up spoke volumes, "God, they're incredibly heavy!"

The bodies of Deanna, Janine, and Leslie were now perfect Galactic Dolls. The gold nanoparticles that carried the mutation sequences throughout their bodies worked perfectly. Each sported breasts that appeared much like smaller soccer balls. A doctor explained that their breasts wouldn't sag with time. Their hair was shinier and wavier, reaching their hips. Someone had manicured their long nails. None appreciated the cherry red nail polish, though. The trio also discovered their legs were altered. They had to wear tall heels since their feet would not lie flat on the floor. Otherwise, they could find nothing else altered in their bodies. Later they realized their backs had been strengthened to help support the weight of their large bosoms.

Three other Galactic Doll women from GEnt were present when the doctors revived them. Their purpose was to assist the trio in dressing and adjusting to their new appearances. Further, they briefed the three on Galactic Doll regulations.

That they were dressed in identical red satin, form-fitting gowns didn't surprise Leslie. After all, that seemed to be the most frequently seen color and style.

Once dressed, one woman explained the regulations.

"We're to flirt with those in the corporate world. But it's illegal for us to engage in sex of any kind with the clients. They told me they aren't assigning you to any corporation executives but still I have to go over these regulations. If you're eventually assigned, you'll also be medically examined twice a week to verify the no-sex rule. Your job is to look gorgeous at all times, to flirt as your clients wish you to, and to make them look and feel good. I'm told a new version of us will be available soon— Galactic Sex Dolls—and those are allowed to have sex with the clients and those they wish."

She continued, "On a personal hygiene level, you are *required* to keep your nails at least an inch long at all times. Mind you, they can be longer if you wish, but never shorter. Once a month, we visit our nail salons and have a manicure to keep them at the required length. Further, your hair must never be shorter than your upper hips. While you can put it up in various styles, it must stay this long. We visit the hair salons once a month and have split ends trimmed and such. They'll maintain its proper length for you. Of course, you can have it longer, if you prefer.

"Finally, you're required to wear gorgeous, elegant gowns at all times. You can never be seen wearing slacks, a blouse, jeans, skirt, or other commonplace clothing. The sole exception is that you may wear swimwear to the lakes, beaches, and pools. If you violate these regulations, GEnt will drop your sponsorship, and we all know how disastrous that is. We have a reputation to live up to—the most elegant women on the planet. We all must do our part. Questions?" Seeing none, the women departed.

"Come on," Janine said. "Let's find a mirror and see what we look like, though since we're clones, you must look like me."

"I want to see myself," Deanna insisted. "God, I look awful."

Leslie giggled. "We're like fetish now."

"Come on. I want to see how Bev is doing," Janine said.

"You two go ahead," Deanna said. "I have to see how the device development is coming along. Later, let's meet at that store where she said we could buy our apparel. We'll need a new wardrobe. My treat. We'll buy out the store, sisters. We'll get things for Bev too. God, walking is a bitch in these heels."

Leslie giggled. "Yes, small steps, but like you'll get used to it. I like did. At least, they always like put the gel pads in the toes. My boobs are like so heavy I'm afraid they'll like tip me over."

Deanna glared at her, annoyed. "Well, if this is what we have to endure to get them to stop killing us, it's worth it. I've lost four sisters, and I sure don't want to lose any more of you. I love having sisters." All three grinned.

Felix saw them as they came out of the hospital to his waiting EMAC. He exclaimed, "Wow, I like love how fetish you look, Leslie. You're like even more of a fetish queen now, but are you like sure you can manage?"

"I like keep thinking I'm falling over." She laughed. "I'm like used to this, but my sisters aren't. Best lend Janine and Deanna a hand getting in. Deanna's like heading to First Division HQ."

"You like got it. Gosh, it's like getting hard to tell you three apart."

Deanna glared at him. She said, "I know. This is a problem. As soon as we can, let's get our nails painted different colors and wear different colored gowns. Felix, you'll need this EMAC this afternoon, because we're going shopping and plan to buy out the store." He groaned, then chuckled.

When he dropped Deanna off, Russell was already there waiting for her. "You look terrific, Mrs. Cartwright." She glared at him. "Honestly, you look good, but that's the whole point of this modification. Anyway, you'll be glad to know about a day before you woke, that GD lawyer, Sam, dropped by the hospital while you were in a coma. He verified they had properly modified you three. He's departed Tau Ceti, so that's a good thing. Can't stand lawyers myself. Bottom feeders. Come on. The colonel wants to brief you and introduce you to the development staff."

Deanna's annoyance grew. She had no choice but to walk much slower than she'd ever walked before. Her steel tipped heels constantly announced her coming. Yet, she knew she had to endure this for the sake of her sisters and the male clones. But that didn't mean she had to like what GD had forced her to become.

***

Leslie continued on into Bev's room, while Janine stopped to visit Hank. When Janine stepped into his room at the assisted living complex, Hank said, "I've missed you so."

In fact, Janine was self-conscious, bordering on embarrassed to have Hank see her like this, but then this was the way she would always look.

"I thought I'd go crazy not seeing you for over a week. You look so different, Janine. Am I allowed to say wow?"

That wasn't what Janine was expecting. Hank didn't reject her garish appearance. She chuckled. "Yeah, but I feel like a lady of the street or something. Just look at what they did to us."

"Well, you have more curves. And I like your hair, so long, wavy, and lush. What did they do to it? Come here. You need a hug. I can tell that much."

She walked up to him, pressing her bosom into his body so he could slip his arm around her. "You really think I look somewhat acceptable like this?"

"Janine, I love you no matter how you look. I think you look great. Now you walk almost as slow as I do."

"Thanks. I fretted my garish look would turn you off. It does me."

"Hey, you look wonderful. I'm the half-person here."

"Oh, stop that. You know you're not that."

After kissing her, he changed the topic. "So does this mean that whenever Mrs. Cartwright gets her device working we'll leave?"

"Yes. We're taking you and Bev out of this death hole. I hope it's sooner than later."

"Say, Janine, I was thinking lots about you and this situation while you were gone. I'm afraid this whole Galactic Doll thing could backfire on you. From all I've ever heard, they are the toys of the corporate executives and rich men. So I was thinking—how about us getting married? Then, they can't make you be someone's sex doll."

He felt her whole body relax. "Oh, Hank. That would

make this so much easier for me. I keep expecting some guy to come by and cart me off or something. But are you sure you want me looking like this?"

"Are you sure you want me looking like I do?" Hank countered. They kissed again and agreed to get married as soon as possible.

"Come on. Let's go tell Leslie about it. Gee, I guess I do walk at your speed now."

Hank smiled, as he crutched towards the next room with Janine's heels clicking on the floor.

"Leslie, guess what? Hank and I are going to get married!"

"Ooh!" Leslie exclaimed, giving her and Hank a big hug, almost knocking him off his foot. "That's like *so* wonderful. Congratulations. Now you like won't have to worry about someone forcing you to become their corporate Doll, right?"

"Three minds think alike," Hank commented. "That's what I thought while you three were gone."

Leslie said, "I'm like texting Deanna about it and Felix too. Darn, texting with these long nails is like hard. Oh, Bev is like doing better today. She's like glad to see me. Maybe like when enough time has passed, her mind will like return to normal."

***

In fact, Bev's mind didn't return to normal during the ensuing months. The trio was on Brussels for months before a successful test of the device occurred. However, the true test would come whenever the Sixth Invaders launched their next ground attack. For now, the enemy seemed content with their northern position, defying all logic.

Deanna did splurge on her sisters, insisting they have as wide a variety of elegant clothing as permitted to Galactic Dolls. It took a crew of men to load the many crates of the women's new clothing into the light cruiser. While the men were loading the ship with the crates, Janine helped Hank navigate the tarmac and into the ship. Leslie and Deanna led Bev, who was still doped up on psych drugs. At Deanna's insistence, the doctors were weaning her off them. While Bev saw men around her, she just mumbled her usual words.

Almost six months after they originally left Earth, the group returned home and to Chicago. Deanna was seven months along. That alone helped the many people who worked in the Cartwright Skyscraper to recognize her from her sisters. Before, hairstyles and dress had been a quick way to identify the women, but now they looked even more alike.

One day passed while they moved back into the forty-ninth floor. During the past six months, her uncle had all the extensive damage repaired, though he was annoyed that GD gave the huge company back to Deanna and not to him as they had promised. Thus, Deanna saw no signs of the explosion and fire that had killed Peter and the others.

Once settled in, Deanna was ready to do what was necessary to find Molly and the other younger clones along with the Ted clone.

"We're going after Molly while I can still waddle along," she jested.

"You waddle far faster than I can walk," Hank said.

Her annoyance melted; Deanna cracked a smile.

Just then, her security man announced over the intercom, "A Sam Deckerson of Galactic Defense is here to see you. Says it's urgent."

"Okay, send him up."

"I'm embarrassed to have him see me looking like a whore," Deanna whispered to her sisters.

"We like look good. He like should be envious," Leslie whispered back.

Deanna glared. *I'll never look good again. She has no idea how awful it is trying to do my work with long nails. I hate being stared at whenever I walk anywhere, but the darn heels give me away. I look like a whore. Wonder what that lawyer creep wants. To gloat, most likely.*

"Hello, Mr. Deckerson," she said formally, her voice icy cold.

"It's time we work together as agreed to. I don't like this any better than you do but we have to follow orders. We're picking up Miss Parkinson and four other clones from a South Pacific atoll. More importantly, we're picking up two doctors, Nelson and Janet Padella. They are top genetic mutation and biological nanoparticle workers. We need them. They're on that island. It's their private laboratory."

Janine said, "You can't be serious! Those are the doctors who cloned us. They should be tried for their crimes against humanity." Taut lines appeared on her forehead.

"Tisk. Tisk. Mrs. Cartwright agreed to work with whoever we choose on the war effort. The security of Earth depends on those two doctors. So we're retrieving them from their island. Mind you, Mrs. Cartwright, you signed a contract not to seek retribution."

"Damn it. You knew about this when you met with us on Brussels, Tau Ceti," Deanna said. Her eyes drilled into his. He was lucky she couldn't shoot fire from them.

Sam shrugged his shoulders. "The art of bargaining has its rewards. Now then, can you be packed by ten tomorrow morning? We want to leave from New O'Hare at that time. It's a long trip."

"We'll be there," Deanna said through clenched teeth. She added, "Accidents are known to happen."

Sam sneered back. "Indeed, they are."

After he left, Janine asked, "What was that all about?"

"I was letting him know that I could arrange for these wicked doctors to have a terminal accident. He was reminding me that GD could just as easily arrange one for us. Still, we both understood each other. I don't like this, but we have my company back, lots of money in the bank, a secure, safe place to live, and no one is trying to kill us. Doesn't mean I like the price we're paying."

Chapter 14 Rescued

Late February, 2351

The Cartwright Airliner settled down on the landing strip beyond the lab and compound. As they approached the atoll, they spotted a large mansion at the opposite end of the island. Via the one cryptic email from Ted over six months ago, they suspected their sisters and Ted lived in that home. As they got closer, they saw a tall wire fence around the lab and other admin buildings. Only one building was accessible to those walking down from the mansion. Later, they learned this was the store that carried groceries and apparel. As the ship landed, Deanna noticed an EMAC engine generator and solar panels providing power for the island.

***

Molly's turn to do the grocery shopping came. As she arrived at the store, she saw an Airliner with the Cartwright logo on it landing just at the edge of the main office building and lab. Her heart raced as her mind grasped what this might represent. She wanted to run back to tell the others, but in her heels, it would take forever for her to walk all the way back to the mansion. By then, the ship might be gone, so she moved over to the fence where she could see who arrived.

As she watched the side door opening and the retractable steps rolling down, she saw Drs. Nelson and Janet Padella coming out of the admin building. Neither looked pleased. Their faces taut, she heard them cursing. Molly concluded this wasn't an expected or desired arrival. Her heart beat faster.

A man she'd never seen stepped down first, walking briskly over to the doctors. Molly felt a twinge of grief. She could never walk fast again. Then, her heart raced. She saw the pregnant Deanna carefully descending. She recognized Deanna's favorite color, a light blue.

Oh, my god! What's happened to her? She looks like me, but she still has her arms.

Molly fought against yelling out to her, figuring Deanna needed to concentrate on the stairs. Giant breasts and tall heels didn't make going down a steep set of narrow stairs an easy task.

When she saw Deanna reach the safety of the ground, she yelled. "Deanna. Deanna. Over here. It's me, Molly. Over here."

Deanna looked and saw her. She gasped and then shrieked. True, Molly looked very much like she and her sisters did, a Galactic Doll, but Molly had no arms.

At the top of the stairs, Molly saw what must be Janine and then Leslie making their way out of the Airliner, though now she couldn't tell them apart. Even from this distance, Molly heard both of them cursing. Molly yelled, "I'm okay. I'm so glad to see all of you. What happened? You all look like me."

Deanna reached the fence and barked to the doctors, "Open this fence immediately! Send a vehicle down to the mansion and bring the others up here. Now, you fools!"

Both doctors looked at Sam, so Molly did, too.

"You heard her," he said. "Open this gate and send someone to bring the others here. Then, let's go inside. We've much to discuss, presuming you both wish to continue to live."

If that's his best try at a threat, it's rather lame, Molly thought.

"Oh dear god, Molly, what have they done to you?" Deanna asked. She hugged Molly.

"I could say the same thing. Did they get to all of you? Are we all turned into Galactic Dolls now?" Molly asked. "Oh, come here. Give me a hug, you two. How can I tell you two apart?" Janine and Leslie did so.

Leslie said, "It's like horrible what they've done to you. I like can't imagine how you're managing. What like happened to us is nothing like compared to you. Janine like wears green gowns, and I like wear red ones. Oh yes, Janine and I are like married. Deanna's like saved us all—you too. GD isn't like going to try to kill us anymore, but they've already maimed you. Don't worry. We'll like be here for you. We'll like be your hands now, won't we, Janine?"

Molly chuckled, "I'm doing okay. I met Ted Billings,

and we want to get married. Lots of good has happened here, too, Leslie. It's not been all bad, thanks to Ted and our three younger sisters. They're incredible. So who are the lucky fellows?"

Leslie explained, "Oh, they're like coming down the stairs now. It's like hard for Janine's husband, Hank, to negotiate stairs. He's like a war victim, so my Felix is helping him down. See, there they are."

"Gosh, what happened to him?"

"It's part of the long story we have to tell you," Janine said. "He was in the army fighting the Sixth Invaders. They captured him and did this to his body."

"Wait a second, Leslie. Isn't your fellow one of the male clones? He looks an awful lot like Frank, only he's got a mustache."

Leslie giggled. "He is, but he's like cute. He's like a security guard for GEnt. We're like in love. He like has my photos I did for Shiny Magazine posted on his wall. But like what happened to your arms?"

Deanna added, "Yes, what happened to your arms?"

"She cut them off—Dr. Janet Padella. She also cut off Ted's hands, and she's cut off the hands of our three younger sisters after they were born."

Deanna pivoted and glared at Janet, who trembled and backed up several steps.

Sam stepped in, "Remember your contract, Mrs. Cartwright. No retribution on those who have harmed your clones and the male clones."

Through clenched teeth, Deanna said, "Accidents happen, even to doctors."

Sam said, "Come, come. We have work to do. Why don't your people walk on down to the mansion? I'll take the eighteen blood samples inside and get the Padellas working on them."

"I'm not letting those samples out of my sight," barked Deanna. To the others, she said, "You take that small electric cart there, go down, and visit our sisters and Ted. Tell them everything that has happened. I'll be along later. Maybe. I don't trust GD or these insane doctors."

The doctors, Sam, and Deanna headed inside the administration building on their way to the genetics laboratory. Leslie, Janine, Felix, Hank, and Molly took the cart down the two-mile length of the island, Felix driving.

"We go swimming down there at least once a week," Molly said. "The water is warm and the beach, perfect. The weather is a paradise."

"But how can you like swim?" asked Leslie.

"I float on my back and paddle with my feet. It's pathetic, but I'm able to enjoy the beach and waters. The others do it that way too."

Ted called out from the front doorway, "Hey everyone. We have a lot of company. What the heck..."

Molly saw his eyes focusing on Felix, who looked like Ted used to, except for the mustache. Then, Ted saw Hank and the other two Galactic Dolls who looked almost identical to Molly and her three younger sisters.

After the cart stopped and everyone got off, Molly moved over to her four companions. "These are my two other sisters, Leslie and Janine. Deanna is back at the genetics lab. This is exciting. Okay, introductions and then you *have* to tell us what's been going on. We're isolated here, but we have good Internet service, thanks to Ted, but we're limited to university connections.

"Because of him, they've been able to attend online college classes. Can you believe this? Our three younger sisters each have two doctorates, and they're working on a third."

Molly introduced Randi, Eve, Celeste, and Ted to the others.

Ted said, "I used to look like you, Felix, but now I'm a freak. Still, Molly wants to marry me, so I'm one very lucky fellow."

Molly said, "Come on inside. Have a soda. Tell us about *everything*. What happened after I texted you? Did they get you out of the building? Catch the assassin? Stop the bombing?"

They congregated in the spacious living room. Molly impressed Leslie with how she handled her drink. The younger sisters carried out cold cans of soda, cradling them in their arms. Eve rested one on Molly's shoulder, and she held it by squeezing her head against the can and her shoulder. After sitting, she popped the tab using her toes and, using her foot, lifted it up for a sip.

This was a new experience for Molly. With the four staring at her, she felt embarrassed, but she knew she'd have to get used to this. From now on, staring would always happen. She found the unwanted attention very hard to endure. Molly saw that Celeste also noticed this and hoped this embarrassed feeling could be handled with more therapy. If not, she'd just have to endure it.

Time flew while Leslie and Janine related what had happened to them, beginning with their worry over not hearing from Molly that night. Hank told them about the battle with the Sixth Invaders, and how their sister, Kick Ass BB—or Captain Beverly Blossom Blythe—saved most of the companies on three occasions. Molly and the three younger sisters gasped when they heard how badly Bev's mind had been altered.

Evening came before Deanna joined them, bringing along supper for everyone, compliments of the base's chef. As expected, everyone stared at Molly and the four as they used their feet to deal with the meal. They had seen nothing like these five.

After eating the chicken, potatoes, gravy, and coleslaw meal, Molly related her six months on the atoll, praising the therapy skills of Randi, Eve, and Celeste. Then, Ted outlined his many years here as a prisoner, and he, too, praised their therapy skills.

He finished by saying, "Maybe they can do something for Bev. I expect they can erase the genetic mutation trauma you three endured and what must have been an awful pain for Hank."

When he finished, Celeste, Eve, and Randi told them about their lives. Deanna's face twisted and cringed when she heard of the many lies the Padella doctors had told her younger sisters. Per the contract she'd signed, everyone knew they couldn't get justice for these victims of the insane doctors.

"Incredible," Deanna said. "You really do have two

PhDs each. This is unbelievable. Very well done. Molly, Janine, Leslie—you should take a hint from our younger sisters. Knowledge is vitally important."

Leslie giggled. "I'm like not smart like them. Sorry."

"Not everyone is cut out for the universities," Janine added.

Molly laughed. "All I ever wanted to be was a PI. Now that's been taken from me."

"I don't know why you can't continue to be a PI," Deanna said. "Your office is still there as you left it. I got the rent caught up for you. Thanks to Felix, we have the equipment you left behind when they abducted you."

She continued, "Ted, Eve, Randi, Celeste, I want you to move into my Cartwright Skyscraper where you'll be safe. I've tripled the number of security guards on the place. I'm wealthy, so I can help each of you with your financial needs. For the time being, I think we should stick together. None of us trusts Galactic Defense, not remotely. Plus, some fishy things about this war with the Sixth Invaders bothers me. Safety in numbers. We have the resources to respond to situations. And I might need babysitters soon."

Eve said, "That would be wonderful. Randi and I want to keep on with our studies, but we might be able to help Bev. I'm sure we can help the rest of you. While you were in a coma during the genetic mutation process, your minds recorded everything. That unseen stuff can have deleterious effects on you later on."

Randi asked, "Can we see this supposed contract you had to sign, Deanna?"

"I brought copies for you five." Deanna passed them around, watching the four grab them between their arms, but slipping off heels to use their toes to page through them. Molly took it in her teeth before sitting and joining the others.

Soon, Molly commented, "Legal gibberish. All I can say is that we need justice. A complete lack of justice isn't right."

Celeste agreed. "She's right. If civil and personal rights are not recognized and enforced, all justice has lost any point it may have had. Justice and no civil rights or no personal rights simply don't go together. If a person cannot safeguard his own body or those of his family and friends, let alone his property, then he becomes very worried about justice. The only justice is a fair justice."

Molly admired how learned Celeste sounded. Her sister continued, "If a person gets into a position where he knows he cannot get justice for actions done against him, and if he sees others able to get justice against him, then he slides into the revolution mode. This is how you create a revolutionary, a criminal, or a juvenile delinquent. If they aren't allowed to use enough force to get justice, they crash."

Leslie giggled. "I don't like know what she said, but it like sounded good."

Molly grinned. Felix chuckled.

Deanna said, "So you're saying we, as a group, have been harmed, and for our own well-being, we need to get justice, specifically against the Padellas and against GD?"

Celeste chuckled. "Precisely, though with this contract thing, that may be difficult to obtain. If we don't, our own mental well-being could suffer."

A wry smile appeared. Celeste said, "According to the contract's wording, none of us may undergo any reverse medical procedures that would undo the Galactic Doll or other modifications."

Eve interrupted her. "There are other ways. You'll see, Deanna. But let's get off this atoll and away from these beasts who call themselves doctors."

Deanna responded, "Well, we'll be here a few days. GD is having the doctors analyze the blood samples taken from Bev and seventeen other women from the three Sixth Invader attacks. GD wants to know if the enemy is using our own Galactic Doll mutation methods or one of their own. The DNA will tell us what's going on."

Eve piped up. "This is my field. Yes, they must isolate the few specific sequences of DNA that cause the soccer ball breasts and the distorted legs and feet. There is a maker's ID marker in that portion. The hair and nail excessive growth are caused by a simple set of organic chemical stimulants given to the person during the mutation period. If the Padella doctors are any good, they should have the results in two days at most.

If you have any pull, I'd like to watch over them and what they do. I don't trust them."

"Okay. Eve, come with me. We'll take the cart back. I'll see you're involved. Keep the beasts honest. I think this study is very important, though I'm not sure why. This is way out of my league of EMAC design."

She added, "On my way back, I'll bring my Airliner's captain with me. He can marry people. We can enjoy Molly and Ted's ceremony."

Molly beamed. Ted exclaimed, "Incredible! Yes!" He punched his arm into the air, bringing smiles to many faces.

***

On the ride to the lab, Eve said, "Deanna, I know this will sound awful, but you and the others have to let us and Molly do everything our own special way, as slow and awkward as it may seem to you. Our self-respect is on the line, particularly Molly's. She's only had six months to relearn how to do things and still has a difficult time. Pass this along to the others when you can."

"I understand—more today than, say, last year. Every time I'm out in public, I feel embarrassed to have people see me looking like this—as though I'm a prostitute."

Eve sensed the deeply suppressed emotions that lay behind Deanna's simple admission. *Once we're clear of this atoll, Randi and I have to help our sisters.* They rode on in silence, enjoying the evening sea breeze.

Later, the group watched Molly and Ted get married. True, it was a simple ceremony, the first the flustered captain had ever done, but all welcomed it.

***

Two days passed before the doctors, watched by Eve, had the results.

Nelson was angry. "This is an abomination! These—these Sixth Invaders have stolen our work—Janet's and mine. The genetic mutation to produce the Galactic Dolls is our invention. Look here. This is the breast augmentation sequence."

He had nineteen windows opened on his giant wall monitor, tiled so one could see the same sequence in all

192

eighteen and one of his own lab samples.

"It's identical. See this spot. It's an unused section of the gene. See that? That's our identifying mark. We always insert our ID marker in any altered sequence we've ever made."

Janet added, "So that means these Sixth Invaders stole the Galactic Doll genetic mutation gold nanoparticles from a GD laboratory or perhaps from GEnt or GMed."

"Oh, dear god," Sam declared. "I'm all over this." He grabbed his phone and moved away to place a call to the mainland.

Eve smiled. The Padellas hadn't lied. She'd observed the analysis every step of the way and could find no fault in their procedure or comparison. The result was shocking, and she suspected it would have far-reaching effects. Eve headed back to the mansion at the other end of the island, hoping this would be the last time she would have to make the long walk back. *In a way, I'm about to leave my childhood home. I'm not sure if this is good or bad.* She strolled while inhaling the salty air.

***

Deanna said, "Okay, you've heard the report. Time to go home, everyone. Hank will drive the cart back, loaded with your possessions. The rest of us will walk back to the Airliner." *GD won't like these results. They must have had one hell of a security breach or they are in league with these Sixth Invaders. I can imagine all kinds of scenarios with GD. Wait. It might not be GD. What about getting it from GMed or even GEnt? We best not rush to judge this one.*

***

As they walked down the road to the admin and genetics lab for the last time, Eve sent telepathically, 'Randi, are we going to let these Padella doctors get away with what they've done to us, to Ted, and to Molly?'

'No. They need to learn there are consequences. But we can't do anything overtly without harming Deanna's contract with GD.'

Eve replied. 'We won't have to. Have you looked at the gold anchoring dots that used to define the space for Ted's

193

hands?'

'No, not for a long time. Is that important?'

Eve hinted, 'Yes. When they first brought him to this island, I snooped. I overheard them talking about cutting off his hands, so while he was unconscious, I moved the gold balls that defined his hands into one tight location. Then, she cut off his hands, leaving the bunched balls at the ends of his arms. It's the same thing I did to our bodies when we first came here.'

Randi sent back, 'Well, we should have him energize the gold balls and push them back to where they belong.'

Eve countered, 'Precisely, but not until we're safe in Deanna's place. I wonder what would happen to the Padella doctors if we bunched together all the golden balls that anchor their body's hands in place.'

Randi smiled. 'You think their hands would soon vanish, once the anchoring points for the body are removed?'

'Yeah, that's what I think. Or perhaps their hands will curl up into balls. Shall we see what happens?'

Randi turned to Eve and nodded. The two focused on the doctors, doing just that—clumping all the golden balls that defined the outline, the space of the doctors' hands.

***

An hour later, Ted, Molly, Eve, Randi, and Celeste watched the atoll diminishing in size, as the Airliner rose.

Eve said, "Well, this closes this part of our lives. Still, I loved that island."

Celeste said, "True, the island was wonderful. It was just the other people on it who were bad."

"Not us." Molly interrupted, flashing a broad, teasing grin.

"Oh, don't be silly." Eve chuckled.

Just then, the voice of their captain yelled over the intercom system. "Good god! Brace yourselves. There's a large missile heading for that island. I'm applying full thrust."

"I'm being crushed!" Molly said. The force pressed her down into her cushy leather seat.

"The ship should hold," Deanna said. "Wait. If it's a nuclear bomb, we could be in trouble. Captain, turn off the engines and everything electronic!"

Deanna held her breath, releasing it only when the giant Airliner slowed its upward climb. The pressure eased off the passengers, and all lights went off. Then, the ship started falling, accelerating downward. Boom! A gigantic explosion shook the Airliner, tossing the ship this way and that, arresting its downward acceleration for a second.

Deanna said, "Captain, now would be a good time to restart your engines and power up." She looked back at the pale faces of the others. "Don't worry. The ship can float on the ocean. It can survive a fall from this height. Redundant safety features. Still, I don't want to swim back to civilization."

Through her window, Molly watched the ocean rising towards her at an alarming rate. Then, she felt the ship shudder and again felt her body forced hard into the leather seat. Glancing out the window, she saw the ship flying at a dizzying speed just above the waves before it shot upwards. Only then did Molly remember to breathe.

"Well, someone wanted the Padella doctors dead," Deanna said.

"Or someone wanted us dead and missed," Molly countered.

Both women looked at Sam, whose face was devoid of all color. He raced for the restroom. When he returned several minutes later, his face had some pink in it, but his eyes radiated anger.

Deanna asked, "Well, Sam, was GD trying to kill us all in one shot? How does it feel to have a target painted on your back?"

"It wasn't GD," he said. "At least, I don't think so. I will sort this out and let you know."

The way Deanna rolled her eyes, Molly didn't believe she thought he'd share such information with her.

***

Curiously, no one bothered to check what had happened to the atoll complex. In fact, twenty years ago, General Fuller had installed a missile defense system on the island. Until today, everyone on the island had forgotten about it, but the system detected the incoming missile and fired its counter-missile.

Unknown to those on the Airliner, the explosion only shattered a few windows, causing no serious damage to the facilities or personnel.

***

Once safe in the Cartwright Skyscraper and as life attempted to find a new normal, several things occurred. While Deanna, Janine, and Leslie bustled about doing their best to make things easier for the others, Eve, Randi, and Celeste went into action. First, Eve and Randi focused on their own golden balls that outlined the space that their physical bodies occupied, pushing and shoving the ones that were out of alignment or distorted. In the end, they gave each one a shove and watched them jiggle. Those that were out of place returned to the locations they were supposed to have had.

Next, the pair did the same thing to Celeste and to Ted. Eve explained, "We're now able to fulfill our promise we made to you both years ago."

"My stumps feel funny," Ted whispered. The women smiled.

Then, Eve took Bev into her bedroom to see what she could do about Bev's scrambled mind, while Randi dealt with Hank.

Celeste began Leslie's therapy session. "But I like don't need this. I'm like always lucky," Leslie protested. Later, she cried out from the pain of the genetic mutation process.

Several days later, Leslie felt fabulous.

"What's going on here?" asked Deanna, when she joined them for supper. "Something is different."

Leslie giggled. "Eve, Celeste, Randi, and Ted's bodies are like going back to being normal, though now Ted like is desperate for a haircut. And my boobs are like shrinking. That's what I told you. We're like all lucky. No, wait a minute. It's like our bodies are lucky. We like make our own luck, but it's good to know our bodies are like in there pitching with us."

"But we're not supposed to get genetically undone," Deanna said. Her face clenched.

Eve spoke up. "Look, none of what's happening is due to any kind of this world's medical or genetic procedures. Leslie has the right idea. GEnt should think of this as more like a bunch of miracles. But it's each person's own powers that we're helping—"

Celeste interrupted, "We are spiritual beings who have a mind of videos and pictures and who inhabit these bodies." She gave everyone a lengthy explanation, often glancing at Eve to make sure she was saying things properly. "So, I'm learning how to do their therapy thing, practicing on you guys."

Eve added, "She's right. Each of us has the potential to be a goddess or god, only the people on this world that we've met so far seem to have forgotten who and what they are and what they can do. But Randi and I are very excited because you have so much technology we can learn."

Deanna, the engineer in the bunch, frowned. "So how are you re-growing their hands? What about Hank and Molly? How is this possible?"

Eve sighed. "You're talking biology now. As far as I know, there isn't any known drug or compound you can ingest that will regrow arms. However, the human spirit is more powerful than the physical universe."

She took another point of view for Deanna's sake. "If we look at your body, not you or your mind, just your body, it has these tiny gold ball-like dots that it uses to define the space it occupies. I know, you can't easily see them, but with enough therapy, one can. Both Ted and Molly have been able to see theirs. Think of them as though they were rivets holding metal pieces together. If they pop out, the pieces fall apart. Anyway, when I heard Dr. Padella was going to cut off our hands, I forced the myriad gold dots that define the space of each of our bodies' hands into a single spot at our wrists. That way, they would still be there. I did the same to Molly's, but they cut off her arms and so went the pile of gold dots. If we'd been conscious when I did it, the body would have sent excruciating pain through our hands, but we weren't since she was about to operate on us."

Eve continued her explanation. "We jiggled them, and they shot back into their original places. Now, our bodies are rebuilding our hands. What about you three? While everyone was sleeping, we jiggled your anchoring gold balls. With the four of us, that has made the gold dot framework revert back to what it should have been all our lives."

Eve sighed. "I am uncertain why jiggling the gold dots is also undoing the mutations; I'm still studying that. With the five of us on the atoll, I know the Padellas used their original mutation formulation. That version was shipped to other worlds, but only in small quantities. I suspect it was used on you three on Brussels.

"I've stolen close looks at that agent, comparing it to their current version. It's my belief that their original version was weak and that its changes weren't altogether permanent. Over time, the body rejected the mutations, reverting to its original form. That explains why jiggling our bodies' gold dots is undoing the mutation. We're helping it along. Also, when the Padella doctors examined all those samples you brought to the atoll, I noticed these Sixth Invaders were also using that original old version on the captured female soldiers. So I'm hopeful Bev's modifications can be reduced or undone."

Smiling, Eve added, "As far as GD is concerned, Deanna, you can claim the doctors on Brussels used a defective batch of the genetic mutation serum. My conclusion is that I believe these changes can be undone in all of you, but we can't regrow new limbs.

"As we work with each of you, we will help you discover who and what you are, and if possible, how you can remedy things you consider aren't right with your bodies. None of this has anything to do with your medical profession, so you don't have to worry about GEnt repercussions since GEnt is now your sponsor and not GD. GD has no direct authority over any of us."

"Except making us help with the war effort," Deanna added. "That's still something I can't wiggle out of."

***

By the time two weeks passed, even Deanna understood. She re-experienced the mutation pain and unconsciousness and erased its effects. The terrible loss of Peter was handled, bringing a sense of closure to her. When Eve drilled Deanna on mocking up small golden balls and putting them in a rectangular solid surrounding her body, Deanna spotted several of her body's gold anchor balls that were out of place.

Eve suggested she give them a shove.

"Gosh, they're moving inwards. Oh, I get the feeling that's where they're supposed to be."

Days later, Deanna's bosom was back to what it had been before the mutation. Even her legs returned to normal by the time Jana was born in mid-April. She had her hair cut short, back to her usual bob haircut. When Eve finished giving her therapy to handle childbirth, Deanna felt like a new woman. Invigorated and full of life, she was ready both for motherhood and for uncovering the truth about what was going on.

In fact, when Jana entered the world, Ted looked like a man again, though he didn't grow a mustache. That way, everyone could tell him from Felix. Likewise, Janine and Leslie had their bodies restored, though Leslie kept her DD bosom so she could continue photo shoots for GEnt. Celeste, Eve, and Randi had their bodies reset to what they should have been for three young women. Even Bev's body was restored, though her arms and legs lacked the powerful muscles she once had had.

Vitally important, Eve's therapy worked a miracle on Bev. Because of that, Deanna and the others now knew what the invaders had done to the female soldiers. True, she'd endured the genetic mutation trauma to her body, but that was minor compared to the painful mental implant she'd received.

Via the therapy sessions, they learned the Sixth Invaders had put her into a machine, attached electrodes to her head, and drugged her. Then while blasting her head with excruciating painful electricity, headphones replayed the silly message she had constantly babbled so many times. The words she had spouted and the actions she craved from men were contained within the words they had implanted into her mind, buried and enforced by the massive induced pain and drugs.

It took several long days for Eve get Bev to face and confront that nasty trauma. When Bev re-experienced it in all its detail, the implant lost all ability to affect her. Bev returned to the land of the living, and no one was happier to be normal again than Bev.

By the time Jana was born in mid-April, 2351, only Molly and Hank's bodies hadn't been restored. True, the

Galactic Doll modifications to Molly's body were gone, but she still didn't have arms, though she kept her hair long. She liked draping it over her shoulders, hiding her lack of arms. Likewise, Hank's body was still missing his left arm and right leg. Both had their therapy sessions and, with those physical exceptions, were doing very well.

Hank said, "Look, stop worrying about me. I'm getting along fine. I'm taking history classes and on my way to becoming a history professor. I have the world's greatest wife. So, Eve, get on with your own studies."

Eve then worked more with Molly.

"Look, I can see all these gold ball things around my body, and we've jiggled them all," Molly said. "But I see none of those ball things where hands or arms should be. Nothing has changed these past weeks, so I guess I'm not supposed to have them, but I'm determined to resume being a PI because I want to help people. Besides, we owe you more than we can ever repay. You've salvaged our lives."

Eve chuckled. "No, you salvaged your own lives, but I see your point. Celeste wants to delve deeper into this therapy thing, so maybe she'll learn something that can help you later on. Is it okay if she keeps working with you each day?" Molly agreed.

***

With that settled, Bev took Molly aside. "Say, are you still planning to continue to run your PI business?"

"Bev, I just have to get back to being a PI. I have to help others and to get justice for them. If I don't, there's nothing to live for. Not really."

"I know what you mean. We've both got that drive. That's why we're so alike, compared to our sisters. You stick with me, and you'll be back investigating again."

"It's what I've always wanted to do. I owe Ted a great deal. It seems GD had me set up to be in the army like you, but Ted altered their files. How about you? Did you always want to be a soldier? And why do they call you Kick Ass?"

Bev chuckled. "Yes, always. I had an older brother who had all these toy soldiers. I never took anything from anybody, especially higher-ranking officers. Most of the time, I was dead on, dead right, including this last time when I got captured. Kick Ass. I used BB because Bev didn't sound good. Hell, Beverly or Blossom or Blythe sounded even worse, but I could sort of tolerate Captain Blythe. So how come you are called Cool Head?"

Molly chuckled. "Because in tight situations, I always seem to be relaxed with a cool head. I was that way throughout high school. I don't get flustered like some of our sisters do and was a crack shot with my 9mm Glock, but now I'm pathetic. Deanna has reservations about whether I should resume being a PI."

"Now that is something, Cool Head. You and I should train together. Just look at these arms and legs of mine. Pitiful. I've not been this weak and out of shape since before Eighth Grade. I'm going to have to really work out to get my physical form and endurance back. Say, I know a lot about martial arts combat. Together, we can get both of us into shape and turn you into a deadly weapon. I bet if you didn't have your gun, you were done fighting."

Molly laughed. "How'd you know that? Yeah, I depended on it. Frank always told me I needed to take self-defense courses, but I never did. I'll admit it's damn scary being like this."

"It'll help your self-confidence, too, Cool Head. Of all our sisters, you and I are more alike than the others. Hell, I don't know a fraction of the stuff our younger sisters do. Besides, book learning was never my thing. Don't get me wrong. Deanna is incredible, the way she can design things. Me? I never could. You stick with me, Molly, and in no time we'll both be kicking ass again."

"Okay. I'm game, but remember, it's frightening for me."

"I don't give a crap about that. You shouldn't either because people will try to use it against you. Come on. Let's change into workout clothes."

Thus began the toughest workouts Molly had ever experienced. She and Bev ran up the back stairs from the ground floor to the rooftop. Running back down the stairs was far more challenging for Molly, who had a tough time keeping her balance. Then, the pair ran laps around one little-used floor. When June's balmy days arrived, the pair spent several hours outside running along Lake Shore Drive. Bev was careful to always push Molly, but never beyond what she could do. In July, Bev built them an obstacle course, further challenging Molly's balance and endurance.

What changed Molly's opinion of herself turned out to be the martial arts training. Bev worked on Molly's kicks until Molly could shatter a two-by-four with one strike. While the many hours of workouts on the mats resulted in bruises all over Molly's body, she progressed in agility and skill, until Bev almost couldn't knock Molly off her feet unless she took Molly by surprise.

Bev's strength and endurance returned gradually, though her muscles still were not as pronounced as they had been when her sisters first saw her on the videos.

By late August 2351, Molly resumed her PI work, though Bev often tagged along, since her duties as a security guard for Deanna were very boring. Molly had another motive for returning to her PI work. She wanted to find the assassin who had murdered so many of them and discover who had fired the rocket at the atoll.

Part 4

Vic Broquard

Chapter 15 Fourth Reich

Late April, 2351

Around the time Deanna gave birth to Jana, daffodils shot up, declaring the end of the cold Chicago winter.

"Kyle, you tone it down. You're just beggin' for trouble," Mel said. He was Kyle's roommate at the University of Illinois Chicago Campus. "Look what happened to Bob. You could be next, and I sure as hell won't lie to protect you. Don't say or post anything for a month. After that, Kyle, I don't care what you say; just don't screw up my chances to graduate."

"Well, Bob was honest and right in his criticism of GD," Kyle Dorn said. The twenty-one-year-old more or less ignored his conservative roommate.

In a month, both men were to graduate with their degree in electrical engineering and were sponsored by Galactic Electronics. Already, Mel had accepted a job offer, activated upon graduation.

Kyle knew Mel wouldn't do anything to back him up, but if he could only get him to see what was going on in the world and in Chicago in particular, why, maybe word would spread. Maybe there was some hope of changing other people's minds.

Trying a different approach, Kyle said, "Back in 1776, anyone was free to say anything they wanted. As long as it wasn't slanderous of course. You could *talk* about committing a crime all you wanted, but it was only when you actually *did* something that the cops got involved. A crime was something one did, like robbing a bank. Look where we're at today. If you even whisper such a thing, you'll get arrested and jailed."

"No, Kyle, not jailed. You whisper stuff like that—you're insane and should be terminated. You have to be nuts to talk about robbing a bank. Why would any sane person want to rob a bank? So I think CEO Hardy is right. Insanity is our enemy, and we all have to do our part in spotting those who have gone crazy. Kyle, you're darn close to it, if you ask me. Like I said, shut up for a month, will you? I have to study. You should too." His left hand shot out parallel with the ground, palm facing down, and with his little finger pointing to the floor, emulating the silly gesture GD CEO Hardy often made.

**

Mel opened one of his electronic books and tuned his roommate out. If privately Mel thought Kyle was already insane, he wouldn't say anything to anyone about his suspicions. Why? If they found Kyle was crazy, then he would be interrogated, if not also declared nuts.

The corporation authorities believed in Guilty by Association (GBA)—an idea that went back centuries to the War on Terrorism, when if you had a friend who was a terrorist, then you too were considered to be a terrorist, unless you could prove you weren't. Many individuals spent decades trying to prove they weren't Guilty By Association or guilty until proven innocent, though most gave up and pleaded guilty. How do you prove that nothing is there? Mel wanted no part of that.

**

Kyle knew how much Mel feared GBA. In fact, everyone on campus feared it, but that's just the way life was. The corporations saw to that. Since Mel was no longer paying any attention to him, Kyle changed the subject.

"Gonna watch Hardy's speech tonight? It's supposed to be important."

Deigning to look up, Mel merely nodded.

At seven, the newscast began. Few students bothered to gather in the dorm lounge to watch it on the big screen; most preferred to catch it on their laptops or touchpads. Mel and Kyle watched it in the privacy of their dorm room.

Mr. Hardy, the middle-aged CEO of Galactic Defense, Chicago, appeared before a wall of microphones. The man's serious look meant the news would not be good. As usual, he began by shooting his left hand outward, parallel to the floor, palm down, and pointed his little finger straight downward. He then began his remarks.

"My fellow Sol Empire citizens and Earthlings, the Sixth Invaders have struck again, crossing the Rios River of North

Continent on our sister world, Brussels, Tau Ceti. Our First Division was there to stop them but failed. In a devastating loss, thirty were killed, but a hundred-six were brutalized. These Sixth Invaders are the vilest creatures in the universe. The holographic GEnt video I'm about to show you was taken during this recent attack. It is beyond graphic, so if you have a weak stomach, don't watch. Yes, the video has gone viral on Brussels."

As the edited 3-d holographic video played showing the removal of an arm and leg of the captured soldiers, he continued. "Yes, these foul fiends are cutting off an arm and a leg of our brave soldiers. They're barbecuing and eating the pieces. These Sixth Invaders must be slaughtered to the last one. Encased in their body armor and with breathing cylinders on their backs, we still have no idea what these fiends look like. Grim.

"Today, I'm calling for all young men and women to visit your nearest GD headquarters and volunteer for a four-year term of service as a GD soldier. All other sponsoring corporations have agreed to honor such a commitment on your part. Their sponsorship will resume upon your service termination. We are desperate for your service as a Sol Empire soldier. Help us defeat these hideous invaders before they reach Earth. Sign up today. Your Sol Empire needs you.

"Next, as of today, all corporations will be charging a two percent tax on the sale of all goods and services. The funds will be used to help the defense of Earth and the Sol Empire. Everyone now has a way to contribute to our defense.

"Finally, my Executive Order 1026 directs the Earth Drone Army to conduct a definitive and final war on these Sixth Invader Terrorists. With the recent unprovoked bombing of the Cartwright Enterprise Headquarters here in downtown Chicago, these Sixth Invaders have shown they can strike anywhere. This local war here in Chicago will be conducted without endangering a single soldier's life. Rather, our many drones will begin continuous surveillance runs over Chicago, ensuring the safety and security of all citizens. The drones overhead will protect us all. Troublemakers will be discovered and face their Termination Day. We must remain united if we're to win this war and win we will!"

Again, he made his weird left-hand gesture, pointing his finger to the ground. Kyle didn't know what it meant. He figured it was a quirk of the CEO's personality. An applause machine ended his presentation. He took no questions from reporters.

Mel and Kyle turned off the video-cast. Mel looked up with a grimace on his face. He said, "Did you see what those fiends, those Sixth Invaders, have done? Finally, our CEO is acting to end terrorism here in Chicago and end the war with these brutal inhuman beasts. I don't mind paying more to help fund our brave soldiers. I feel safer with the drones always overhead." Mel emulated CEO Hardy's left-hand gesture.

Kyle groaned, knowing he'd get nowhere with Mel. *The world has become a dictatorship, and everyone seems to think this is a good thing. Real insanity. Why can't people see what the corporations are doing to us? I have to take a stand against this, but how? He's got a good point. If I say much, they're likely to declare I'm crazy and terminate me. But I can't keep quiet. Ah, I can make an anonymous posting to my Friends Book page, pretending to be a concerned citizen and use a fake IP address.*

Far into the night, Kyle worked on his new posting, finally uploading it to his page, pretending it was from someone called Anonymous Freedom Fighter.

***

As Kyle entered the EE lab for his 8:00 class, a classmate asked, "Kyle, have you seen what someone has posted on your Friends Book page?"

Several other electrical engineering students, having also seen the posting, whispered about it and nodded to Kyle.

Kyle played dumb. "No, just got up—almost late for lab. What's it say?"

"You best take it down fast—if ya know what's good for you," a student said.

The professor walked in, curtailing the whispered chatting. When the lab finished, several gathered around Kyle, as he brought up the new posting on his laptop. Already, it had received over a thousand "likes." A dozen others had commented on it. These comments interested Kyle, who pretended to read the posting. It read:

In 1776, our ancestors created our nation based on personal freedoms and with a government that had checks and balances on those who were elected to rule. Today, the corporations and GD CEO Hardy have abolished all that. In short, in its place they've established the Fourth Reich. Just as Hitler attempted to exterminate all Jews, Hardy is trying to exterminate anyone who doesn't support the corporations and their actions.

Now we have to pay a two percent war tax, lining the pockets of Galactic Defense. Isn't that corporation's stated purpose the defense of the Sol Empire? Hardy is telling you that GD isn't prepared to defend us. He wants you to join his army. In my book that corporation is treasonous.

Who has all the money in the country? Who controls our futures? I say it's time for a people's revolution. Enough is enough!

We know where Hitler led his people. Do we really want Hardy leading us there, too? I say no!

If we don't take a stand now, all will be lost, just as it was centuries ago in Nazi Germany. People, wake up. The Fourth Reich has arrived on the Earth!

Below the post, some of his friends had posted comments, most urging caution, suggesting this post was tantamount to treason and that the GD security forces would deal with the anonymous author. This wasn't the response Kyle had hoped for.

With six others watching him, he deleted the anonymous post. However, everyone knew other sites had probably picked it up. Kyle suspected that by suppertime a hundred other sites would have re-posted it. Kyle hoped those would get more reactions than he'd gotten on his own page.

Downcast, he headed off to his next class.

The following Monday, CEO Hardy again held a brief conference. "My fellow Earthlings, the Sixth Invader threat is escalating. GD has now established the number of volunteer soldiers needed to exterminate these fiends. The numbers are shown on your screen. I'm here today to ask those of you who have engineering skills, pilot skills, navigation skills, or one the many other skills shown on the screen to volunteer for the four-year service. Help defend Earth and the Sol Empire from these vicious Sixth Invaders. I've been instructed to announce that GD's cut of soldiers' pay will be reduced by twenty-five percent. Yes, that means our soldiers and volunteer soldiers will have some of the highest actual take-home pay of any profession in the empire. Take advantage of this soon. Thank you."

Again, he ended the presentation with his trademark left-hand gesture or salute as Mel called it.

"Well, I kinda expected that," Kyle muttered to his roommate.

Mel shrugged his shoulders. "Probably for the best."

Kyle also shrugged. *President Hardy set himself up as the de facto dictator, but no one seems to care. I can't move to another land. It's just as bad there as here. The corporations are empire-wide. Damn.*

"So are you volunteering, Mel? I saw electrical engineers are being requested."

"I've already got my job offer." Mel's face flushed.

Kyle suspected images of the mutilated soldiers from Hardy's video were flashing in Mel's mind. They certainly were in his. Only a fool or someone who was desperate would sign up to fight these monsters. Via the Internet, Mel and Kyle had watched the raw 3-d holographic video made during the three previous First Division attacks, which highlighted their humiliating defeats and the resultant Sixth Invaders mutilations and cannibal actions against the captured Sol Empire soldiers. Grotesque beyond words.

What to do? Galactic Supplies had sponsored Kyle's parents before they forced his father to retire from his manager's position four years ago, but now his parents were ill with dementia. He stopped visiting them on school breaks last year since neither recognized him. Worse, even after introducing himself, they were unable to carry on an intelligent conversation with him, merely babbling corporate platitudes. A fellow student from London told him about conditions in England, which differed little from Chicago.

Perhaps, I should go to a South Pacific island. Hell, even that's no good. Global warming has swamped many islands. I swear the world has gone totally insane!

"I need a plan," he said.

"What's that?" Mel asked.

Kyle saw that Mel was pretending Kyle's utterance made some sort of sense.

"A plan? I'll say you need a plan. After that anonymous posting on your page last week, I'm surprised the GD security guards haven't swarmed us. Say, you got your EE senior lab project ready to go? My presentation is tomorrow."

That wasn't what Kyle wanted to hear. Kyle grimaced. *He's right. I need long-range plans. The GD guards are likely to come calling, especially since I called Hardy our Hitler dictator.*

He responded, "Yeah, all set. You've accepted a job offer from GE, so I suppose I should make some similar plans."

"Little late to start applying for jobs. I told you to do it back in January. By now, you'd have one lined up. Still, it can't hurt to get started. I emailed you my list of Galactic Electronics corporation contacts. Good luck with getting a job. At least, GE is still sponsoring you."

Cash, phone, computer, clothes, water, backpack— heck, camping gear would be nice, too. Kyle began making evacuation plans. If the world was going under, he, Kyle Dorn, wasn't about to become another mindless victim.

By late the following afternoon, Kyle had drained his bank account, which held the nest egg he'd gotten from his aging parents, and bought a backpack, now stuffed with essentials. His idea of going camping would have to wait until he graduated, but he began making a list of what to buy, checking them out at the local Bushwhackers. He planned to make his move in two weeks.

***

The next morning as he headed off to his early morning senior lab, Kyle spotted a blue and gold EMAC with the GD logo on it landing in the visitor's lot close to his dorm. He pulled his hood tighter over his head as he walked, though occasionally glancing over his shoulder, as did many other students. Three men in their blue and gold uniforms marched straight into his dorm. A knot formed in Kyle's stomach. Halfway to his lab, Kyle decided to cut class. He had to see what the GD men were up to.

Are they after me? I'd better not go to class. They'll surely show up there. They can get my schedule from Admin.

He circled back to his dorm and found a spot in an alley by a dumpster. From there, he could see the main entrance of his dorm. Kyle waited, his stomach twisting even tighter. An eternity passed before he spotted the three men rushing back to their EMAC as fast as they could walk. Running about in their fancy uniforms would not display the ultimate confidence for which GD security guards were known. He watched their vehicle head off in the general direction of his EE lab. Kyle ducked into a side door and headed up to his room.

"Hey, the GD guards were here looking for you," someone called out to him as he ducked into his room. He didn't bother to answer. He grabbed his backpack and stuffed a couple last minute items into it. Turning, Kyle walked out of his room for the last time. *I hope Mel won't get into trouble over this.* He ducked down the back stairs and checked outside before heading out into the late April morning.

Kyle had no actual plan for this eventuality. In fact, he didn't think GD would bother with him and his anonymous posting, even it if was so critical of the establishment. Yet, here they were. One thing was certain: Kyle had no intention of meeting with these men. He had no death wish, but he had no plan either.

Kyle headed for the MTES, taking a direct route to the Loop where he entered his favorite coffee shop, not far from the Lake and its many attractions. Sipping the warm brew, Kyle pondered his next move. *I can head out to my folks' old home in Palo Heights. It still hasn't sold. I bet it'll be a while before they look for me there.* Emboldened, Kyle took his coffee and headed off on the MTES once again.

As he stepped onto the moving sidewalk leading to his parents' street, he passed a large information billboard. He inhaled sharply. There was his picture—his college entrance photo—prominently displayed along with a dire warning about his being a subversive and a potential terrorist or even a Sixth Invader, to be considered armed and extremely dangerous. Kyle smirked. He never owned a gun, let alone fired one. *Glad I turned my phone off. They can't track me. I have'ta get a burner phone soon.*

A half hour later with his new phone stuck in his backpack, Kyle walked up to the rear of his childhood home. He slipped inside, hoping the realtor wouldn't bring someone by to see the place today or anytime soon. "I need time to figure this out," he explained to the walls, tossing his empty cup and old phone into the plastic trash bag, the only item in the home.

He sat on the floor, took out his computer, and searched for ideas online. True, he could still make Bushwhackers, buy enough gear to get by, and head out, but to where? After trying a few searches, on a whim, he entered "how to escape the corporations and GD." One item appeared and clicking on it took him into the Dark Net side of the Internet, a fact that did not escape him. The site only displayed a phone number. Curious more than anything else, Kyle dialed it on his new phone.

Chapter 16 Testing

Shen Wang, a Chinese psychiatrist, said to his brother, "We need field tests of our Exchange Machine. In case of trouble, we do it far from Peking. We have our agent in the City of Angels carry out test." Both continued to practice their English, anticipating the coming trip.

Yuan Wang, the engineer of the duo, brought electronics into their research. Together, they claimed to have invented several machines, one of which was the Exchange Machine, whose prototype needed testing on subjects—just not on themselves.

"Agreed. LA it is. I visit our local LA office and arrange for test."

"I come with you. If this works in field, we begin long-duration lab tests this year. We need kinks fixed before our bodies get too old," Shen said.

"Indeed. If works, we can live forever."

"But only if we get new, youthful bodies. Here in Peking, that not too difficult, but is hard in western lands. Come. I will write a thorough checklist to follow to make sure the machine works right."

"Say, how we get volunteers in City of Angels?"

Shen said, "Leave that to me. You make sure Exchange Machine works. Dead bodies harder to explain in LA than Peking. I must practice my English for this trip. Must speak proper to get test subjects."

Yuan laughed.

The next day, the two fifty-year-old, rather short men and their Exchange Machine departed Peking in the Airliner of the Wang Foundation, a subsidiary of the Galactic Medicine corporation. Via a phone call, Shen alerted his US connection, Jasper Jones—if that was his real name which Shen doubted. He wasn't complaining; rather he suspected the six-foot, lean man was a con artist looking for ways to avoid the corporations. In the city of millions, such was possible to do, though Shen knew it was difficult to avoid the long hands of the corporations. He was thankful for a way to field test their invention with no repercussions to themselves.

"Yes, Jasper. We arrive later tonight. We bring a new machine we want to test," Shen said.

"Okay boss. I'll be expecting ya," Jasper said. When he heard the Chinese accent, his hands shook a little. After hanging up, he said, "What do they want over here? This can't be good. Well, best get the place fixed up. Not what I wanted to be doing today." He set about gathering up weeks' old garbage and vacuuming the long-abandoned storefront, which he sometimes used—illegally of course.

***

Jasper met his bosses at LAX, helping them transfer the machine from the Airliner to his rented EMAC. The roar of spaceships landing or taking off prohibited conversation. Once at the storefront with offices and living quarters on the second floor, Shen explained what he needed done.

"Tomorrow, Jasper, you must get two narrow beds—cots okay, too. Not for us, but for our test subjects. We explain everything to you then. Now, we sleep."

Jasper decided not to waste the daylight. As soon as he could get them done with their experiment, they'd leave him alone, which he preferred. Experiments sounded dangerous. Besides, he thought, they can go wrong and then trouble follows. Jasper wanted nothing to do with that. His motto: avoid GD security guards and the cops.

***

"Perfect, Jasper." Shen inspected the two single beds Jasper had purchased from a used furniture store. He said, "We arrange them like so, on either side of my new machine."

"So what does it do?" Jasper asked, baffled by all the loose wires coming out of both sides of the device.

"This our new Exchange Machine. We connect two people to it, one on each side. I turn it on, and presto, the two people swap bodies."

"Huh? That's impossible."

"Until now it impossible; not any longer. We here to test it. We need two test subjects."

"You're not using me." Jasper grimaced; his hands

shook.

Shen said, "Of course not, Jasper. We need two volunteers. Two people desperate to change their identities. We test it on them. Say, one is a wanted man. We swap him into another person's body. He still himself, at least, we think so, but now the corporations cannot get him. They use DNA and fingerprints to identify the person. When they arrest the proper body, during interrogation, they discover the person now inhabiting the body they identified is not the guilty person, but someone else. Did you know GD guards use truth drug on those they arrest to make certain they've captured the guilty person? Via our new machine, the test subjects get a second chance, and the corporations will not know their new body's identity."

"Damn, that's a useful invention."

Shen suspected Jasper was wondering if he could get one for himself. He said, "Quite true, quite. So we need two volunteers, two people who very much want to change their physical identity."

"Can't you pick up two people off the street and do it to them?"

"We could, but then we would have to terminate them, and you would have to dispose of their bodies. Messy. They would spill the beans as you people say. We need two desperate to change their identities. That way, once we do it, they'll keep their mouths shut. They have stake in no one discovering what has happened to them. Neat. Clean."

"I see. But how you gonna find two like that?" Jasper's nervousness subsided. He wasn't going to be one of the victims—yet.

"We use our brains and the desperation of others. Post a special ad on the Internet," Shen said. "One angle is to look for someone who is being chased by the corporations."

Jasper chuckled. "Aye, that'll be enough to make anyone desperate. The corporations are downright nasty."

Shen ignored him. "Another is people who want out of a physically inhibiting situation. We will post in both arenas and see what happens. If we do not get a pair of responses in a week, we will try another method. But then, Jasper, you will have to deal with body disposals." Jasper grimaced. "Now, if you will excuse me, I have to make two websites."

Two days passed before the new burner phone rang. "Hello," Shen answered.

"Is this the people who say they can give me a new body?" The young woman's voice sounded hesitant.

"Indeed. This, we most can do, miss, but much depends on your physical condition."

"Oh. I'm in excellent shape. I run a mile every day and work out too. It's just that—well, you know, I'm physically limited in ways I'd rather not be if this thing doesn't cost too much." Her voice now sounded more relaxed, just as Shen intended.

"I am sure we can keep your cost down. That not a problem at all. What is your situation? Who are you? My name is Lennard."

"Holly Ann Durbin. I'm twenty-one. I have a web page, and you can see what I look like. I hope this isn't going to be a problem."

She rattled off her URL. Shen entered it and then smiled.

"I can see why you wish replacement body. You realize your donor must agree to swap. I should warn you it is rare for person to want to swap their body for another. In your case, the person might well be most desperate for the exchange."

"But if he or she is a criminal—I don't want to be arrested."

"Of course, you do not. Not to worry; that is handled by the corporations' use of truth drug. If by chance they should pick you up, they will see you are not the person they are looking for, despite any DNA or fingerprint match. So, Holly Ann, you are most safe. Have you considered your donor's body might be male? Will that be problem?"

Shen needed this detail ironed out. Getting someone who was desperate enough to swap bodies with Holly Ann would be quite a challenge. Her website was called Unarmed Holly Ann. She had no arms, a genetic birth defect, and the site held homemade 3-d holographic videos of her doing most normal things using her feet as hands and toes as fingers. She even had a license to fly an EMAC.

"I don't care about gender, but who's going to want to take my body? I mean, if I want to exchange this one, who will want to trade places with me?"

"Leave that to me, Miss Durbin. That my job. We may have to act on this soon. Your web page suggests you in Flagstaff. Correct? We in LA. Can you come to us? Or will you need help with that?"

"Oh don't be silly. I'm not helpless. I can get there. Give me your address. I can be there in six hours. Just call when you're ready."

"Excellent. We call you when we have an exchange partner for you."

Shen saved her phone number and suggested she get her personal affairs in order so when he called back, she would be ready to come to LA.

Once she was off the phone, Jasper spoke up. "Good Lord! How you gonna find anyone who would want to swap bodies with her? She's got to be helpless."

"Leave that to me," Shen said. *My goodness, this'll be a superb test. Most definitive, too. If I can find a male body for the exchange, that'll make this the ultimate test!*

Later, speaking to his brother, he said, "Of course, will the transference be permanent is the key question. In a case like this one, he is sure to want out of the exchange almost as soon as he gets transferred into Holly Ann's body."

"Indeed, that must be impossible without our machine—I hope. He will be stuck with her body, just as she will be stuck with his body. That is the way it is with bodies."

Though Yuan and Shen hoped this was true, they had no proof—yet.

Three days later, Shen received another phone call. This one came in on the number associated with his Dark Net posting.

"Hello. Yes, we are in business of exchanging bodies. What is your situation? Just who are you?"

He smiled; the caller was male, perfect for this proposed body swapping experiment. Opposite sexes and with one body severely handicapped—this test would be most valuable.

"Ah yes. I look at the Chicago GD Wanted site. You are right. They most want to get you, Kyle. From much experience, I can tell you what they will do to you. I have seen it many times. If you are lucky, you will be made into a trash recycler, the lowest of the low. More likely, they will terminate you. Your education will be wasted."

Shen used his knowledge of human behavior to good advantage. He needed Kyle to be more than willing to accept the body swap he was about to propose. Only Holly Ann and Kyle had responded, though that wasn't unexpected. The vast majority of people in the US were already under the total control of one of the major corporations. Only the younger kids weren't yet in the system, and of course, the many executives and CEOs.

***

Kyle's stomach tensed up again. *Trash recycler? I've seen some of them and how they live; they have to scrounge through college dumpsters looking for anything salvageable just to survive. My god, they'd do that to me in a blink.* He swallowed. "So tell me about this thing you do. What's involved?"

"We have an invention that exchanges two people's bodies. Yes, you wake up in a different body, while your donor wakes up inside your body."

He explained how use of a truth drug would obviate any worries about the criminal justice system and most lawyers too.

"It's painless but most permanent. Once you swap bodies, there's no going back. We provide you with new identity, new papers. We recommend neither party return to their city of origin. Whoever takes your body should not move to Chicago. You should avoid moving to the city where your donor comes from."

"Okay. That makes sense, so what does all this cost? Isn't this illegal?"

Shen said, "Your cost will be nominal. While this poses problems for the corporations, there are no laws about exchanging bodies."

"Isn't this dangerous?"

"No danger to either party. But I must be honest with you. Finding another person willing to swap bodies with you is most challenging since GD Chicago wants you *dead* or alive."

"I didn't think about that. Can you find someone?" *Who in their right mind will want to swap their body with mine? Only someone who's as desperate me.*

"All right, Kyle. I can make you an offer of a replacement body. Your donor would be female. Will that be a problem for you?"

"Huh? You saying I'd be a she when this is done?"

"Yes, and she'd be a he. You would have a most perfect disguise. The corporations never figure out this exchange."

"True, but I'd be a woman. I'm not sure I can handle that."

"Well, she would be a man, and she not sure she can handle that either. Kyle, one other point you must consider. We have been looking for matching donors for weeks. You most lucky this one come up. I expected you must wait many months for someone to agree to exchange bodies with you." Shen played to Kyle's fears. It worked perfectly.

"Months? I can't wait that long. The GD guards will find this place in another day or so. I can hide here for a while, just not that long, so I'll have to take this one," Kyle agreed, struggling to imagine being a female. It did not compute.

"One more detail. She wants to swap bodies and gender for a good reason. Her reason most different from yours. Write down this URL. Check out her website. Then, if you still interested, call me back. We can make the swap as soon as you get to LA. If you pass on this one, one might not be available for many months, perhaps a year or more."

Kyle had no idea he was being played. "I can't hold out for months—days, well maybe. Okay, I'll check it out."

Kyle hung up. A minute later, he gasped. *No wonder she's desperate to swap bodies!* His stomach knotted hard. After catching his breath, he explored her professional-looking website. He saw that, despite appearances, she seemed able to do normal things, just very differently, as her many holographic videos showed. She was in excellent shape. In fact, she was attractive, except for her lack of arms. Holly Ann was quite shapely.

"So why does she want to swap bodies? Oh damn!"

A GD corporation EMAC landed on the driveway. Hastily, Kyle packed his few items and ducked out the back door, eluding them once again. That Shen might have anonymously alerted them to his location did not occur to him.

Two blocks away, Kyle whispered to himself, "That was too darn close! I don't see I have any choice but to make this swap. I sure as heck don't want to be killed. What has our world become?"

He dialed Shen's number while continuing to walk down the alley and hopping onto the MTES.

"Yes, I'll take the swap, but I want her to help me adjust."

"That is only fair of her. How soon can you get to LA?"

"That's the problem. They're onto me. I'm on the run again. I think they'll be watching for me at New O'Hare."

"Okay. Let us see what we can do from here. How far south can you take the MTES?" Shen brought up a Google map of the greater Chicago area.

"The line goes down to Peoria, a southern suburb," Kyle said.

"Okay. You go to this place called Joliet. We send EMAC to pick you up. Stay out of sight. Someone will call you later."

***

After hanging up, Shen said, "Jasper, take the EMAC to Joliet, south part of Chicago. Pick up this volunteer, Kyle Dorn." He gave Jasper the phone number and other explicit orders. "Top speed. The GD corporation is onto him. He may not last more than a day before they corner him. Make much haste unless you want to swap bodies with Holly Ann."

Shen watched shock appear on Jasper's face; he had impinged just as he had intended. He knew Jasper would do everything humanly possible to bring Kyle back to LA fast.

***

Kyle spent most of the afternoon traveling down to Joliet riding the slow moving MTES. Night fell by the time he arrived, dark and cold, still early spring. He found a school and hunkered down, hiding behind a dumpster, his burner phone in his hand, ready to answer the call.

My god, Kyle, what are you doing? All I wanted to do was to stick up for human rights—for what's right. Now, I'm about to become a helpless woman just to avoid GD guards and termination. What am I supposed to do after that?

Unbidden tears trickled down his cheeks. He wiped them away, before realizing that after this swap, he'd never be able to do that again. That brought more tears. Time slipped by him, until his shivering roused him, just as his phone vibrated, announcing the lifesaving phone call.

He didn't recognize the voice, and his stomach knotted again.

"Is this Kyle?"

Hesitant, he said, "Yes."

"Good. My boss sent me from LA to find you and get you back there fast for the body exchange. Where are you? I'm hovering over what I think is Joliet."

"I'm by the school. Can you see the school and playground from up there?"

"Give me a minute or two."

Five minutes later, Jasper sat the EMAC down on the school playground, and Kyle ran towards it, shivering from the cold and hunger. He'd not eaten much for the last two days.

Once he ran up the bay ramp, the tall, lean Jasper closed it.

"So, you're the most-wanted man, eh? You're freezing. There are blankets in that bin and food in the galley in the rear. Help yourself. I've got to get us airborne before anyone comes after us for landing on a school's playground."

Shivering, Kyle nodded, heading for the blankets, while Jasper walked back to the pilot's seat.

"Taking off now."

An hour passed before Kyle was warm and full. Jasper had brought along sacks of fast food, which worked out well since neither man could cook. Then, Kyle wandered up to the pilot's seat.

"So have you done this many times? Swapped bodies?"

"I'm under orders to say nothin' much about it. I'm just a driver if you follow me. That way, I can't be held responsible for whatever you've done, but it must have been something to get the Chicago GD guards hot on your tail."

Jasper struggled to keep a straight face. As a con artist, this wasn't too hard to do, just terribly funny, from his point of view—that and a relief, since he had Kyle and thus wouldn't be forced to swap bodies with Holly Ann.

Kyle saw Jasper wouldn't say more, and exhaustion set in. He headed back to sleep. For the first time in days, Kyle slept soundly, waking only in the morning when sleepy-eyed Jasper set the EMAC down close to the storefront in one of the many strip malls of LA, most of which were abandoned.

***

Shen met Kyle as he stepped down the ramp of the EMAC. He saw what he expected to see, a distraught young man of twenty-one, who was in need of a shave and a bath. Kyle looked like a typical college senior, in this case, sponsored by Galactic Electronics.

"I am Lennard. This way, please. You must clean up. You want your donor to desire your body and go ahead with the swap."

"Thanks. They nearly got me in Palo Heights."

He entered what appeared to be an abandoned storefront. There were no auto parts for sale here. Automobiles were a thing of the very distant past, though, in grade school, most people had seen pictures of what they had looked like.

Shen led him to a bathroom. Kyle had clean clothes in his backpack.

A half-hour later, he finally met his donor. Shen introduced them.

"Holly Ann Durbin, this is Kyle Dorn. Kyle, Holly Ann. I let you get acquainted. I come back in thirty minutes."

He turned and left them standing and facing each other. She saw a youthful young man, not overly handsome, but fit. He was six feet and lean, with short brown hair and light blue eyes. He wore jeans, a U of C sweatshirt, and tennis shoes.

"Do you run?" she asked.

Kyle chuckled, "Not if I can avoid it. I'm—er, was a

college senior—EE, electrical engineering. I was a couple weeks from graduating with my degree when this happened."

He saw a young woman who could well have been a model. She was fit, not an ounce of fat on her body. She was well endowed. Her dark brown hair shone. It was long, falling to her waist in gentle waves. Her eyes were enchanting, such a light blue that Kyle couldn't stop staring at them. Her face was round with thick brows and lips. She wore jeans, t-shirt, and flats.

"Wow. You could be a beauty queen or something."

"Except for the lack of arms," she said. "I guess I can get your body into shape, physically. You don't have any illnesses or problems?"

"No, healthy. And you?"

"No. Mr. Lennard showed me why GD is after you. Did you really try to knock sense into people?"

Kyle laughed. "Yes, I tried, but no one listened. Everyone thinks the way corporations run and control everything is just perfect."

Holly Ann giggled. "I think your notions of us becoming the Fourth Reich might well be true, only the corporations are the Reich. Still, I'm with you. Anyway, I'm on the run, too. Galactic Entertainment wants to sponsor me. They want to make me into one of these new Galactic Dolls. I'd rather die than become some corporate executive's sex Doll. So that's why I'm so desperate to do this. I didn't know people could swap bodies but I'm sure glad we can. This will work out well for me, since once we do this thing, they can never make me into a sex Doll. But Kyle, are you sure you want to swap with me?"

Kyle's face flushed. "No, not if I had any real choice. No offense, Holly Ann, but who would want to live life with no arms? I saw your videos on your website, so I know you're somehow able to be independent. Still, I don't know how I'll ever be able to live as you are."

Holly Ann sighed. "I know. I was afraid of that. Look, I'll make you a deal. I've got a small touchpad loaded up with my videos and every holographic video I've ever been able to find of how we armless people do things. This way, you'll have a library of how to do it videos. Also, I'll stick around with you for a while, helping you adjust. After all, I was born this way, and I know no other way to do things. I expect you'll be very frustrated until you catch on. Besides, we're not supposed to return to Flagstaff or Chicago."

The relief on Kyle's face told Holly Ann she'd made the right decision.

"That would be terrific. I'm terrified of becoming helpless but then I see your videos; you do everything so differently. I'll need all the help I can get. Do you think I'll still be able to do electrical engineering?"

"I know nothing about that, Kyle. Sorry. But not much has stopped me. Sometimes, I have to spend a good deal of time figuring out a way to do something. I had to move a big comm display once. While I could use my toes to unhook the connections, carrying it out to the EMAC was quite a challenge for me."

"Wow. How could you carry it?"

"I couldn't, silly. I slid it over onto a pushcart and rolled it out to the EMAC. It took me an hour to do that, though. But if they turned me into one of those Galactic Dolls, I wouldn't be able to do much by myself, since they make them wear very high heels. I use my toes and feet all the time. They said my sponsor would hire a personal assistant for me. If so, I'd be both a slave and a sex Doll. No way. I'd rather die first, but then I found this incredible offer. Have you ever heard of exchanging bodies? I haven't, and I couldn't find anything on the Internet about it either."

"Nope. They want to make me into a trash recycler or terminate me. I'd rather die than waste my life like that. Besides, I'm a trained electrical engineer or nearly so."

"So are we going to do this?"

Kyle chuckled. "It's better than dying. Does either of us have much of a choice? I'm willing to do this if you are, but I sure will appreciate all the help you can give me learning to adjust. I don't want to be helpless."

***

Neither knew that Yuan had installed a hidden microphone so Shen could listen in on their conversation. Both might have had a clue they were overheard because it was at this precise point that Shen knocked and entered the room.

"Well, Mr. Lennard, we're ready to do this," Kyle said. *It's this or die, and I want to live.*

He bowed politely. "Okay, follow me. This only takes a few minutes and is painless, but irreversible. Once done, it done. No going back."

He led the pair into the bedroom where they had the two beds on either side of their Exchange Machine.

Out of habit, Kyle asked, "How does it work?" Seeing the electronic device brought out his innate curiosity.

Shen said, "Each of you, lie down on a bed. Heads this way."

Yuan and Shen hooked a dozen electrodes up to each head though later improvements would use a device that looked more like a crown or hat.

"Okay, you hooked up. When I turn it on, you see a brilliant white light. Follow the white light to your body. You cannot go wrong. Are you ready?"

Kyle suspected he should be asking another question, but couldn't quite formulate it. Later he did, but never asked it: How much is this going to cost? In fact, the brothers didn't ask for any monetary payment for this experimental body swap. Why? This exchange was the perfect test. Shen was keen to know the outcome. Yuan flipped the Power On button.

***

Kyle felt a surge of energy flowing through his head. Just as it began to register as intense pain, he saw a brilliant white light. At least, that's how he later described it, a pure white, incredibly aesthetic light. He felt drawn towards it; he knew he couldn't resist it, for it was so pure and beautiful. Did it move? He couldn't tell since he could see nothing else and hence had no way to detect motion. He had never sensed something so wonderful, and it filled him with total awe and utmost respect. The white light dimmed. Oh, how he tried to make it persist, to stay brilliant and pure, but to no avail. The light dimmed, and he began to feel what might be a headache, but even that faded away. The room came into focus once more.

Not really thinking, Kyle said, "That was so beautiful.

226

What's supposed to..." His soprano voice faded off, and he realized he was lying on the other bed. "Oh!"

From the other side of the machine, he heard his voice say, "Wow, that was so beautiful, so pure. Is it going to work? Oh!"

No, that's now her voice asking that—not mine anymore. Oh god, I'm going to be completely helpless. What have I done?

"It worked. I'm in his body. Incredible. Fantastic," Holly Ann said. "I've got arms."

Kyle-in-Holly's-body rolled his head to one side and saw his body's arms wiggling about in the air, reminding him of some babies he'd once seen. Until now, he'd taken arms for granted. He swallowed hard and struggled to sit up on the narrow bed.

After a minute, Holly Ann and Kyle sat facing each other across the Exchange Machine, while Shen and Yuan Wang stood nearby, big smiles on their faces.

Shen spoke up. "Yes, it worked, just as we wished. We make your new names so we do not get confused. Have you thought what name you wish for your new body?"

Feeling rather foolish, Kyle said in his new soprano voice, "Er, no, I haven't. Are we supposed to pick new names?"

"Me either. I didn't really think this would work. Perhaps, he should keep my first name, Holly Ann. It might be less confusing that way. I can keep using Kyle. It might be hard learning to respond to a new name."

Shen continued to smile. "I agree. You must disappear, so we use different last names. How about Holly Ann Beck and Kyle Chesterfield?"

A pair of "fines" echoed in reply. Shen continued looking at the young woman.

"Holly Ann, you can expect to have more difficult time adapting to your new body. Rightly so. She has touchpad filled with how-to videos. As a doctor, I can say Holly Ann's twenty-one years of doing things in her unique ways are most implanted in the body's brain, much like walking, running, riding a bicycle, or any other learned physical action. Instead of panicking, relax and let new body take over, since it knows what to do."

Kyle spoke up. "I promised to help him learn to adjust too, if that's all right, doctor. I'd feel awful if I took off with his body, leaving him to panic in my old body. Sometimes, I did feel like panicking, though frustrated would be more accurate."

Shen responded, pulling on his chin. "That most wise idea. We going to make new ID cards and send you to different cities, but Kyle has point. Holly Ann looks scared; she most appreciate your help in learning how to do what she must. Yuan, make them motel reservation nearby. I make new ID documents. You two—stay put and get used to your new bodies."

After the two brothers left the room, Holly Ann swallowed hard. "Thanks, Kyle. I've never been as scared as I am now. I feel so helpless, but I've seen your videos, so I know you're able to do nearly everything I could do."

Kyle giggled, "I know you are. It must be terrifying for you. I expect it's much like being in an accident and waking up in the hospital having lost your arms. Don't worry. I'll not leave you until you have it all down."

"Thanks. You're right. That's exactly how I feel. It's as if I've been in an accident and have woken up to find I've lost my arms. Downright scary. Everything feels so strange. I've got boobs too."

Kyle giggled again. "Double-D boobs to be exact. I found out they're not even the minimum size GEnt insists all their Galactic Dolls have. I found them annoyingly large. I suspect you will too—in a while, that is. Come on. We should get up and move around and get more used to these bodies. It's so weird, Holly Ann, having these arms dangling down. Say, do they get in the way when you're sleeping? Is there anything I need to know about living with arms?"

Holly Ann chuckled. "No, I've never had any trouble with my arms. Gosh, this is so weird. I keep trying to move my arms, and they aren't here. What a strange feeling."

Again, Kyle giggled. "Sorry, Holly Ann. I've never had that feeling because I never had arms—until now that is. Come on. Let's walk a bit."

***

Once in another room, the Wang brothers chatted. Yuan said, "So far so good. They show no sign of diving back into their original bodies."

"Quite true, most good sign," Shen said.

"But I thought we were separating them right away, not putting them up in same motel room. Are not we risking everything? We do not know how long they can stay in the other's body."

Pulling his chin, Shen answered. "I do not think so, Yuan. This way, we can further test the exchange. I am curious if they will dive back into their original bodies if they are in close physical quarters. We must keep watch on Kyle, or rather the new Holly Ann. She is the one most likely to dive back into her old male body. If they stay in their new bodies for several days, we may conclude they can never go back on their own, not without reusing our Exchange Machine. That is the one question we must have answered before we use it on ourselves, Yuan. This is perfect test."

"Indeed. I make the reservations. Should we install monitoring devices before they check in?"

"There is no time. Get us a nearby room. We can watch them that way. I make their ID papers now."

***

A half hour later with their new identification documents in their pockets, the pair followed Yuan's directions to the nearby motel. As they approached their door, Holly Ann panicked.

"How can I even open a door?"

"I always took my shoe off and used my foot and toes," Kyle said. "I'd show you, but this body is so incredibly stiff and inflexible. Can't even get its leg above its knee to insert the keycard and twist the latch. Come on. I've got it this time. I'm so sorry, Holly Ann. I should never have answered their ad. We've made a huge mistake."

Holly Ann sat down on the bed. "That, Kyle, is an understatement. I know I was running from the GD security men, but maybe I could have hidden in another city, such as St. Louis, or something. Wait a minute. You probably didn't really have any choice but to do this, Kyle. The Galactic

Entertainment corporation is everywhere, so just moving to another city wouldn't have done you any good at all. They'd still try to turn you into a Galactic Doll. You're very attractive—er, well, except for the missing arms."

Kyle sighed, tossed the key card on the table, and slumped onto the bed beside Holly Ann.

"I know. They would have. You're right; they'd turn me into a Galactic Doll no matter what city I was in, but still, this is wrong. I don't have any right to do this to you. Look, Holly Ann, I've been this way my whole life and have figured out how to do most everything, but you haven't. I imagine you're quite frightened."

"Kyle, you have a penchant for understatement. I'm terrified. If you weren't here with me, I'd be freaking out."

"Well, I won't run off and leave you, Holly Ann, not until you're confident about everything. You'll need to get more clothes sometime. I packed a change in the backpack, and you've about nine thousand credits in there too. That's all I had saved up. The corporation took everything else."

"You've got a change of dirty clothes and nearly ten grand in my—er, your backpack. If my parents' house ever sells, perhaps you can get your hands on that money, too. I guess we're okay on the money side for a while. Oh no. I have to go to the bathroom. Help. How?"

That awkward situation handled clumsily, both were hungry. Kyle said, "I always ate out. I've no idea how to cook anything, except boil water for tea."

"Hey, we have that in common. I lived in a dorm and ate their lousy food. I'd say let's find a diner around here, but I've no idea how I can feed myself. Well, I've seen your videos, but seeing them isn't actually doing it myself."

"Right. Okay, how about I go find us some fast food? I'll bring it back here, and you can make your first stab at doing it. While I'm gone, watch these videos and practice the motions. If you get bored, see if you can write your new name on the pad there. Back as soon as I can. You'll be all right, won't you, Holly Ann?"

"Sure. What can go wrong in here?" As soon as she said that, she wished she hadn't. Plenty could go wrong because she felt helpless.

Chapter 17 Adaption

"I don't know how you could do all this," Holly Ann exclaimed. Kyle had brought back a chicken dinner, and thus Holly Ann had her first experience learning how to feed herself using only her feet and toes. While Kyle was gone, she had watched several videos Holly Ann had made illustrating how she dined, but watching a how to do it video wasn't the same as doing it yourself.

Kyle fought hard to keep the water out of his eyes. He felt horrible, knowing his actions had put her in this untenable position. *I've made a terrible mistake in doing this body swap.* He tried to hide the guilt he felt. Worse, this new body was so inflexible that he couldn't use it to show Holly Ann how to do things and had to rely on the videos.

The awkward dinner finished, Kyle said, "You did well, Holly Ann. Just give yourself time and practice. It looks as though my body remembers how to do things. So just relax and see if it doesn't respond to you better that way. Honestly, we've made a terrible mistake exchanging bodies. I feel so guilty over what I'm putting you through that my stomach aches."

Holly Ann sighed. "Yes, a huge mistake. Perhaps tomorrow, we can go back and beg them to swap us back. I can't see why they wouldn't do that for us. Besides, they should have foreseen all the trouble I'm having."

"Okay. First thing in the morning, let's get this undone. Meantime, we have to get you ready for bed. Women have certain things they do before turning in."

Holly Ann's face crimsoned. "I've no idea about that. I strip down to my underpants and hop into bed."

Kyle giggled. "I'm afraid you have much to learn how to do before you can hop into bed. I'm sorry about keeping my hair so long. It takes a lot of upkeep and time every day. Vanity. It's the only part of my body I admired."

"Why? You're gorgeous. Well, except for the missing arms. I'll admit that. Still, you're beautiful."

232

"Look, Holly Ann. Who in their right mind will want to date or marry a handicapped woman, pretty or not?"

"Someone who loves you. That's what everyone says. I've never found love, but then I've been studying all the time for the last four years. Say, did you have a job or something before? I mean before you came here to LA from Flagstaff."

Kyle sighed. That seemed a distant lifetime ago though it had only been a few hours. "I got my math degree six months ago. I wanted to be a math teacher, but so far, no corporation would give me a chance. As soon as they saw I was handicapped, they rejected me. I've been living off the insurance money from my parents' death—killed in an accident three years ago."

"Bothers? Sisters?"

"No. They had to follow the Corporate Guideline of one child per family, though now it's been upped to two children. They were conscientious about global overpopulation. Between us, I think they were terrified of having another armless child. The doctors told them it was genetic, so that's another reason no one will want to marry me—er, you, now. You'll probably have armless children, too, if you ever have any."

"But didn't you want to get married and have a family anyway?" Holly Ann asked.

In spite of Kyle's valiant efforts, salty water trickled down his cheeks, though he resisted the instinctive urge to bring a leg and foot up to wipe it away.

"When I was a little girl, I had such thoughts, but I knew I was too different for any of that to happen. The best I could hope for was to live independently, which I've done. You will, too, once you've had enough practice." Kyle tried to sound a positive note.

Holly Ann said, "From the videos, I'd say you're a genius at working out ways for you to do what others take for granted—a real genius. Still, I wouldn't lose all hope of finding the right person and having a family. Oh!" Holly Ann flushed. She realized she was now talking about herself since Holly Ann now had a perfectly fine male body: his.

"We should try to get some sleep," Kyle changed the

painful subject. "First thing in the morning, we'll see about getting our bodies back. Come on. I'll help you get into bed without tangling up your hair."

Kyle helped Holly Ann lie down, but then his face flushed, and Holly Ann saw the bulge in his underpants.

"Does it always do this sort of thing? It's as if it's got a mind of its own."

Holly Ann chuckled. "Yeah. Every time I see a pretty woman, it goes bonkers. Guy thing."

"Well, it's embarrassing."

"I told you; you're very attractive, except for the arms."

The next morning, Kyle left Holly Ann struggling to get dressed and her hair brushed out, while he went in search of something for their breakfast. When he returned with fast food, he praised Holly Ann.

"Wow. You did it—dressed and hair brushed pretty well. Good going."

"I'm exhausted, Kyle, and starving. Let's eat and then go get our bodies back."

Around ten, the pair stood outside the storefront.

"What's going on?" Kyle asked. "It's empty. That's a For Sale sign. Where did they go? Come on. Let's ask the folks in the neighboring stores if they know what happened."

Both stomachs knotted, threatening to upchuck their breakfast.

A nearby store manager explained, "Well, it's been empty for decades. We saw several people in there yesterday. Figured they were checking the place out. Probably didn't want it. There are so few of us independent store owners left now. Guess I'll have to close up shop by the end of the year. With everything becoming sponsored by the big corporations, business has dried up."

After thanking the man, the pair headed back to the motel.

Holly Ann said, "I don't get it. What's going on? We were just in there yesterday." Her stomach knotted once more. *If we can't find these men and their machine, I'll be stuck in Holly Ann's body forever!*

"I don't understand it either. Let's redo our two web

searches. Surely, we can find where they've moved to, can't we? I suppose what they're doing is illegal, so maybe that's why they're being so clandestine about their location. You think so?"

Holly Ann said, "Could be. I've never heard of this body swapping before. I can see how it will play havoc with the corporations. We just have to find them again."

Back in their room, the pair entered the same Google searches as they had used to initially find these men. To their shock, both searches returned nothing at all. They sat back and stared at each other's screen.

"Make sure I spelled it right, Holly Ann."

"Make sure I typed it right, Kyle."

They had. Both sat back in silence for several minutes. Next, they tried the phone numbers they'd called. They received a disconnected message.

Holly Ann exclaimed, "We're so screwed. Who were those men anyway? Are we some kind of experimental guinea pigs?"

"It would seem so. I feel so horrible about what I've done to you that my breakfast is about to come up."

"Hey, don't be so hard on yourself. It's as much my fault as yours. Wait. It's their fault. They were playing on two people who were in desperate situations. I think they took advantage of us, Kyle."

"Well, what can we do now? How do we undo it? This is so weird looking at my body that now isn't me."

"They used electronics to make us swap bodies. That much I know. I wonder just how permanent this body exchange is. As far as I know, we're the first to ever get such a thing done. So maybe it's only temporary, and in a few days, we'll slip back into our own bodies. Can you feel or sense me— er, I mean this body?"

"Not really. I think I can imagine how it feels, sort of. Maybe we need to be very close to each other," Kyle suggested.

Holly Ann flushed. "Well, I must admit it felt good to be sleeping beside you last night. I wish I had arms to hold you. Say, maybe that's the trick—hold each other tightly. Want to try that?"

"Anything to get us returned to our original bodies," Kyle said, throwing his arms around Holly Ann and pulling her body into his. He whispered, "Anything?"

"I kind of feel you—er, I mean how my body, which you have, feels. Is this making any sense?" Holly Ann asked. "Wait, your body is having some kind of reaction—oh." Her face flushed crimson.

Kyle said, "Wow. So is yours. Maybe that's how we can get swapped back, you know, by being intimate with each other. Do you suppose that might work?"

Kyle's face reddened, but he was ready to grasp at any conceivable possibility to undo the body swap.

"It can't hurt to try. I'm at a loss for any other ideas, but I've no idea how to do anything like that with a woman's body."

Kyle giggled. "Same with me, but I suppose we can work it out. While we're doing it, see if you can get back into your body, and I'll do the same with mine. We just have to return to our own bodies."

An hour later, the two lay cuddling. Both had had a new experience, but they were still stuck in each other's bodies.

Holly Ann ventured, "Well, that was intense, and for a moment, I thought I might be sensing my original body again. Not too sure of that, but it sort of felt as if I was—well, maybe."

Kyle admitted, "Same here, though honestly, I never ever expected to have a man making love to me. Now you've had an experience I often longed for."

"Well, perhaps we should continue to make love as often as we can and see if we can eventually make it back into our original bodies," Holly Ann suggested, torn between a terror of being stuck in this body and the new sexual experience. Also, she found that she admired Holly Ann for what she'd overcome and her brilliant mind, except now their bodies were switched—so confusing.

"Agreed. I was going to correct you and say our own bodies, but right now, this is my own body, just as that one's yours."

"No kidding. But confusion is the least of our worries—mine anyway. Say, did you ever get your IQ measured? You must be a genius to have learned and invented your ways to do everything. I'm amazed."

Kyle giggled again. "Once. When I was a junior in high school. 151. So you're right about me being a genius, but what are we going to do now? I'm scared."

"Not much, until I can get good enough to get by doing things. We should spend our daytime hours working with me doing the whatevers. You be the teacher. One thing is certain. We have to get me being more or less independent or all is lost, really lost. I won't pretend to say I'm not petrified."

"Of course, we have to get you being independent. I was never terrified. Frustrated. That's what I often felt, but then I always figured out a way to do something. Come on. Let's work on your skills." *How brave he is.*

***

Meanwhile, in the next room, the Wang brothers had been eavesdropping on the pair using a wall amplifier. Shen said, "Excellent. They're having sex, and still, they can't slip back into their original bodies. I believe we have the machine perfected. Shall we head home?"

"Yes, let's. We must carry out long-term experiments. Will the transference hold for a year, five, ten years, or more? We can best make those tests in Peking at our foundation." The two men slipped out of the motel and returned to China.

***

Still feeling guilty about what they'd done, Kyle spent the next month working with Holly Ann. Every day, Kyle saw that Holly Ann was improving, getting better with each action. While they continued to be intimate every night and early morning, during these times, each only had a vague sense of their original bodies, but that was better than the "no sense" that they had for the rest of the day. Still, after four weeks, neither could see any real change in their ability to slip back into their former bodies. Further, they tried to find the Chinese men via their original Internet searches four more times, again with no success.

***

"So what are we going to do?" Kyle asked. It was night, and he cuddled with Holly Ann. "It's been a month. I have to admit you're adapting very well. When we started, I was scared you wouldn't catch on to how I used to do things—that you'd just give up or something, but you didn't. I'm impressed."

"We need to do something, but honestly, Kyle, I've fallen for you. I can't imagine continuing on without you with me, but I know you deserve to have your own life and not to be stuck with me. You deserve a real woman, not me."

"Don't be silly, Holly Ann. I've fallen for you if you hadn't noticed. Maybe we're in love with our original bodies." He giggled.

"Do you suppose?" Holly Ann asked.

Laughing, Kyle said, "Of course not. I was teasing you about our original bodies though maybe there is some truth in that. I'm in love with you. Anyway, you're right. We need to make plans. It's been a month. We can't stay here forever."

"Heck, I still want to fight these corporations and how they are running everything. It's not right. We've lost so many of our freedoms. Ours is a world of mostly unthinking people. I got into this mess because I felt I had to speak out, to protest what was being done, but no one listened. I still want to make a difference. How about you?"

"Now I could be a math teacher, but they'd probably arrest me first because I'm you. I don't think they would terminate me because I don't know squat about your electrical stuff or what you've done. But the real problem, Holly Ann, is you. Eventually, GEnt will get you. Considering how attractive you are, I'm sure they still want to make you into one of those corporate sex Dolls. They told me that before I fled Flagstaff."

"I'd be helpless then, that's certain, but I wanted to work in electronics. Well, I suppose without hands that's out. But that's what I wanted to do." Holly Ann sighed.

"Well, where could you get a job doing that? Sorry, I know nothing about it, except turning on the light switch sends electricity down wires somewhere to the lights."

Holly Ann thought before speaking up, knowing the risk she was taking with Kyle.

"Well, the Chicago vicinity has many ongoing construction projects. They're installing the MTES to rural areas. EMACs are only for the wealthy and the corporations, so

I suppose there should be many possibilities. I don't think any major labs will hire me as I am." She shrugged her shoulders to punctuate it.

"Going to Chicago would put me at risk if I follow all this. Right? GD is looking for you. Still, I'm sure they'd decide I'm not you and let me go."

"I've no right to endanger you."

"I had no right to swap bodies with you and make you have to live as I did."

"Hey, you were as desperate as I was. It's done. We have to move on somehow. It will be easier for me in Chicago, since I'm familiar with the city, but we could try another city."

"After what you've endured, we should do what's easier for you, Holly Ann. We simply must. So if you think Chicago is the place, let's do it."

Kyle tried to sound firm and resolute, but images of GD torturing him swept through his mind.

Holly Ann chuckled before sobering. "Sorry about laughing. I realized that if I stop trying to do something and just let the body do it, thanks to you, it knows what to do. Come on. Get your computer running. I've just had a bright idea."

Using her feet, she lifted hers up, sat it on the floor, and got it opened up. Slowly, she typed in a search. That done, she saw that Kyle was patiently waiting with his computer. Holly Ann laughed again.

"I see what you mean about everything taking so much longer to do. Okay, enter this search sequence."

Kyle did as asked, but noticed that even though Holly Ann was doing much better using her feet and toes, in fact, she was ten times slower than she had been before swapping bodies. Still, he saw this little improvement as a positive step. Holly Ann was relaxing and catching on. Yet, Kyle still felt guilty about exchanging bodies.

Holly Ann read the web page. "Ah ha. Isn't this interesting? So someone has made up a Galactic Doll disguise. It says that no one can tell any physical differences between them and the real Galactic Dolls. No drugs involved, but it says they will help you learn how to act like one. Shouldn't we take advantage of this before we make any other moves?"

Kyle finished reading it and sighed. *If only I'd thought of this before. Then I wouldn't have had to swap bodies, endangering him with my own Galactic Doll mess.* "Yes, it sounds promising. According to this, they just make your body indistinguishable from any other one. I see where you're headed with this, Holly Ann. If your body seems to be a Galactic Doll, then GEnt will leave you alone. It says they can hack into the GEnt site and make you official, too. We should check it out. Their address is around here. Looks as though you can get anything in LA. I'm getting us directions. Ah, we can take the MTES. This way, you'd look like a Galactic Doll, but you wouldn't actually be one. It might work."

An hour later, the two entered Hank's Nails & More, a decrepit store that had seen better days. An effeminate young man stepped into the main room with six empty chairs.

"How can I help you?" His eyes rested long on Holly Ann's unusual form.

Knowing this would be embarrassing for Holly Ann, Kyle spoke up. "The website said you can make fake Galactic Dolls." Hank nodded, so Kyle continued. "GEnt wanted to turn her into a Galactic Doll. We'd like to avoid that. Your solution seems almost too good to be true."

"Ah, they have good taste." He flirted with Holly Ann, who had no idea how to respond. She stood shyly beside Kyle. "Follow me."

He turned and headed into a back room, closing the door after the pair entered. A large computer installation sat on a table against one wall while another wall held a large selection of Galactic Doll apparel. A table occupied the middle of the room. Hank indicated they sit across from him, and Kyle pulled a chair out for Holly Ann.

"Excellent choice," Hank began. "For a grand, we'll have you all setup. That covers the required body modifications, one set of appropriate apparel, and your official registry as a Galactic Doll with GEnt. You can also opt to have GEnt sponsor you, that is, give you a monthly stipend. If you do, then realize they could make demands of you. On the other hand, if they aren't sponsoring you, they can't do that. I've got a contact at LA General who will handle the modifications to your body. Now, which of you will undergo this change?"

"Huh? Holly Ann, of course," Kyle replied.

"Well, I had to ask." Hank responded with a wry grin. "We often get men undergoing the change, too. Are you sure you don't want to become a Galactic Doll yourself? In fact, you can keep your maleness and still appear to be a Galactic Doll; they can even change your voice."

"Er, no. Just Holly Ann here."

Holly Ann asked, "Can we have a private minute?"

With a teasing grin, he agreed and left the room.

"Look. If you looked like a Galactic Doll, then there would be almost no chance the corporations could recognize you as Kyle Dorn."

"But I'd look like a Galactic Doll. Oh, I see. I'd only have trouble in restrooms. Wow, that would be a huge disguise, wouldn't it?"

"That's what I was thinking. We have to weigh how likely a corporation is to hire you as a male to be a math teacher versus hiring you as a Galactic Doll. Still, it would be weird—looking like a Galactic Doll and yet being a male down below."

"Yes, that would be problematical. I think we best not try that yet. We can always come back again."

Kyle let Hank know they'd finished discussing it.

"A grand and we'll begin."

Kyle handed over a thousand credits from his savings. He still felt guilty about forcing him into her armless body, and this was the least he could do to make amends. If this worked, then Holly Ann would be off the hook with GEnt.

Another two hours passed before the pair met with a doctor at LA General. He had done several tests on her and now counseled them. He spoke in a bored monotone.

"Okay. Hank told me Holly Ann wishes to appear as though she was an official Galactic Doll."

"Yes, that's the idea." Holly Ann's voice sounded timid.

"Okay then. First, Holly Ann, I must tell you that in your case an arm transplant isn't possible." He pointed to two sets of x-rays. "Your shoulders lack the concave sockets for arms. Yours are flat so there would be no way to attach replacement arms, assuming you could pay the ten million credits per arm for that operation."

Neither Holly Ann nor Kyle had ever heard of arm replacements. Even so, both felt an emotional letdown and didn't comment.

The doctor continued, "There's one slight hitch. Did you know that you are pregnant?"

Kyle's face flushed. Holly Ann crimsoned, and she mumbled, "Er, no. Is that going to be a problem?"

"A slight problem, but I can see you two are or would like to be a couple. If you're married, then GEnt will mark Holly Ann as having retired from the Galactic Doll profession, providing you both an extra layer of protection."

From his tone, she thought he must see this sort of situation every day.

"Since you're pregnant, I always err on the side of caution. My suggestion is to wait until you have the baby to get this done. I'll let you discuss this for a minute, while I'll go get your other test results."

He rose and left the two sitting in the small, antiseptic-smelling room.

"Oops. What have we done?" Holly Ann blurted out, "I told you I knew nothing about being a woman."

"Well, the doctor has a good point. If we're married, then you're even more off the hook, so to speak." Kyle swallowed hard. "Holly Ann, will you marry me?"

Holly Ann broke into a laugh. "Sure, Kyle, but I never thought it would be backward as this is. Sure. We should. We'll both have far fewer worries this way."

When the doctor returned, Kyle explained, "We want to be married."

"Excellent. The hospital has an on-site official who can perform the ceremony, making it legal. I've already done the required blood tests. So why don't I take you there?"

Time flew by. The official married them, but not before asking for their choice of a last name for Holly Ann, who chose to be known as Holly Ann Beck-Chesterfield. After the couple shared a quick kiss, he handed Kyle their marriage license and entered their names into the planet-wide database of married couples.

Alone at last, Holly Ann said, "Perhaps we should wait on the surgery. Look, if we're married, they can't expect a married woman to become a Galactic Doll, right?"

"Point taken. Okay. We'll wait."

As the two breathed in the fresh, dry air outside LA General, Kyle chuckled.

"Well, Holly Ann, I never expected to leave there a married man or woman. I can't believe we didn't take more care, but what's done is done. We're going to have a baby—well, you are. I suppose you don't have to keep it. After all, they said my birth defect would affect my children."

Holly Ann chuckled along with Kyle though her face flushed.

"Well, I didn't expect to leave married either, but now I can see this makes even more sense for us. At least, one of us is likely to be off the hook with GEnt. Why wouldn't I want to keep the baby? Gosh, I'm going to be a mother. Now that's even freakier than all the rest."

Kyle hinted, "Well, our baby might lack arms."

"So? You're damned pretty. So what? Oh." Holly Ann flushed. "I'm you now. I see what you mean. Well, if you could manage without them, so can our children. Only I know nothing about having a baby. What do I eat? You'll have to help me with this."

Kyle flushed and hugged her.

When they returned to the nail store, Hank gave Kyle back most of his donation but encouraged them to return after the baby or sooner if Kyle wanted to become a Galactic Doll, too.

When they arrived back at their motel room, Holly Ann looked at herself in the mirror.

"What do I look like? I don't seem to be any larger around the middle."

Kyle leaned over her shoulder in front of the full-length mirror. "You're still pretty. Don't worry. You won't show for months. He said the baby is due next January, but we must get maternity clothes at some point. Oh, and baby clothes. I guess

I will have to get a job. I'm supposed to support you. That's the usual husband's role, isn't it?"

"Don't worry. We'll figure something out. At least, we have one of us handled."

Holly Ann sat down before continuing. "Kyle, what has our world become? The corporations control every aspect of our lives. We can't survive without one sponsoring us, and yet if we allow them to sponsor us, we're obligated to do whatever they wish, when they wish it. If this isn't the Fourth Reich, then I don't know what is."

Kyle sighed. "I'm sure glad I avoided becoming a Galactic Doll when the Flagstaff GEnt people told me that's what I'd be. Still, I feel awful that you've taken my place. I had no idea things in our world were this bad—really, I didn't. I knew it wasn't good. Once Dad retired, Galactic Supplies moved them into their assisted living home. Less than a year later, Mom and Dad stopped recognizing me when I visited them. But maybe they had just enough mind left to have their bad accident..."

Holly Ann picked up his thought. "So they were able to have an accident—to end their torment."

Suppressing tears, Kyle nodded.

"I understand. My parents stopped recognizing me about a year ago. At first, they knew me, and I visited them once a month. Then, dementia entered the picture, at least, that's what the doctors told me. Damn, Kyle, now I get it. Maybe it's all been misdirection."

"Huh?" he said, looking into her eyes, thankful she wasn't pressing for details of the accident.

"Misdirection. Focus everyone's attention on the Sixth Invaders and their terrorists. Then, no one will see what they're doing to our world and the Sol Empire."

"Turning it into a corporate-controlled society?" Kyle made sure he was following Holly Ann's reasoning.

"Precisely. What we should ask is who is doing this and why?"

Kyle shrugged his shoulders. "Sorry. I don't know. I was always more interested in learning all the math I could. You know—calculus and differential equations. Even topology. I should have been paying attention to all this. High IQ isn't everything, is it?"

"Don't knock yourself. You did what you needed to do to live independently. Honestly, I don't know how you ever figured out how to do many of the things you have. Genius. Anyway, as I see it, we have half our battle solved, namely me. Now, let's put our heads together and get you fixed up and safe somehow. I'm not about to let them get you, Kyle. Besides, I'm dependent upon you, especially since we're having a baby. We'll need a house, stable income, and safety from the corporations and this insane society. I don't think I'll be able to get a job in electronics, not without hands."

Kyle giggled. "Not too many females in electronics, as you said. Don't forget—society now thinks of you as a woman— a married woman expecting a child. I think that will make it even tougher to find a job in your field."

Holly Ann flushed. "Heck, if you would have said that to me a month ago when I made that anonymous posting on my Friends Book page, I'd have said you were nuts. Now look at me."

"A gorgeous woman." Kyle teased her. Both laughed. "So what are we going to do about me? Our roles are reversed. I never thought I'd be seen as the man in a marriage, but then I never expected to be married either. It's obvious to me we'll never be able to switch back to our own bodies. We're stuck as we are, so I have to start thinking as if I'm the man."

"No, Kyle. We're a *team*. I think that's the best way to look at our situation. I need you and you need me. Come on. Let's put our heads together. We have to get you fixed up, too."

For hours, the pair searched the Internet for hints, for clues, for some way to avoid GD arresting and torturing Kyle. He sighed, giving up hope except for the drastic surgery option, but Holly Ann continued to plod away, operating her computer using her toes and voice commands, frustrated with her pathetically slow speed. It took all her willpower to keep her focus on the computer and not her physical situation. *I have to figure out something for Kyle; he's giving up. We're doomed if he does—no, I'm doomed if he does. Be honest with yourself.*

"Hey, Kyle, look at this. Apparently, the corporations leave company presidents and critical personnel alone. Kyle, I think I have a way out for you. We make you a company president or a critical man in a company."

"Fat chance of that, Holly Ann. I've never been a company president, and I'm certainly not critical to any endeavor. I just know math."

Holly Ann sighed. "Okay, you're right. Forget that idea. Instead, we will capitalize on your math skills. I think I know how we can do that, but we'll have to go back to Chicago."

"Well, before we do that, we're both going to need many new outfits. We've been living out of our backpacks. I keep washing clothes every other day."

"How did we ever get into this mess? I think I could scream about now," Holly Ann said.

That did it. Kyle's near continuous suppression of guilt feelings failed at last. Tears streamed down his face. "I'm so sorry, Kyle—I mean Holly Ann. I was being selfish and petty; I should never have done this to you. I'm so sorry." He sobbed.

Holly Ann felt a strong urge to put his arms around her and comfort her, but again stark reality slammed into her. She had no arms. He was in her body now. Instead, she leaned into Kyle, whose arms seemed to have a mind of their own, encircling her, latching onto her body. *Best let her cry some. This is so confusing.*

Kyle let her go, pulling back his arms and wiping his face on his shirt sleeves. "Sorry. I sometimes get too emotional. This is still so strange for me, Kyle—er, Holly Ann, rather. You're right. I feel like screaming too. I keep thinking that perhaps this is all some terrible nightmare. I'll wake up soon. We won't—wake up—will we? Besides, it's so weird calling you Holly Ann, because that's me, and I've got to keep reminding myself I'm Kyle."

"I feel the same way. I don't know how to be a woman, just as you don't know how to be a man. Yet, we're doing okay so far, making it go right for each other. Besides, I'm in love with you. That has to count for something, doesn't it? After all, if we hadn't done this, why, I would have never met you. No matter what else happens to us, I treasure loving you. Always will. No matter how confusing this all is. Now, it's us against this insane society."

Chapter 18 Unusual Solutions

Holly Ann knew Kyle depended on her. He'd given up all hope of finding a job that didn't involve GD arresting him and torturing or terminating him. Besides, without a sponsor's monthly stipend coming in, they had spent their savings on motels, food, and now clothing. She spent long hours surfing the Internet, searching for ideas.

Corporate executive positions were dependent upon family connections. The duo had none and no such prospects. Holly Ann kept coming back to the singular fact that Kyle wanted to teach math, preferably at the high school level, since universities required advanced degrees. She retrieved Galactic University's high school curriculum and discovered Kyle qualified for such a position, if only GD hadn't listed Kyle as a most-wanted criminal.

There seemed no answer that would ensure Kyle's safety unless she could find a way to make him a corporate executive. The more she looked, the more depressed she became.

Mid-June, Holly Ann admitted defeat. "Well, Kyle, I've tried everything I can think of, but whoever set up this corporate-controlled society has thought of everything, except the fake Galactic Doll angle."

"I figured so. Don't worry. You tried. That's what matters to me."

"I want you safe. I need you, and I love you. This will sound crazy, but what do you think about the insane idea I just had? If they are insisting most teachers be women, what about you undergoing the operation to become a fake Galactic Doll and then applying for your teaching position? Perhaps they'll hire you to teach math at a high school."

"You've got to be kidding? Right?" Kyle looked at her. A devious smile spread across his face. "Oh, that's the most diabolical idea yet, dear. It could work, but only if they'd hire a Galactic Doll as a math teacher. Wait, what about us? Our marriage? Children?"

"Change everything except that part. Then, we could still raise a family. Plus, if it doesn't work out, you could have the body modifications undone."

"Well, I don't know. Are you sure about this? I'd look like a woman. Others would see us as having an unusual marriage."

"I can't think of anything else to keep you safe. Okay, Kyle, I'm being selfish, too. I depend on you, more so when our baby comes."

"I think we should check it out further. We don't want to rush into something as drastic as this, do we?"

"True. But we shouldn't waste too much time. They'll be hiring teachers for the fall terms soon. As far as I can tell, there are more men needing jobs than there are male positions, so the corporations are ordering men to get their gender changed so they can become employable. Either that or join the army and fight the Sixth Invaders. More insanity, but this works in our favor, don't you think?"

***

The third week of June, Holly Ann sat beside Kyle's recovery bed at LA General. The same doctor who they had met before worked on Kyle, again treating this as though it was routine. In fact, Holly Ann now knew that it was routine, thanks to corporation orders. The doctor had altered Kyle's voice. She now sported a massive bosom as did all Galactic Dolls. They chose not to have some of his ribs removed or have his pelvis and hips reworked to give his body a more feminine appearance, but his hair and nails had been lengthened.

Kyle's manhood was intact. Kyle had insisted on that, much to Holly Ann's relief. She suspected he continued to hope they might one day be able to return to their own bodies though Holly Ann no longer had such illusions. During her Internet searching, she'd found no trace of the men who had performed the body swapping process. While she was often quite frustrated with her physical limitations, she accepted what had happened. Time to move on, she often told herself.

"Wake up sleepyhead. It's done."

Kyle's eyelids fluttered. "Oh. Oh! My voice." Kyle became more alert and felt her body with her hands. "I ache all over. What do I look like? Is this going to work?" Kyle had a new high-pitched voice.

"I think you look scrumptious, dear. You have to look gorgeous if you're to pass as a former Galactic Doll. Come on. The doctor said we could leave as soon as you get dressed. I'm glad we brought along a starter gown from Hank's place."

The moment the two arrived back at their motel room, Kyle's first action was to look at his image in the full-length mirror.

"My goodness, I do look like a woman, don't I? The only way to tell I'm still a man is if I remove my panties. This is incredible. Thank you. For the first time in months, I feel safe. We're in the corporate system as married, and I'm a retired Galactic Doll. No one will bother us further."

"Precisely."

Kyle chuckled. "Say, we have to get me many new clothes. I wish we didn't have to exhaust our funds on dresses for me."

"Right. Let's go get some. Then, let's send out resumes. We need to find you a math teaching position somewhere."

"That look. Holly Ann, what are you thinking?"

Holly Ann flushed. "You look like a woman, and I'm getting incredibly turned on."

Kyle roared. "A man in a woman's body. Touché. Just you wait until bedtime." Both laughed, but they set to work on the next phase. With their funds nearly exhausted, they had to find a job or jobs.

By the middle of July, they had sent out several dozen resumes, picking key institutions. Holly Ann decided Kyle should teach at one of the more prestigious high schools where her students might be brighter than the average. At first, they avoided both Chicago and Flagstaff. Then, because Kyle had no chance of being recognized in Chicago, they also sent off two resumes to promising schools in the Windy City as well.

By August, Kyle had received three offers for the fall term. Although Kyle hadn't made his choice yet, both he and Holly Ann relaxed. His comment reflected his increased self-respect.

"After I accept one of these, we'll have a stable income,

and we can begin a real life. Come on. Let's look at these three cities, dear, and pick out the one that's best for us."

Chicago was among the three. Kyle weighed the offers and chose Cook County Elite High School. His deeper motivation was to get Holly Ann back into her familiar city. He hoped this would help her.

Chapter 19 On the Trail

August 2351

Molly's endurance improved significantly. Her self-confidence rose in parallel to her ever-increasing skills in her martial arts. Bev trained and pushed her hard. Everyone saw the improvements in Molly, and she and Bev received constant praise from their sisters and the men in their lives.

At last, Molly decided it was time to resume her PI business, at least part time. While she and Bev continued to train half the day, in the afternoons, Molly hoped to be back helping others. Showered and dressed in her usual gray skirt, silk blouse, and flats, she headed off to her office, pleased with all the sewing Janine had done for her. Her tops, blouses, and shirts now had no arms or sleeves. Nothing to flop around and get in her way.

Molly paused at the door to her office. *God, I'm really doing this. Opening my PI doors again. Lord, I hope Ted and Bev are right about this and that I can do it. I can't fail. I just can't. I might as well be dead if I can't do this. Okay. Unlock the door.*

She faced her front door, slipped off a shoe, unlocked the door, slipped the shoe back on, and entered. A month ago, Deanna had hired someone to clean and dust, and today, a faint odor of polish greeted her. Molly smiled but then spent a half hour picking up all the mail lying on the floor just inside the mail drop. She resisted cursing that this took twenty times longer than it should have. Just as she began to sort out the mail, someone knocked.

"Come on in. I'm open again."

An older woman, perhaps in her fifties, walked in. She wore a gray dress that did little for her appearance. She wore no makeup, but she had dyed her hair blonde; Molly could see the brown roots appearing.

"Welcome to Molly Parkinson's Private Investigations and Security. I'm Molly. Have a seat. How can I help you?"

"I have a very touchy situation. May I count on your discretion?"

"Of course, that goes without saying. When you hire a PI, we try to be as discreet as possible. Please don't let my lack of arms bother you. I do very well."

The woman flushed; Molly sensed she'd been thinking about that.

"My name is Eloise Dorn. I would like to hire you to find my nephew, but if you find him, you can't tell anyone but me about him or where he is."

"Okay. Please tell me about him. Do you have a recent photo?"

She slid a photograph across the desk, hesitant as though uncertain how she should hand it to the PI. Molly slipped off a shoe and picked it up between her toes.

"I'm right toed," she jested. Eloise flashed a brief smile.

Molly said, "He's a young man, in school I'd guess from the background."

"Yes, he attended the University of Illinois Chicago campus. He was studying electrical engineering and was to graduate in mid-May, but he disappeared in late April. I should explain."

With a sigh, Eloise outlined what she knew of Kyle's actions and protests against the corporations. She had seen his Friends Book posting and knew GD had branded him a terrorist, wanted dead or alive, though that had been months ago. Kyle had not been in the news since late April. GD guards paid her a visit, but she knew nothing about his disappearance.

"So he vanished with GD hot on his tail. Always one step ahead of them, I guess. Anyway, I'd like to hire you to see if you can find him. Why? My husband recently passed away, and I've come down with incurable cancer. Kyle was always my favorite nephew. I want to leave my estate to my three nephews, but we have to have a way to get the money to Kyle when I die."

"I'm so sorry for you. How long have the doctors given you?"

"Three, maybe four months. You can see the urgency, can't you? GD must never know about this. Lord, they would probably terminate him, and he's done nothing wrong. I can't understand why speaking your mind has become a deadly crime."

"No, I don't either. I'll find Kyle for you, Eloise."

Eloise smiled and then asked, "How much will it cost me?"

"How about twenty-five credits a day plus expenses? Say a hundred up front? I'll return any excess if I find him in less than four days."

"Honey, that's cheap, but I appreciate it. Here's cash. I don't want GD to find out that I've hired you, so I'll always pay you in cash. If they find out, we could both be in trouble, but between us, there's not a damned thing they can do to me. I'll be dead shortly anyway."

She slid the bills over to her along with a card with her contact information on it. A second card had his dorm room at the school, just in case she needed it, along with his GD-confiscated bank account records. Eloise showed herself out, leaving Molly staring at Kyle's photograph.

"He's rather cute," she commented aloud. "Okay, to business. Let's see what GD says about him. Back in April. Okay, computer, let's get to work. Damn, I'm so slow compared to what I used to be doing. Ah well.

"It feels so wonderful to be back doing what I love to do. Well, I can see why GD went to Palo Heights. That's his parents' unsold home."

Molly entered her PI ID number and gained access to the City Surveillance System. After entering the date, time, and location, the system replayed the video from three different cameras. Her computer had three holographic displays playing back what had been recorded while Molly watched and controlled them with her right foot.

Flashy GD entrance. No wonder Kyle knew they were coming. Why not use a bullhorn to announce you're arriving? Idiots. Kyle must have sneaked out a back door.

She used voice-activation to pause the playback and to bring down the local menu. No cameras out back. She opened another window and examined the MTES system. Smiling, she brought up video from a different camera. Within a minute, she spotted Kyle and his backpack, frantically running down the moving sidewalk and looking back over his shoulders.

Molly endured a long, frustrating afternoon, taking many times longer to carry out what she used to do while going through surveillance videos. But by suppertime, she'd followed him all the way to Joliet and had verified he had no relatives or connections to anyone in that suburb.

After the next day's workout with Bev, Molly returned to her work. She had a spring in her step as she walked into her office building. *God, I love this.*

She resumed her search for Kyle, beginning in Joliet. Molly discovered an unverified police report of an unauthorized EMAC landing on the school grounds late at night. A frustrating hour later, a new video stream played; she found an observation point that showed the school grounds. Although it was dark, she saw what was likely Kyle briefly meeting another man and getting into that EMAC. She zoomed in on the ID on its side but could only make out part of its number.

Again, the going was far slower than she wished, but she found the EMAC was registered to someone in the greater LA area. If she could have read the last three digits, she could have pinpointed to whom it belonged. No such luck. Molly sat back, pondering why Kyle had gone to LA and what her next move should be.

"If he's fleeing, then there must have been a reason he went to LA with that man. It has to involve a way to hide, but what? Flights have to be logged," Molly explained to her computer.

She took another hour to get into the Southern California EMAC logs. Once more, she entered her ID and breathed a sigh of relief. She was in. Guessing that the EMAC probably landed in LA the following morning, she entered the date and the partial EMAC ID number, pressing Search. Molly waited.

"Gee, Molly, you have learned patience," Bev's voice broke in on her thoughts.

"Oh hi, Bev. Pull up a seat."

"Just dropping by to see how ya doing on your new

case. Honestly, I'm bored—okay, mega-bored. Anything I can do?"

"Not yet. I'm waiting on California." Molly explained what she was doing.

"Darn, you're a hot PI. I'd never have thought of that."

"Ah, finally. Here's the report of arriving EMACs—ones that have that partial ID number. Now I'm getting somewhere. Only one. Let's see where it landed."

"You can do that?"

Bev pulled the guest chair around so she could look over Molly's shoulder.

"Yes, my PI license allows me access to surveillance data and a few other things. First, I have to jot down that location. Darn hard to write like this. Okay, now we dive into the nearest video camera systems."

***

Bev watched Molly. Her heart ached to see her sister taking so long to get this task done using her toes. Had Molly seen her face, she'd have seen Bev fighting against stepping in and just doing it for her.

***

"Whew. Here we go. Now let's see if we can find Kyle and this man."

The video began playing on her computer.

"So you have to sit here and watch?"

"Yes, that's what a lot of PI work involves. Sit and watch hours of video for just the key clue. If you don't have patience, you can't be a PI. Hey, look. We're in luck. That's Kyle. His photograph's over there. That certainly looks like him. He's going into a building with that man. Now comes the hard part."

"What's that?"

"Now we have to ID the store and watch endless hours of video to see Kyle coming out and where he goes next."

"Why don't I try to ID the store? How do I do that?"

Molly told Bev what to do, while she continued to watch the video, sped up by a factor of five.

"Weird. It's an abandoned store. No one's been there for decades. Not scheduled for demolition, though. Guess that

256

doesn't help at all."

Molly chuckled. "Oh, yes, it does. He's fleeing GD guards. He must have found something there, probably illegal—something that'll allow him to elude detection. I say illegal 'cause it's abandoned. So now we watch for his exit."

"There—there. Isn't that him?" Bev pointed to the screen, quite excited.

They had been watching the stream for over an hour. Molly stopped it, backed it up, and played it at normal speed.

"Yes, that's Kyle, but he's with a woman. Wow, she's like me."

"This is exciting. I'm used to fast action, but still, this is interesting."

"Yeah. I love moments like this when I uncover something. Now we follow them using street MTES cameras."

"They're going into that motel room." Bev pointed out the obvious a half-hour later.

"They are together, Bev. One room, one bed. It's a cheap motel, so the bed can't be a double or king. Hence, they're together. We need to identify this young woman. We've got two clues going. Kyle has met a woman, and they're staying together in a cheap motel. Interesting."

Bev glanced at the clock. "Say, we best head home. Supper will be waiting. Mind if I tag along with you tomorrow? This is fun. Besides, I'm bored sitting around the skyscraper. I need action."

Molly laughed. "Sure, Bev. I know what you mean. I wish I was capable of more action—like I used to..."

"Oh, I think in time it'll get faster and easier for you. It's like basic training. Grunts have a horrible time with it at first, but by the end, they are old hands with it all."

"God, Bev, I hope so."

"Say, want to go out drinking with me tonight after supper?"

"I'm not up to that. Not yet."

"Okay. I'll bring you back a beer."

"Brown ale, please."

***

The next afternoon, the sisters resumed their investigation.

Molly had Bev searching through video, trying to follow either person when they left the motel. Meanwhile, she worked on identifying the young woman. Using a spare computer, she backtracked the video. By suppertime, she'd discovered the woman had arrived in LA via public transportation. She'd come from Flagstaff. Considering her age, she ran a facial recognition search against high schools in the area and found her name, Holly Ann Durbin. She was an only child, deceased parents.

"She's got a birth defect. That's why no arms. How are you doing?"

Bev said, "Well, Kyle left and picked up fast food. They both left the next day and returned to that abandoned building, but couldn't get in this time. From their gestures, I think that upset them. Anyway, they went back to the motel. He keeps bringing them fast food. I'm following them on the MTES into downtown LA. I've no idea where they are going or why. Wait. This is really weird. They're going into a hospital. Molly, why would someone fleeing GD go into a hospital? Neither of them looks injured, though that's hard to tell on these poor quality images."

"Dunno. Maybe they are sick or something. Let's see if we can pick them up leaving," Molly suggested.

Later on, Bev found them departing the hospital. Molly needed hospital records. If the pair entered the hospital, then there had to be records. But her PI license didn't allow her access. She made a quick call.

Coyly, she said, "Oh Ted, dear, I've got a small job for you."

Soon, Ted ran into her office, his own computer in a backpack.

"Hi, love. I need you to hack into that hospital and search their records. We need to know anything having to do with Kyle Dorn or Holly Ann Durbin."

Ted gave her a sly grin. "You got it. LA General, here I come."

"Don't get caught."

"I learned my lesson."

An hour later, he looked up. "Molly, no one was there

with the last name of Dorn or Durbin. But there was a Holly Ann Beck and a Kyle Chesterfield. Believe it or not, they just got married. So what does this mean? Helpful?"

"Dear, you've cracked this case. Yes, we're trying to locate Kyle, who's fleeing GD security. So he's changed his name and gotten married. Not sure why he's gotten married. Now we have a name. Ten to one he'll feel confident he's thrown GD off his trail and be overt in using his new last name."

Bev said, "How do you know all that?"

"He's done all this." She made a sweeping gesture with her right leg and foot. "A last name change and a new ID gives people a false sense of security. He'll use it, making our job easier. But it's anyone's guess why he got married or what his next move will be. We'll just have to keep on with our hunt."

"She's damn good!" Bev said.

Ted said, "I knew that back in high school. Now, I'm the luckiest man in the world."

***

On their walk home for supper, Molly explained, "Kyle's actions are starting to make sense. Fleeing from the Chicago GD forces, he found a connection in LA, one that led him to this Holly Ann woman. Next, they marry. In many ways, his marrying makes Kyle fit in with society far better than before when he was an outspoken critic of the corporations, assuming this young woman isn't herself a similar critic. My gut feeling is that she isn't. In a real way, Kyle is joining our society in ways he simply wasn't while in school. What I still haven't discovered is how these two came to know each other. There's no sign Holly Ann was ever in Chicago or that Kyle was ever in Flagstaff. More research is needed."

Bev said, "Wow, that's a fascinating line of reasoning. I'd never have drawn that conclusion, but when you explain it, why, it seems obvious."

"Thanks. Maybe tomorrow we'll find that connection. Then, so much more will make sense."

In fact, things made much less sense, for the next afternoon's studies of surveillance footage showed Holly Ann and Kyle going into LA General together, but Holly Ann came out with another woman, a Galactic Doll. As they reviewed more footage, Molly got a good facial view of this new woman.

"Oh, my god! That's Kyle. Look at his face. Ignore the rest of her. Focus on the face."

"Unreal! He's had a gender change? Now that'll throw GD off his trail!"

Molly said, "That's quite a drastic change, one I didn't expect. He must be terrified GD will find him. We best keep on looking. If they're married, they'll need to find jobs. He or rather she will likely look for a job that needs an electrical engineer while she will probably try to put her math background to good use. Teaching perhaps. We'll see."

Bev asked, "But where will they look for jobs? Flagstaff? Chicago? Surely, he—I mean she—wouldn't come back here, would he, er she?"

Molly pressed her lips together, deep in thought.

"Bev, you've a good idea. They could move almost anywhere in the US though it's unlikely they'd go much farther. But people are creatures of habit. I'm sure Kyle feels more comfortable, more at home, in Chicago than LA. Holly Ann feels more at home in Flagstaff. Why go to this extreme and get a sex change? So you can safely return to your familiar city with almost no fear of recognition by GD forces. Bev, great idea."

Bev laughed. "Sorry, that wasn't my idea. I didn't even think of that."

Both women laughed again.

Molly said, "Okay, tomorrow we'll look to see if they get a job in Chicago or Flagstaff. My wager is on Chicago."

"Why?"

"Because Kyle got the sex change, not Holly Ann. I think he did that so he can return here, but we'll see."

As they headed home, Bev asked, "So you ready to hit the pubs with me tonight? I'll buy."

Molly laughed. "No. Why not just bring a six-pack of ale home with us?"

***

The next day, Molly discovered that Kyle Chesterfield had just accepted a position at Cook County Elite High School teaching math. She was due to begin classes in five days.

Bev said, "I don't quite get it. Kyle is teaching math. But he's got an electrical engineering degree. I'd have thought teaching math would be Holly Ann's choice."

"I agree. This is another reason I love being a PI. Surprises. People are always full of them. Come on. We have to find them."

A phone call produced Kyle's orientation interview: date, time, and place.

Molly said, "If we take the MTES, we can be there before the interview is done."

As she and Bev headed out the door, Bev asked, "Aren't you going to tell your client we found her nephew? Tell her where to meet him?"

"Nope. In this business, you trust *no* one, not even little old ladies who claim they're dying of cancer. She might be telling the truth, and then again, she might not. First, we'll get Kyle's side of things."

"Wish I could've gone to a high school as fancy as this one," Bev said.

The pair arrived across the street from a modern school. Its red bricks were pristine as though they'd just been laid or someone had power-washed them recently—probably the latter. Playgrounds looked more like manicured golf courses than soccer fields, baseball diamonds, volleyball courts, and basketball courts. These reminded Molly of a passage in her high school history book that described professional adults playing these sports and who were watched by millions of fans, but that was centuries ago.

As the pair stepped off the MTES and walked up the last block, they spotted Holly Ann standing beside the street, watching the main doors of the school. Molly continued her forward pace, and Holly Ann idly glanced towards them, but then she turned to face Molly, staring wide-eyed at her.

"Hello. I'm Molly Parkinson, Private Investigator. You must be Holly Ann. We're trying to find Kyle. His Aunt Eloise Dorn is dying of cancer and wants to leave her estate to Kyle and two other nephews. He or she is still in the orientation interview, right?"

"Wait, I don't have an Aunt Eloise or whatever you called her," Holly Ann said.

Confused, Molly said, "She hired me to find Kyle. She gave me his school photograph and bank records."

"Anyone could have gotten those. I tell you I don't have any such aunt." Her face reddened.

"Hold on a second." Molly's face frowned, her eyebrows rising perceptibly. "What do you mean you don't have that aunt? You're twenty-one-year-old Holly Ann Durbin, recently called Beck and now that you're married, Chesterfield. Kyle Dorn changed his last name to Chesterfield and had his body modified into that of a Galactic Doll."

Holly Ann's face reddened even more as Molly's words impinged on her like baseballs. "I—I—I'm Kyle. She's Holly Ann. Okay, you can turn us into the GD guards." She sighed and slumped.

Just then, Kyle Chesterfield walked out of the front doors. No mistaking her enormous bosom. She wore a blue satin gown, typical of Galactic Dolls, and the requisite matching tall heels. As she walked over to the group, her broad smile changed to worry lines. Molly also saw that her nails were quite long.

"Kyle, it's up. They know everything," Holly Ann blurted out.

"Oh god, Holly Ann, what do we do now? They just hired me."

"Hi, I'm Molly Parkinson, Private Investigator. I'd shake hands, but I've misplaced them. My sister, Bev."

Her jest brought a smile to Holly Ann's worried face, as well as Kyle's. Molly continued.

"Kyle, your Aunt Eloise Dorn hired me to find you. She's dying of cancer and wants to leave her estate to you and two other nephews."

Kyle looked bewildered, glancing repeatedly at Holly Ann.

Good god, Kyle has no idea what I'm talking about.

Before Molly could think of anything to say, Kyle said, "Holly Ann, do we have an Aunt Eloise?"

Lame. Molly sensed how lame Kyle's question was. She

262

was certain Kyle didn't know what she was talking about. Bev stood motionless, looking confused.

"Honestly, Molly, I told you I'm Kyle. I was Kyle Dorn. Look, I almost have my EE degree, and she's going to be a math teacher. I swear I don't have any such aunt. Probably GD hired you so they could capture me, only now they'll try to take her instead. This is so confusing. We're married, too."

"Now wait a minute. We saw street camera video of you meeting Holly Ann in LA outside an abandoned store. You can't be her."

"Okay, okay. We swapped our bodies there in LA. Each of us found a strange ad on the Internet that offered a body exchange. I was desperate. The GD guards were hot on my tail, and Holly Ann wanted a new life because GEnt wanted to sponsor her as a Galactic Doll. She wanted to teach math and not be a sex Doll. So we both fled to LA. These two men had this Exchange Machine."

Holly Ann explained what had happened, how wonderful and beautiful that white light had been, and waking up to find they were in each other's bodies.

"I can't tell you how helpless I felt," Holly Ann said. "Oops. You already know. Anyway, by the next day, we both realized we had made a horrible mistake. We went back to beg them to undo it, to swap us back, but they vanished. Like it never happened. We tried everything to find a way to swap ourselves back, but nothing worked."

Kyle interrupted, "I should never have done it. I mean I grew up like this, a birth defect. I learned to be independent, but Kyle didn't know how to do anything. It was horrible. Once we realized we couldn't undo it, I stepped up. I have to be the man now. We found out that if Holly Ann is married, then GEnt couldn't make her into a Galactic Doll. She's safe, except she's pregnant with our child. I knew he or she would fare better in Chicago, so we looked for a math teacher's job for me. I got the fake Galactic Doll changes made there in LA. We hoped no one in GD would recognize Kyle's body. I'm still male, though, in case we ever can get this thing undone."

Holly Ann said, "So what are you going to do about us? Turn us into GD?"

"Hardly," Molly said. "Do you have a place to stay?"

Kyle answered, "No. Motel. We were going to see about renting a place if I got the job, which I just did, but they insist I wear Galactic Doll outfits to school. Something about setting an example for many young girls who also want to become one when they graduate."

"Okay then. How about coming to stay with us? We're living with our sister, Deanna Cartwright in the Cartwright Enterprise skyscraper. I can guarantee you'll be safe there. Bev and I need time to find out just who that woman was and what her aim is in finding you. How can people swap bodies? Our sisters might be able to help."

Chapter 20 Unraveled

When Eve, Randi, Deanna, and the others heard Holly Ann and Kyle's lengthy story, Deanna insisted the pair live in the skyscraper.

She said, "Molly and Holly Ann can share ideas, ways, and means. Comradery."

Eve said, "We know some therapy that will help you both." Telepathically, she sent, 'Randi, we need to discover what this new machine does and why they're making such a machine.'

Randi sent back, 'Absolutely.'

Holly Ann sighed, much relieved. "Thanks. We need help. I've never felt so helpless in my life. It's crazy. If I can stop panicking—just relax and stop trying to do something, the body has a mind of its own and knows how to do it. Weird. But sometimes I feel scared, too. Worse, I love electrical engineering. Like this, I can't do much of anything. I feel awful forcing everything off on Kyle. I should be supporting us, not her. This is so confusing."

"Eve, is this body swapping thing possible?" Deanna asked.

"Remember, we are composites. There is a physical body, a mind of mental images or pictures, and the spiritual being, the personality, that which is aware."

Eve continued, "But we call it body stealing. Force someone out of their body's head. Then, the thief slips into the body's head, leaving the original person stranded without a body."

"So is this possible?"

"Is it easy? No. Is it possible? You bet. They used a machine. Notice Kyle and Holly Ann said they attached the electrodes to their heads. I've no doubt they're telling the truth. What bothers me is there's an electronic machine that can switch two people."

"They called it an Exchange Machine, and that they were just swapping minds," said Holly Ann.

"The potential for abuse and misuse is gigantic, especially with corporations running everything," Molly said.

Deanna asked, "How so?"

"*Corporation A* needs control of something owned by *Corporation B*. *Corporation A* swaps one of their personnel with the unsuspecting owner of *Corporation B*, and as that other owner, gives control of it over to *Corporation A*. Then, they swap bodies again. No one will believe the ripped-off owner. Who ever heard of body swapping?"

That sobered everyone.

Breaking the silence, Kyle asked, "How come so many of you look so alike?"

That was an effective conversation changer. An exchange of the group's many adventures filled the rest of the evening.

***

The next morning Bev and Molly cooled down from their brisk two-mile run along the side streets.

Bev asked, "How did ya know your client wasn't who she said she was? And what're you going to do about it?"

"First, I knew something was off when I heard the first words out of Holly Ann's mouth. She said, 'I don't have an Aunt Eloise.' I was looking at the woman we identified as Holly Ann from Flagstaff, but she used the word 'I.' Big tipoff, Bev. I would have expected to hear, 'He doesn't have an Aunt Eloise,' assuming she was familiar with Kyle and his extended family. Second, she said 'don't have.' Red flag. Thus, my client could well be lying to me. As their story came out, I became certain my client isn't who she says she is. This is why I *so* love being a PI. The rush I got from finding them and meeting them—wow. Anyway, it's up to us to find out who Aunt Eloise is and who she's working for if you're still up for more PI work."

"Absolutely, but not until we finish your martial arts workout this morning." Molly growled through her teeth. Yet, she couldn't deny this was helping her cope. Everything depended on her keeping her balance, so hard to do without arms to arrest a fall.

Bev added, "I get a similar feeling when we win a skirmish, a battle, or even a training exercise. What a rush. I loved being a soldier."

After showering and having lunch, Molly watched Eve and Randi taking Holly Ann and Kyle aside for their first therapy session.

"They will benefit from this," Molly said, and Bev smiled. "Okay, we're off. Come on. Time to find out who this client is."

At her office, Molly began by backtracking street surveillance video around the block where her office was located. Bev spotted the woman leaving Molly's office building. Next, they split the task. Molly searched for the woman's arrival and then followed her back from whence she came, while Bev followed her path after she left the meeting with Molly.

By suppertime, both women were frustrated. They'd each tracked the woman back to a home, discovering that a Mrs. Appleby lived there. A widower, she looked just like the Aunt Eloise. However, they discovered nothing more about this woman. Worse, the woman had no visitors for days, both before and after the visit with Molly, though twice she had had groceries delivered. Disgruntled, the pair headed home.

After dinner, Molly saw Bev heading out to the pub again.

As she and Ted got ready for bed, Ted said, "Bev sure drinks a lot. Heard she's not getting in until the wee hours of the morning."

"I think she's really bored. I'll talk with her tomorrow."

The next morning Molly launched her power kicks into the mats held by Bev.

"You know what I'd do about this client?" Bev said. "I'd set her up. Call her up, saying you found Kyle. Arrange a meeting, say in the lobby of the Cartwright building. Flood the lobby with disguised security people. When they arrive, wham!"

She slammed both mats together with her hands.

"Has Deanna got any of the truth drug stuff? If so, use it on whoever comes."

Molly laughed. "Bev, I like your idea. We only have a couple days before school starts and Kyle will have to go to work. It would be ideal if this whole thing was resolved before then."

She took Bev's proposal to Deanna, who agreed. "Yes, we need to get this situation resolved quickly. I've thought a lot about this swapping bodies thing. We should be worried about that, not this silly business of Kyle's being so outspoken and critical of the ruling corporations. Let's make it happen tonight."

After Molly told Bev that Deanna was behind the plan, she saw a different side of Bev—the Kick Ass side. All afternoon, Bev charged around the lobby, instructing the many guards on every detail of the operation. She pulled in every off-duty guard Deanna had. Close to sixty men and women, some wearing night vision goggles, all heavily armed, were strategically positioned around the lobby, disguised in various ways, such as janitors and maids.

While Bev was arranging the surprise welcome, Molly went to her office and called up Aunt Eloise to relay the "good news."

"He's staying at the Cartwright Enterprise skyscraper off Lake Shore Drive. I've arranged for him to be in their lobby at 6:00 p.m. Can you be there by then?"

"Oh, this is so wonderful! Thank you ever so much. Yes, I'll be there at six. Thank you, thank you. And how much more do I owe you? I'll bring that along too."

"Another hundred would be appreciated." *I should charge this bitch a hundred thousand, but I gotta play along.*

Molly ducked out of her office early that afternoon.

Once in the Cartwright lobby, she told Bev, "Okay. It's on for six. Will you be ready by then?"

"Absolutely. If they hit us with a dozen men, we're prepared. If they try to gas us, we're prepared. If they try to storm the rooftop, we're ready for that. If they put snipers on nearby rooftops, we're prepared. I have a bulletproof glass wall between the outside glass walls and where Kyle will be. The only thing we're not prepared for is one of those dog whistle things the Sixth Invaders have because Deanna doesn't have one of her new portable EM machines here. Otherwise, we'd be prepared for that too. I'm having almost as much fun as I had in the army running my company of soldiers."

Molly laughed. That much, she could see. Now they had to wait, allowing the three hours to pass.

"So, I heard you've been getting in really late."

"Yeah, kinda drunk, too. Except for today, it's been goddamn boring. I miss all the action, but I sure as hell ain't joining up for another stint in GD's army. Not with those idiots in command. How about coming out with me one of these nights? Bring Ted with ya."

"Maybe. I'll ask him. He's cramming away on the robot things. Me? I've had all the book learning I want. I just want to help people."

"Same here."

As the hour approached, Bev ducked down beneath a desk, surrounded with comm devices, staying in communication with her security forces. Around five, Molly brought Kyle down, positioning themselves behind the bulletproof glass wall. Periodically, she heard voices over Bev's devices. "Rooftops clear." "Alley clear." "Street clear." And so it went, as the minutes drifted by, and six o'clock approached.

As several clocks sounded the hour, a man wearing an expensive business suit walked into the lobby. Glancing around, he spotted Molly and walked over to her and the Galactic Doll standing beside her.

"Ah, you must be Molly Parkinson. I'm VP Russell Godwyn of Galactic Entertainment, Chicago Office."

Russell was a big man, slightly overweight, with a pudgy face and a countenance that demanded respect. He looked somewhat familiar to her.

Seeing the confused look on her face, he said, "Is Deanna around? She knows me. It's best we begin there."

"Yes, I'm Molly. She's standing by. We're supposed to be meeting someone. Can you go on up yourself? The elevators are that way."

She nodded her head, annoyed that she couldn't just point to them any longer. She still found little things that bothered her.

"You're waiting to meet me—this business about Kyle Dorn. Send for Mrs. Cartwright."

In a flash, dozens of guns appeared, along with Bev and her gun.

Bev barked, "Deanna's on her way. Don't try anything. We're fully prepared here."

"Whoa. I'm unarmed!" He grinned, raising his hands. "Trouble is, other than Molly, I can't tell the difference between you sisters. Are you the one that used to be called Kick Ass?" She nodded. He continued, "Impressive. You're the first of the captured female soldiers who has regained her mind. The others are still ranting and demanding sex unless they are kept doped up. So yes, I'm impressed. Ah, Deanna. Thank goodness for your bob cut. It's nearly impossible to tell you sisters apart, save for Molly here. Please, let them know who I am. Then, we all should sit down and discuss this."

Deanna said, "Yes, he is VP Russell Godwyn of Galactic Entertainment, Chicago Office. He's been of invaluable help to us all, though Bev wasn't coherent when he was with us, and, Molly, you were on the atoll. Russell, what the devil are you doing mixed up in this?"

"As I said, we should all sit down and discuss this."

"Stand down," Bev barked, a sad note in her voice. Guns lowered.

"We'll use the second-floor conference room. This way," Deanna said.

As Holly Ann entered and moved to the side of the Galactic Doll, Russell asked, "Another one?" Deanna nodded.

Everyone wanted to hear what was going on, so the room filled up. When Deanna closed the door, Russell began his explanation.

"Hello, everyone. I should be formal. I'm VP Russell Godwyn of Galactic Entertainment, Chicago Office. I hired a retired actress to play the role of a dying aunt of a Mr. Kyle Dorn, an electrical engineering senior at the University of Illinois Chicago Campus. She hired Molly to find Kyle Dorn. I had two purposes for doing this.

"First, as you know, GD dropped sponsorship of Molly and her PI business, and GEnt took it over. My bosses were doubtful that Molly could continue to be an effective PI. They viewed her physical limitations as inhibiting her ability to

270

perform such a role. So in part, this affair has been a test to see if GEnt should continue to sponsor her in this role. I'm pleased to say she passed with ease. I guarantee your PI sponsorship, Molly."

"Russell, you have no idea what this means to me. I'm back being able to help others and get justice. I'm alive, and I still have my reason for living. Not sure what I'm going to do if I run into Sixth Invaders. I can't hold my Glock, let alone fire it. Anyway, I've much to uncover. I aim to make the corporations pay for what they're doing to us."

Russell smiled and nodded. "Second, GEnt was *keenly* interested in locating Mr. Dorn. Why? As far as we can tell, all he's guilty of is posting critical comments about the way the corporations are running the world and the Sol Empire. GD's response was *total* overkill, considering his minor infraction. We might have expected GD to severely scold him or perhaps censor him until he graduated. Yet, they made Kyle public enemy number one. We asked ourselves why? And we got no answer.

"At GEnt, we continued to follow the story. Frankly, we were amazed at how resourceful the young man was in evading the GD goon squads. He vanished from sight and remained so for many weeks. I can tell you this much. We have several contacts within GD, who have told us GD has forgotten about him, so wherever you have Kyle, he is relatively safe.

"We would like to meet with him and try to find out just why GD reacted so unexpectedly. Did Kyle run off with a secret weapon, some classified documents, something? Hence, we hired Molly to locate him, which if her phone call to the actress was truthful, she has, though I don't see him here."

Holly Ann sighed. "I'm here. I know I don't look like me anymore. Kyle's got my body now and has become a fake Galactic Doll, so GD can't recognize me."

Russell stared at Holly Ann. He gasped. After swallowing and glancing around the room and seeing all the stern faces, he said, "What's going on?"

"Body swap," Holly Ann answered.

For an hour, she and Kyle retold what had happened to them.

She finished up. "So now Kyle looks like a Galactic Doll and has landed a math teacher's job, but they want her to look like one at work. I've no idea why GD was after me like they were."

"Is this body exchange thing even possible, Deanna?" Russell asked, rubbing his forehead with his handkerchief.

"We don't know how," she said, "but I've subtly tested Holly Ann. She has the knowledge one would expect of an EE graduate. Kyle doesn't, but Kyle's good with math or she wouldn't have gotten the teaching job. I know they tested her skills. I've some pull in Chicago, Russell. While I don't know how this machine of the two Chinese men works, it's clear they have switched bodies. On a cruder level," she glanced at Holly Ann and added, "no offense intended, but Holly Ann was born without arms and before this, has led an independent life in Flagstaff. Yet, if you watch Holly Ann today, as we have, you'll see she is often confused and seems to be adapting poorly to her lack of arms. This is unexpected from someone who has lived independently for twenty-one years. So on two levels, Russell, I have concluded that these two have indeed swapped bodies."

She continued, "It's incredibly confusing. So we agree with their methods. She's called Holly Ann, not Kyle. And Kyle answers to Kyle and not Holly Ann. The current situation is that Kyle looks like a Galactic Doll, but he is still a male. We've decided to call her a her, too. Less confusing."

Wiping his brow again, Russell said, "Got it. Anything we can do to lessen the confusion for these young people. Congratulations on getting married, too. As a GEnt vice-president, I can tell you Holly Ann is safe from the corporate system. She's married and that is most significant. That she's expecting their first child makes her doubly safe, so you can relax on her account. Kyle's side is much more problematical. The corporations are aware of the black market Galactic Doll fakes. It's only a matter of time before someone discovers that Kyle is a fake one.

"I agree with his, er her, choice. The Galactic Doll disguise is ingenious. I'm sure that'll never cross GD's mind. However, we need to ensure that she's not a fake one. Kyle, the test for a Galactic Doll is a specific gene that's responsible for the breast enhancement. On behalf of GEnt, I would like to offer you a free conversion to a Galactic Doll form, maintaining your maleness, of course. We can also lower your need to shave. Considering your current form, the genetic modification shouldn't take more than a few days. Once we do this, you'll look much as you do now, but a simple blood test will prove you're a legal Galactic Doll.

"If you agree to it, GEnt will sponsor you as a retired, married Galactic Doll. That will guarantee your immunity from GD hands."

He looked at Holly Ann. "Holly Ann, I'm sorry. I doubt there's much that modern medicine can do for your situation or that of Molly's. You've seen the horrible treatment our soldiers have had in the hands of the Sixth Invaders. Hank here is one example. Thus far, GMed hasn't been able to do much of anything for them. You have lots of company, and many are working on limb regrowth procedures, but I wouldn't hold your breath on those. Anyway, what do you say, Kyle?"

She replied, "Sure. I can't lose. These people trust Mr. Godwyn. Holly Ann, we have to start trusting someone, especially now. I'll do it."

Russell said, "Excellent. I'll arrange it for tonight. We need speed since you start teaching Monday. Holly Ann, I'll get back with you shortly."

He stepped out of the room, made several quick calls, before rejoining them.

"It's all set. Cook County General is expecting you as soon as you can get there. Holly Ann should accompany you. Deanna, you can send along your people too. Let's get these youngsters off on the right foot."

Deanna sent the two off in a company EMAC, but Bev and five security men went with them. Meanwhile, Russell stuck around to continue talking.

"By now, you have probably guessed there is organized resistance to the corporate heavy-handedness. Well, GEnt is behind it, leading the way. We're conducting investigations into illegal activities, but with this terrible war, our ability to bring about change is limited. When Kyle—I mean Holly Ann—returns, we need to talk more with her. There must be a reason GD went after him so hard. We have to discover why.

"If we haven't enough going on, this new body swapping thing has me frightened. What is to prevent someone from living forever? When their body gets old or ill, they swap into a new, younger body. Speculation: could someone swap bodies with our top corporate leaders? Like the Sixth Invaders? Lord, that scares the willies out of me."

Deanna responded. "Russell, we think alike. Count us in on your resistance movement though I suspect you have done so long ago. We'll help in any way we can. Bev is back with us. A miracle. She's working out every day, building her strength back up. Plus, she's working with Molly."

"Excellent. And yes, we're counting you among us."

"Might I ask a delicate question?" He nodded. "These spies you have—would they possibly be some of these new Galactic Dolls?"

Russell flushed. Deanna had her answer, but he verified it. "Yes, you are most observant, Mrs. Cartwright, most. GEnt sponsors the corporate Galactic Dolls. Mind you, only a few are spying for us. They are in delicate positions. They risk their lives, so we must keep this a secret. Other corporations are using some of them as their own spies. While only GEnt is allowed to sponsor the Galactic Dolls, there's nothing to prevent another corporation from subverting them for their own uses. Even so, we have a good idea which women are being so used, and there's not many. GD is the biggest offender."

Around nine o'clock, Bev and Holly Ann walked back into the conference room. Bev announced, "Kyle is in the genetic mutation coma now. She's due out of it around this time Sunday. Something about her body needing little re-arranging. So what have we missed?"

Russell said, "Good, good. It's as I thought. Well, Holly Ann, quite a bit. I've revealed that some of us in GEnt are the resistance you've been looking for. We're using a few Galactic Dolls to spy for us, but for heaven's sake, tell no one. They're risking all for us."

"Wow. Now that makes sense," Holly Ann said. "So others also see how messed up many corporations are?"

"Yes, quite true. In your case, we have to figure out why GD went after you as they did. You didn't have secret documents in your labs did you?"

Holly Ann chuckled. "Hardly."

"You or your classmates weren't working on a secret project in the lab?"

"Nope."

Russell scratched his head, frustrated.

Molly spoke up. "You want me to investigate?"

"No, that would be too obvious. It was risky having you track him down. Son, er, ma'am, there must have been something you were involved in that so got the attention of GD."

"Nothing at all. We were taking the last of our courses. We had Senior Lab."

"What's that?" Russell asked.

"Oh, that's the invention lab. Each of us has to create a final project from scratch. At the end of the semester, we make an official presentation of our work to the whole class. It's supposed to be similar to what we'll face in the real world."

His face tightened up. Russell asked, "What was your project about?"

Holly Ann laughed. "It was meant as a big joke on everyone. Students take this lab work too seriously, so I developed a special nano-circuit that used almost no power. Whenever anyone sent any kind of signal anywhere within its range, it would pick up the signal, convert it to a digital format, change it into the audio range, modulate it, and rebroadcast the original message in a voice that sounded like an antique cartoon character. Hilarious. My device is so small it fits inside a button on my shirt. It was just a joke, something to liven up the lab, and it worked too. But kids hated me for messing up their lab presentations. Like I said, it was nothing, but technically, it met the lab's requirements."

Deanna exclaimed, "Good god!"

Everyone turned to look at her, including Russell, who said, "This isn't a joke?"

"Lord no. Yes, while Kyle—er, Holly Ann—meant it as a joke, in fact, its uses are enormous. Change the voice, adjust its range, and you have a perfect spy device—one that isn't known or likely even detectable. Holly Ann, did you leave your device in the lab? Where are your plans for it? Russell, this has empire security etched all over it."

Holly Ann flushed. "The design is mostly in my head. I have part of the design on my laptop. The working prototype is inside my laptop. I was supposed to give my presentation a week after I fled Chicago. I was going to show it to everyone then. Why? Is it that important?"

In an unusual display of emotion, Russell exclaimed, "Son, this is very important."

Molly turned to Bev. "See. I told you there is always an underlying reason behind men's actions. Now we know. Can I have one of these spy toys? It would be handy."

Several laughed at her, but Russell said, "Deanna, I think it best if you work with Holly Ann here and see if you can get this device working. I don't have to tell you it should be considered top secret. I'll see you have all the funding you need on this one. Good Lord, the damage GD could have done using this device is staggering. No wonder they made Kyle public enemy number one."

Molly asked, "So why have they forgotten about him?"

Deanna said, "I'll see she has her own lab. We'll get on it tomorrow—Monday at the latest. She should be with Kyle when she wakes from the mutation coma."

Russell rose. "Well, I must be off. Ladies, gentlemen. Honestly, nothing this group does should surprise me any longer. You've quite a group, Deanna. Keep me posted."

No one noticed that no one answered Molly. Instead, Molly saw Bev had brought back two six-packs of ale. She shared them with Ted and Molly.

Sunday afternoon, Molly, Bev, and Holly Ann went to the hospital to wait on Kyle's recovery. The doctor met with Holly Ann.

"She's done just fine, a perfect Galactic Doll. We removed the voice box clamps that were raising her voice. The mutation handled that. Her legs have mutated. She must

276

always wear tall heels. We've lengthened her hair to the proper minimum length. Kyle will have to shave infrequently, compliments of the mutation. She should be coming around within the hour. Once she feels like it, she's free to leave. Any questions?"

Holly Ann had none, and the doctor departed. The three waited beside Kyle's bed. Within a half hour, her eyes fluttered, and she awakened.

"Holly Ann? Molly, Bev. Is it done? What do I look like? My voice sounds different, less strained."

"You're perfect. The doctor said so," Holly Ann explained.

A half-hour later, they had her on her feet and dressed.

"Boy, now I do have to wear these heels," Kyle declared. "Holly Ann, I'll keep an arm on you for balance."

Holly Ann giggled. "Sure. Funny I'm helping you for a change. Go figure."

Once they were back inside the secure skyscraper, Holly Ann told Kyle what they'd discovered about his lab project.

"Deanna is going to provide me with a lab so I can perfect this device of mine. I'm not sure I can do it. No hands."

"Use your toes, silly," Kyle said. "I know you can do it. Time, patience, and practice."

Molly said, "Stop and think how." Both women chuckled.

On Monday, Holly Ann walked Kyle to her high school, providing a steadying body to help him adjust to the tall heels. She was there to walk Kyle home when school let out. This soon became their special activity. Kyle's provisional status turned into a permanent position.

Vic Broquard

Part 5

Vic Broquard

Chapter 21 Inventions and Changes

As things settled down, Deanna held a group meeting. "There are many anomalies, discrepancies, weird things, injustices, and invaders happening without explanations. And there's the potential of Eve's therapy. We have here a fine collection of very bright minds and skills. We have relative safety and all the funds we need. Let's put our minds to work and see what we can come up with."

As usual, her ability to lead came to the fore, along with her unique design skills. Everyone pitched in, applying their own special skills to the multitude of questions and problems at hand.

Molly and Bev continued working together. Mornings, they exercised and trained. Afternoons, they continued their investigative work. In the evenings, Molly and Ted sat with Eve, Randi, and Celeste, sharing the new ideas they'd uncovered in their various studies that day, just as they had done on the atoll, though more and more, Molly felt out of place.

The autumn slipped by, and changes appeared, beginning with Deanna. In October, Jana was six months old. At first, Molly watched Deanna attempting to run her business as though nothing had changed, but between nursing, diapers, and lack of a good night's sleep, Deanna's position on motherhood altered.

One evening at the supper table, Deanna announced, "Look, I don't think it's healthy to raise a child inside a fifty-story skyscraper. Jana needs a yard and a real house. I can always find a nanny and take the MTES to work or even a shuttle craft. Of course, you're welcome to continue living here."

"Since no one is like trying to kill us any longer," Leslie said, "Felix and I like want to move out, too. We like want our own place. My folks' costume store like still hasn't sold. As some of you know, five apartments are like connected to it. We're like going to move in there. I like want to do more photo shoots, and we both like want to go clubbing. Plus, we're like thinking of starting our own family."

Janine said, "Hank and I will join them. We'll rent one of Leslie's apartments. I've gotten a receptionist job offer from Ace Temp Workers. We're thinking of starting our family, too. Like she said, this is a good time for the move. Besides, Leslie and I aren't smart like everyone else. But if you ever want help, just holler. Even for babysitting, Deanna."

Molly said, "Gosh. I'll miss you, but I know how you're feeling. Ted and I are thinking about starting a family, too. Let's stay in touch every day."

"Of course," Leslie said. "We'll like have you over for supper on the weekends."

***

The next day, Eve, Randi, and Celeste met to discuss what their plans should be. Eve said, "It's my goof with Molly. We haven't been able to restore Molly or Holly Ann's arms. What else can we try?"

Randi said, "You know on Kaseeb, we always consulted Ulima Al Atia. She came to this world on your ship, Karla—er, Celeste. We should ask her if she has any ideas."

"Great idea," Eve said. "Have to use telepathy. I lost touch when we jumped ship and took the baby bodies."

Hours later, Eve reported. "I found her. She's in Switzerland. Her suggestion is to have them mock up the missing limbs, have the new limb do some action, and then un-mock or vanish the limb, over and over, thousands of times. I'll run it on Molly tomorrow, and you can do it on Holly Ann."

For several days, Eve and Randi ran the process on the two women. While the two women felt better, were happier, and more alive, arms didn't magically appear.

Molly declared, "Look, Eve, I appreciate what you've done for me, but I'm just going to have to accept it. This is the way my body is. 'Stop and think how,' as Ted keeps telling me. Maybe you can help the other female soldiers like you did with Bev."

Randi and Eve agreed with her suggestion. Since those victims were still on Brussels, Tau Ceti, Deanna made flight arrangements for the two. In late October, the pair flew there to work their miracle therapy on the many victims housed in assisted living homes on Brussels.

Meanwhile, Galactic Medicine's VP, Joan Hammerschmidt, asked to meet with Celeste to discuss the miracle therapy. An excited Celeste joined them at supper.

"Guess what? I've accepted a commission from GMed to set up a therapy research center in St. Louis. I'm to train others in our therapy methods and to develop additional ones. And I get paid to do that. Incredible. GEnt has okayed it, so tomorrow I'm off to St. Louis. If any of you need me, just text. I can get back here in a few hours."

She received many congratulations, just as Randi and Eve had. The remaining sisters helped her pack and saw her off in an EMAC the next morning.

Thus, as the last week in October arrived, only Molly, Ted, Bev, Holly Ann, and Kyle still lived in the skyscraper, though Deanna was there during the daytime hours, along with hundreds of other workers. Holly Ann ducked into her lab just as soon as she returned from walking Kyle to school. Ted continued to study robotics, leaving Bev to aid Molly during the daytime hours. Bored, at night, Bev headed to one of several local bars, often returning drunk and late at night.

Nevertheless, Bev rose early Monday morning and insisted on doing their physical training before heading to the PI office.

When the pair arrived at Molly's office in the afternoon, Bev said, "So are we going to track down these Chinese men and their body swapping device?"

"Since they're in China, they're beyond our reach. Right now, I want to focus on the anomalies that have been piling up. We've been ignoring the war with the Sixth Invaders."

Bev flinched. "I'd just as soon forget about that. It was awful."

"Yeah, every day Hank reminds me the war exists. He's one brave man."

"Hey, Cool Head, you're one brave woman."

"No, I don't have a choice in the matter."

"Well, Hank doesn't either."

"Let's see what has been happening with the war on Brussels, Tau Ceti."

"Changing the topic, I see. Okay. Let's," Bev said.

The pair spent the afternoon reviewing GEnt footage of the war effort. It had been many weeks since Bev had been returned to them from the Sixth Invaders. During this time, the Sixth Invaders had spread out, taking over the fields just beyond the Rios River. For an invading army, they weren't in any rush to conquer land. A mile in eight months wasn't much of a thrust into enemy territory. But they did erect force fields over their encampments, preventing GD from bombing them or otherwise harming them from the air.

A month ago, GD had launched another offensive, intending to drive them back across that northern river. It had failed, though Deanna's portable EM pulse generators knocked out several of the dog whistles, saving the lives of several companies. Another company hadn't been so lucky. One hundred six men lost an arm and opposite leg, while thirteen women were turned into Galactic Dolls, their minds implanted just as Bev's had been.

As the two walked home via the MTES, Molly said, "So, the war's continuing, but the pace is nuts."

"Way damned slow. Why would anyone invade another world, deliver devastating blows, and yet take months to move a mile? No damn sense. Hey, I was good at soldiering. We're missing something about these Sixth Invaders, and it's gotta be huge. But what? Why hasn't the First Division counterattacked and wiped out that small invader ground force?"

Molly added, "And what do they look like? Why do they always wear full body armor? How did they get our Galactic Doll genetic mutation stuff—whatever it's called? What's behind their dog whistle thing? Why are they mutilating our male soldiers? Why not just kill them? Why are they turning our captured female soldiers into Galactic Dolls that are nuts? Are they cannibals? How did they get our latest healing technology—that nano stuff? What are their ultimate objectives? Do they have a version of this body swapping machine?"

Bev interjected, "Do ya think ya have enough questions?" Both laughed. "I can see why Deanna's so worried. What will happen if they invade Earth? I wonder how GD's recruitment program is doing. Rumor has it that they can't recruit anyone."

"Don't forget the whole injustice thing. Remember. Janine said the corporations are killing off anyone after they reach sixty. My money is on tons more injustices—many hidden. I'm glad Hank is researching them. Then, as you said, what do we do about the Chinese who have this body exchange machine? Don't forget Kyle or Holly Ann's spy device. Also, I want to find the assassin who killed our sisters. Oh, then, there's the unanswered question of who fired that missile at us on the atoll. Gosh, Bev, there's so much to figure out."

"And they all seem important."

As they reached the skyscraper home, Ted joined them. After kissing Molly, he said, "What all seems vital? I came in at the end. I say we have a picnic along the lake tomorrow."

Molly said, "Now that sounds like fun. It's been ages since I was on a picnic. Let's. Soon, it'll be too darn cold."

***

On Halloween morning and after Holly Ann returned from walking Kyle to high school, she stopped by Molly's room, where she and Bev were getting into their workout clothes. "Hi, Molly. Say, can you come to my lab for a few minutes? I want to talk with you, privately."

"Sure, Holly Ann. Gosh, you're starting to show."

Her waist-length, dark brown hair shone, and her light blue eyes were enchanting, but that she was expecting was obvious. In contrast, Molly's wavy raven hair reached just below her hips, but as usual, she had it draped over her shoulders hiding what wasn't there.

"Yes, entering the seventh month. We've picked out names. Carl or Anna, but if the sonograms are right, it's going to be Carl. Just three more months."

Molly followed Holly Ann into her suite, taking a seat opposite Holly Ann. "Thanks, Molly. Okay, as you know, I've gotten the nano spy device working for Deanna; she's handling its manufacturing. That's not why I asked you here today. I think I know how to do the body swap thing. I've figured out how it can be done, how the Wang brothers did it but I've told no one else because I wanted to talk to you first. I think I can swap you into another body. Do you want to do something like that? Should I even try to make such a machine?"

"Wow, Holly Ann. Incredible. You've figured it out already. But hey, I don't want to swap bodies. Look. I wouldn't wish my body off on anyone. I couldn't sleep if I did that. Besides, I'm in love with Ted, and he, me. I almost made a huge mistake with Frank, but I got a second chance with Ted, and, well, he's just the most incredible man ever. So no, I sure as heck don't want to swap bodies with anyone. That would jeopardize our marriage. What about you and Kyle? Do you two want to swap back? If so, you should do it if it's safe."

Holly Ann flushed. "We would have jumped at such a chance last summer, but now, no way. Kyle has her lifelong wish to teach math at a high school. As much as I might wish to be normal again, I'd never do that to her. I love Kyle too much to swap her back into this body, depriving her of her chance to teach. Never. You should see her face when she walks out of the school in the afternoons. It's as though she's in heaven. I'll never take that from her, not ever. Somehow, I'll muddle along as you and I are doing. It's a royal pain, but I'm still being slightly productive, thanks to Deanna's lab. But I'll admit I'm getting a little worried about how I'm supposed to handle a baby and being a mother."

Molly grinned. "You'll do fine, Holly Ann. Besides, there are lots of arms around here to help out."

"True. But we need our independence, don't we?"

"Absolutely."

"All right. Should I proceed with its development at all? If you and I don't want to swap bodies, then do I need to go on with my development?"

"Now that's a damn good question. Look, those Chinese men have a device that works. You and Kyle are proof. Who knows what uses they'll put the machine to? I think the safest bet is to verify the technology works and then make it widely available and cheap. That way, no one person can hog it and use it for their own nefarious purposes like an unlimited weapon."

Holly Ann frowned but brightened up. "I see your point. But if it's available, what's to keep people from misusing it?"

"Nothing at all. At one time or another, I bet every invention has been subject to misuse. Ask Hank about that; he's the history buff. The main thing is to make it available so these Chinese men can't claim a monopoly on it, especially if someone sees it as a way to become immortal by swapping into a new body when theirs gets old.

"Besides, I don't trust those two Chinese men. What they did with you and Kyle is criminal. What else do they have in mind? Fair scares me to think about that. No, the route to safety is to make it widely available and cheap." Molly sighed. "But someone's likely to misuse it. What we need is a medical breakthrough that regrows arms."

Holly Ann laughed. "This body never had them. When I entered college, if I would have known I'd be like this four years later, I might have gone into medical research instead of EE."

Both women laughed. "I bet you wouldn't have. You're too into all things electronic."

That brought a big smile to Holly Ann's face. "You got me on that one. Okay, I'll get to work on it. Thanks for being so frank with me."

"Any time. You and I need to stick together. I won't say anything about this until you tell everyone else. Okay?"

She agreed and Molly left, joining Bev for their morning workout.

***

Mid-November, Holly Ann again asked Molly to meet with her after breakfast. "Oh, bring Bev with you. Meet in my lab, please."

Glancing at each other, Molly and Bev shrugged their shoulders and headed for the lab down on the forty-fifth floor.

"What's this all about?" Bev asked while the pair waited for Holy Ann to get here.

"No idea, but with Holly Ann, it's probably important."

"Hi. Sorry that I'm so slow," said Holly Ann.

The long, brown haired woman waddled up to them.

Bev opened the lab door for them.

"Okay. I need Bev for this test, while Molly and I will be the safety crew, just in case. You see, I believe I've also discovered how the Sixth Invaders' dog whistle thing works. I found it while working on my version of the body exchange machine. I haven't told anyone but Molly about it, but I'll make the big announcement at supper tonight."

"Way to go, Holly Ann," Bev said. "So how does it work?"

"I've been playing with sound frequencies as part of my experimental work. I've created this special generator that will sweep upwards in frequencies like you said the dog whistle does. The frequencies end up in the kilo-yottahertz range, the key frequencies for body swapping and other effects."

Bev rolled her eyes. "Yeah, whatever range." Molly smiled.

"So Bev, with your permission, I'll test it on you. What we want to know is this what you can recall experiencing? As a safety factor, Molly and I will don headphones that'll block most of the sound. If either of us thinks you're in any trouble, we'll immediately hit this kill switch. If you experience any trouble, just nod or raise your hand; we'll hit the kill switch."

Bev grimaced. "Okay. But I sure don't want to end up like I was when the invaders were done with me."

"I won't let that happen to you. You've my word on it."

"All right. Let's see if it works," the ex-army soldier said. She gripped her chair tightly and clenched her teeth, expecting something painful.

Holly Ann flipped the switch and activated the programmed sequence. Initially, Molly felt low-frequency vibrations, much like bass at the rock concert that Frank had forced her to attend. As the frequency rose, the tactile sensation vanished, though she briefly heard faint, audible sounds from the edges of the sound-dampening earphones. She kept her eyes focused on her sister, watching her facial expressions.

At first, Bev smiled and flashed them a thumbs-up sign, which she took to mean this was what she'd heard when she had fallen victim to the Sixth Invader's dog whistle device. The smile vanished, replaced by a rather bored look. Then Bev's eyes had a blank or dazed look, and Holly Ann ended the program, noticing one dial that marked the highest frequency used during the sweep.

When the machine stopped, both women removed their earphones and looked at Bev, who appeared to be in a trance. Molly and Holly Ann had enough therapy sessions from Eve and Randi to know they shouldn't say anything at all but wait in silence for Bev to rejoin them. Molly's stomach tightened into knots. Had they somehow harmed Bev? She saw Holly Ann also grimacing.

Five long minutes passed before Bev shook her head, rubbed her hands across her face, and then slapped her cheeks.

"Wow! That was it. It started out low like that and swept upwards until we couldn't hear it any longer. Gave me a false sense of security—both then and now. Then, it came— that incredibly pure white energy thing, so beautiful, so perfect, so indescribable. I never wanted it to end, but I guess it did. How long was I out?"

Holly Ann giggled. "Five minutes. You gave us both a scare. Wow. I've discovered the secret of the dog whistle weapon. I bet if we gave you orders to follow while you were knocked out, you'd carry them out like a slave. Incredible."

"Not so incredible when you are on the receiving end," Bev said. "Now find a way to defeat this machine of yours."

Molly asked, "So this is how the machines swap bodies?"

"Yes. Have two separate generators, each attached to different heads. Raise the frequency to the right level where both are seeing the aesthetic, white waves. Then, use a stereo effect, making it seem as though each one is moved into the other body, and allow the frequencies to lower.

"Bev, when the Sixth Invaders had you knocked out by these waves, they used it to implant a behavior pattern."

Bev flinched. "Yeah, and one that can only be undone by Eve and Randi's special therapy sessions. Going through that was a bitch."

That evening over supper, Holly Ann explained what

she'd discovered, backed up by Bev's testimony. Further, the group set up a hyperspace relay teleconference with Eve and Randi so they could hear this news.

Eve said, "Incredible, Holly Ann, but once again, we have technology advancing far beyond the knowledge and abilities of the spiritual beings."

Deanna backed Holly Ann. "While that's true, it's vital that her discoveries become widely known. We can hope others will find ways to defeat this stuff. It's like hypnotism, isn't it?"

"Hardly," Eve said. "Hypnotism is relatively harmless. Once you show the person what the 'gimmick' was, the person regains control. With the implants that Bev and the others received while knocked out by these aesthetic waves, there's no way to undo it, short of our therapy. It's damned near permanent."

Randi said, "But she's got a point, Eve. The more this technology is known and spread, the greater the chance it won't be used and that others will help uncover other ways and means of defeating such brainwashing effects. Plus, I doubt many people swap bodies."

Deanna said, "Okay then. Holly Ann, develop two versions. Make one a generator anyone can use to put someone into a trance. I hope others can use it to find a way to defeat or, at least, neutralize its effects on people. Make another dual version that can swap bodies. This should fall under the purview of GMed, but I don't trust any corporation at the moment with the possible exception of GEnt."

Molly wondered how soon others would misuse these inventions.

***

Mid-December, Christmas break began for Kyle. The Principal at Cook County Elite High School sent her home with a startling graph. Over supper, she showed it to Ted, Molly, Bev, and Holly Ann. Deanna saw it the next morning.

Kyle said, "I can't believe this. Look at the trend."

The graph showed the number of high school senior girls who requested the Galactic Doll mutation upon graduation each year. Twenty years ago, none had it done.

"It's an exponential curve."

"What's that mean?" Molly asked. High school math wasn't her forte.

"It means this year, we can expect nearly every graduating girl to get the Galactic Doll mutation. I checked into it. Only a handful of girls are going into that line of work. Some are being sponsored to attend college. Others are going into occupational training schools, such as nursing, while many are being hired as normal workers—even sales clerks."

Molly laughed. "Okay. So what's that mean? Have the girls gone crazy or something?"

Kyle said, "At first, I thought it was peer pressure. I checked, and it's the same with other high schools. Soon, all young women will be Galactic Dolls, but only a few are working as corporate Dolls. Maybe it's a beauty thing. Maybe they think guys are attracted to Galactic Dolls."

Holly Ann laughed. "We are."

Ted grinned. "She's got a point. You look smashing, Kyle. I think we should look into this further. Someone or something has convinced these young adults that the best way to survive or get ahead is to look like a Galactic Doll."

Bev roared. "Ha. I'd like to see a Galactic Doll being a soldier or even a security guard. Bet the army doesn't have them. Bet you won't find them in any corporation's security unit."

"Could be their mascots." Ted chuckled.

Molly said, "Ted, this is serious. What's happening to our common sense? Have the high school girls gone bonkers on us? I hated having monster boobs. Deanna felt humiliated and embarrassed. I guess Leslie didn't mind. Still, you know what I mean, guys."

Kyle suggested, "Maybe peer pressure. We need to look into this mess tomorrow."

"Bev and I'll get on it after our workout."

The next morning Deanna said she'd ask GEnt about it, and Russell dropped by to explain.

Once settled in the conference room, Deanna said, "So Russell, what's this all about? Kyle came home with a startling graph."

She slid it across the table to him. Molly, Bev, Ted, Kyle, and Holly Ann waited for his answer. Molly watched his facial reactions. His raised eyebrows and the lifted corners of his mouth suggested he knew about it.

"Well, this is the graph GEnt has suggested the various high school principals create and send home with their teachers. The goal is to bring teachers up to speed on recent developments. GEnt is still in control over this genetic modification, though GMed performs it.

"What began as a unique career path some years ago has taken on a life of its own. An exponential growth rate among graduating seniors. We've surveyed the seniors and found a mixed bag of reasons. Some want it so they look more attractive. Others want it so they can land the husband of their dreams, while many believe it will help them get and keep the job of their choice. A few cite peer pressure—that everyone's doing it. There's no single overriding reason.

"In contrast, except for women who want a career change, there have been few adult women who have asked for this genetic modification. But even that is changing. Already this year, adult women modifications are increasing rapidly. What bothers me and many others in GEnt, is the future. If this continues, all women in the next generation will be Galactic Dolls."

Molly noticed Deanna grimacing. The CEO said, "Russell, I have no problem hiring women who have had this mutation, as long as they're able to do their job. I can't forget what GD demanded of us last year, turning us all into Galactic Dolls. If so many are having it done, what about the rest of us older women?"

Russell ran his hands over his face, pausing before replying. Molly thought perhaps he was stalling, working out a way to say something. He sighed.

"I shouldn't be telling you this, Deanna. You didn't hear this from me. Tomorrow night, GD CEO Hardy's holding a press conference on this very point. We've seen a rough draft of his speech. He'll be citing these statistics and urging all women to have it done as a Christmas present to themselves or their husbands. GEnt has been ordered to gear up for a big rush, as has GMed."

"Good lord! Are they going to force all women to have it?" Deanna asked.

"The draft didn't say that. Between us, I wouldn't be surprised if he did."

Molly cursed, and Deanna said, "Someone should give Hardy that genetic mutation. See how he likes it."

Russell's stern countenance shattered. He laughed heartily. "I agree. That would prove most interesting."

"No good can come of this," Molly said.

With that sobering thought, the meeting ended. Bev and Molly changed clothes and began their late morning jog.

Bev asked, "Is there any way we can find out how this ridiculous Galactic Doll thing got started? I mean in such a big way. That graph showed that a few years ago, only a few had it done. Some pervert must have pushed it. You know—made it the popular thing to do."

Molly didn't answer right away. "Good question, Bev. I've no idea how we could uncover that. Maybe we could find someone in GEnt who knows. But you know, I'm starting to see what Eve means."

"'Bout what?"

"Like Eve says, our world has incredible technologies, but we know next to nothing about ourselves—spiritual beings. And there's almost no humanity left in our world."

That evening, everyone gathered around a big screen to hear CEO Hardy's press conference. Deanna stuck around to hear it before heading home to her nanny and daughter. Molly thought Hardy had an imposing countenance on his squarish face and wasn't handsome. As usual, be began with his trademark left-hand salute, if that's what it was—arm and hand parallel to the ground with his little finger pointing down. It still looked weird to Kyle or rather Holly Ann.

"My fellow Sol Empire citizens and Earthlings, tonight I am here to celebrate the direction our young high school senior women are taking. Nearly unanimous. That's how dozens of high school principals have described it. All want to be genetically modified into gorgeous Galactic Dolls, who used to only work for corporate executives.

"Why should their beauty be monopolized by these executives? The young women of Earth have spoken. Their message is loud and clear. They all want the benefits of looking fabulous. I believe that within one generation, all women will be Galactic Dolls, the epitome of feminine beauty, grace, and poise.

"Yes, Galactic Entertainment still retains the obligation to okay each such request. But I've ordered a change in corporate sponsorship of Galactic Dolls. All corporations will sponsor Galactic Dolls in all professions. Expect to see these gorgeous women as your salesperson, your clerk, your nurse, your pharmacist. All professions are open to them, as long as they can do the work.

"In light of the desires of our young seniors worldwide, tonight, I've signed Executive Order 1201. It states that all women above the age of eighteen are highly encouraged to become Galactic Dolls if they aren't one already. Contact your GEnt representative and get your approval to become a gorgeous Galactic Doll. GMed has geared up to handle you. Give our world a Christmas present this year. Become a beautiful Galactic Doll.

"Some women may not wish to become a wonderful Galactic Doll. EO 1201 also states you must contact your GEnt representative and get their approval to opt out of this program. I speak for everyone when I say the world wants and appreciates the beauty of a Galactic Doll.

"Finally, tonight, I am proud to present the Distinguished Service Award to two doctors, who have dedicated their lives to furthering our skills with genetic modification and nanoparticle healing methods. If it weren't for these two doctors, we wouldn't have any Galactic Dolls. Their legacy is having raised feminine beauty to new heights. In fact, today, the world is using their newest Galactic Doll mutation formulation, which I'm told works much better than their original formula."

The camera panned over to the doctors, Nelson and Janet Padella. Several curses echoed how Molly felt.

She said, "I can't believe this."

"Look. Look at their hands," Ted said.

Hardy continued speaking. "They are retiring today. Old age claims us all. Arthritis can be a crippler."

Meanwhile, an aide hung a medallion around each doctor's neck and handed them the award, but their hands were curled up into tight balls. Neither could open them to grasp the award, but pressed their arms together around it. In the background, a machine made loud clapping noises.

"Wow, what happened to their hands? Can't they move them?" asked Holly Ann.

"Thank you and good night."

He took no questions, and Deanna turned off the comm center. A torrent of curses echoed around the room.

Molly said, "I bet Eve did something with the gold anchor ball thingies that defined their hands. Still, they're criminals, and they get an award for it. Crap."

"True, but they can't do much of anything any longer," Deanna said. "Odds are they're in an assisted living home and will be dead soon. Still, the damage they've done—I wonder if there really is karma."

Chapter 22 Plots

In the year 2320—or thirty years before Molly was abducted—a group of Sixth Invader scouting warships encountered the outer fringes of the Sol Empire. A few ships attacked several Sol Empire cruisers, damaging them. These initial attacks tested the state of this new empire. With strength data gathered, the warships withdrew, having done their job of contacting a new space-faring civilization. They moved on into a different section of space looking for other such systems to be conquered, while the Sixth Invaders then sent in their second wave, in this case, Recon Force 125, led by Commander R'Ina.

Commander R'Ina stood six-six. Her well-muscled, gray-skinned body demanded the respect of her troops. Her hair was rather short and jet black, also the color of her eyes. By Earth standards, her bosom was gigantic, each breast the size and shape of a soccer ball. Each hand had six fingers, long and dexterous. She was twenty-five and one of the youngest recon commanders of the Sixth Invaders. Commander R'Ina had a dynamic and compelling charisma. No one dared doubt her decisions. She had already dispatched one who had. She was unattached in 2320 and had no marriage prospects yet, but considering those of her race tended to live around two hundred Earth years, this wasn't a problem for her.

In the Sixth Invader civilization, females ran and controlled everything, while the males nurtured and educated their children, took care of their homes, and handled most domestic duties. Their males also sported soccer ball sized bosoms for three reasons. First, primary nursing duties fell to the males. Second, their children had voracious appetites while infants. Third, the females usually had twins more often than single births, though they helped their mates with the needed breastfeeding.

Thirty personnel comprised Recon Force 125, of which twenty were female—the actual soldiers and engineers. The ten males were their domestic staff and science officers.

Commander R'Ina's Chief Science Officer was G'Karn, also twenty-five, slightly shorter, and recognized as the most likely male to catch Commander R'Ina's fancy. Like all Sixth Invaders, his skin was gray, his eyes and hair, jet black. Like all males, his hair was straight, thick, and long, touching his hips. He wore a light colored dress, often favoring a light yellow that blended with his skin color. The females wore space fleet uniforms, consisting of black shirts, pants, and knee-high boots. Star patches on their collars differentiated their various ranks in the service.

A recon force was always armed with the latest electronics and technology. Their giant cruiser could operate in stealth mode, invisible to more primitive societies, such as the Sol Empire. Each soldier was equipped with a ULTU—a Universal Language Translator Unit—and a Morph Unit, which would alter their apparent physical appearance to the average of the local humanoids around them. The Morph Units allowed them to intermingle undetected in local populations. They also had personal invisibility devices.

Six months after their arrival on the edge of the Sol Empire and after extensive monitoring of communications, Commander R'Ina sized up the situation with her crew.

"This Sol Empire is truly weak, a fledgling space-faring people, prime for our takeover. The empire is controlled from a central planet called Earth, the third planet from the star they call Sol. It's up on your monitors now. That's our destination. As usual, you may expect we'll be on that world for many years. Our job is to gather all the intelligence High Command will need to conquer this empire."

Captain L'Grina, her pilot, grumbled, "And when might that be?"

Commander R'Ina glared at her. "One or two decades, Captain. I know you'll be bored, so I'll assign you other duties while we're landed. Now then, already we have learned much. Their entire society is completely *backward*. Honestly, I can't believe the human females have allowed such backwardness to persist, but they have. In this empire, men and women have reversed their roles. Men run most everything."

She had to pause. Raucous laughter swept over the

entire cruiser. Captain L'Grina laughed so hard that she doubled over, unable to stop. After a time, she blurted, "So that's what Chief Science Officer G'Karn found so funny last week."

The Commander nodded, but several minutes passed before she could regain control of her briefing. Even she chuckled.

She said, "Giant corporations control this empire, apparently from Earth. Our first task will be to identify these corporations and those who are actually running this empire. We will stay cloaked. We don't want these people to know we're on their base world. Some of our warships will occasionally engage their merchant ships out on the fringes of this empire, giving us time to infiltrate them.

"Chief Science Officer G'Karn will make our official log entries. Your first entry should be along these lines." She outlined what she had said. "Technology Classification Level: Space-faring-one, just able to travel via Hyperspace. Conclusion: Conquer Earth and the Sol Empire is ours."

"Yes, Commander," G'Karn said. He made the entry.

"You know," Commander R'Ina said, "This Sol Empire is not only backward but will be so easy to conquer that we—yes, we—a mere recon force, can conquer it." With this declaration, both women extended their left hands outward parallel to the ground and extended their little finger straight down, their official Sixth Invader salute.

Many cheers erupted. No recon force had ever done this before. If they succeeded, these twenty soldiers would become famous among all Sixth Invaders. But G'Karn thought she had delusions of grandeur.

***

One month later, Commander R'Ina ordered their cruiser to land in a remote area in western Illinois. They kept the ship cloaked, and she stationed armed guards around the ship twenty-four/seven. Via their small shuttles, which also used their stealth construction, spy groups fanned out over Earth. Slowly, Commander R'Ina received data allowing her to make key decisions.

"My goodness, G'Karn, this planet is insane. Males run

298

everything that's critical or vital. Females frequently stay home and raise their children. Can you believe that?"

G'Karn shook his head. "I can't believe how these Earthlings are wasting all their most valuable talent. Forcing men to do the work of a woman—I agree, this civilization is goofy."

"Glad you see that, too. We've identified fifteen major galactic-wide corporations, but only one has a female in charge, and she's inconsequential. Worse, few females hold high positions within these corporations. Totally nuts."

He said, "Maybe not totally insane. Galactic Expansion controls all the other corporations though Galactic Defense is second in control. That makes sense. An empire must focus on expanding its worlds or succumb. No company can continue for long if they are staying the same size or shrinking. At least, that's what our financial planners say."

Commander R'Ina sighed. "All right. I'll give you that point. These nutty men are doing that right."

More field messages arrived, and G'Karn routed them to their big screen display.

"Commander, this is interesting—just what you need. The Sol Empire corporations use a hierarchy. Your scouts report that local corporations control only a zone on a planet, often a large city. Each world has a worldwide corporation that controls all its locals. Earth's locals are controlled by those in Moscow. The many worldwide corporations are then controlled by the Sol Empire corporations based in Chicago."

"Excellent. Now, we're getting somewhere."

Commander R'Ina made Chicago their base of clandestine operations. She ordered most all her operatives into the large city. Once there, she issued more orders.

"Chief Science Officer G'Karn, I want you to infiltrate their Galactic Medicine corporation. Find out where this civilization is on genetic modifications and such things. Are they able to engineer body modifications?"

"Yes, Commander."

Activating his disguise machine, he began exploring Chicago and its people, as well as visiting Galactic Medicine's laboratories. In less than a week, he reported back to

Commander R'Ina.

"Pathetic. They've just perfected human cloning. That's how far behind they are. Not a hint of Fetal Regeneration Stimulus. Barely scratching the surface on biological nanoparticle procedures. Grim."

"Hum," the Commander said. She puckered her lips and frowned. "Well, that puts a damper on things. No, wait. I want you to give them some hints on Fetal Regeneration Stimulus as a way to bring about genetic modifications to their bodies. Heck, while you're at it, get them up to speed on the use of gold and silver nanoparticles. Especially for healing."

"Aye, aye, Commander. I've isolated the two top medical personnel—the ones who have perfected human cloning, which, as I understand, is an outlawed procedure in their society."

She laughed. "Chief Science Officer G'Karn, you almost have the mind of a female." Commander R'Ina meant that as a high compliment. He flushed. "If these two will perform illegal procedures, then they are very likely to do so with a real genetic mutation processes. Just what we'll need, if we're ever to correct this fouled up society. So who are these two people?"

"Doctor Nelson Padella and his wife, Doctor Janet Padella. I'll get on it right away. I'm sure if I show them the procedures and methods and then vanish, they'll make use of them as if they had invented them. Heck, we won't even have to use our Transference Machines on these people."

"Excellent, G'Karn. See to it." *I best not tell him we've accidentally lost or misplaced one of our Transference Machines over in a country called China. It'll probably amount to nothing since these Earthlings are so dumb.*

The next day, disguised as a human intern named Dr. Kane, G'Karn began educating the two doctors, the best potential people to make use of genetic modification techniques and nanoparticle methods. First, he left a dissertation on the use and construction of the Fetal Regeneration Stimulus on his computerized workstation, where the two doctors could see it. A week later, he left similar documents up on his holographic display. These outlined the methods of using gold nanoparticles to hold the dormant potential genetic modifications and the Fetal Regeneration Stimulus, which would cause the body to rebuild itself. Via IR or infrared activation beams, the gold nanoparticles would release their particles into the human's body, and Fetal Regeneration Stimulus would mutate that body according to the encapsulated genetic specifications.

The following week, he left similar documents up on his display. This time, he took pity on the humans, who knew so little about this vital technology. Why? At the hospitals, medical centers, and even the research labs, he saw doctors crudely amputating appendages that had been damaged in construction accidents. This time, the documents outlined how to use silver compound nanoparticles and the graphene mesh for extremely rapid healing.

In each case, he left the documents partially completed, as if Dr. Kane was still developing them. What he left out of each document were rather trivial details, which he presumed the Padellas could provide. Then, he pretended to be transferred to another facility. Later, he returned in his stealth suit, observed the pair of doctors, and smiled when he heard them discussing how they believed they were inventing these vital and new techniques.

Meanwhile, Commander R'Ina issued another order. "Captain L'Grina, since you have little to do now we're stationary here in Chicago, I want you to take a stealth shuttle to this China place and see if you can locate our missing Transference Machine. Not a word of this to the science team. Report privately to me."

She saluted, grinned, and left, excited to have something to do. A week later, Captain L'Grina reported back.

"Commander, I've recovered the unit, but two Chinese men found it first. I'm sure they have figured out what it does. I stole our unit back from them, but they've begun building their own copy of it. What should I do? Kill them? Blow up their lab?"

Commander R'Ina rubbed her face before answering. "Males, you say?"

"Aye."

"Well, no harm done, since they're merely males. Leave

them alone. They aren't connected to the ruling corporations. Just return our machine to the cruiser. We'll pretend it was never lost. Besides, these Earthlings wouldn't have the slightest idea how to use them."

***

Commander R'Ina spent a year gathering statistics on the Earthlings and studying their operations, particularly those who ran the galactic-wide corporations. Satisfied that she understood as much as possible without being within those organizations, she held another planning meeting with her key officers, her Chief Science Officer, and his two assistants.

She began the conference. "The statistical results are in, and frankly, I'm appalled at the treatment of females in this society. G'Karn, I want you to develop a genetic mutation sequence for these Earth females. I want them to have ideal bodies, ideal physical forms, which in some cases will result in far healthier bodies. I'm code-naming this Project Galactic Doll, a reference to one of their popular girl dolls. For Dingle's sake, give them proper, optimum breasts. Also, I'm intrigued by their unusual fetish high heels. Find a way to include them in the genetic mutations. If Earth women are ever going to rise to their full potential, we'll have to give them a strong push."

"Aye, Commander. We'll get to work on it," G'Karn said. He gave her a pleased look. "I can't believe how terrible these Earth men treat their females. It's disgusting."

Captain L'Grina said, "Actually, G'Karn, it's revolting. We should do something about it. You heard our Commander." He nodded to her.

Commander R'Ina smiled and continued. "Next, we will infiltrate two of their corporations, namely Galactic Expansion and Galactic Defense. Ready the Transference Machines. I'll take over Galactic Expansion's CEO Armstrong, while Captain L'Grina will take over Galactic Defense's CEO Hardy."

Captain L'Grina's face twisted as though she'd swallowed something foul. "Oh, for Dingle's sake. We're going to be in male bodies?"

"It can't be helped, Captain. Yes, it will be hideous for us. So I've decided that each night, we'll pop back to our bodies and have a good round of sex. G'Karn, I'm choosing

302

you. When I pop back, pull your panties down and your dress up. You've got to keep me sane. Captain, you can choose any other male to help you keep your sanity."

He flushed, but could do nothing about her choice. A Chief Science Officer had almost no power beyond science matters.

G'Karn readied two prison cells on board one of their shuttles. At night and invisible, he entered each CEO's office, planting a concealed remote emitter from a Transference Machine over their chairs. He also planted spy devices. The next morning, Captain L'Grina and her team hijacked two workers, drugged them, and put them into the shuttle prison cells. G'Karn hooked their bodies up to the Transference Machines and to a pair of medical machines that would keep both men unconscious, but alive.

His two assistants sat before spy monitors, observing the two CEO men. With all ready, via his wrist device, he signaled both Captain L'Grina and Commander R'Ina, who joined the small group in the shuttle, parked on the roof of an abandoned warehouse close to the skyscraper section of Chicago.

G'Karn affixed the helmets to each woman's head, making sure the other leads went to the device in the ceilings above the CEO men. If he switched them into the wrong CEO's body, he'd be in deep trouble. Thus, he moved slowly, double-checking each action.

"Oh, get on with it," Commander R'Ina barked.

He powered up her unit first. A powerful aesthetic wave of the whitest energy flooded her being and mind. Although she couldn't see or perceive anything other than this incredibly beautiful, pure light, she sensed that she was moving—perhaps. When the energy faded out, she was sitting in a chair behind a huge desk in a strange office on the one hundredth floor of the Galactic Expansion corporation. She cringed as she sensed the body of CEO Armstrong.

"For Dingle's sake, this is hideous but necessary," she complained, startled by her new bass voice.

"Copy that," she heard via the spy device. One of her subordinates manned the post, ready to give her whatever help was needed. Commander R'Ina flushed.

A minute later, Captain L'Grina occupied GD CEO Hardy's body. Her distaste was far worse than her commander's was.

Each of the replaced men found themselves jammed into an unconscious male body, along with that body's original owner. None of it made the slightest sense to either man, and both were content to stay unconscious, believing they were sleeping. Neither had any idea they would remain so for decades. Meanwhile, the two junior officers placed the women's bodies on two cots, where they would rest until G'Karn transferred them back for a brief period each evening.

That night, he did so. Commander R'Ina returned to her own body while that of CEO Armstrong slept in his office chair.

She barked, "Panties down; dress up! For Dingle's sake, that was awful." She dropped her pants as fast as she could. G'Karn had no choice but to salute and obey.

Later, she briefed her troops on what she'd learned. Then, he transferred her back into the CEO's body. Thus began a nightly ritual for the commander and captain though eventually they had to "go home" and deal with the men's wives and families.

***

As the days passed, Commander R'Ina devised a plan of action, one that would enable them to take over the Sol Empire.

"Look, we need to completely discredit the male leaders of these corporations. And I know a way we can do just that. G'Karn, we'll need to take over the CEO of Galactic Robotics. Put together a team that can build robot soldiers that can be controlled remotely from here. If I'm right, we can make the credibility of the male leaders of these corporations effectively zero."

"That will take time to do," Chief Science Officer G'Karn said.

"We've plenty of time. Make it happen."

"Aye, sir. But what about modifications to male bodies?" he asked.

304

"Nothing for now. If we do this right, our Recon Force 125 will conquer this Sol Empire!"

Everyone cheered and saluted with their left hands.

***

Commander R'Ina's plans continued to move forward, albeit at a slower pace than she might have desired. At random times, Sixth Invader warships appeared in Sol Empire space and attacked a few merchant ships before vanishing. These attacks lent credence to the notion that the empire was under attack.

About five years before Molly's abduction, that is, in 2345, G'Karn's crude robots were nearing completion. At a night meeting, Commander R'Ina issued more orders.

She said, "Look, we need to develop an aesthetic wave knock-out machine for use on the battlefield. This is critical to our success at discrediting the males of Earth. We need to administer severe shocks to their soldiers during the battles—at least some of them. Female soldiers are to be genetically modified into Galactic Dolls, which should be their proper body form, anyway. Since they're being soldiers, we will need to scare other females from joining the army, so after genetically modifying them, let's implant them to think of nothing but demanding intercourse several times a day.

"We need to frighten their males from signing up to be a soldier, so let's amputate male soldiers' limbs—an arm and leg. They still need to be mobile and not helpless. The goal: strike terror in the minds of enemy soldiers, so corporations will find it next to impossible to recruit more soldiers and so their existing soldiers will fear the Sixth Invaders."

Captain L'Grina said, "Hey, since the army has streaming video cameras on their officers, why not make them think the robot soldiers are cannibals? As you amputate appendages, make it seem that we're cooking and eating them. That should really shock their soldiers, males and females alike."

Chief Science Officer G'Karn grimaced. "I wish to go on record opposed to this brutal treatment of these humans."

The female soldiers laughed.

Commander R'Ina said, "Noted. You can put that in your log, G'Karn. That's why you aren't the commander or even a soldier."

Again, the women laughed heartily.

She continued, "Another thing, there is an inordinate amount of corporate corruption. It's rampant in the two we're monitoring. It's almost unbelievable what these men do. There probably isn't an honest male in any of these corporations. We must plan for that, too."

"What about the LDF divisions?" asked Captain L'Grina.

"What are those?" asked G'Karn.

The Commander explained, "Local Defense Force army divisions. Earth has nine hundred eighty-two of them. The numbers vary world to world. These are part-time soldiers, charged with local defense. They also respond to emergency situations, particularly bad weather-related events. Sometimes, they are used to keep law and order, but the last time they were used for that was a century ago. They are definitely second-rate soldiers, of no consequence to us.

"The Sol Empire has never faced any outside threat. They only have one ground army, the First Infantry Division, which we will deploy to Brussels, Tau Ceti when we unleash our disguised robot ground attack there. You pick a location, G'Karn."

"Aye, sir." His left hand shot out horizontally in a salute.

The meeting ended. However, after studying that world, he chose to invade in the far north of North Continent, where there were very few civilians, but instead largely giant, automated farmsteads. Again, he felt sympathy for the humans they were about to mutilate or kill. The more he got the devices prepared for the commander's soldiers, the guiltier he felt. Again, he logged a protest in their official log, though no one was likely to see it until they returned to home world, and he had no idea when that might be.

***

November 2351, Captain L'Grina, who occupied Galactic Defense CEO Hardy's body, met with Commander R'Ina, who occupied Galactic Expansion CEO Armstrong's body. They used their human names in case someone overheard them.

Mr. Hardy said, "Mr. Armstrong, we've run into unexpected problems with our implanting of captured female soldiers on Brussels, Tau Ceti—shocking actually."

"Oh, you mean the implanted Galactic Sex Dolls."

"Right. Something has gone wrong. Someone is undoing our implants."

"That's not possible, not even for us. I monitored the results on many females taken to assisted living homes on Brussels," Mr. Armstrong said. "They were perfect implants."

"Well, I couldn't believe it either, so I checked further. It seems one of those pesky female clones, a Beverly Blossom Blythe, was brought back to Chicago by her fellow clones. Her body is no longer a Galactic Doll, but I suspect that bad batch of mutation agents on Brussels was the culprit, since her fellow clone bodies have also lost their Galactic Doll appearance. But Beverly's mind is normal. From all reports, she is back to her usual self. I've sent out spies to the bars she frequents at night. By all reports, all traces of our implant are gone."

"What? How can that be?"

"It's worse. I checked with our agents on Brussels. All the other implanted female soldiers are also cured. No traces of their implanted behavior remain. Two those female clones may have been responsible for undoing the implants."

"Oh get real, Captain! These humans can't possibly undo one of our powerful mental implants. I'll check into that aspect. Now then, what's the recruitment factor? We've killed or maimed over a thousand of their First Division troops."

"Ah, now there your plan has worked to perfection. Almost no one is resigning when their enlistment period is up. I've upped the ante—particularly pay—but as we expected and desired, the fear factor looms large. GD has only replaced about one percent of the losses suffered in the war. Perfect."

"Excellent indeed."

***

Mid-December 2351, the present day, CEO Hardy sat back in his leather chair, sipping his morning coffee, brought to him by his Galactic Doll secretary, Linda. Last night's speech had gone well. He'd notified Lazy Oaks to up the "meds" on the

Padella doctors so that dementia would take them in less than a year. Like many others, they had served their purpose and were no longer needed. Long-range plans were coming to fruition.

His computer beeped, indicating incoming mail. He leaned forward and tapped a key. Ah, the manufacturing reports from Galactic Supplies. He scanned the pages, noting the seven-figure totals in the various categories, and nodded, firing off his approval to Galactic Supplies and Galactic Manufacturing. Both corporations had followed his orders, dating back a score of years, and had ramped up production of high-quality leather heels, satin gowns, and other intimates for Galactic Dolls.

For a moment, his mind returned to his initial meeting with their CEO heads. "But this makes no sense," the Galactic Manufacturing CEO had said. "There are only a few of these new Dolls."

Hardy remembered smiling in response. "Give it time. Do as I ask. You'll make a fortune."

Although disbelieving, the two had tooled up to mass-produce Galactic Doll apparel in exponentially rising volumes.

Hardy took one last look at the seven digit figures on the reports and switched to another report estimating the number of women remaining to be converted to Galactic Dolls. He smiled. It was a good fit. The backlog would be with Galactic Medicine. They could only handle so many genetic mutation patients at one time. Although he wanted the conversion to proceed rapidly, he knew it would take several months.

He sat back in his chair, pulled out a burner phone, and dialed his boss at Galactic Expansion.

"Armstrong. Hardy here. I've got the latest figures in this morning. I can guarantee you that the supplies of high-quality heels and Galactic Doll apparel will more than meet the coming demand. Galactic Manufacturing and Galactic Supplies are both reporting record profits. As we suspected, GMed will be the slowdown. It's too costly to build more medical facilities. Still, I believe my estimates on the completion of the Galactic Doll project will be accurate—late

February—March at the latest."

"Excellent, Mr. Hardy. I take it they're using the new formulation, the one that creates larger breasts? The Padella doctors rather botched G'Karn's original formula back then."

"Yes, of course. That older formulation, which sometimes didn't remain permanent, has been destroyed. I'm told breast sizes should match the size of the person's head. They are engineered not to sag with age, and they tell me that each weighs about ten pounds. GEnt has been asked to have older Galactic Dolls return to their nearest medical center for a checkup. When they do, they'll be injected with the new mutation agents. I'm told that only if their bodies haven't retained their proper shape will they drop into a mutation coma. Even so, the duration is expected to be short, perhaps only a few hours. We'll see. Still, it's good we caught this strategic error before very many females were converted."

"Excellent. From the news conference last night, I take it the mind persuasion devices have been working out as expected in the high schools. What about our scheduled nighttime drone flights?"

"Yes, working to perfection in the high schools. The graphs show the results. The operation is being conducted during the girls' gym periods. No one's the wiser. The reports suggest no girl has counteracted the implanted commands. It's a genius plan if you ask me. The drone flights are scheduled to begin this evening. We should have all women demanding the mutation soon. We're staging the flights so we don't overload any city's medical capacity." He stopped his foot from tapping on the floor but found his hands fidgeting with his tie.

"Excellent. It's time we put these Earth females into their proper roles: positions currently occupied by males. I need you to handle another action; I want someone promoted at once."

"Yes, of course."

***

VP Russell rung his hands and dabbed the sweat from his forehead. He sat across from Bev, Molly, and Deanna in her office on the fiftieth floor.

"Yes, I got this call from GD CEO Hardy this morning.

He framed it as an order, but as we both know, one corporation can't order another. Still, you should consider this offer."

"This can't be good. Not after last night's speech," Bev said.

He dabbed his brow again.

"Maybe it is. As we all know, our war with the Sixth Invaders isn't going well. In fact, we're losing it, but you know that firsthand. GD is having a gigantic problem recruiting new soldiers to replace the losses suffered. Plus, no one is resigning when his or her contract expires. Bev, I believe GD is becoming desperate. Hence this offer."

Again, he wiped his perspiration with his handkerchief, before continuing.

"Bev, GD wants you to immediately get genetically modified into a Galactic Doll. Once that's done, they want to promote you to colonel and place you in charge of the Forty-second Regiment. It seems the infantry regiment is about to mutiny if they don't get a leader they can respect. You've made an indelible impression on your fellow soldiers. They want you and no one else to lead them. Here's an image of your new uniform."

He laid his phone on the table so the three women could see the 3-d hologram of a young Galactic Doll dressed in a blue satin gown with gold trim and matching tall heels. She wore a traditional officer's hat, her hair tied in a tight bun.

The woman looked professional, Molly thought. She said, "While women should be Galactic Dolls, Bev, you can't do it."

"She's right," Bev said. "While women should look good, the stupid generals are in charge. They'll make me lead my regiment into a slaughter, just like they've done in the past."

Again, Russell dabbed his forehead. "I agree, all women should be gorgeous Galactic Dolls. I was told you might react something like this. CEO Hardy said that if you take this position, you'll be given complete and total control over all assets you believe necessary to carry out whatever mission the generals request."

"Does that include artillery support, drone support, air support?" Bev asked.

"Yes, total control. The generals will give you the target, but you will tell them what you need, and then you run the whole show. Plus, Hardy said your pay would be quintuple what you were making as captain."

He lowered his voice. "Bev, this is an incredible offer. In all my years at GEnt, I've never seen a deal like this. I believe Hardy is desperate for a victory and will give you carte blanche to do it. As you heard last night, soon almost all women will have this done. This way, you'll have a good position. I suspect you could make general."

"I've got one stipulation. Eve and Randi are on Brussels helping the other female soldiers recover from the Galactic Doll implants. Once those women recover, I want them to have a chance to continue to serve under me, if they still want to help. Get Hardy to agree to that and I'll do it."

"Bev, I know women should look good, but are you sure about this?" asked Molly.

"Yes. I'm bored out of my head around here, except when I'm helping you. That's why I joined the army. I'm not cut out to be a PI, but you are. Besides I can see we need to become Galactic Dolls. This way I get to be on top of it. But how I'm supposed to fight eludes me. I can't see Galactic Dolls fighting in the field, but we'll see. Women should look good."

Russell made a pair of quick calls. "Okay, Bev, Hardy approved your request. I've arranged with GMed for you to undergo the genetic mutations this afternoon. Allow eight days. Your new aide is Corporal Gail Jackson. She'll be with you when you wake from the coma and will help you with the new uniforms or dress gowns as they're now being called. A light cruiser will take you to Tau Ceti."

"Boy, they sure want her fast," Molly said. "So many of us want the mutation now, before Christmas, right?"

"No kidding," Bev said. "Still, maybe I can kick some Sixth Invader butt. Don't worry, sisters. I'll call you often. I love you all. Wow, I can't believe they want me in charge. Well, it's about damned time we kick their ass. Besides, I'd like to keep the battles on Brussels and not here on Earth. Women should look good while doing it."

Deanna smiled. "Ditto. I don't want to see those Invaders marching down Lake Shore Drive. Just be careful, Bev. If you need any changes to the EMAC transports, give a call. And you're right. All women should become beautiful Galactic Dolls. We should look good."

"It's good to have a genius billionaire as my sister."

Everyone chuckled. Molly and Ted accompanied her to the medical facility, returning home after she slipped into the mutation coma.

Molly checked on Bev once each day, but on the eighth day, Corporal Jackson joined them, lugging a duffle bag of new apparel for Bev.

"Hi. You must be Molly. I'm Gail."

"Hi, Gail. My husband, Ted. You take good care of my sister."

Gail laughed. "You can count on that. I can't believe they're allowing us gorgeous Galactic Dolls to be in the army."

"Well, your uniform looks great," Ted said.

She wore a blue satin gown that fit her curves snugly. The gown revealed her rather massive cleavage. Gold trim outlined the uniform. Her blonde hair touched the top of her hips while her ankle boots with their heels matched her gown. Gail wore no makeup but had her long talons painted red. Her hat was folded, tucked into her gold belt, along with a Glock, but Molly couldn't tell its caliber. Molly felt a pang of loss; she missed her own Glock.

"Thanks. I've measured Bev and got her a new uniform. After she wakes up and feels like it, we'll visit the quartermaster and pick up more. The cruiser leaves at 0900 tomorrow."

"You look good in your uniform," Molly said. *What else can I say to her? She seems genuinely excited about this.*

"Thanks, Molly. This is just the greatest, isn't it? Imagine, Galactic Dolls going to war. She's terrific, you know— Kick Ass BB. Everyone's heard of her—how she single-handedly saved the entire battalion. It's such an honor to be her aide. I've been taking target practice all week, and I do hope I'm up to her expectations."

Molly smiled. "Well, do me one favor. Make sure she doesn't drink too much."

Gail laughed. "Okay, but I think we all do that—drink too much. Also, you don't have to worry about men taking liberties with us. I know we're gorgeous and all that, but no intercourse is permitted with Galactic Dolls; we're tested twice a week."

Bev stirred and woke. "Wow, they're big, aren't they?" she muttered as she pulled out of her grogginess. "Hi, Molly. Ted."

Gail saluted. "Corporal Gail Jackson, your aide, reporting for duty, sir. Got your new uniform in the duffle bag, sir. Shall I help you dress?"

Molly and Ted backed out of the room while Gail set to work on Bev. The two heard occasional growls from Bev. Gail opened the door, and the pair got their first look at their sister in her new uniform. In fact, she looked much like Gail: blue satin, form-fitting gown that highlighted her bosom, and her matching blue ankle boots with their tall heels. Her hair was tied up in a tight bun. Her uniform had five times as much gold trim as Gail's had.

"Don't know how I'm supposed to fire my Glock with these nails," Bev grumbled.

"We'll take gunnery practice on the way, sir. I'm doing pretty well with it. We will be issued blasters when we arrive."

"Bev, you look good," said Molly. "Just be damned careful. And stay away from those dog whistle things. And don't get yourself killed. Come here; give me a hug."

Molly and Ted watched the pair check out of the medical facility before they headed home.

The soldiers visited the quartermaster. At lunchtime, Bev and Gail joined Molly and all her sisters at Luigi's Pizza Parlor. Here, they said their tearful goodbyes.

As Molly and Ted rode the MTES back to the Cartwright Skyscraper, Molly said, "I hope she comes back alive and in one piece. Galactic Doll women do look beautiful."

***

CEO Hardy sat back in his leather chair. He'd just received official notification that Bev had departed in a light cruiser, bound for Brussels. He dialed a number on his burner phone.

"Armstrong, Bev is now a Galactic Doll and is heading to Tau Ceti as we speak. Mission accomplished, though I can't see what this is all about."

"Hardy, it's come to my attention that Ted Billings is back from that South Pacific island and that Molly Parkinson is back, too. The pair has married. Have you forgotten he hacked into your GD system years ago? And she terminated General Fuller for you. Yet, both are back here in Chicago."

Hardy ran his hands over his mouth before replying. "Well, yes. They're back. I've refrained from terminating them because too many questions would be raised by the other clones."

"You assured me those two had the Galactic Doll mutation and that they removed Ted's hands. How is it they aren't Galactic Dolls and that he has hands?"

He pulled out a handkerchief and mopped his forehead and face. This body sweated heavily, something Captain L'Grina found hideous.

"Well, I had that provision in their signed contracts. Something must have gone wrong with the mutation process. Perhaps the Padella doctors botched it. You still want them terminated? That missile strike on them when they were on that South Pacific atoll failed."

"Of course not. We don't want to draw attention to ourselves right now. No, we need them unable to cause us any further problems. Here's what I want you to arrange."

***

"Deanna, there's been an attack—residential floor. You need to see what's going on," a security guard said.

Deanna had just arrived at her skyscraper for work when she found him waiting for her at rooftop door.

"Anyone killed?" She jogged along with the guard to the elevators.

"No, but we think they might be in comas."

"How?"

"Through a hole in the glass on floor forty-nine, boss. Looks like someone hovered just outside the window and used a glass cutter on it. Jenson was on guard duty on that floor. He

314

took a nasty blow to his head. Medical personnel are tending to him now. Probable concussion. Ah, here. This is where they entered."

She saw several EMTs tending to her guard. Cold December air blew in from the gaping hole. They walked down the hall and stopped at Molly and Ted's section.

A medical attendant looked up from their bedside.

"Ma'am, looks like they're in a coma. I see no signs of trauma."

"Get them transported to Cook County Medical Center right away. What about Holly Ann and Kyle?"

She stopped further down the hallway. Kyle was awake, but Holly Ann was in a coma, too. Kyle was frantic with worry.

"Deanna, what's going on? Someone attacked us in the night. They injected me with something, too, but I'm not affected."

"Take her and Kyle to Cook County, as well. I'll ride with you, Kyle. I can't believe we've been attacked again. Come on. Snap to it."

The medical technician nodded, and with Kyle's help, lifted Holly Ann onto the stretcher.

Deanna and Kyle fretted in the hospital lounge for well over an hour before a doctor joined him.

"Mrs. Cartwright, Mrs. Chesterfield, I've good news. They'll be all right. They are in genetic mutation comas. We've verified they were given the new Galactic Doll genetic mutation serum via a single injection site."

"Whew. I thought it might be deadly or something," said Kyle. "That explains why I didn't go into a coma. I'm already a Galactic Doll."

The doctor smiled. "Yes, that's correct. The usual period is eight days. You're welcome to visit them anytime."

After looking in on the three, Kyle and Deanna headed back to the Cartwright Skyscraper, where the CP and a detective were wrapping up their investigation. As she expected, the detective had no clues to follow but promised to search street cams. Then, after arranging for the window to be replaced, she let the others know what happened.

The following morning, Deanna and Kyle headed to the

hospital to check on the three. The doctor met them in the hallway. His face radiated excitement.

"This is incredible—a real medical miracle of enormous importance."

"What? What are you talking about?" Deanna asked.

He swallowed hard. "Mrs. Billings and Mrs. Chesterfield—their arms are regrowing. Heck, I don't even know if that's the right word for it. Come. You have to see this for yourself."

He led them into Holly Ann's room. Kyle stared in disbelief. Holly Ann now had small baby-like arms attached to her shoulders.

The doctor said, "If she's regenerating or rebuilding or regrowing her arms, then our best guess is that her body will need large amounts of nutrients. That's what all those tubes are doing. Since this has never happened, we're only guessing what their bodies might need."

They walked next door and peered in on Molly and Ted. Molly, too, had tiny arms attached to her shoulders. Deanna covered her mouth, gasping.

"Yes, this is an incredible breakthrough—a miracle," the doctor continued. "We've definitely verified they were injected with the new Galactic Doll genetic mutation nanoparticles. The lab has verified the Padella markers. Earth has made millions of Galactic Dolls, but I guess no one has ever thought to use it to regrow limbs.

"We've called in two genetic specialists to study this further. If their findings match ours, we have a cure for all those who have lost one or more limbs."

Deanna chuckled, "As long as the men don't mind being a Galactic Doll themselves. Men might not appreciate that detail, but we women will."

"Don't worry. I've also alerted all the major corporations to this incredible discovery. More tests must be done to confirm these results. Certainly, we'll have to study what nourishment must be provided. How long they'll be in their comas isn't known. My guess is that eight days won't be enough."

"This is a miracle for my Holly Ann. I can't help crying,

Deanna." Kyle dabbed her eyes several times.

Deanna said, "Doctor, as soon as you want another test subject, I think I can provide one. War victim. Arm and leg gone."

"Okay. I'll log that on the chart here. As soon as the two geneticists get here, they'll want to conduct a controlled test."

He took down her contact information.

After returning to the Cartwright building, Deanna set up a conference call with all her sisters, particularly Janine and Hank. She told them of the break-in, the forced Galactic Doll mutations, and then dropped the startling news.

"Yes, both Holly Ann and Molly have arms regrowing, if that's even the right word for it. They're small arms, much like Jana had when she was born."

Shrieks of joy echoed.

Deanna said, "Hank, I told them about you. I'm certain that soon the geneticists will want to conduct a controlled test. I suggested you might be interested. The downside, you'll look like Ted did when we rescued him from the atoll. Yes, a Galactic Doll, but one with two legs and two arms."

Hank yelled, "I don't care what I look like. To be a whole person again—I'd give anything for that. What about the hundreds of other soldiers like me?"

"I'm sure that once they verify this works, they'll make it available to all the soldiers that the Invaders harmed. I'll keep you updated. For once, the break-in and attack will have an accidental beneficial side effect. But the cops don't have a clue about the attack."

Hank chuckled. "I bet Molly will—when she recovers."

The next day, when Kyle and Deanna visited the patients, the two women's arms were longer and thicker. Two geneticists hovered over the pair, taking blood samples. One noticed Deanna.

"Excuse me. The doctor said you have a man who might be willing to undergo a test?"

"Sixth Invader war victim. Yes, Hank West. Arm and leg missing."

"Terrific. Can you get him here today? We'll begin the control testing at once. This is just an unbelievable breakthrough. But our records show that Molly underwent this Galactic Doll modification once before."

"Yes, but they cut off her arms *after* mutating her," Deanna said.

"Ah, that explains it." She logged that on her chart. "If they'd done it backward, the world would have known about this long ago."

Deanna nodded and left to fetch Hank and Janine.

Two hours later, Janine watched the two geneticists injecting the nanoparticle serum into Hank's arm. He smiled at her.

"See you on the other side, a whole person again. Love you."

She leaned over and kissed him. After they passed the infrared beam over his body, he slipped into a coma. A crew entered, hooking many tubes to his body.

As Janine left the room, one geneticist walked up to her. "Mrs. West. You've heard CEO Hardy's request that all women undergo the modification. I was thinking this would be a good time for you to have it done. It only takes eight days. Hank will be here much longer. Then, you can surprise him when he wakes. We all want to take the plunge and do it. I'm scheduled to have it done in three weeks."

Grinning, Janine agreed. An hour later, an envious Deanna watched her sister slip into a similar coma.

"I wish it was my turn," Deanna whispered to Janine, who smiled back. "Women should look good." Deanna then frowned, wondering why she said that.

When Kyle and Deanna dropped by to visit the next morning, they found Leslie already there, holding Janine's hand. She looked up and smiled.

"Like isn't this wonderful? We're all like incredibly lucky. Molly, Holly Ann, and Hank will like be whole. I'll like have it done as soon as everyone here is healed and back home." She chatted on, but Deanna stopped listening, wondering how soon she could get this done to herself and if Russell would like her afterward.

***

CEO Hardy sat back in his leather chair, mopping his brow.

Things were going unimaginably wrong. He stared at his burner phone, swallowed, and dialed.

"Armstrong, the 'accident' occurred without a hitch. But there was an unexpected complication."

"Yes, I've heard," said Mr. Armstrong. "The genetic mutation is triggering a body rebuild, much like a fetus does when it's been harmed. We don't care about the Chesterfield woman. What about Ted and Molly? How are you going to handle them?"

"Don't worry. I'll handle it. But have you heard? They are testing it on one of the war victims, one who's missing an arm and leg. Should I stop such testing?"

"Don't be silly, Hardy. Our empire needs a miracle about now, but I would suggest the Billings couple lose theirs again. Arrange it. Now then, you're holding the Midwinter Formal Ball on January 1. Correct? Invite the Billings couple. You'll gain plausible deniability, something you need."

***

When Deanna, Kyle, and Leslie arrived at the Medical Center on the seventh day since the break-in, Holly Ann's arms were about half the size of a comparable adult, highly encouraging. Hank had both an arm and leg growing on his body. Deanna had watched the news. Already reporters had spread word of this potential cure for the war victims, thanks to GEnt. However, neither Ted nor Molly was in their bed in their room. After a time, Deanna inquired.

"What do you mean they were taken up for surgery?" their doctor screamed.

The red-faced nurse pointed to her computer screen that showed they were both in surgery.

"What's going on here? Find out who ordered that procedure."

With that, he raced down the hall, heading for Surgery. He arrived and was just about to don surgical garb and rush in when the surgical team came out.

"What's going on with my patients, the Billings couple?" he asked.

"Both are in recovery. I'm not sure why the surgery was ordered, but it was a success. The silver compound

319

nanoparticles and the graphene mesh are holding nicely on their shoulders. Where would modern medicine be if it weren't for these two inventions?" the surgical doctor said.

"What do you mean? What was done to them? Whose orders?" the doctor asked.

"Their arms were removed at their shoulders. It was on their charts and scheduled for this morning. Check with scheduling if you have a problem with it."

He verified the surgery and accompanied the unconscious pair as attendants wheeled their beds back down to their room.

***

"What have they done?" shrieked Deanna.

An anxious group jumped up to see Ted and Molly.

"Oh, dear god," said Kyle.

"Someone like ought to pay," Leslie added.

The hospital director joined them. "I'm so sorry about this unfortunate mix-up. I've called the police, requesting a thorough investigation. In time, the guilty parties will be uncovered and dealt with."

Thus, the director began a lengthy discussion, primarily with Deanna. She knew what was likely his goal: avoid a costly lawsuit.

Leslie sat beside Molly and Ted and cried.

She whispered, "So sorry, Molly. You almost like had an incredible miracle. And Ted, it's going to be like awful for you, too. I'll be here for you both."

***

The small group gathered around Ted and Molly's beds. It was the eighth day. The mutation had reshaped Ted's body. His brown hair reached his hips, while his bosom was equal to Molly's, though both were noticeably larger than they had been before on the atoll. His legs and feet, like Molly's, had been altered. Neither could put their feet flat on the floor. Except for his lack of arms, Ted looked much as he had when Deanna had rescued him from the atoll. Same with Molly. The only visible difference was her somewhat larger breasts. He had a high-pitched voice. Later medical scans revealed his pelvis had widened and a pair of ribs had dissolved, making

320

his body appear much more feminine.

Ted awoke first. "What happened? My voice? My arms?" He screamed in a shrill soprano tone, waking Molly.

Deanna helped Ted to sit up while Leslie did the same with Molly. Both now faced each other.

Molly gasped. "What happened to us?" Her body trembled a little.

Deanna took her time and explained what had happened, beginning with the nighttime attack and ending with what little they knew about the hospital error.

"Once we get you dressed, you have to stop by and see Hank and Holly Ann. Janine is here, too."

Molly said, "Well, Ted, I'm back to being the way I was on the atoll. So are you, only you're worse off. I guess now I get to keep reminding you to 'Stop and think how.'"

Ted managed a faint smile.

Deanna got them dressed in identical red satin gowns with matching heels, the default apparel.

"Okay, let's visit Holly Ann. She's next door. Are you going to manage?"

Molly rose to her feet. "Wow. I thought I was done with this wobbling, but I guess not. I'll be all right as soon as I get reused to it. You should put a steadying arm around Ted."

"Please," he said. "Molly, I had no idea you felt this terrified there on the island. I'm petrified right now."

"Stop and think how, Ted. I managed. So can you. I want to see the others before we go home."

Walking extra carefully, the pair entered the adjacent room where they stared at the unconscious Holly Ann.

"Wow. She'll really have arms," Molly said.

"And you should have had, too," Deanna said.

"You don't know who broke into our place? The forty-ninth floor? Incredible. Well, I'll see what I can uncover."

"Please, Molly. I guess this is one case where the damage done was much less than the potential good. Hundreds of war victims now have hope for the future."

"While we struggle," Ted said.

Later, they looked in on Janine and Hank.

Molly said, "Look at that. He's growing a new leg and

arm. He's gonna be one happy fellow when he wakes up."

"So will Janine," Ted added.

"Say, what about injecting us again with that genetic agent stuff?" Molly asked.

Deanna sighed. "I already asked about that. The two geneticists insist that many others get cured first. Sorry, Molly. Let's get you two to the apparel store and then home. Be thinking about what color gowns you want. I'll treat you both to a couple dozen each. Plus, I was told they have boots for winter use, but we'll have to get Ted some heavy cloaks like you have, Molly."

"Make somebody pay, Molly," Ted grumbled.

Chapter 23 Strange Developments

"We can manage," Molly said. *God, we just have to!*

Deanna fretted over the two. True to her word, she paid for two dozen gowns and accessories for each of them, including undergarments. As always, the heels were of high quality, real leather. The boots came in two styles: ankle and knee height. It snowed on their way home, so the two were glad they'd purchased several pairs.

Once home, Janine, Leslie, and Kyle helped them store their new clothes, packing their old clothes in boxes. Ted couldn't wear his male clothing, and Molly's wouldn't fit her bosom.

"Thanks for insisting they put a police guard on Holly Ann's room," Molly said to Deanna.

Deanna smiled and returned home to Jana.

"Okay. Remember, we're like a phone call away," Leslie said.

"Hey, and I'm just down the hall," Kyle added.

"We'll get by. See you in the morning," Molly said.

Soon, the pair was alone, sitting on the edge of their bed.

Molly said, "Well, dear. Looks as if we're back to where we started. I expected to be here like this; I'm supposed to be a Galactic Doll, but not you. Are you going to make it?"

"I made a lot of use of my arms back then. This is freaky. Now I appreciate what you were going through when you woke up on the atoll. Hey, if you can make it, I can, too. Glad my looking like a freak again isn't turning you off. That always bothered me."

"I love you, sexy man. Come on. Let's see if we can get ourselves ready for bed without calling for Kyle."

An hour later, the two sat on the edge of their bed, ready to turn in.

Molly said, "I'm proud of you, dear. You did it."

Ted laughed sarcastically. "Yeah, only took us an hour to do a couple minutes' work." He sighed. "But I did it. Some of this is coming back. Maybe I'll have the hang of this in a few days."

"Don't worry about it. It may take you much longer to do things than it did when you were on the atoll. Anyway, what I want most right now is a kiss and..."

An hour later, they lay side by side.

"That was harder to do than expected," Molly said. "I can see now how much I depended on you to help me manage. Still, we did it. Now, how do we cuddle?"

In the morning, Kyle checked to see if they needed any help.

Ted answered. "I've got to see if I can figure out how to do things. We'll yell, if we need you. Thanks."

Molly watched him closely and saw how hard he fought to keep his emotions suppressed. She encouraged him constantly, remembering how he'd been there for her on the atoll.

Around nine, the pair finally walked out of their bedroom and into the communal kitchen where the Cartwright chef had a breakfast laid out for them. Kyle had finished hers and was sipping coffee, waiting for the pair. She wore a light green gown.

"Ted, you look good," she said. "Brown suits you. Molly, I like you in blue. I think we should wear our boots today. It's snowed six inches, and it's around twenty degrees outside. Expecting lake effect tonight. I think it'll be tricky navigating the snow in these heels. Worse for you two, I'll bet."

"Okay. Give us a few minutes to eat and change shoes," Molly said.

Ted commented, "Well, I had to use my feet and toes to dine before, so I hope it's just a matter of remembering how. But my stomach is in a knot. This is frightening. I feel so helpless. Boy, do I ever appreciate you, dear."

"Stop and think how, love. That and lots of practice. Yes, sometimes I still feel spooked and frightened, but we'll manage. Slow and easy does it."

"Before when we had no hands, I was mostly annoyed. I could still reach out, touch, and move things maybe two to three feet away from me. Now, I feel like my reach has collapsed down to just the vicinity of my body—my head, nose, shoulders. It's as if my outreach to the universe has shrunk to almost nothing. Oh yeah, and my boobs, too."

He laughed as he looked down, and it brought a grin to his face.

"Ted, this is one reason I love you so much. Brilliant. I felt that way from the moment I woke up on the atoll. My outward reach collapsed from three feet all around me to darn near nothing. It makes everything so strange and frightening. And it still occasionally bothers me. As you say, I can reach out with just my nose, head, and boobs. You're a genius. But know this: I won't rest until I find out who did this to us. Payback will be a bitch. I promise you."

***

Days passed. Christmas loomed nearer. Each day, Kyle and Deanna helped Ted and Molly travel to the Medical Center, where they checked on Holly Ann, Hank, and Janine. When Janine came out of her coma as a new Galactic Doll, they helped her get new outfits. Right on schedule, a delighted Leslie underwent the procedure, coming out of her coma the day before Christmas. Felix was there to help her and get a new wardrobe. Then, on Christmas day, both Hank and Holly Ann woke up.

Hank said, "Well now I look like a Galactic Doll, just like Ted and Kyle, but I'm a whole person. I can't tell you how wonderful this feels." His smile was gigantic.

Holly Ann was quite surprised. "I wonder what this will do to our baby, Kyle. This is incredible. I have arms. Wow. And they've no idea who did this to us?"

"None at all," Kyle said.

Later when Kyle and Holly Ann were alone in their bedroom that evening, Kyle asked, "Now that you have arms, should we use your new machine and swap back to our original bodies?"

"No way. You have your dream job. I would never take that from you. I can now do my work a thousand times easier. So forget such ideas. Come here. I want to hold you. I never thought I'd be able to do that."

***

None at all was Molly and Ted's expectation of the special delivery invitation delivered to the Cartwright building the day after Christmas. Kyle took the parcel from the GD deliveryman and opened it for the two. Deanna and Holly Ann joined them, curious about the delivery.

"What's it say?" Holly Ann asked. "Hold it up so Molly can read it."

```
Dear Mr. and Mrs. Billings,

GD CEO Hardy invites you to attend the GD
Midwinter Formal Ball on January 1.
    Since this is a formal ball, the dress
code demands ball gowns be worn, especially by
Galactic Dolls. If you don't have one, they
may be purchased at your local Galactic Doll
Apparel store.
    This is your night to shine, so dress
fancy, and enjoy the finest evening of the
year. I will expect to greet you at the doors
of the downtown GD Ballroom at 6 p.m. sharp.
Bring this invitation, your ticket to an
elegant evening to always remember.

    Sincerely,
    Phil Hardy
    CEO Galactic Defense Chicago
```

"Huh? What can GD possibly want with us?" asked Molly.

Deanna said, "It's only the fanciest dance in the city each year. I was invited one time. I'm surprised by this, too."

Ted said, "I don't think I want to go, not after all the terrible things GD has done to everyone."

Deanna ran her hands through her short hair. "You have to go, Ted. While this looks like an invitation, in fact, it's not. About five hundred attend—at least when Peter and I went. All the major corporate CEOs and VPs will be there with their wives. You can't turn it down, not if you don't want GD on your case. Look at it as a way to familiarize yourselves with the corporate leaders."

"But I don't trust GD or that man," Ted said. "He might be responsible for doing this to us and now wants to see how we look and gloat over what he's done."

"Ted, no one has made any connection to GD about the break-in here," Deanna cautioned. "Don't jump to conclusions. We'll get your ball gowns today so you have time to get used to them. I'm not sure you'll be able to manage in them. I had a difficult time and clung to Peter the whole night."

Holly Ann said, "Say, why not put some of my new nano-spy devices on them? Then, we can listen in to everything that's said. Maybe we'll learn something. Hey, how about video spy-cams too?"

"I like that," Ted said.

Later that afternoon, Deanna, Leslie, and Felix accompanied the pair to Ball Gowns and More down in the Loop. As the five entered and saw the elegant gowns adorning the front windows, Molly concluded this store catered to the wealthiest clientele. Plush red carpeting, golden chandeliers, and saleswomen wearing gowns that made her Galactic Doll gown look cheap vied for her attention. Molly thought they should have a sign posted on the door: 'If you have to look at the price tag, you shouldn't enter this store.'

The saleswomen were also Galactic Dolls, though Molly thought two of the four had recently become one and were still adjusting. Most of the gowns billowed out via either petticoats or hoop skirts. When the lead saleswoman heard what Ted and Molly needed, she made a wise decision.

"Most of the women who'll be at the Formal Ball will be wearing these gowns." She pointed to a selection whose hoop skirts made them billow ten or more feet at the floor. "In your case, I think you'll find these too difficult to manage. Might I suggest something that would be easier for you to handle?"

Deanna spoke for them. "Please. Thank you. This is their first Formal Ball."

An hour later, they left with two designer gowns, a light blue for Molly, and a light brown for Ted. They were the same design with a bared shoulder. The bare shoulders were on opposite sides, giving the illusion of a matched pair, an idea that appealed to the young couple. Unlike the tight form fitting gowns they normally wore, these were loose fitting, which also appealed to the pair, though the heels that matched didn't.

"Oh, this is the very latest style," the saleswoman insisted. Each had an ankle band about an inch wide, ensuring the heel couldn't slip off. For the pair, this meant they'd lose the use of their feet and toes and would be dependent upon others while they wore them. "Every woman there will be wearing this style."

Reluctantly, the pair agreed to the shoes.

***

During the next few days, while Molly worked with Ted to get him more comfortable, Holly Ann was very busy in her lab. Something Deanna had said fired her up: all the major corporate CEOs and VPs will be there. She knew the identity of only a few of these executives and saw this as an excellent opportunity to learn more. She put together four tiny spy cameras. Used in conjunction with her nano-audio device, she planned to record the images of everyone there, along with what was said.

The downside of her two devices was the range of their signals. Thus, she wired up a signal booster box, battery operated. The afternoon before the ball, she and Kyle took a stroll through snow-covered Chicago, passing by the entrance of the GD Ballroom. On either side of the main entrance, workers had piled up large mounds of snow. She bent over and buried her booster box in the drift. Its battery would power it for at least three days. The box boosted the signals from two spy video cameras and two of her nano-audio devices.

Once back, Holly Ann set up her recording devices and tested them. Then, she explained to the pair what she had planned.

"Look, this is a great opportunity to record everyone who is there. I'll put a tiny video spy cam on each of you, along with one of my new nano-audio devices, and will record everything from all four devices. Already I've put a signal booster in place. Your job is to mingle and see all the executives. You know, like 'Hello. I'm GD CEO Hardy.' After

328

the ball, we'll have an inventory and images of most of the corporate executives."

Molly said, "Are you sure you haven't been a spy? Perhaps in your last life?" Both chuckled. "It's brilliant. We'll know who the major players are. Even Deanna doesn't know more than a few of them."

***

On January 1, Leslie and Janine arrived after the early supper. They dressed and pampered Ted and Molly. Leslie stood back and admired Molly's appearance. "You like look beautiful, stunning in fact. I like how you drape your hair to hide your shoulders. I keep expecting to like see your arms appearing."

"Yes, but with these new heels, we won't be able to take them off," Molly said.

Holly Ann joined them, bringing the four tiny devices. She fastened them onto the two.

"Make the others help you. Okay, the video cam records whatever you're facing. The nano-audio isn't directional."

Janine adjusted Ted's long hair to drape over his shoulders, emulating Molly's hair.

"I'm nervous," Ted said. "I'm going to this ball, and everyone'll think I'm a Galactic Doll, a woman, but I'm not. Plus, we're both helpless in these new heels."

Leslie giggled. "But you like make a dashing couple. Make those men like take care of your needs. Like ignore the fact you're a male, Ted. Pretend like you're an actor, and play it for all it's worth."

Kyle joined them. "Gang, it's snowing again. We should escort them to the GD Ballroom, just in case. It's going to be slippery out there tonight, even though the MTES is covered."

"Thanks. But you'll have almost as much trouble with the snow as we will," Molly said. Everyone laughed.

"The price for looking fetish," said Leslie. "You two like look very fetish tonight—like two stars."

Kyle and Holly Ann walked on either side of Ted while Janine and Leslie escorted Molly. The sidewalks were slippery with an inch of new snow, but they only had a block to cover before reaching the MTES. Molly and Ted each wore a heavy cloak, affixed by a clasp at their necks. By the time they

329

reached the building, everyone's legs were freezing. Bare legs and a Chicago winter didn't mix, but for this special occasion, the women in attendance didn't mind.

Kyle handed the door attendant the Billings invitation. "Knock 'em dead, you two."

As they entered the foyer, a coat man took their cloaks.

"You'll have to undo them. No arms," Molly said. "Put the receipts in our bags."

Each had a small bag that dangled from their waist. Others lined up behind the pair, so Molly was relieved to move on inside the spacious ballroom, decorated in a winter theme. White giant snowflakes hung from the ceiling, and various colored lights swept across the dance floor. Their heels clicked on the floor, but soon the sound of hundreds of the steel-tipped heels upon the marble drowned out theirs.

At the main entrance doors, they paused behind another couple. The man wore a tuxedo, but the Galactic Doll woman wore one of the giant ball gowns the two had seen at the store. Seeing her in it convinced both they'd made the right decision. When they reached the front of the line, he stood there smiling.

"GD CEO Hardy. And you are? Oh, I know. The Billings couple. No hands to shake. Still, very pleased to meet you. Tonight, you're my guests at this ball. You look elegant. Enter and enjoy my Midwinter Ball."

He waved them onward with his left arm, which twitched as though he stopped himself from making his weird gesture. He was neither handsome nor homely, perhaps average. His gray suit wasn't.

Molly thought, *probably costs as much as my dress, but he looks better on the comm system monitor.*

The ballroom's floor was shiny white marble with flakes of silver that reflected the sweeping lights. Across the huge space, tables of food and drink lined one wall. Along the wall to their right, thirty musicians were warming up and tuning. Already many couples were here.

Ted looked at Molly, and she, he. As they had promised each other, they checked to make sure their long hair was draped over their shoulders as though hiding their arms, had they had them. Already, Molly noticed most of the Galactic Doll women had their hair up in a myriad of styles, and they looked young. Only two older women weren't Galactic Dolls. Before the night ended, she estimated two hundred fifty women attended, but only five older women were normal. This Galactic Doll craze had swept through the executives' wives.

"Hello. You look ravishing."

A young man stepped up to Molly, introducing himself as a junior executive with GEnt. Before the evening ended, she and Ted estimated several dozen young men were checking out potential matches among the young women.

Thus began a long evening for the pair. No sooner had one executive stepped up to them and introduced himself when the next did so. Once the musicians began, Ted never got an opportunity to dance with Molly. To his embarrassment, a young man stepped up, introduced himself, put his arms around his waist, and proceeded to dance with him. Flustered, Ted said little and tried to smile.

Likewise, Molly was the center of attention among the men. She, too, did her best to smile. *At least we're recording their images and their positions.* Soon, she found herself separated from Ted.

After most of the men had introduced themselves and danced briefly with her, a young man stepped up to her. She estimated he was in his mid-twenties. His face was handsome. His black hair shone, and his trimmed mustache looked perfect on him. Like the other men, he wore a tuxedo. His black shoes reflected almost as much light as the silver streaks in the marble floor.

"And you must be Molly Parkinson-Billings. I'm Casper Hugo, Junior, CFO of the Empire GD. You are one stunning woman. I love how you look. And your lush raven hair. Hides your lack of arms. My compliments. I heard you're a private investigator."

He slipped his arms around Molly, pulling her in close to him, forcing her enormous bosom up against his chest. She couldn't pull back from him and had to breathe in his cologne.

"Yes, I still am a PI. Why? Does that interest you?"

He began to waltz, and she had no choice but to follow.

Either that or have him step on her toes, but that might not be so bad. Even with the built-in gel pads that came with every pair of Galactic Doll sandals, her feet were aching. She suspected that by now all the women's feet were throbbing. As he twirled her around, she got a view of the entire packed room. Alas, there weren't any chairs, save for those used by the musicians. He continued to chat while they danced, throwing compliment after compliment at her.

When this piece ended, Hardy announced an intermission. Everyone moved towards the back where the food and drink lay waiting.

"Come with me. We'll get some refreshments, Molly," Casper insisted.

He still kept one arm around her waist. She knew she'd not be able to break free, not in heels.

"I'm afraid if you're taking me to the refreshments, you'll have to assist me. I'm unable to remove these shoes to use my feet." *There, that should be enough to get rid of him.*

To her surprise, he filled up a plate of delicacies, balancing a glass of red wine in the middle. He still kept his left arm around her waist, forcing her body up against his side. After they stepped back, he stopped and released her, but rubbed an appetizer against her lips. Rather than make a scene, since she saw several others watching them from the corners of her eyes, she opened and accepted it. He then helped her take a sip of the wine.

"Superb vintage. Hardy serves only the finest red wines at these dances. Still, you are finer than any of these wines—a rare orchid."

He continued to alternate between their mouths, all the while lobbing praise after praise her way. When the music began again, Casper continued to keep his arms around her, forcing her to close-dance with him and him alone. Several other young men who had already danced with her came up to them, saw Casper, and hastily retreated.

Towards the end of the evening, he said, "Molly. Dump Ted. He looks like a Galactic Doll, not a real man. Marry me. I'll give you everything your heart can desire. I'm the Chief Finance Officer and third in command of Sol's Galactic

Defense. One day, I'll be running it, and I'd love to have you at my side when I do. I have a mansion, my own shuttles, and EMACs. You can live the life of utter luxury that a stunning woman like you should be living. Just marry me. I can give you anything you desire. Tell me, and it's yours. I won't take no for an answer."

What the hell? "I'm a happily married woman, Casper. Thanks for the offer." *There, that should put an end to this.*

"Not a problem. Just dump Ted and marry me."

"If I had hands, Casper, I'd slap you. Consider yourself slapped."

He grinned broadly. "Such a fine spirited, stunning woman you are. Mind you, I never give up. I always get what I want, and I want you. You'll see."

"Please, help me find Ted. It's late, and the party is almost over. That's what I want now."

"As you command, my princess." He glanced around the room and moved her along with him as he navigated about until at last, his eyes landed upon Ted. He whisked her over to Ted. The Doll dancing with Ted nodded to Casper and moved away. As she did so, Casper's other arm shot out, encircling Ted's waist, pulling him up close to his body, opposite Molly.

"My princess commanded me to find you, Ted. Allow me to help you get your coats."

As they stood in line to retrieve their cloaks, through the doors, Molly saw that the snowfall had picked up. Her feet throbbed mercilessly, and she hoped she and Ted could make it home without falling down.

"Allow me," Casper said when the coat man brought theirs. He slipped Molly's around her shoulders and fastened the clasp, before doing the same for Ted. "Look, it's nasty outside. I've heard it's rather treacherous for you Galactic Dolls to traverse snowy sidewalks. Allow me to take you home. My EMAC is waiting."

While Molly wanted to get rid of this man, she saw Ted limping. *We'll never make it home on our own.* "Okay. We accept. Take us to Cartwright Skyscraper. The EMAC can land on the roof."

When they stepped outside on the snow-covered roof,

Molly watched several other women in their billowing dresses. Each had a man holding on to them. She spotted several slips, caught in time by their men. Thus, when Casper pulled her and Ted even tighter against his body, she didn't resist, as he led them to an EMAC. Down below, six inches of snow had accumulated on the sidewalk, trampled into an uneven slippery mess by those who left via the front doors.

A half hour later, a security guard on the Cartwright Skyscraper's rooftop EMAC lot let them inside. Since Holly Ann had been recording everything, Leslie and Janine were just inside the doors waiting for them.

"My feet are freezing and throbbing," Molly said.

"I might not be able to walk to our room," Ted said.

"I've got you," Janine said, but Kyle joined them, slipping an arm around Ted's other side. Between the two, they supported him, as they made their way to the Billings suite.

Leslie said, "Let's get you like undressed, a foot massage, and then a bath."

"Heavenly," Molly said.

***

When Molly and Ted got into bed, he felt like talking. "What an evening. I can't believe all the women who just had to dance with me. Four to one, women to men. They kept saying I was gorgeous, beautiful, and such things... As if they thought I was a woman—one of them—a Galactic Doll. And they kept pulling me up close—collision of the boobs. And they kept sliding their hands over my butt. Plus, I never did get to dance with you. What did that Casper fellow want with you?"

"He monopolized me for over half the dance." She told him what he'd said about dumping Ted. "I thought telling him I was married would have ended it, but nope."

"Well, I'm proud of you. Let's snuggle before I fall asleep."

Chapter 24 Key Observations

Beginning the next day, Holly Ann and Kyle went over the six hours of video and sound recordings. Kyle suggested they make a hierarchy chart of each corporation with the CEO at the top. Days later, they plastered one entire wall of Holly Ann's lab with photos labeled with the person's name, corporation, and position. They found only a few holes in the top layers of management. Only one galactic corporation had a woman as its CEO, and that Galactic Doll ran the Galactic University. She had been forced to become one against her will she had claimed when she had introduced herself to Molly, but now she thought having it done was perfect.

When putting up the images of the women at the ball, Kyle made another discovery.

"Look at this. There's not a plump woman in the lot or a skinny one either. All their bodies are similar in shape and so young. Never seen two unrelated women look so similar. I'd expect some with larger hips, others with larger abdomens, a few with thicker legs—a variation, but all these women including us have similar body shapes and youthful. So I'm going to see if GMed can explain it."

Kyle returned late that afternoon with the answer.

"You'll never guess what I found out. This Galactic Doll genetic mutation reforms bodies. The geneticists told me they've seen very overweight women lose all the excess weight. Sometimes, the women are very annoyed with that. She's also seen very thin women with small bones put on weight and add bone density because of the Galactic Doll mutation. So what we've seen with the women at the ball isn't a surprise. My contact said that sometimes the women are healthier after their conversions. Nothing like standardized body forms. Weird."

***

On the morning of January 3, Casper dropped by the Cartwright skyscraper, requesting to see Molly Billings. While he was the last person she ever wanted to see again, she had no choice but to visit him in the main lobby. She wore her usual form-fitting light blue satin gown and matching heels.

"Ah, the flower of my life appears. You look as lovely as ever, Molly."

His parka was open, revealing his business suit.

"What do you want?" She used a cold tone, hoping he'd just go away.

"I've come by to ask you if you'd like a tour of GD headquarters. Few get the chance to visit our building."

Molly heard the clicking of Ted's heels as he joined them.

"So you want to take us on a tour of GD?" Ted asked.

Molly forced herself to keep a straight face. Casper's face twisted; he looked first at Ted and then at her. He wanted nothing to do with Ted. Yet, the man wasn't stupid, Molly thought, for he hastily changed plans.

"Sure, Ted. Why don't I take both of you on a tour of GD headquarters?"

"I'd like that," Ted said. "Excuse us a few minutes. We'll get our cloaks."

Molly knew Ted well enough to know he had something devious in mind. No way would Ted want to voluntarily visit the lion's den.

"Sure, back in a few minutes. We're kinda slow," she said.

Once they entered the elevator, Ted pushed their floor button with his nose, and he explained his idea. They stopped by Holly Ann's lab, telling her what they were going to do. She attached her spy devices and began the recordings. She affixed another set to their cloaks in case they kept them on. After they left, she followed them, keeping her amplifier box close enough so as not to lose the signals from the spy devices.

A security guard escorted Casper up to the rooftop, where he had his EMAC parked. Ted and Molly joined him there. Once again, Casper helped them into his vehicle. During the short flight to GD, Casper chatted with Ted.

"You know, you should divorce Molly and marry yourself a Galactic Doll who has arms. I'd expect she would be of enormous help to you. I can't imagine how you manage. You and Molly must need so much help with life. Why not remarry someone who can help you with your needs? Of course, she should be one of these gorgeous Dolls. You deserve it."

Ted clamped his jaws and said nothing. Molly debated whether to chide Casper, but decided not to do that. Landing on the rooftop of GD ended his conversation for the moment.

Here, GD followed the same protocols that Deanna had established at Cartwright. A security guard escorted the group to the main lobby where Casper registered them, affixing a visitor's card to each gown. Then, he led them on a tour, showing off the booths displaying various weapon systems designed to protect the planet. The exhibits that illustrated the Sol Empire were scaled down to fit in the many alcoves. Once they finished here, Casper took them up many floors.

"Ted, I did a background check on you. I thought you should have the chance to see the giant computer system you hacked into when you were a kid—the hack that cost you your hands and made you look like a woman. Here it is. The massive computer complex. Mind you, it's now impenetrable. We have you to thank for that. Your hack exposed our weakness, which has been fixed. Never been hacked since then."

At first, Ted's face felt hot, but as Casper chatted on, Ted smiled. Casper had no idea he'd hacked into this system many times while he was on the atoll. The CFO had no notion that Ted continued to make GD pay for the university educations of Eve, Randi, Celeste, and himself.

Casper didn't show them the cafeteria. Molly suspected he had hoped to wine and dine her, but Ted's appearance canceled that idea. Soon, he took them home.

"So did you get it all?" Ted asked Holly Ann the moment he got back.

"Sure did. Making a copy of the audio files now. Video copy is on that flash drive." When the process finished, Holly Ann carried the two drives to Ted's workspace and copied them onto his computer. That done, Ted buried himself in the recordings, looking for clues.

***

Meanwhile, Molly had time to do what she did best:

337

investigate. She focused on two events. Who broke into the Cartwright building and injected them with the genetic mutation nanoparticles? Who orchestrated the Medical Center operation to remove their arms? Her PI license allowed her to check on active Chicago Police (CP) cases using their online system. She continued to remind herself: patience.

The CP had used surveillance video to track the EMAC back to its point of origin. It was stolen the morning of the attack. Molly suspected they'd stolen it just before carrying out the attack. Hence, she looked for street surveillance in the vicinity where the GMed EMAC was kept. Hours turned into days before she found what she wanted. She slowed the video stream down and watched as three men hijacked the vehicle. "Gotcha," she declared to her laptop.

A few hours later, she tracked the men back to GD headquarters. She played it forward and watched the men exiting the building. She made a copy of the videos, putting together the damning evidence. *If I can only identify these men.* For a minute, she struggled to keep tears from swelling. If Frank were alive, she could have him run facial recognition on the men.

She spent another hour getting the best still images of each. Then, she asked Ted for help.

"Can you hack a system that can run facial recognition? I've got images of the three men who attacked us."

"Okay. I think I know a way. Say, what do you make of this sound?"

He played her a section of the recording Holly Ann had made when they were looking through a window at the giant GD computer system.

"Sounds kinda mechanical. I've never heard it before."

"Thanks. I'll let you know if I can ID these men."

Molly went back to her laptop to find an answer to the second question. This one was far trickier. It happened at a medical facility run by GMed. It was a serious breach of security, one that could well lead to huge lawsuits, as Deanna threatened to do on their behalf. Thus, getting the inside information on how it had happened would be closely guarded by GMed. Rightly so. What she needed was someone on the inside who would discuss what they had found so far.

She pondered the various people she knew or had met. She'd been introduced to most of GMed's top management at the ball, but she suspected they wouldn't divulge anything to her because of the lawsuit angle. Molly sat back and thought about the situation.

Look, the Medical Center is fully automated. All patient information is computerized. So someone must have entered the system and brought up our pages. They must have submitted the amputation orders and scheduled the surgery. One more day and Ted would have come out of his coma. So the guilty party must be familiar with their whole system and work for that Medical Center. How to find them?

Molly closed her eyes and pondered this question. Then, she had an idea. Money or a threat. Both possibilities seemed reasonable, but she decided to look into the financial gain angle. "This world so lacks humanity," she said to her laptop.

She looked up the Medical Center's website. Perfect. They had a listing of all their employees, listed first by doctors, then nurses, lab technicians, the administrative staff, and so on down to janitors. "Could a nurse be capable of pulling this off? Possibly. A doctor, of course, but they make tons of money anyway. Lab tech—no. Admin personnel? Yes." She made a list of doctors followed by top administration personnel, and then nurses.

She knew she couldn't get access to their bank records. Even Frank would have had to get a warrant. She stared at her screen for several minutes. Then something Frank had told her popped into her mind. Copies of large deposits and withdrawals from all banks were logged at one financial site so that the corporations could more readily spot suspicious activity. Molly searched for the site, found a link to it, and arrived at their secure site. She attempted to log in using her PI license, hoping she didn't have to have Ted hack his way into these bank records.

"All right!" she said to her laptop. "Something goes my way. Let's see what we can find." Correlation. She needed to see if anyone on her Medical Center list of potential suspects received a large deposit. The smallest amount appeared to be one hundred thousand credits. The larger ones were seven figures, but those were inter-corporation transfers. Realizing she didn't have the programming skills to deal with this, she made a copy of that file and her potential suspects file, emailing them to Ted.

"Ted, I need your programming genius."

After she explained what she needed, he set to work on the program.

"When I had hands back in high school, I could whip this out in minutes. With my toes, it's taking much longer. Okay, there you go. It'll take each Medical Center name and see if that name appears in the bank records, displaying only matching data. So you think this will uncover who did it and who paid for it?"

"That's my bright idea. Ah ha. Looks like we've got one match so far."

"Best let the program run. Could be more. Say, got a question for you. Why would GD be sending out robot signals over a hyperspace relay unit?"

"Huh?"

"Yeah, I've isolated what that background noise was—you know, from the recordings Holly Ann made while we toured GD and stood close to their computer system. It recorded something which I've figured out is binary encoded robot control commands—or BERCC. I almost have my PhD in robotics, so I'm familiar with their communications modes. Definitely, commands were sent somewhere via hyperspace relay. I can't tell where the signals were going or what they meant; those commands would be specific to the robot receiving them."

"But we don't have real robots marching around. Do we? Robots are just factory things."

"True. Most robots are in the manufacturing and distribution companies. But Galactic Robotics is close to having an operational human-form robot."

"What would it do?"

"It's top secret, but from certain clues we grad students have picked up, it'll have two arms and legs, walk like a human, and do simple household chores. There's talk it could one day pilot spaceships. Ah, the program is done. Looks like you've only got one hit. I'm emailing it to you."

Molly stared at the result. The bank account of the Medical Center's number two administrator, George Fielding, showed a deposit of two hundred fifty thousand credits on the day before the two had their surgery. Coincidence? Molly knew she found the person who had arranged for the two to lose their precious gift. But who sent the funds? The Chicago Galactic Defense headquarters sent the funds, no disguising that fact, but she couldn't go blaming hundreds of people who worked for GD. Somehow, she had to pin it down to the person who orchestrated it. Within GD, whose account was it? Molly didn't know how she could find out, and Ted hadn't been able to identify the GD men who had broken in and injected the four of them while they slept.

That evening Ted couldn't sleep. After sharing a passionate time, Molly went to sleep, but he lay on his side, alert. Something bothered him. Robot commands. Hyperspace relays. What could it mean? His mind drifted, replaying mental images he had of the newscasts GEnt showed of the battle with the Sixth Invaders on Brussels, Tau Ceti. The cannibals. The Invaders who always remained inside their battle armor suits. Ted found it curious these Sixth Invaders never took advantage of any ground captured nor did they land in overwhelming numbers. Then, a wild idea flashed in his mind. Finally, sleep came.

Ted dropped by Holly Ann's lab first thing in the morning.

"I need to know how hard it would be to build a local jamming device that blocks these frequencies coming through on a hyperspace relay unit."

He told her the precise frequency range.

"Oh, that's darn easy, a freshman project. Why?"

"Can you instruct someone in how to do it—like long distance—like on Brussels, Tau Ceti?"

"Sure."

"Would army engineers be able to make it—if you tell them how?"

"I know nothing about them. But if they had access to the components, it wouldn't be hard to make. Why? Anything to do with Bev? Colonel Bev?"

"Yes, Holly Ann. Come on. We need to talk to Colonel Bev right away."

When Deanna arrived, they discovered she had a hyperspace relay communications unit in her office on the top floor.

"We use it to contact our subsidiary companies on other worlds in the Sol Empire. I'll have my operator make the connection to Bev. She'll let you know when she has her on the wire."

Ted and Holly Ann waited outside the small room for what seemed an eternity.

"Okay, she's on the line now. Remember, there's about a five-minute, one-way delay. Go ahead and talk. She'll respond in five minutes, but allow for another five minutes for her words to get back here," the operator said.

Ted said, "Bev. This could be critical. Before you make your next attack on the Sixth Invaders, I want you to have your engineers build a device and activate it just as you attack them. It could be nothing or it could be vital. I'll put Holly Ann on and have her instruct your engineers in how to build it. She says it's simple. Over."

Thus began an hours-long communications cycle. When Colonel Bev signed off, Ted relaxed.

"It may be nothing at all, Holly Ann, but then again, it could be important. Time will tell."

An hour before lunch, an unexpected phone call took both Molly and Ted by surprise. Molly answered her phone, and a holo image of a young woman rose up.

"Hi, Molly, this is Helen Hugo, Casper Hugo's wife. We met and danced at the Midwinter Ball last week." Her voice sounded cordial.

"Oh, yes, I remember you," Molly replied, moving into the room where Holly Ann had assembled images and name tags of the executives they had met at the ball. She spotted Helen's image up near the top of the GD hierarchy, close to CEO Hardy. "What can I do for you?"

"I would dearly love for you and Ted to join me and a few other wives for a lunch at Barnaby's—our treat of course. We would like to get to know you both better. You are most intriguing people. And we do have something we'd like to discuss with you—privately—Doll to Doll. Can you meet us there at, say, noon? Please, you mustn't say no."

As much as Molly wanted to say no, her PI curiosity pricked. She couldn't put her finger on just what. Intriguing people? Privately? Doll to Doll?

"Okay, we'll be there at noon. Thank you for asking us, Mrs. Hugo."

"Oh, just Helen, please. And may we call you Molly and Ted? Unlike our men, we don't hold with such formalities. Friendlier, don't you think?"

"Okay, Helen. That's fine with us, too. See you at noon. Bye."

Ted said, "Now that's the strangest call we've had. Those women—my god, they wouldn't stop dancing with me. They kept sliding their arms up and down my backside and butt, teasing like. Guess they can't do that in a public restaurant."

Molly chuckled, imagining Ted in the clutches of their hands.

The weather cooperated. Bright sunlight reflected off the snow pack, in sharp contrast to the deep blue sky. The sun had melted the ice from the sidewalks and MTES roofs, but the forecast called for another round of lake effect snow later in the day. Snug in their heavy cloaks, Ted and Molly walked to Barnaby's, perhaps the most expensive restaurant in Chicago, close to the lake and within the Loop. They only served real food, never any of the usual synth food. As they walked up to the brass-trimmed doors, a doorman opened the doors for them.

"Welcome to Barnaby's," he said in a pleasant voice.

While Molly appreciated and even needed the doors opened for her, she wondered how a man could do this mindless job all his adult life. It seemed like a waste of a life, especially with the automatic doors most establishments had.

"Ah, here you are. Right on time. I'm Helen, in case

you've forgotten me. This way. We've reserved the Manor Room."

She was a little taller than Molly with platinum blonde hair, possibly bleached, and deep blue eyes. Molly guessed she might be in her late twenties, but she definitely wore too much makeup as far as Molly was concerned. Her satin gown was cherry red as were her matching heels, nails, and lipstick. She also wore three rings with large gems: one diamond, one emerald, and one ruby. Gold bracelets and necklaces adorned her arms and neck. She wore her hair up, just as she had at the ball.

The Manor Room resembled a medieval castle, complete with a fireplace and crackling fire—actually real— and a giant stuffed grizzly bear in one corner. Six women sat around the table, but they all rose when Helen entered with Molly and Ted. Without asking, Helen removed their cloaks and hung them on the rack near the door. Both Ted and Molly shook their heads forward and down, left and right until their hair slipped into place over their shoulders.

Several women helped them get seated. Ted, however, recognized all six women. They were among the many women who had danced with him at the ball.

Helen introduced the women. "This is Elaine, Betsy, Jane, Phillis, Sam, and Julie. We've ordered the chicken cordon bleu if that's acceptable to you. There's none finer in all Chicago."

While the women eyed Molly and her blue dress, their eyes lighted on Ted in his brown gown. Molly saw a uniform sea of cherry red, the most popular color choice for the Galactic Dolls. Each woman wore her hair up, but styles varied from woman to woman, and each dress was a bit different, too.

Helen said, "You must forgive us. We've never been around someone like you. Will you need us to help you dine?"

Molly chuckled. "Hardly. We're independent, as long as we can use our toes as fingers. I hope you don't mind."

The next half hour was embarrassing for the two. The seven women couldn't help watching them as they ate.

Well, it must seem weird to them, Molly thought. *I hate being stared at.*

Over tea, the meeting began. Helen said, "We can talk freely in here. Our men can't hear us. I should begin by saying we and many other wives and women within GD Chicago were not pleased to be forced to become Galactic Dolls, though now we all just love it. I, for one, lost thirty pounds during the mutation and still feel skinny as a rat. Our bodies were changed in subtle ways. True, a few in GD desired the mutation—ladder climbers, we call them. Molly, many of us were fighting mad over this. But now, for some strange reason, we think becoming Galactic Dolls is just the thing to do, that it's perfect."

"She's right," broke in Julie. "At first, I didn't want to look like this—like a whore. All right, so now all women look like us. Until two weeks ago, I didn't like it. Many of us didn't. Now, every one of us feels this is simply perfect. How strange."

Betsy said, "And they had the gall to genetically modify my two daughters. They're still kids. Thirteen and fourteen. Some of us were furious over that, but now I feel this is wonderful for my girls. How can this be?"

Sam said, "I used to be a nurse before I married Henry. What a mistake that's turned out to be. Anyway, after we met Ted at the ball, I did a little investigating. This genetic mutation really does a job on both men and women. I've seen many big women, some nearly two hundred pounds, end up looking as thin as we are. In fact, out of the millions of Galactic Dolls, as far as GMed can tell, not one is overweight or underweight."

Julie chuckled. "Maybe that's a good thing."

Sam glared at her. "Nothing like making all women have very nearly the same body proportions and looks. That we're all about the same size and shape must make the dress manufacturers happy. A couple weeks ago, we would have liked to get our claws on the man who thought boobs should be this big." Many heads nodded. "But now, we feel they're just perfect. Isn't that just the strangest thing?"

She continued. "But I looked into what the mutation does to men's bodies. We can see that Ted looks just like one of us. We saw that much at the dance, didn't we?" Heads nodded. "But what we also didn't know is that the mutation

345

has done other things to men's bodies. Ted, did you know that your lower rib has dissolved? You have the same number as we women have. I believe that's so your waist can be as small as ours are. Also, your pelvis region has widened, enlarging your hips. You probably wondered why we were running our hands over your derriere at the ball. Well, we wanted to make sure your form was like ours. Mutated male bodies look identical to females."

Helen said, "What we'd like to know is can Ted still function as a man?"

Ted flushed.

Molly answered, "Absolutely. That part is still male. Why do you ask?"

Jane, the youngest of the women, giggled. "We think he's like a sex toy, a male Galactic Doll."

Ted's face became even redder.

Helen leaned over, her head inches from Molly's. "Weeks ago, we hated what our husbands did to us. We would like to teach them a lesson by turning them into male Galactic Dolls like Ted is. I know. Today, we love our forms, but still, we want to make them pay."

Betsy leaned over. "No arms, so they can't fight back and beat us. So we're in control, not them. I've had too many bruises from my husband when he gets drunk."

"We're tired of them telling us what we can and cannot do," Julie barked. "Besides, it was criminal to amputate your arms while they were regrowing."

Helen said, "Can you help us, Molly? You're a PI. Can you find something on them we can use to force them to get it done? We're prepared to pay you any fee. We've had all we can take. My feet ached for days after that ball. How dare they force us to be on our feet all those hours! Not a damned chair in the hall."

Molly said, "Wow. I had no idea. I—we figured most corporate women wanted to become Galactic Dolls. We knew most normal women didn't until recently. You're serious, aren't you?"

"Damned right we're serious," said Sam. "Only we don't know how we can do it. Our men are just too powerful. We find it so strange that weeks ago we hated what was done to us and now we embrace it—like our minds have been messed with somehow."

Molly glanced from woman to woman, staring into their eyes. Her gut told her they were being honest. No lies. They weren't just telling her what she wanted to hear to gain her confidence. An idea gelled.

"I'm not after money, ladies. I want justice. That's what's missing in our screwed up world. Humanity is gone. Somehow, I want to bring the guilty parties to justice. Maybe we can work something out. I need some inside help you might be able to give me."

Sam asked, "If you find the men who did this to you, are you going to kill them?"

"Oh, how I want to," said Ted.

Molly said, "But we both know that's the easy way out. They need to learn. What better way to learn than to spend the rest of their lives as an armless male Galactic Doll?"

"Count us in!" Helen said. Six others also agreed.

***

That evening, Molly received an email from Helen. It listed many bank accounts, just as promised. She stayed up late correlating these accounts with the various payments, building a solid case against six GD men, including Casper Hugo. Although CEO Hardy loomed in the background, she couldn't pin anything on him, not yet anyway.

The next morning, Molly slept in, but Holly Ann's cries woke her. "Help. It's happening!"

Carl Chesterfield, Holly Ann and Kyle's son, arrived that morning. Molly knew Holly Ann didn't know what to expect, and as a result, she was so involved in her work in her lab she almost gave birth on the job. When she cried out, many came to her aid, including Ted and Molly, who felt helpless to do much of anything for her. They watched EMTs wheeling her off to the Medical Center. Molly and Ted got to the center just as Kyle arrived, slightly out of breath, her face glowing. Together, they learned Carl arrived healthy but in the transport.

"He's cute, Holly Ann," Molly said.

They found mother and baby lying together in a private room.

"Well, I did it, Kyle. He almost came in my lab. Does that mean he wants to be an electrical engineer like me?"

Everyone chuckled. But Molly felt a strange kinship with Holly Ann. Motherhood. *Can I possibly handle a baby?*

Days later, Kyle discovered that he had no choice but to help breastfeed Carl. Until now, this aspect of male Galactic Dolls hadn't been known.

Chapter 25 Successes

"Okay, Colonel Kick Ass, we've got six of those signal jammers built," Lieutenant Carlie said. She was the engineer Bev assigned to this special project.

Ted was so insistent about the devices that she'd gone along with it. Bev knew the Forty-second would soon be ordered to assault the Sixth Invaders' encampment, and so much rested on her shoulders. The horrid results of the earlier attacks festered in every soldier's mind. The women feared becoming insane sex freaks, while the men were terrified of losing an arm and leg, as hundreds upon hundreds before them had. That all the female soldiers were now Galactic Dolls further pressured Bev, who was determined to show the world they were more than some man's sex toy. She had to or lose her own self-respect.

She ordered, "Okay, make sure an engineer in each battalion has one. They are to activate it the moment we launch our attack."

"Aye, sir. Mind me asking what they're supposed to do? Nothing uses that frequency."

"Not sure myself, but I trust its source. Just do it."

Lieutenant Carlie saluted and left.

Bev studied her clay model of the area around the Rios River where the Sixth Invaders had made their base of operations. In her mind, the trouble with earlier assaults was a total lack of coordinated combined arms. She positioned toy soldiers representing each of her battalions, surrounding the enemy. Next, she positioned ten drones with their bomb loads over the encampment's center. Finally, she moved six heavy artillery pieces into position. They couldn't use their normal indirect fire from the safety of five miles away—they'd likely hit friendly soldiers. Rather, she moved them in close, right on the ridge line, where they could fire their disrupter shells down at specific enemy targets. She had laser cannons mounted in EMACs ready for takeoff; they would drill holes into the enemy's armor suits.

Bev reviewed her artillery and laser cannon orders: direct fire at dog whistles and their operators and also enemy transports.

Lieutenant Gail Jackson saluted and entered the headquarters tent. "Sir, the engineers have delivered the jammers to the battalions. Do we know what they do? I've been asked that a lot."

"No idea. Okay, can you see these orders are delivered to the six artillery commanders and the six EMAC captains? Thanks. Now, what am I missing?"

***

Planning must end and actions begin. Bev knew that, but with the load of responsibility on her shoulders, she delayed as long as she dared. The First Division general had ordered an all-out assault on the enemy; she had to deliver. At last, she set the date for January 25, 2352.

Early that morning, GEnt film crews arrived in force, setting up their coupled feeds to those of her monitoring stations. As usual, every officer, lieutenant on up, was wired for sound and video, each person's feed going to a specific big screen monitor inside the giant HQ tent. Here, Bev could see the battle from every angle, and she could issue direct orders to any of these leaders.

"This is Harvey Smith, your North Continent, Brussels, field reporter. We're in the Forty-second Infantry Regiment headquarters with Colonel Kick Ass BB, who is leading this assault on the Sixth Invaders. As you can see, this is quite a challenge for her, though admittedly she looks very good in her new uniform. Many are asking how a Galactic Doll can be an effective soldier. Well, we're here today to see.

"We have a live, direct feed to the video streams coming into the Colonel. But we insist on inserting a ten-second time delay so we can filter out inappropriate scenes.

"As many of you know, Colonel Kick Ass BB began her career last year as a company captain. She received the distinguished valor medal for single-handedly holding off the enemy while several companies evacuated. She was taken prisoner after a dog whistle rendered her unconscious. Returned to us as an insane Galactic Doll, she has recovered from it. That same special therapy salvaged the other female soldiers who were subjected to it, too.

"I have it on good authority that many of them rejoined when they heard Kick Ass returned and was in charge of the regiment. Will she be able to reverse the direction this war's been going? Until now, every skirmish has been lost with severe casualties.

"In fact, recruitment is down so much that GD has had to make many unusual offers. I can't say I blame men for not signing up. Hundreds upon hundreds of men have lost an arm and leg in these confrontations with the enemy. That's enough to ensure this reporter will stay clear of the actual battle.

"We owe thanks to the sisters of Colonel Kick Ass. Their discovery that the Galactic Doll genetic mutation also regrows missing limbs is monumental in scope, giving these men a new chance on life. These valiant men paid a steep price; some are calling them male Galactic Dolls.

"Hold on a second. Yes, we're hearing the company captains reporting in. I think something big is about to happen."

"Third battalion is in position, Colonel."

"Check," said Bev.

One by one, the various leaders checked in.

"Okay, we're set. Engineers, activate the jammers."

Six voices acknowledged their compliance.

Harvey said, "I'm not sure what that exchange was all about. This is the first we've heard of jammers. I'll try to find out. Lieutenant Jackson. Lieutenant Jackson, what are the jammers supposed to do?"

She glanced at him, but ignored his question, focusing on what Colonel Kick Ass might need next. The many monitors became a hive of activity. Soldiers raced towards the line of the enemy, blaster guns blazing. Artillery shells pounded the heart of the encampment, blowing up enemy transport vehicles. Bev wanted to make sure there was no retreat possible for the Invaders. Drones hovered overhead, and six dropped their payload on the giant medical-like machines the enemy had used to amputate arms and legs. For unknown reasons, the enemy's deflective shields didn't go up as they had in previous attacks.

"What the hell is going on?" Kick Ass screamed, as her eyes roamed from monitor to monitor. "No one's firing back! Captain Jones, gimme a close up on that inert Invader. Okay. See if you can remove its armor. We want to see what these cannibals look like."

Harvey said, "Zoom in on that monitor. Follow what Colonel Kick Ass is doing and looking at."

Bev said, "What the hell is that thing?"

Captain Jones said, "I think it's a robot or something. It's inert now. Blasting its head off."

Boom. The severed head rolled away.

"All battalion captains," Colonel Kick Ass barked, "remove the body armor and knock the robot heads off. Capture the dog whistles and get them back to HQ fast."

Harvey said, "I can't believe what I'm seeing! These Sixth Invaders are robots of some kind. Whatever Colonel Kick Ass is doing, for the first time in the war, it's working. The Invaders haven't fired a shot. Just look at the robot heads falling left and right. Within mere minutes, Colonel Kick Ass and her Forty-second Regiment have retaken all the ground lost and have eliminated the Sixth Invaders' ground force. Unbelievable, just unbelievable. I've no words to describe what we're seeing. Soldiers are smashing the robots with abandon."

Colonel Kick Ass said, "Okay, engineers. I want you to turn off the jammers for a second. If you see any reaction from the robots, turn them back on again fast!"

Suddenly, beheaded robot bodies wiggled and jerked. Some of the "eyes" in the heads looked left and right, but couldn't relay signals to the rest of its body. Several that still wore armor opened fire but went inert the moment the jammers came back on.

Bev yelled, "Way to go, Ted and Holly Ann! Yahoo! General, you seeing all this? We're eliminating the entire ground invasion force. We've been fighting a bunch of robots! Captain Jones, get me a close up of one of their big guns."

"Kick Ass, they look like our own guns but with cosmetic changes. What's going on?"

"Round up a dozen examples. Bring that dog whistle

too, Captain."

"Zone One secure, sir."

One by one, the six battalions reported in. All firing ceased.

"Collect up all the bits and pieces. Get the engineers working on identifying what we've got. General, if you're hearing this, we need tech support out here fast. Repeat that, Captain Jones."

"Sir, this robot has GR logos on many of its parts. Yes, Galactic Robotics. What the hell's going on?"

"Sir," another captain interrupted. "We've located a hyperspace relay box here. It's on and active. What are your orders?"

"Shit. General, get a tech team out here like yesterday or we're going to have to blow up that relay box."

"Colonel BB, do not damage that relay box! That's a direct order. Do not touch it. We're sending a team now. ETA ten minutes. Hold until then. I repeat. Do not harm that box. What's with those jammers? Where did they come from? What are they supposed to be doing?"

"My sister's husband, Ted Billings, sir. He and a friend, Holly Ann Chesterfield, detected signals in an unused frequency band emanating from GD headquarters in Chicago, Earth, and designed these jammers. My engineers built them to their specs. He told me to turn them on before I launch my attack. I've proven they work. When my engineers turned them off, all the robots attempted to activate, and they shot at two soldiers before they turned the jammers back on again. That's all I know about them. If you want to know more, contact Ted Billings in Chicago. He's staying at the Cartwright Skyscraper. Another thing, if you contact them, tell Deanna Cartwright that I'll send along one of the dog whistles for her to study since she invented our only protection against them to date."

Bev smiled, knowing that now the army couldn't leave Deanna out of the picture with those machines.

"Well done, Colonel. Well done," the general said.

***

Off camera, Harvey said, "At long last, we're winning the war with the Sixth Invaders. Someone should get an interview with that Ted Billings fellow and his associate, Holly Ann Chesterfield. Relay that to GEnt Chicago, Earth."

A technician headed off to do that while Harvey went on camera again.

"You're seeing incredible breaking news brought to you by Galactic Entertainment, live from North Continent, Brussels, Tau Ceti, where we've just witnessed Colonel Kick Ass BB's assault and total elimination of the entire Sixth Invader ground force here in the north."

He continued his broadcast though there was little to see beyond soldiers carting bits and pieces off to waiting EMACs.

An EMAC landed close to the center of the invader encampment. Techs in their yellow uniforms rushed out. While several stopped to examine the robot remains, three went to work on the hyperspace relay box. Colonel Kick Ass kept her captain standing close to the men so she could overhear them. If GR or GD was somehow involved, she didn't dare trust anyone but GEnt people.

She overheard their talk. "Running the backtrace now. Start the record logger. Good. We're recording the signal now. Backtrace ongoing. Tracking the time delay. One minute." He continued calling out the minutes.

"Lieutenant Jackson, any idea what the minutes mean?" Bev asked.

"Not certain, sir, but I think the longer the delay, the further away the other party is. I know the time delay to Earth is five minutes. I heard that once."

"Five point two minutes. That's gotta be Earth."

Another voice said, "Okay. Send the info to GPan Earth. Order a full trace on this signal before we lose it."

Bev said, "Captain, stay with those three techs. I want to know what they hear on the trace. I think we're about to discover traitors in our midst."

"Aye, sir."

Chapter 26 "You Can't Always Get What You Want"

Casper Hugo's infatuation with Molly Parkinson-Billings rose to a fevered pitch, especially when he learned his own wife had taken her to lunch. Molly had ignored all his heartfelt pleas though he didn't intend to marry her. She would be his consort, his play toy, and a way to make Helen more pliable to his whims. He'd make her the happiest woman in the world and the most satisfied, too. *I'm handsome, wealthy, and the CFO. What more could any woman want? Molly. I don't get why you aren't running to me.*

He sat alone in his office, part of his large suite on the ninety-fifth floor of the GD skyscraper.

"I'll have to take matters into my own hands. I can see that. Helen said she uses her toes, so we mustn't allow that. I know. The heels with the ankle bands like the women wore to the ball—she can't take them off. Time to get what I need. Molly, tomorrow night, you're going to be mine, and you will love being with me, wishing you'd taken my offer when I first made it. And you'll want for nothing. Helen'll be your personal assistant. No more doing all those silly things with your feet because you will be the beautiful Doll you were meant to be."

What worked before should work again was Casper's thinking. He had helped Hardy arrange the earlier raid on the four in the Cartwright Skyscraper, so it was a simple matter of arranging payment for those three men—that and obtaining chloroform. The strike hour: midnight.

***

The stolen EMAC hovered close to one window on the forty-ninth floor. Through the thick pane, the men spotted the long hallway with various suites branching to either side. One man pointed out the right suite and then held the suction cups in place. His partner forced the diamond tip cutter in a giant square about four feet high. A tug pulled the slab of thick, heavy glass loose. Maneuvering it via the suction cups, the man stowed it inside the vehicle, while the other man grabbed the rag and chloroform bottle. Both men stepped into the hallway. Neither knew Deanna had reacted after the earlier break-in by installing motion sensors on all the windows on this, the living suites floor.

When the two men stepped inside, they heard alarms going off. One drew his gun with a silencer on it. "Damn. We best make this fast."

As they ran down the hall to the right suite, the second man poured chloroform on the rag. They dashed into Ted and Molly's bedroom, just as the noise roused the pair who struggled to sit up.

Bang. The silenced shot hit Ted in his chest, making a weird crunching noise. Molly's eyes darted to her left. A line of red expanded across the sheet. She screamed but the other man pressed a rag over her face. With her legs still beneath the sheets, her little resistance proved futile. Darkness swept over her. Dropping the rag and bottle, the man lifted her up, draped her over his shoulder, and headed out the door, while the gunman kept watch, holding the door open.

Cartwright security guards dashed into the hall from the far end but chose not to shoot. Molly's inert body blocked any clear shot. The other kidnapper fired off a clip, aiming in the direction of the guards who dodged them. As he did this, the man carrying Molly passed by him, jumping into the waiting EMAC. The remaining gunman dove through the hole and into the EMAC just as it took off, rising rapidly, and thus giving the guards no opportunity to fire back as they fled.

They landed on the top floor of the GD skyscraper. Casper, who spent the last hour pacing back and forth, rushed to the door, just as the men opened it. He relaxed. They had Molly, his new play toy.

"Cover her with this. No prying eyes. This way."

He tossed a sheet and watched the two men wrap her up. Again, the man carried her over his shoulder, following Casper into the building, while the driver and gunman left to dispose of the stolen vehicle.

"Sit her there on that chair. I'll take it from here," Casper said.

Now alone in his private bedroom, his eyes sparkled; a gigantic smile formed on his face. He pulled the sheet off his prize and studied her naked form for a minute. Then, he retrieved the shoe box and put the red heels on her feet, strapping the two-inch bands around her ankles.

"There, now you can't use your feet against me."

He waved smelling salts around her nose, waking Molly.

***

Casper didn't see Helen peering into the bedroom from a crack in the door. Yet, she saw his crazed expression, the wild glee in his eyes, as he ran his fingers over the unconscious body, the insane smile on his face. He didn't know she was listening to his every word from twenty feet away.

"Wake up, my precious Doll."

***

Molly's head jerked. The smell was awful. She opened her eyes and struggled to make sense. Ted was shot, bleeding, the rag, the bright lights, that voice.

"You! You killed Ted! You bastard."

"There, there, Molly. I gave you plenty of opportunities to divorce Ted, but you didn't. So I took matters into my own hands. Now you're my toy, my private Galactic Doll. Oh, if you'll notice, I've locked your heels onto your feet. Helen told me how adept you are with your toes. I'll have none of that from you. Tomorrow, you'll have everything a Doll could want, even someone to assist you. No more of those goofy antics with your toes. I can only imagine how embarrassed you've been to have to do such strange actions in public. Well, never again."

Molly decided not to scream or say another word. She guessed she must be somewhere inside the GD building because she spotted their logo on the side of a desk opposite the queen-sized bed. He was right about her feet; she couldn't easily undo ankle straps, ensuring she couldn't remove her heels. *No sense furthering his ego.* Molly remained silent and observant, knowing if she were going to get out of this mess and bring Casper to justice for killing Ted, Cool Head would have to do it. She gazed around the room.

The blue satin bedspread and matching sheets

357

suggested Casper had a sensuous streak. The thick, light blue carpet smelled fresh, as though recently cleaned. Her eyes took in a walk-in closet filled with many suits, mostly grays and browns, along with white shirts. Five pairs of polished black shoes lay side by side in perfect alignment. On the other side, the large desk held a computer and swivel chair, which rested on a large plastic pad. Nearby, two other chairs, like the one she sat on, rested against the wall. Behind her, a private bathroom beckoned with golden fixtures, complete with tub and shower. Molly detected a faint odor of cleaning solvents. She concluded a maid must service this room. Casper would never deign to clean a toilet bowl.

Molly saw no gun, no knives, and nothing that could be a weapon unless one counted the trash can sitting beside the desk. That alone was a key observation, for Molly realized she could take him out. *Bide my time.*

"Get into bed," Casper ordered.

Molly rose, walked to the bed, and sat down on one edge near the foot. Normally, she'd use a toe or perhaps her teeth to pull back the sheets. Instead, she sat waiting like a black cat poised and motionless, but ready to pounce on the unsuspecting. She watched him undress. He removed his shoes, placing them in the neat line in his closet. He slipped his phone out of his pocket, setting it on his desk. With practiced motions, he undressed, hanging each item in its proper place, ready for laundering. Wearing only his underpants and grinning, he walked over to join her by the bed.

From the look on his face, she suspected he was wondering why she was still silent. Casper continued to taunt her.

"Can't you even pull down the covers? Oh, I see you're still wearing your heels, so you can't use your toes."

She saw her silence unnerved him. He goaded her.

"Guess you'll have to sleep in your heels, but please don't poke holes in the sheets. They're expensive satin."

Still, Molly had no reaction, but she rose off the bed.

"Don't worry. I'll have someone feed you in the morning, but you'll spend the rest of your life in my suite here."

Still nothing. He leaned over, pulling back the sheets.

The panther struck.

Bev's hours spent teaching her to fight using her feet weren't wasted. She swung her left leg up and around, executing a circle kick using the top of her foot. She timed it perfectly. Just as he stood back up, her left foot struck the left side of his neck. He collapsed onto the bed, out cold. Molly lost her balance and landed in a heap on the soft floor. She struggled to her feet and walked over to the desk and his phone. Molly made a futile attempt to use a heel to dial, but gave that up, instead using her tongue and nose.

"Deanna? Molly. Casper Hugo kidnaped me. I'm somewhere in the GD building. He's killed Ted. I need help."

"Oh, thank god, you're alive. Are you wounded? Holly Ann and Kyle are with Ted at the Medical Center. He's one lucky man. He fell asleep with his laptop on his chest. The bullet went through the laptop, but only grazed him."

"Incredible. Is he going to be all right? I'm okay. He's got heels locked on with ankle straps, so I'm stuck here. I knocked Casper out. Can someone rescue me? I just heard a gunshot!"

Helen stepped into the room, holding her hand up to her lips. "It's okay. I'll help you."

Molly said, "Deanna, Helen's here. She'll help me, too, but we've got to get justice."

Deanna said, "I rather figured that's where you were taken. We're on our way, almost there. If Helen can—wait. Good lord! There are a hundred policemen and Local Defense Force men swarming the GD building. Call you back."

***

Chief Science Officer G'Karn said, "Field tests of the new robot soldiers have been successful, Commander R'Ina. But humans have uncovered our robot soldier plot, resulting in the complete destruction of our test robots on Brussels, Tau Ceti. Molly Parkinson-Billings and Ted Billings are proving formidable opponents. Your orders?"

Commander R'Ina smiled. "I expected this to happen. Now, we enter the next phase in our plan to totally discredit these corporations and their men. Here's what we're going to do next. I'll promote Molly to become the temporary head of GD and to investigate the robot scandal, based on her believability factor. Likewise, her clone sister, Beverly Blossom Blythe must be promoted to general of the First Division. We have a lot to do and little time. Get Captain L'Grina ready to abandon Hardy's body and swap him back when someone arrives to shoot him."

She then called up Chicago's Police Superintendent. "CEO Armstrong here, GPan. Yes superintendent, Mr. Hardy, the CEO of Galactic Defense, has betrayed the Sol Empire. It's likely that many others in GD are involved in this incredible Sixth Invader hoax. I want you to mobilize the entire Chicago PD and Local Defense Force. I'll send along GPan security men to coordinate the takeover. We'll raid the place around 2:00 a.m. Understood? And make sure no one escapes, either on foot or from the roof in an EMAC."

"Aye, sir. On it," the superintendent of the CPD replied. "Oh, good heavens!"

Over the phone, Armstrong heard the news playing in the background and smiled as he hung up. He pressed a button.

"You buzzed, sir?" Hank responded.

"Yes, I have a situation for you to handle. You must not be seen."

He outlined what he wanted done, knowing his top assassin wouldn't fail. Next, he called Hardy, or rather Captain L'Grina.

"Get ready for the reverse swap. Five minutes."

"I'm watching the news now. Superbly done, Commander. These foolish men in GD will be completely discredited or worse. Have you figured out a replacement?" When she heard the name, she laughed. "Genius, Commander, pure genius. Oh, the swap has started. See you—"

She floated off in the pure white aesthetic energy flow. Mr. Hardy, who had been unconscious for more than two decades, found himself awake, but his body had somehow aged more than twenty years. Confused, he struggled to make sense of the situation, feeling his arms and legs, as though just discovering he had them.

The comm center was still on and reporters were still discussing the treachery of GD and their Sixth Invader robot hoax. Mr. Hardy wasn't stupid. Something was completely wrong. He rose and muttered, "I'm getting out of here now."

Just as he reached the door, it opened. A man with a silenced gun stood there. He fired, but caught Mr. Hardy's body before it fell.

Meanwhile, Armstrong, or rather Commander R'Ina, rose and headed to GPan's hyperspace relay room, where he placed a call to Brussels, Tau Ceti.

"Ah yes. This is Mr. Armstrong, CEO of Earth's Galactic Expansion corporation. I've just heard the awful news. I'm handling Galactic Defense on this end. Expect a total overhaul of that corporation. We will look into any complicity by Galactic Robotics, too. Based on past performance of GD generals, I want two immediate actions handled. I want you to arrest First Division General Spitzer on a charge of incompetence. Then, I want this Colonel Beverly Blossom Blythe promoted to First Division general. Have it done with full military honors and broadcast empire-wide by GEnt."

"Aye, sir. Within the hour. The situation here is almost indescribable."

"Yes, yes, but we must act swiftly. Get it done. Goodbye."

Armstrong hung up, again smiling. Later, his phone rang. "Ah, Phillips. How's it going?"

"Potential problem, sir. Mrs. Deanna Cartwright is here. Claims CFO Casper Hugo kidnaped Molly Parkinson-Billings and shot her husband, Ted. Apparently, Molly has subdued Casper, but she is trapped inside GD. Orders?"

Armstrong thought for a moment. "Brilliant, Phillips, just brilliant. I would never have expected her action. In fact, this makes everything much simpler. Your first action: get to her and see she's safe. Tell her GPan has temporarily appointed her to be the CEO of GD and to use her PI skills to flush out the guilty parties. She's to handle justice any way she desires. Best have her call me. Tomorrow morning, we'll hold a press conference. Much will have to be explained. I'll expect her call. Goodbye."

He sat back, his hands pressed up behind his head. *This couldn't have worked out better if I'd planned it. In one day, I have my choice in as First Division general and a perfect choice for temporary GD CEO. Credibility in spades. Robotics will be tricky, but if Molly's PI work pans out, she'll handle it for me.*

***

Helen entered the private bedroom of her husband, her eyes watching Casper as though she expected him to rise any moment.

"Is he really out? Are you okay?"

"Knocked him out with my foot. He's gonna have a sore neck. Get me out of these heels, please."

Helen undid the ankle straps and turned on the news. Both women gasped. Molly said, "Way to go, Bev!"

However, Helen saw Molly shivering and asked, "What're we going to do for clothes? I'm much shorter than you are."

Molly studied Helen for a moment.

"I doubt I can wear yours. I know. Use his cell. Recall the last number. It's Deanna."

Helen's long nails clicked on the glass.

As it rang, Molly smiled. "Deanna. I need clothes and heels."

Deanna laughed. "We figured that out for ourselves. We're on the way to you now. Hold tight. Just entering the building. Never seen so many policemen in one spot. What floor are you on?"

Helen heard and said, "Ninety-fifth. Suite A."

"At the elevators. A bigwig from Galactic Expansion is with me. Wants to talk to you. Important, or so he claims. See you soon."

"I'll wait by the door, Molly. Will you be okay alone with him?"

"Yes. I'll kick him again if needed."

Casper showed no signs of waking.

Soon Deanna peered into the room. "All clear?"

Molly grinned. "Yes. Come in. I'm freezing. Thanks."

"A VP of GPan, a John Phillips, is talking with Helen now. He's demanding to talk with you. Told him not until you're dressed. I embarrassed him. There you go. Forgot to bring a hairbrush."

She draped Molly's hair over her shoulders. Molly sat down at the desk, while Deanna brought in the man, but Molly had no idea what Galactic Expansion could want with her. From Deanna's expression, Molly guessed she didn't either, but she was sure Deanna would stick by her.

A tall, thin man wearing a gray suit marched into the room. His pant creases appeared pristine as though coming directly from a tailor even though the clock on the desk showed 2 a.m. His elliptical face contrasted with his muscular frame, and beady black eyes took in everything at a glance. Molly's first impression was here was a man who wielded power.

"Hello. I am VP John Phillips of the Chicago Galactic Expansion corporation. Our office services the entire Sol Empire. I am here at the request of our CEO Mr. Armstrong. And you are Mrs. Molly Parkinson-Billings, Private Investigator, correct?"

"Yes, sir. I'm Molly. How do you know me?"

"GPan oversees all other corporations. It's our job to know. We've been keeping an eye on GD CEO Hardy, but until today, we had nothing on him. You used to be sponsored by GD but were dropped. We found that suspicious and looked into it. We've not been able to uncover all the details. But from GEnt, we know you have proven to be an exceptional PI."

"What if I am?"

"I'll be brief, Molly. May I call you Molly? You may call me John."

Anything to get this over. I need to see Ted before I fall asleep on my feet. "Okay, John. Can we make this quick? My husband was almost murdered this evening. Besides, it's late."

"Molly, since GPan oversees all other corporations and considering what's just happened on Brussels, Tau Ceti, and here in this office tonight, Mr. Armstrong has appointed you to be the temporary CEO of Chicago's Galactic Defense corporation."

Deanna's eyes bulged. Her lower jaw dropped. Molly's eyebrows rose. "Huh?" she mumbled. Of all the things she thought she might hear from this executive, this wasn't even in the same universe.

"Yes, as of this minute, you are the temporary official CEO of GD here in Chicago. GPan suspects there has been massive corruption and criminal actions perpetrated out of this office and over many years, most originating from the deceased CEO Hardy. Your task, Molly, is to use all your PI skills to root out this corruption—how Hardy ran the Sixth Invaders, and every other criminal action you can uncover.

"Search and uncover all those illegal plots. Find the guilty parties. Bring justice for everyone. You're in charge. You decide what each guilty person's justice should be. Wipe out the rampant, covert corruption within Chicago GD. Once that's done, your assignment will be complete.

"Your monthly pay will be that of CEO Hardy's. You have the complete backing of GPan. With that, your authority is absolute and will be recognized as such.

"Now then, specifics. We must visit Hardy's office on the top floor tonight. In the morning, say ten o'clock, we will hold a press conference at which time I will make your appointment public knowledge. You may bring any others onboard your investigations as you wish. Molly, your task is enormous, but Mr. Armstrong has complete faith in you. Only someone with your incredible PI skills can be trusted to clean up this mess."

"Wow. You're joking about all this. Right?"

"Do I look like I'm joking? Now then, we must visit Hardy's office. Mrs. Cartwright is it? You may join us. I'm told it's not a pretty sight."

As they headed for the elevator, he continued briefing them. "When CEO Hardy learned Colonel Beverly Blossom Blythe destroyed the Sixth Invaders and discovered they were robots controlled by a computer system in this building, he took his own life. That's what I've been told."

The elevator doors opened, revealing a plush hallway. Two men wearing the purple uniforms with the gold trim of GPan and holding blasters, not guns, stood guard.

"No one has entered this floor, per your orders, Mr. Phillips." He also saluted.

"Excellent. This is Molly Parkinson-Billings, the new CEO of GD here. Only she and her associates are allowed access to this floor until she says otherwise."

"Aye, sir."

"Okay, Molly, this way. Nothing has been touched. As you can see, we believe he shot himself in the head to avoid facing the enormous consequences of his actions. With your approval, I'll have the CP crime scene technicians analyze this room and remove the deceased."

"Don't let them remove anything from this floor. Who knows what could be important," Molly said. The man had a hole in his head, but something looked a little off. "Tell the CSI people to verify this man shot himself."

"Why do you say that?"

"Obviously, he was shot in the head. Forehead. Between the eyes. If I were going to shoot myself, I might stick the gun in my mouth or at the side of my head. I can't imagine holding it to my forehead and seeing the bullet coming at me. Also, you'll notice no powder burns around the edges of the entrance wound. Gun wasn't up close. He doesn't have very long arms. Have CSI check this out."

"Incredible, Molly. Mr. Armstrong certainly has picked the right person to unravel this horrible mess at GD. Now, I'll let you go. Oh yes, here's your badge."

His hand moved forward holding a clip-on ID card, but he wavered, uncertain how to give it to her. His face flushed. Deanna took it for her, pinning it onto her dress top.

"Thank you. See you here at GD at ten tomorrow morning, Molly. Thank you."

Deanna slipped an arm around Molly's waist, nudging her into the open elevator. She put her finger to her lips.

Molly nodded, but said, "First, visit Helen."

A GPan security man stood guard just outside the Hugo suite. He noticed Molly's ID badge and followed them inside. They found Helen still watching over the unconscious Casper though she had tied his hands together. Molly and Helen exchanged whispered words.

Ted and I need justice for what Casper Hugo did to us. Helen needs justice even more than we do. Sending Casper to the penal colony isn't going to rehabilitate him, but Helen's idea just might. I know it's inhumane, but this might teach him a lesson. He just might regain his lost humanity. That would satisfy me and Helen, I expect. Okay. I'll do it.

"Guard, take him to the Medical Center. Helen will go with you. She knows what treatment he is to receive. Make sure it's done per her request."

"Yes, sir," he replied, saluting her.

Molly nodded, and she and Deanna left for the elevators. Neither said a word until they reached the MTES and the snowy early morning. As the pair rode the moving sidewalks, Molly said, "I don't believe what's just happened."

"Neither do I. GD has a gigantic problem. If it's true that Hardy has been running these Sixth Invaders, wow. How did they do the implant thing? How did they create the dog whistle machines? The machines that did the amputations? Of course, if GD was behind it, no wonder the Invaders used our Galactic Doll mutation and our latest healing tech. So much makes sense, but you'll have your hands full ferreting out the truth."

"Deanna, I don't have any hands."

Deanna looked at the serious face of Molly; both burst out laughing. Deanna's phone rang.

Kyle called and said, "We're bringing Ted home from the Med Center now. He's fine."

She relayed that to Molly, who relaxed.

***

Once home, Ted was waiting for her. They pressed their bodies together, exchanging a passionate kiss.

"I thought you were dead," she said.

Ted chuckled. "I fell asleep with my laptop in my lap. The assassin put a hole through it. Kind of cut my chest up a little. Doc says I've got a cracked rib, but otherwise, I'm fine. So what happened with you? Kyle said that Casper fellow was behind it."

Chapter 27 Reconstruction

"I can't believe it!" Molly said.

Deanna, Leslie, and Janine gathered around the comm center display watching the early newscast relayed from Brussels, Tau Ceti. They had just seen their sister promoted to general of the First Division. Bev looked good in her blue satin dress uniform with yellow trim. She had her hair up in a tight bun beneath her cap.

The reporter asked, "So, General, can you tell us how you wiped out the entire Sixth Invader ground force? And did you know they were robots and not people or cannibals?"

Behind a wall of microphones, she said, "Combined arms. Use every weapon we have. Even drones. Don't hold back. Good field position. Plus, I took the advice of my sister's husband, Ted Billings, and his friend, Holly Ann. Their jamming device turned the tide. Without it, the battle would have been very bloody. We're still picking up robot pieces. What's left is just their space fleet. Not my thing. Ask the admirals about those. I'm thrilled our mutilated soldiers are getting their missing arms and legs regrown. That's what's important."

Deanna interrupted them. "We best get going, Molly. We don't dare be late."

"See, I told you we're like lucky," Leslie said. "Bev's lucky. Ted's lucky. Molly's lucky."

Janine grinned, fastening Molly's cloak around her. Kyle did the same for Ted while Deanna slipped on her parka.

Janine said, "We'll be watching the comm center, Molly. Knock 'em dead. Congratulations, too."

Molly smiled, pleased her sisters were here to see her off.

Once on the MTES, Molly admitted she was afraid. "This is intimidating. I don't know if I can handle it."

"Oh, you'll do fine. Just think of it as another PI investigation," Deanna said. "You've got Ted to handle the computer hacking. You have a chance to bring the guilty people to justice though what that means in our world isn't clear."

She added, "Molly, you be darn careful. Some may be out for revenge for taking them down. If you're right, someone shot Hardy. Who? Why? I have never trusted any corporation though GEnt seems okay so far. If GPan is supposed to oversee all corporations, then why did they miss everything Hardy did? I find that suspicious."

Molly replied, "I don't trust them either. We'll see. Gosh, that's a lot of reporters. Now, I *am* nervous."

Ted squeaked, "You and me both. I get to be embarrassed before the entire empire—a man who looks and sounds like a Galactic Doll."

"Sorry, dear, but I'm desperate for your computer skills."

John met them, ushering them into a side room where they deposited their cloaks. He then led the pair out before the wall of digital cameras, microphones, and reporters.

I hope he does all the talking.

"Good morning. I am VP John Phillips of the Chicago Galactic Expansion Corporation. As you know, an awful lot has happened during the last hours, some of it horrific. At this time, much evidence points to the Chicago Galactic Defense corporation and its head CEO Hardy. He was confronted with these allegations yesterday. His response was to commit suicide—at least, it initially appears to be a suicide.

"It is GPan's responsibility to oversee all corporations. In this case, we've failed in our duties. Considering the breadth of the potential nefarious and criminal actions committed by members of Chicago GD, GPan's position is to bring in an outside person to run GD and to get to the bottom of all allegations and charges against this corporation and any others involved in these conspiracies, such as the Sixth Invaders.

"GPan has chosen someone who has an outstanding record of investigations, someone who will not be intimidated and who will never back down, someone who will find and reveal the truth for us, someone you can trust.

"Last night, CEO Mr. Armstrong appointed that person.

I give you Mrs. Molly Parkinson-Billings who runs her own Molly Parkinson Private Investigations and Security company; as of yesterday, she is the temporary CEO of Chicago Galactic Defense corporation. She is tasked with a thorough investigation of GD, rooting out the guilty parties, and bringing them to a justice as she sees fit.

"I give you Molly Parkinson-Billings and her husband, Ted Billings, a computer expert who holds a PhD in Software Development and who is completing his doctorate in robotics, rather germane to this investigation."

The reporters politely applauded before sending volleys of questions their way. "Any truth to the rumors that GD was behind the entire Sixth Invaders? That it was all a hoax?"

John waved his hand to Molly, indicating she should answer it. "We've only heard what you've heard. We need time to investigate. Yes, my sister, General Beverly Blossom Blythe, used a signal jammer invented by Ted and our friend, Holly Ann. It stopped the robots from receiving their control orders, allowing her infantry to destroy them. Initial reports showed those jammed signals came from the large computer system in this building. We'll investigate that."

Another asked, "Aren't you and Ted helpless? How can you run this investigation?"

"No, we aren't. We do just fine." Molly flushed, rather annoyed.

"Did CEO Hardy take his own life?"

"That is an ongoing investigation," John answered.

"What was their objective with the Invaders?"

John fielded this one. "We have no idea. That's why GPan wants a complete and *outside* investigation. We will hold further press conferences when we know more facts. Now, let's let Molly get to work."

Molly and Ted joined Deanna while John continued to field more questions. Deanna carried their cloaks on up to the top floor. CSI personnel continued to scour the office for clues, and Hardy's wife had already packed their personal things and left. Hence, the pair set up shop in what had been Hardy's dining room. Deanna opened their laptops for them.

"Thanks, Deanna. You can take off now. You've your

own company to run. We'll manage here."

"You call if you need anything, Molly. You both watch your backs."

Ted said, "We will."

"Okay, dear. For each guilty person, we need to assemble complete files detailing their crimes. We'll get a whiteboard up here and generate a giant timeline. We need to make everything as clear as possible. If we don't, no one will ever trust GD again."

Helen walked in, followed by a dozen other women. "Hi, Molly. Their husbands forced these women to become Galactic Dolls. Of course, now women should be Dolls. Nevertheless, they want their husbands to receive the same treatment as my Casper."

Molly chuckled and looked the women over.

One said, "Look at me. I'm a pathetic shell of the woman I used to be. Lost a hundred pounds from the mutation if I've lost an ounce. I'm so skinny the Windy City will blow me away if I go outside. But yes, I know we all look beautiful now. It's just I should have had a say in it."

"Look at me," cried another woman. "I used to jog and run every day. I was healthy. Now I can't. Still, I know all women should be Galactic Dolls, but it's not fair. I want him to pay. I just know I'm going to die young."

Molly chuckled. "Okay, okay. I get it. Helen, have them write their husbands' names down for me. Make two lists, so Ted can have one. Then, I'll issue the orders and have them taken to the Med Center. Mind you, ladies, once done, it's permanent."

"We're permanent Galactic Dolls," one declared. Then, she amended it. "But we're supposed to be Galactic Dolls, aren't we?"

Later, Molly learned GPan guards hauled a dozen protesting GD executives to a Med Center. Doctors injected each with the gold nanoparticle genetic Galactic Doll mutation as it had become known. Further, seven days into their usual eight-day comas, doctors amputated their arms at their shoulders, completing their orders, as demanded by their wives. No one dared speak out against official GD orders.

Molly received confirmation of this from the Med Center.

Molly began her comprehensive document by listing these men and their criminal actions against their wives. Further, she noted that these women had requested their husbands receive this punishment. Later on, she added many more crimes to their files.

By the end of the first day, the CSI people finished their work, and a cleanup crew performed their miracle, making the office usable once more. Then, Molly and Ted made this their base of operations.

The next morning, two reports arrived on Molly's desk. The ME and CSI both agreed that CEO Hardy had not shot himself, despite ballistics matching the gun found on his floor to the bullet in his head and the positive GSR test on his hand. Molly smiled. Her initial observations were correct. Finding who had shot him was of little immediate importance because she had far bigger questions that demanded answers.

***

Four months later—April 15, 2352—Molly, Ted, and John held a lengthy press conference, during which Ted displayed on a giant screen much of the incriminating evidence the pair had uncovered. Molly gave the presentation, while Ted ran the audio-visuals for her, though he added a comment here and there.

Molly began, "CEO Hardy ran most of the action from here in Chicago, making use of other people's skills on other worlds. Let's discuss the robot army disguised as Sixth Invaders. Mr. Hardy set up a shell company to buy the necessary parts from Galactic Robotics. There is no direct evidence yet that GR knew what their parts were being used for. Their products are in widespread use in manufacturing. From the recovered parts, GR is now investigating the potential construction of human-form robots for home and industry.

"The parts were shipped to the penal colony on Mercury. As you know, that facility is at a high latitude where the temperature range is manageable. Inmates did the work. The robots needed an activation signal, which always came from GD's computer system here in Chicago, sent via

371

hyperspace relay. We know the robots were then controlled from an EMAC in orbit above Brussels, relay fashion. That abandoned vehicle has been located and warrants are out for the dozen men who ran the operations on Brussels and carried out the mutilations and death of our soldiers.

"We still don't know how Hardy invented the dog whistle technology, but we know researchers at the penal colony on Mercury tested it on inmates. Perhaps, they developed the powerful implant technology used on our female soldiers and the dog whistle machines that rendered our male soldiers unconscious. Our own people have duplicated this technology, resulting in a new medical technology called body swapping.

"We know Hardy used our own silver nanoparticle healing technology and the Galactic Doll gold nanoparticle genetic mutation technology developed by the Padella doctors. Among the dozen men and women we're searching for are two medical doctors and one psychiatrist. Ted is displaying their names, faces, and descriptions on the big screen. GPan is offering a reward for them, dead or alive.

"We've discovered that Mr. Hardy launched a missile strike on a South Pacific atoll to try to murder us and the Padella doctors. Then, when we uncovered too many things, Mr. Hardy ordered a raid on the Cartwright building, injecting us all with the Galactic Doll nanoparticle genetic mutation agent. Later, when I began regrowing arms, he panicked and arranged to have surgeons remove Ted's and my arms, paying the administrator, George Fielding, two hundred fifty thousand credits to arrange it.

"The question I've been asking myself is why? *Why* did Hardy do all this? What did he hope to gain? He spent—or more accurately stole—almost a trillion credits on this project. The why remains unknown. If he hadn't been murdered, then we might have discovered that answer. Was he murdered so we wouldn't find that answer? My personal feeling is that's what happened. Someone somewhere doesn't want that known.

"As you may have heard, three hundred three GD men were complicit in this mess and related criminal activities.

GPan insisted that I dole out their punishments. No one deserves to die. I believe life is sacred.

"I looked into the rehabilitation rate for criminals sent to the prisons on Mercury. Frankly, it's about zero. If I sent someone there, either they would die there or they would be back later committing more crimes. So I gave the guilty a choice: appropriate prison terms on Mercury or become a male Galactic Doll, figuring they'd have a much more difficult time committing crimes as one of us. Who knows, maybe they'll rehabilitate this way. I was surprised, though I shouldn't have been, that most opted for the prison sentence.

"I also uncovered other crimes against specific people. These too have been handled." By that, Molly meant crimes against herself, Ted, and the female and male clones. "Because GD wanted to include everyone in the Sol Empire in its massive DNA database, General Fuller wanted the clones dead to protect what he saw as the invaluable research of the Padella doctors, who had pioneered the silver nanoparticle healing tech and the Galactic Doll mutation gold nanotechnology. Further, a couple years ago, Mr. Hardy ordered me to murder retired General Fuller, the man who ran the illegal cloning project over two decades ago. I refused to become a murderer, and he shot himself.

"Recompense. This brings us to the legal ramifications of CEO Hardy's actions. I'm not qualified to handle such matters. GPan lawyers are hashing this out with GD lawyers. I'm told that some form of remuneration will be made at some point. When? Well, you know lawyers." That brought a laugh from the reporters.

Molly then asked for questions though John moderated them. When the conference ended, Molly requested John join her in the CEO office.

"Before we delve into why CEO Hardy did all this, there's another matter I uncovered. This business of killing everyone by the time they're sixty-five. Giving them drugs that destroy their brains, dementia. Retired at sixty, drugged, and terminated by sixty-five."

Molly felt her blood pressure rise. She couldn't forget her own parents and their dementia, nor could she forget many others. If only she could make this public knowledge, then maybe someone could end it. Molly was smart enough to know something as widespread as this practice was must have a reason, perhaps a critical one. Hence, she decided to discuss it with John before going public with it.

"Damn, Molly. You're far sharper than we ever imagined. So you discovered this, but you didn't bring it up before the cameras?"

"No. If I did, it could cause mammoth problems for all corporations. I wanted to ask you about it first. If you can't convince me why we should be killing our older people, then I will go public with it. Yes, that's a threat." She stared into his eyes.

"Bring up Finance Document 11043, Ted," John calmly replied.

For a moment, Molly fretted that John wouldn't have enough patience to allow Ted to do it. She and Ted were slow with most actions that others took for granted.

"This is the source or the reason that's often cited, Molly. Centuries ago, men and women lived sometimes into their nineties, even hundreds. But usually their quality of life wasn't good. Many had to live in nursing homes that ate up all their life savings. All manner of diseases plagued them, many eventually resulting in their deaths. The healthcare cost to handle the older people is shown at the bottom.

"Those trillions of credits per year could pay for a dozen deep space exploration ships. This current policy of sixty and out allows the corporations to subsidize every person, guaranteeing them a job, a roof over their heads, and food on the table. If we allowed people to die of natural causes at ripe old ages, the entire economy of the Sol Empire would crash. Every person would end up being responsible for their entire living costs—no subsidies.

"Medical costs are problematical. The cost of a heart attack is around a hundred thousand credits. People couldn't pay such a bill. If the corporations covered it via healthcare, they'd go bankrupt overnight. Either that or jack up prices of their goods to cover those expenses, but then workers would be able to buy less. It's a circular path to destruction.

"So we keep quiet about it. True, a few have discovered the truth. Nothing has come from it. I loved my parents, but I'm a realist. We all die one day. I'd rather my children have a good life than live so long that my quality of life deteriorates."

Molly sighed. "I won't say anything about it."

John nodded, solemn-faced.

"Next, I want to explore Hardy's murder. We suspect he was silenced for what he knew. The why of his actions are unknown. I think we've only touched the surface of Hardy's conspiracy."

"Maybe on your own, Molly. GPan is very pleased with your investigations, but it's time to wrap it up. GD needs a new CEO and to begin their lengthy recovery. GPan will have to oversee the corporation for years to come. Mr. Armstrong wants to talk to you."

Molly wanted to protest. Her investigations were hardly finished, but from John's words and actions, she knew it was over. John activated his phone. The holo image of the CEO appeared hovering in space.

"Hello, Molly. I'm Mr. Armstrong, CEO of GPan."

"I'm here. My investigations aren't done yet."

"Your work has been exemplary, Molly, but we need to get GD operational again. I always reward those who do stellar work, as you and Ted have done for the empire. If you decide that you don't want to return to your small PI company, GPan will sponsor you in whatever new endeavor you wish to do.

"For instance, GPan has a Galaxy Detective Squad that travels throughout the empire handling tough cases that cross world boundaries. You have a standing offer to join them. Just say the word. Families are welcome in the GDS. Ted could have a position with them, too, if he wants.

"I wish I had the means and power to restore your arms, but alas, I do not. It's a miracle that the Padellas' research has such a byproduct. I've urged GMed to study the Galactic Doll genetic mutation in hopes they can isolate and develop a procedure to regrow missing body parts, not just arms and legs. If that ever produces results, I will see you and Ted get the treatment as soon as possible."

"Thanks. I will research the GDS, but I've never heard

of that group. I take it you'd prefer Ted and me vacate GD today?"

"If you would be so kind. Right now, the Sol Empire is vulnerable to an outside attack—what with GD being in such disarray. There still are real Sixth Invaders out there."

"Okay then. Thanks and we may get back to you on that offer. Goodbye."

***

Commander R'Ina, currently in Mr. Armstrong's body, sat with Captain L'Grina, who used her Morph Unit to appear to be a human. From her facial expressions, Commander R'Ina saw her captain was greatly relieved to be done having to be in Mr. Hardy's body.

"Well, I had to dismiss Molly from the CEO position," said Commander R'Ina. "She accomplished her purpose, but she was getting too close to the actual underlying causes. See, Captain, we're making progress. Earth women can be very able people."

"Yes, Commander, but this Molly is almost too bright. She's come dangerously close to uncovering us. I had to implant some suggestions into her mind to keep her from following certain leads, like where GD got the implant technology, the dog whistles, and such. She's trouble."

"Yes, well, we'll watch her. She has done a tremendous job discrediting GD and other men. We're ready to enter our final phase of operations. I hope these Earth people put women into all these vacated GD positions. How's Chief Science Officer G'Karn coming on his two final projects?"

"Robots will be ready soon. I've put a rush on the bio agents. He complained bitterly but is doing it."

"Excellent. Another year and the Sol Empire will be ours." Both smiled.

Part 6

Vic Broquard

Chapter 28 Many Changes

Molly and Ted traveled home from GD on the MTES. Ted said, "I think they didn't want us to look into Hardy's murder too closely. That's why he sacked us."

Molly chuckled. "I agree. We still don't know why Hardy did it or what he hoped to accomplish. Nor do we know where he got the dog whistle things. Or even how they developed those giant amputation machine things. Lots of questions remain."

"How about stopping at StarLight's Coffee Shop?"

"We're lugging all these computers. Well, I suppose we can ask them to help us. A cocoa would hit the spot now, but I'd like a brown ale tonight."

The automatic door opened, and they joined the line. As they reached the counter, a young woman came up to them. "You're that Molly Parkinson detective, aren't you? Running GD?"

"Yes, but my temporary assignment has just ended. Two hot cocoas please."

"Let me help you. I'm Mary Trout, a geneticist at GMed."

Molly said, "Thanks. We're loaded down with our stuff. We have to use our toes, and in these cloaks and boots, it's more difficult. Do you want to talk with me?"

She flushed. "Yes, how did you know? Never mind. This way." Mary led them to an isolated table near the rear, took their cloaks off, and got straws for their drinks, before sitting down herself. She, too, looked the perfect Galactic Doll, but she wore a light blue gown matching her eyes and contrasting with her golden blonde hair.

"While you sip, I'll explain. I have my PhD in genetics. There's a big push on reworking the Padellas' nanoparticle genetic mutation sequences. But there's something else that no one is talking about."

Molly nodded, and Mary continued. "Us, I mean the Galactic Doll, is a genetic mutation. The Padella breakthrough causes a body to regenerate, like an injured fetus in the womb, but it's still a *genetic* mutation."

Molly frowned and saw that Mary correctly interpreted that as a sign that Molly didn't get her point. "It's a genetic mutation. Our babies inherit our genes. So our children will inherit our Galactic Doll mutation."

"Damn, that's not so good. If we have a daughter, Ted, I'd like her to make her own choice, even though women are supposed to look good."

Mary said, "Not going to happen. Her body will be a Galactic Doll, too. What's not yet clear is how soon they will develop our giant mammary glands. My hunch is that they will grow rapidly as they near puberty. I also think their legs will be deformed like ours are. They'll have to wear tall heels when they first learn to walk."

"Well, that sucks," said Molly.

"Actually, it's worse."

"How can it be any worse?" asked Ted.

"If you have a boy, his body will also be a Galactic Doll. These genetic mutations are dominant."

"You've got to be kidding!" Ted said.

"How come no one told us this before?" Molly asked.

"No one's talking about that side-effect—not until it manifests itself. Many of my peers don't think it will happen. In fact, I've been ordered to never mention these things. There's no proof, they say, but I think they're fooling themselves."

Molly said, "Crap. From the last reports I've seen, all high school senior girls are expecting to be Galactic Dolls as soon as they graduate. Well, they should look good."

Mary sighed, took a sip of her cocoa, and continued. "I know they should. I checked on that, too. There's no stopping it now. Every girl sees this as in her best interest. In fact, millions of graduating girls are already scheduled to have it done, starting mid-May. There's hardly an adult woman who hasn't done it or is waiting her turn. It's as though women have lost all common sense. Well, I shouldn't be so harsh. We're supposed to be beautiful Dolls. I've done it, but then it was understood that we graduates would have to set an

380

example. Besides, I'm sure they wouldn't have hired me if I hadn't. And now, I'm sure women were always supposed to become Galactic Dolls." She looked confused when she said that last sentence.

After a pause, Mary looked into Molly's eyes. "Do you realize what this means twenty years from now?"

Molly said, "Everyone will be Galactic Dolls."

Ted said, "All men will be Dolls. How will any heavy work get done? How can they perform as guards and soldiers? Geesh, the ramifications are enormous."

Mary said, "Now you see what I see. It scares me, but what can we do about it? Who will listen? You didn't hear this from me. I'll get fired if they find out. Besides, women are supposed to become Galactic Dolls."

"We can try," Molly said.

"I did that, but if you ask other geneticists, they say it's too early to say anything. That I'm being paranoid. That I should wait and see and not raise a panic. Besides, GMed has ordered all geneticists everywhere to work on finding a cure for the degenerative brain diseases that wipe out the minds of older people. I suppose that's a good thing since it's a pandemic. Still..."

"Point taken," Molly said. "If your peers discount it, then we have no hope to change things."

"I know I should have come to you sooner—when you were still running GD. Maybe you could have done something."

"Who knows? Meanwhile, you should focus your efforts on developing a way to undo this mutation. Even better, find a way to regrow lost body parts without turning the patients into Galactic Dolls, too."

Mary giggled. "I know. I'll try to do that. Can we stay in touch?"

Molly gave her their number and email addresses which Mary jotted on a napkin and put it in her purse. Mary helped them into their cloaks and made sure they made it back to the MTES before she headed off in the opposite direction. None of the three noticed a man following Mary.

***

Since Deanna had told everyone that GPan ended Molly's temporary appointment, Holly Ann arranged a big celebration dinner. Leslie and Felix, along with Janine and Hank, dropped by to share dinner with Ted and Molly. They brought six-packs of brown ale for her.

Leslie said, "Isn't that just like a man? Sacking you like when you've just done a wonderful job. Well, we're still lucky. Just look at Ted. Super lucky. Laptop like stopped the bullet."

Ted smiled and said nothing, so Leslie changed topics. "I've like got another photo shoot coming up, so my luck is holding. Anyone like want to come to the fetish dance with Felix and me Saturday night? My costume shop has like lots of fetish outfits now. We're like expanding our line of apparel."

Deanna said, "Well, I need to get my body modified, too. It's scheduled for tomorrow."

"I thought you wanted nothing to do with being a Galactic Doll," Molly said.

"I don't—er, didn't." She flashed them a sheepish look. "But all women should be beautiful Galactic Dolls."

Molly said, "Humanity is long gone. That's what. We'll be there for you, Deanna."

Just then, Celeste entered. "Hi, everyone. I'm back for a visit."

"How's St. Louis treating you?" asked Janine.

"Still being lucky?" Leslie asked.

"Amazingly successful, but I'm more interested in these two." Celeste pointed to Molly and Ted. "I'm back so I can work with you two. With more therapy, we may undo what's been done."

Ted said, "Thank heavens."

Molly added, "Kind of pissed me off. We got dumped from GD just when we were ready to work on who murdered Hardy and other key details. I'm more suspicious than ever."

Celeste asked, "Any word from Bev? Will she be coming back to Earth? I've missed all you guys, and Ted in particular—those balmy nights sharing what we had learned each day."

Ted sighed and smiled. "Me too, Celeste. Any word from Eve or Randi? Miss them, too."

Molly added, "I wish all my sisters were here, at least on

the same planet. Two years ago, I believed I was an orphan, alone except for Frank. Now I've got so many of you."

"We know," Janine said. "I think we all feel the same way. We're all different, but we're all family."

Sipping his ale through a straw, Ted said, "I'm going to have my doctorate in robotics soon. Got the paperwork done. Galactic Robotics has taken a lot of heat over the Sixth Invader mess. Hence, they're calling in us graduates to study the robots that Bev captured. I think they want to make useful robots for the world. You know—robots that look like people and do things for us."

"But what would you like want it to do?" asked Leslie.

"Well, how about a maid or housekeeper?" Ted answered. "Or a cook. We can always use a good cook."

Everyone roared with laughter, for among this large group, none was much of a chef. Although they chatted about robots for a time, Celeste insisted Ted and Molly turn in and get a good night's sleep.

"I want you both rested and ready for therapy sessions in the morning."

"Yes, boss." Molly teased her. "I'll have my ales when we're done."

"That's a good girl. Once I've handled their therapies, I'll deliver it to the rest of you. Think of it as a touch-up, since you've all been in a recent coma. As you can see, I have, too, but one of my trainees ran me through the mutation trauma." They chatted, while Molly and Ted headed to bed.

***

After breakfast and accompanying Deanna to the Medical Center to get her mutation done, Celeste began by having Molly return to when she was injected with the genetic agent and before they later amputated her arms.

"Yes, I'm there," said Molly.

"Good. Go through what happened and tell me what you see, smell, and hear as you move through it."

Like a motion picture—but one filled with unconsciousness and pain, and also the objectionable smells of a hospital and the random background noises—the 3-d film strip replayed in her mind. She had re-experienced the genetic

383

mutation coma before, and Molly flew through that, but slammed into the intense pain of the arm amputations, yawning as that painful charge began to erase from her mind. After re-experiencing it many times, Molly thought it should have erased. Since she wasn't cheerful, Celeste asked if there was something similar and earlier.

After hunting around, Molly spotted a white-gray mass. Soon, she re-experienced that incident.

"I'm sleeping with Ted. Oh, it's like Holly Ann's machine, the dog whistle thingy. I see this really beautiful white energy, so beautiful. Oh, someone keeps saying, 'All women should be beautiful Galactic Dolls.' Gosh, they say that a bunch of times. Then, the incredible white energy goes away, and I'm still asleep."

Molly sat up. Her eyes shot open. "Celeste, someone brainwashed us while we slept!"

Celeste smiled, ending the session. "Yes, I discovered that happened to me when one of my trainees ran out my recent coma. Kind of hoped it might have just been isolated to St. Louis, but it's been done up here, too. I'm beginning to think someone brainwashed the entire world."

By lunchtime, with Celeste's guiding hand, Molly had erased all the trauma she'd endured since Eve had done it when they escaped the atoll.

After a protein-rich lunch, Celeste began again, this time working on mocking up eight gold balls around Molly's body and other bodies. Within minutes, Molly again saw the myriad golden balls that outlined her own body. "Hey, all the ones that should be around my arms and hands still aren't there," Molly said.

"Okay. Let's shake all the balls, just as we did the last time. Give each one a good shove and watch it vibrate around," Celeste said.

"Oh, I feel sick. I did it, but maybe I shouldn't have."

"Good going. Let's shake them all up once more."

Molly did so. "Oh, that's funny. That sick feeling vanished. I feel better but strange."

Celeste ended their therapy session. "Well done. Eve's theory says those golden balls form the nearly invisible framework that holds your body together. They belong to the body itself. Shaking them should force them back into their original positions before the genetic mutation agent moved them to those new positions. Well, maybe. They're using a different genetic mutation formula now than they did when they changed us when we were on that atoll."

"My boobs will shrink and my legs will go back to normal, right? Like last time?"

"That's the plan. If they do, then we'll try the Galactic Doll genetic mutation again and see if it doesn't regrow arms," Celeste concluded. "It should work. Unless..."

"Unless what?"

"Unless this mutation is different. On the atoll, our breasts weren't this big. Anyway, I'll start in on Ted now."

"Celeste, thank you! I feel alive again. I wish every person could experience this therapy of yours."

Celeste grinned. "I know. That's why I'm devoting my life to doing it. I've taught several others in St. Louis how to do it. We're picking up momentum now."

Something that young geneticist Mary had told her popped into her mind. Molly bit her lip and creased her forehead. *All adult women. That was it. All adult women will be Galactic Dolls.* After Celeste left, Molly called up one of her recent contacts in GMed. One benefit she had from being the temporary GD CEO was executive contacts in other corporations.

"Yes, hi. This is Molly Parkinson-Billings. I have a favor to ask. Can you put me in touch with someone in the records department?"

Two hours later, Molly examined the spreadsheets emailed to her from GMed. The number of women who had the Galactic Doll mutation was on the Y-axis, while time was on the X-axis. Each graph represented an area of the world, such as Chicago, St. Louis, LA, and Moscow. A straight line across the top of the graph showed the total number of women in that zone. The graph covered the last three years. True, she already had the graph that Kyle's high school principal sent home with him last December, but Molly was interested in all women, not just high school seniors.

The curve began almost level at the bottom, where only a few women were Galactic Dolls. The graph began rising, more and more steeply, and Molly tried to remember enough high school math to describe the curve. Exponential came to mind, only this graph rolled over near the top where the number of Galactic Dolls almost equaled the total number of women.

Molly sat back and grimaced. Almost all women on Earth had been altered, but some, she knew, had been forced to have it done, women such as Helen. Curious, she contacted the Human Resource department of the major corporations except Galactic Defense, which she already knew about. In each case, during the last year, the corporation had instigated a major campaign to have all their female employees become Galactic Dolls.

Based on what she knew about GD's policies, Molly concluded that a good many of these women were forced to undergo the genetic mutation or lose their job, corporate support, and subsidy.

"Conspiracy," she muttered. "Another sneaky conspiracy. I'll bet anything." Then, she realized the full impact of peer pressure on herself. "I'll have to stay a Galactic Doll or stick out. Crap."

She shared her findings with everyone during suppertime. Many cursed. Again, she felt she missed discovering something major while she was the temporary head of GD.

Kyle took charge and redid Molly's graphs. An hour later, Kyle explained his findings. "For each of these zones, I plotted the date when the curve begins its steep rise or when many women began having it done. It's not the same date. The earliest sharp rise began last year here in Chicago. In January this year, sharp rises began in China. The last zone was southern Africa just last month. Based on what Celeste and Molly have uncovered, whoever is behind this brainwashing took almost a year to cover the world. It wasn't an instantaneous worldwide brainwashing."

"So, I didn't uncover all the nefarious actions. Damn," Molly cursed. "Ted, we missed some." That sobered everyone.

The next day, Celeste finished with Ted's therapy. Molly perked up, listening in.

Ted asked, "Okay, I've jiggled all these gold anchor balls. So my body will soon be back to looking like a male, right? Then, we redo the Galactic genetic mutation to regrow my arms. After that, can we then jiggle them again to undo looking like a Galactic Doll? But will my new arms also vanish when we do that?"

"Golly, I've no idea." Celeste bit down on her lip. "As I understand these gold ball things, they form a framework for the body's physical form. Amputation removes them. I wonder if what happens is wholly determined by the body itself and not us who inhabit and use the body."

"So you're saying my body determines what it's going to do with those golden ball things?" Ted asked.

"I think so. We spiritual beings—we can postulate ideas and things."

Molly interrupted. "Hey, Eve had me mocking up arms and using them and throwing them away a gazillion times. But it didn't make my body grow arms. I felt better, though."

She added, "We jiggled my gold things a bunch, but they don't seem to have changed their locations in the slightest. Not like last time. My boobs are still huge. My feet still can't lie flat on the floor. By now, I should have seen a change. Celeste might be right. The mutation thing might only work one time or this new version can't be undone."

Ted cursed. "So now we're screwed—all because Hardy ordered Casper to cut off our regrowing arms."

"And we'll never know why he wanted that done," Molly said. "Killing Hardy left far too many questions unanswered."

"Wasn't that the point of murdering him?" Ted asked.

Celeste said, "Darn it, Molly. I was so hoping we'd be seeing your body changing by now. Maybe your body has decided this is the way it's supposed to be and won't change its form. If Ted's body is going to change, we should see signs by tomorrow."

Ted chuckled. "I'd say I'll keep my fingers crossed, but I seemed to have misplaced them."

All three laughed.

The next morning when Ted awoke, he began talking. "Nope. My voice is still that awful soprano. Nope, boobs are still monsters. Damn. How about you, dear?"

Molly sat up, her hair slipping down over her shoulders. "Rats. No change. I think we're both screwed this time."

"Kinda figured that. Maybe we could just get them to inject us again. Maybe our arms would regrow, even though the rest doesn't need mutations."

"Come on. Let's get dressed. You have a big day today."

"Yeah, first day working for Galactic Robotics. Don't worry. I'll keep my eyes and ears open. We'll see what kind of robots they want to make. Bet they have me studying the programming code that controlled the robots Bev wiped out."

Molly laughed. "Well, if I was in charge, I certainly would, dear. You're a genius at that stuff."

He smiled, gave her a kiss, and left.

After making tea, Celeste and Molly sat down to chat. Just then, Molly's cell rang.

"Molly! Help! Help me! I'm helpless," a voice cried out, startling both women.

Celeste gave her a questioning look, and Molly shrugged her shoulders. Whoever the woman was, she broke into an uncontrollable sobbing fit.

Then, another woman's voice spoke.

"Hello. Mary Trout asked me to call you. She had your number in her purse. She's at the Med Center. There's been a horrible accident. She's lost her arms. I think she thought you might help her. We want to release her, but we can't. She lives alone."

Molly cursed. "Okay. Be there shortly. Thanks for calling." She hung up. "She's a recent graduate, PhD in genetics. Mary Trout."

Molly explained what little the caller had told her while Celeste helped Molly into her cloak.

"Thank goodness for these moving sidewalks." Celeste chuckled when they reached the MTES and rode along.

When they entered Mary's room at the center, they saw a nurse had her dressed in her light blue, wrinkled gown, but her face was wet. She had stopped bawling but was still sobbing, the kind with jerky breaths.

"She's just terrified. That's understandable. Sign here so we can release her in your care."

Although she handed it to Molly, Celeste took it from the nurse, signing for Molly. Because of the cloak and the way Molly draped her hair, the nurse didn't realize she was like Mary.

"I've got you," Celeste said, slipping an arm around Mary's waist and nudging her to her feet.

The nurse slipped her coat over Mary's shoulders, buttoning it for her. Celeste kept talking in a soothing manner while the trio walked out of the center.

"You're doing fine. Yes, I can see how terrifying this is for you but you're doing okay so far."

Once on the MTES, Mary inhaled the fishy lake smell which she found comforting, the opposite of the sterile odors of the Med Center. Molly kept quiet allowing Celeste to get them safely home and into Molly's suite. Only after they were seated on Molly's couch did Molly speak.

"You're safe here, Mary. Celeste is one of my younger sisters. What happened to you? An accident?"

The crying began again but Mary talked anyway.

"I was walking home after meeting with you and Ted. A man came up behind me on the MTES. He said, 'You should know better than to tell GMed secrets to that woman. I'm to make sure you aren't ever able to work in genetics again.' He did something to me, but I don't know what. The next thing I remember is waking up in there like this. Oh god. I can't live like this. I'm so scared. I'm peeing my pants again. I can't even kill myself."

After Mary got cleaned up, she volunteered more.

"Molly, I've got to kill myself. I'm not brave like you, but I have to warn you first. While I was in the Med Center, I overheard more stuff I'm not supposed to know. No one there wants me telling you about the mutation affecting your children or that they're forcing us to find a genetic cure to the brain degeneration in older people. Since he did this to me, I'll tell you it's just bogus research. The drugs they give them is what's causing them to lose their minds. They're purposely killing off anyone in their sixties. There, now, I'm ready to die only I don't know how I can do it. I'm helpless. I can't do anything now. Please, help me to die."

Molly's phone rang. "Hello. Yes, this is Molly Parkinson. Yes, we just got Mary home. My place. Oh, I see. Okay then." The caller hung up.

"Mary, good news. That was your uncle, Fred. He's coming to pick you up. He and your aunt, Millie, will take care of you now. Let's get you cleaned up for him."

Celeste said, "You can't die. Only your physical body can." She launched into her usual explanation of the three parts of man. "I've helped develop a therapy that can help you erase or wipe out all this trauma and loss you've experienced. After you get settled in with your uncle and aunt, I'll come by and give you some therapy."

"Will it give me my arms back?" Mary said, still sniffling.

"No. But you'll be more alive and vibrant."

"Well, I don't care. I can't live like this. I guess I have no say about it. Uncle Fred works for GR. They've got a lot of money."

"I'm sure it will work out," Molly said.

She couldn't think of anything to comfort the young woman and stuck with social politeness.

Fred arrived. He was a tall man with a round face. Black eyebrows framed his dark eyes, and Molly felt creepy vibes coming from the man, but since he was her uncle, she knew she couldn't interfere.

"Celeste and I'll come by in a few days to see how Mary's doing."

"I'm sure she will appreciate your kindness," he replied.

His voice sounded chilly, but he did keep a steadying arm around Mary as he led her off.

"I don't trust that man," Molly said.

Celeste nodded her agreement.

***

Ted's involvement with Galactic Robotics proved interesting. He and a dozen other new graduates studied the robot remains returned from Brussels along with the robot parts manufactured by GR and widely sold to industry. When he returned from his first day on his new job, he had much to discuss with Molly, none good.

"I think we may have been blindsided by GR during our investigations of the Sixth Invader robots. It's my job to analyze the control circuitry and commands given to those robots. Others who have hands are studying the robots' physical aspects. Worse, we've been ordered to develop robots like those that Bev destroyed. The argument goes: they made terrific soldiers. So why not make our own defensive army of robots? Then, we won't have to risk the lives of our soldiers.

"After what happened to the men and the later recruitment nightmare that GD faced, everyone's buying into that argument. What I find interesting is that we're mere days away from being able to build such robots."

Molly exhaled. "We must have missed a connection. Days? Dear god. Just what we don't need. Mechanical soldiers. What's next? Mechanical cops?"

"Don't jest like that, Molly. I saw plans for a mechanical cop, based on these robot soldiers." Ted sighed. "It isn't all gloomy, though. They're making plans for a house maintenance robot to do maid type duties and several other domestic robots, but I'm not sure of their purposes yet.

"It's my job to work out the control sequences. I don't think this is right, and I'm getting worried. Plus, I suspect I'm being spied upon."

"Well dear, you be darn careful. Now, I'm getting worried again. What did we miss? I'll look into it tomorrow. Oh, I have to tell you what happened to Mary Trout."

Molly explained and added how Mary had pleaded that she wanted to die, that she couldn't live this way, that she couldn't help anyone anymore.

She said, "You know, this help thing is huge, dear. When I fail to help someone, I feel absolutely crushed. On the atoll, I even wanted to die when I lost my arms and believed I couldn't help anyone anymore. People instinctively want to help others. It's a built-in impulse—"

"That the corporations blunt or stop," Ted countered. "Well, not entirely. They support the Local Defense Forces, who respond to natural disasters and such."

"I know. GD wanted to turn me into an assassin. I don't think I could have lived with myself if I'd have killed that general."

***

The next morning, Molly's phone rang. "Hi, Molly. Helen here. Could we meet for brunch? Say ten. Same place. I heard Ted has a job at GR, so it'll just be us ladies. Please, you must say yes."

Grinning, Molly agreed. "See you soon. Bye." *Besides, the walk will help clear my head. Ted's worried, so we must have missed something with GR. Trouble is, I'm not sure what thread to pull.*

She donned her cloak and headed outside. A block later, she stepped onto the MTES, only she rode it to Lake Shore Drive. Here, the humid, rather rotten odor of the lake was strong. She strolled along the boardwalk, now and then pausing to stare at the lapping waves and the pale greenish waters. The frequent spaceships roared overhead, but these she attempted to block out, preferring to listen to the many gulls swooping and sliding through the ocean of air. Since no bright ideas came, she made her way to the expensive restaurant.

"Molly, so good to see you again. You're looking well."

Helen looked peppier than Molly remembered from their last meeting. Her face had more color. Could years have melted from her face? While she still wore the traditional cherry red satin gown, Helen seemed more alive or alert.

"You're looking well yourself, Helen. New dress?" Molly tried to make small talk, but she had never been very good at it.

"Not really. Everyone's here. You remember them. Elaine, Betsy, Jane, Phillis, Sam, and Julie."

One by one, Helen re-introduced her group. After sitting and ordering a tea for Molly, Helen explained why she wanted to meet with Molly.

"Molly, first, we cannot thank you enough for the justice you got for us from our husbands. Each day, I keep discovering bits of me that got squashed or smashed out of existence by

Casper. We're all experiencing similar things. I'd forgotten how much I was into art photography. Used to take hundreds of shots around the city. Even had one gallery show before I met Casper. I can't believe after a month of marriage I'd given it all up. Well, I'm back at it again. Might have a show this fall."

"Great, Helen. Let me know so I can come see it," Molly said.

Julie said, "It's the same with us. I used to love to play Bridge, but after marrying Hue, I stopped. He hated Bridge."

Jane interrupted. "Molly, don't let her talk about cards. She'll go on for hours." The women laughed. "We have our lives back, all thanks to you. Plus, our sex lives are now what we want, when we want it—so different than before."

Julie broke in, "Now that we're in total control, it's heaven, and we have you to thank for that. He's dependent on me. For once in his life, he has to pay attention to me and my needs. It's wonderful and freeing too."

Molly said, "You know it's not humane—what was done to your husbands."

Helen laughed. "Look, our husbands and most corporate executives couldn't care less about humanity. Look what they foisted off on us women."

Julie said, "Helen, it's not all bad. Aunt Gertrude is happy to be a Galactic Doll. Her bosom used to be twice what ours now are. She used to complain she was carrying two drooping mountains. I have to admit she looks so much better now than she did before. And she looks many years younger."

"Couldn't she have... Oh well, nevermind," Helen said. "Say, Molly, we had another reason to visit with you. I've cleaned out all Casper's things and found this thumb drive. It's encrypted so I can't read it, but Casper begged me to destroy it. That was just enough for me to want to give it to you. Maybe your Ted can find out what's on it. Might be important."

Julie took this as the time for her to tell Molly what she'd heard. "Molly, I have—er, had—a close friend over in GMed—studies blood samples and weird stuff like that. She found strange particles in our blood—her job is to take the samples for DNA studies and log them into that big database thing. I don't understand any of it, but it must be very important because I told her to tell her boss about the discovery, and she did, only the next day she's dead. Someone shot her in the head. Five days ago. I helped clean out her apartment and took her laptop. There's stuff about it on there because she told me so. I'm hoping you and Ted can read it and figure out why she was killed."

"Sorry about your friend," Molly said. "Did she say what the strange things were? I'm not a medical person."

"Nope, nano something or other. Science isn't my thing either. I remembered to bring a carrying case for you." Julie slipped the bag over Molly's head, adjusting her hair for her. "Hope you can figure it out."

Chapter 29 Unraveled, but Awful

An hour later, Molly sat at her desk, the thumb drive and new laptop ready for exploration. Molly dove into this new project. While she wanted to do more research on GR and the robots, something pulled her to the new questions. What was encrypted on Casper's drive? What had Julie's friend uncovered that had gotten her killed? She decided to tackle the latter first.

The woman logged her discoveries as a series of journal entries, two of which contained scanning tunneling microscope images of the strange "things." One was from a male subject and one from a female, a Galactic Doll. While Molly didn't know what she was seeing, she could tell the two things were a little different.

Entry 1: In doing my blood work today, I spotted a strange particle in the sample. I checked all my samples. Probably contamination.

Entry 2: Thing is still there in all today's samples too. Going to get an image of the things.

Entry 3: Nanoparticles. Gold. The type used in genetic mutations. Different particles in male and female subjects. Images attached. Purpose: unknown. Going to talk to Julie about this.

Entry 4: Julie said could be important. I checked further today. Discovered the particles are in every sample I've ever taken. Whatever they are, they're in everyone's bloodstream. I took my discovery to my boss at GMed. He seemed interested and said he'd look into it.

Entry 5: Boss said it was nothing. That I should tell no one about what I found. To forget all about it. Today, I felt afraid. I didn't tell him I told Julie about it. Glad I didn't.

That was the last entry. Molly sat back, imagining what happened next—murdered on her way home. She logged into the Chicago Police Department system, thankful her GD upgrade still allowed her access. An hour later, she sat back, acknowledging another dead end. The police had cornered the man and killed him hours after he'd murdered the woman. The apparent motive: robbery. Her few valuables were found on his person. Case closed. Molly cursed. It wasn't closed for her. No one robbed for a few credits, not when the punishment was to be sent to the penal colony on Mercury or to be terminated, especially when the police received an anonymous tip about the culprit's location. Tracks covered nicely.

The next few days, she tried to get access to Casper's drive but failed. Even Ted's attempts to crack his encryption didn't work.

"Brute force," Ted declared, attaching a device that would try all possible combinations, taking days to crack it. However, the device self-destructed an hour later. Casper got his wish.

***

When Deanna came out of her coma, Molly, Celeste, and Holly Ann were there to help her, while VP Russell Godwyn waited for the women to help Deanna dress.

"How does she look?" Molly asked Russell. Deanna wore the usual cherry red starter outfit given to new Galactic Dolls.

"You look stunning, as always, Deanna," he said. The two shared a passionate kiss.

"We've got an announcement," Deanna said. She slipped an arm around him. "Russell and I are engaged."

After congratulations, they headed to the Cartwright Skyscraper for lunch though Celeste just had to call all her sisters telling them Deanna's good news. While they were eating, a hyperspace relay call from Bev interrupted them.

"Hold off on the wedding until I get back, Deanna. That's gonna be soon. They're ordering us home. Should land in Moscow on Saturday. Something about a parade before we're all sent home. See you all on Monday, I hope." Bev sounded quite happy.

"Will it like be on the news?" asked Leslie. Several talked at once since there was a five-minute delay.

Russell said, "That's affirmative, Leslie. GEnt will broadcast it live. General Bev is famous. We're planning to make a statue of her for the lobby area."

"Horse crap!" Bev barked, but everyone laughed. "Gonna have a place for me to stay when I get back?"

"Sure thing. Ted and I are moving into one of Leslie's apartments on Saturday. Kyle and Holly Ann are moving there, too. So we'll have it all ready for you, Bev."

Later, when Molly and Ted turned in for the night, Ted complained. "We've got to figure out what's going on. We've missed something major."

"Somethings major," she corrected him. "Good thing that Eve and Randi will be back on Earth soon. Maybe they can figure out what's in our bloodstreams."

***

When Ted returned from work the next day, he looked somber. Over dinner with Deanna and the others, he shared what he'd uncovered.

"I discovered GR has millions of hair and nail machines in a warehouse. Not exactly sure what they do, but someone said they keep fingernails and toenails properly trimmed. I believe the idea is to put one into every home. They've already got a dressing/undressing robot machine built and programmed. There are millions of those in storage, too. They've got a maid robot that looks rather humanoid. I worked on its control circuitry, but I discovered millions of these are ready to go, once the programming is finished."

"Incredible. Does it have legs and all that?" Molly asked.

"No, it has wheels, but it has a system to allow it to levitate up and down stairs. After seeing these huge numbers, I did some hacking. How does fifty thousand robot soldiers sound to you?"

"What?" exclaimed Deanna. "There hasn't been enough time for GR engineers to study the ones Bev captured, let alone manufacture them. Something is rotten here."

"We must have missed GR's involvement in the fake war," Molly said. "It's my fault. I should have looked harder."

Ted continued. "What scared me the most was discovering plans to make almost a million humanoid robots—with arms and legs. Their programming is the most sophisticated of all these, almost qualifying as artificial

397

intelligence. What's worse, I've no idea what their purpose is. It could be almost anything."

Holly Ann said, "Well, maybe we're getting paranoid over nothing. Except for the soldier robots, I don't see them as being threatening to us."

The next morning, Molly realized she hadn't yet paid a visit to Mary Trout. She and Celeste had promised to check on her, so she called the number her uncle had given them. Aunt Millie answered.

"Oh, she's moved out. Gotten married. It's so wonderful."

Neither Celeste nor Molly knew what to make of this surprise. Lacking further data, they forgot about Mary.

***

On Saturday, Molly and Ted moved into apartment number three. Kyle and Holly Ann were in number four. Leslie and Felix were in number one, and Janine and Hank were in number two. Number five was empty and ready for Bev. All five were identical, small efficiency apartments with a combination kitchen-dining room, a living room, and two bedrooms, and bath. Preparatory to the sale of Leslie's parents' costume shop, which she'd recently decided not to sell, she'd had all five refurbished.

At eight o'clock that morning, the eight gathered around Leslie's large comm center to watch the welcome parade for General Bev and the members of the First Division. GEnt broadcast live from Moscow, and Leslie recorded the newscast.

"There she is!" Leslie said, pointing to the lead car.

Bev and her aide Gail sat on the back seat of a convertible EMAC waving to the crowd on the MTES, which had been temporarily stopped. Both wore their blue satin uniform dresses with gold trim. Thousands cheered as more soldiers marched past the reviewing stands and cameras. The two dozen Galactic Doll soldiers also rode in open topped EMACs since they walked too slowly. Ranks of men marched behind the vehicles.

"I'm glad they like gave them a hero's welcome," Leslie said.

The parade lasted only fifteen minutes, but the whole empire watched via GEnt.

Around noon, Eve and Randi returned from Tau Ceti via a commercial flight. Deanna and Celeste met them at the spaceport and took them to the apartment complex where Janine had a welcome back lunch prepared. Leslie insisted on replaying Bev's welcome home parade for them. Then, Molly related everything that had happened.

"So," Molly concluded, "we need you to figure out what these gold nanoparticle things in our blood are. I figure they must be important or why else kill the woman?"

Eve said, "Can I see her laptop and those images she took?" A few minutes later, Eve gasped. "Wow. These are mutation nanoparticles. Molly, I'll need a lab to analyze these—and samples too."

"If she was right, then those things are in everyone's blood. Hey, remember we heard that the missile didn't hurt anything on the Padellas' atoll. So how about using the their lab?" Molly suggested.

"Good idea. I'll arrange an Airliner," Deanna said. "We should get on this as soon as possible."

Eve said, "You know, it would be a good idea to take the Padella doctors along with us. It's just a feeling I have. Besides, it's their lab. Where are they staying now?"

Molly said, "I'll find out. I'm coming with you."

"Want me to come too?" asked Holly Ann.

"No, you've got to take care of little Carl. I'll be all right. Come on, Eve. Let's go fetch those mad doctors."

Randi insisted on tagging along. She said, "Deanna, you don't have to come with us. I'm now qualified to fly the Airliner. Besides, Jana needs you too. We'll keep you posted."

"Drop me off at Cartwright then, and use my EMAC. Leave it at New O'Hare when you take the Airliner."

***

Molly, Eve, and Randi walked into Leisure Homes, a single story assisted living complex.

Randi said, "It's sure strange seeing all the nurses and aides looking like Galactic Dolls. I want to discuss this with Bev when she gets back."

"Going to be weird seeing these two doctors, after what they did to us all those years being a prisoner on their atoll," Molly said. "Ah, Room 301. Here we are."

The Padella doctors were in their mid-fifties, but because their hands were curled shut, they could no longer care for themselves. Unlike those they held prisoner on their atoll, they made no attempt to learn to do anything for themselves using their feet.

"Hello," Molly said.

The pair sat on a couch staring into space. Both looked up. She saw recognition in their eyes, which opened wide as they raised their eyebrows.

"If you're going to kill us, that will be a blessing," said Dr. Nelson Padella.

"Only please hurry," added Dr. Janet Padella. Her voice sounded whiny.

"Come with us. We're taking you on a trip. We want your help, and we're not about to kill you," said Molly. "Can't say I didn't think of doing that months ago, though."

"Where are you taking us?" he asked.

"Out of here. They are drugging you so you develop dementia if you didn't already know that."

He looked at her. "See, I told you that was likely what was going on and a good thing, as crippled up as we are."

As they passed the nurse station, Molly said, "We're taking them for a walk to get some fresh air." The nurse smiled and nodded.

Once in the EMAC, Nelson again asked where they were going.

Molly said, "To your island research station."

A half-hour later, Molly sat beside the pair in the Cartwright Airliner. Randi began the pre-flight checkouts, while Eve sat on the other side of the two doctors. Molly explained the situation as Eve brought up the two images on the laptop.

Molly finished up. "They had Mary's arms amputated to prevent her from doing anything further in genetic research. They killed the woman who discovered these are in everyone's bloodstream. I want you and Eve to find out what they are."

She changed the topic. "What I always wanted to know was why? Why cut off my arms? Why cut off their hands?"

Janet flushed and her eyebrows rose as she bit down on her lips. Nelson spoke first.

"You see, years ago, the genes of a very lucky man came our way. General Fuller made us a proposal. He needed super-soldiers, lucky soldiers. Since genetic experimentation on humans is illegal, human cloning was suggested. While also illegal, it wouldn't affect a normal person in the way a mutation would. He set us up with a lab and DOD funds."

Janet said, "Our shop was set up on that atoll, where we wouldn't be disturbed. The result on the boys wasn't good, but that cloning was possible was proved. So we expanded to a batch of girls. A couple years later, one last attempt was made, using three girls. Our goal was to get the lucky gene to express itself. It hadn't appeared in the four-year-old boys or the two-year-old girls, so I decided to see if adding physical difficulties would help the gene express itself. Many how-to-do-it holographic videos were provided for the three girls and later that boy."

Nelson interrupted. "That's when the nanotechnology mushroomed. Our future lay there, not in cloning. Besides, the results were not what General Fuller desired. Yes, we cloned identical bodies; it's just they had totally different interests and personalities. Baffling. Frankly, we forgot about all those clones. This new nanoparticle research captured our interest."

Janet interjected angrily. "Until that infernal DNA project came along. We made a last ditch attempt to get the lucky gene to express itself. Ace was hired to shoot at you clones. Mind you, never to hit, just see if your lucky gene would activate. That may have been successful with one of the female clones. We didn't know General Fuller hired an assassin to terminate all the clones.

"Then, they dumped you on us, Molly. True, we needed more experimental subjects, but for our silver nanoparticle healing technologies and genetic mutation work. Here was one last chance to see if that lucky gene would express itself. Obviously, it hadn't since Ted and you were on our island as prisoners. Our orders said you and Ted were never to escape or cause trouble to GD. Perhaps lacking arms would make that gene come to the fore. Honestly, we still don't know why that lucky gene never expressed itself."

Molly raised her eyebrows and pressed her lips tightly. "So we were nothing more than guinea pigs for your research?"

"Naturally. What did you think you were?" Janet said, also raising her eyebrows.

Silence reigned before Molly asked, "So were you both involved in making the Galactic Doll genetic mutation?"

Eve perked up, listening to every word.

Nelson said, "Luck was with us. Building on earlier gold nano dot technologies and the Fetal Regeneration Stimulus—"

"What's that?" Molly asked.

Janet answered her. "A fetus has amazing rebuilding capabilities. If injured, it can rebuild what's been damaged. Fetal Regeneration Stimulus is the scientific term that defines the DNA and chemical processes that cause the reconstruction of damaged tissues."

Nelson continued. "Without Fetal Regeneration Stimulus, bodies injected with the Galactic Doll gold nanoparticle genetic mutation would have no reaction. It is the Fetal Regeneration Stimulus that causes the body to carry out the indicated genetic mutation."

Molly asked, "So where did the Galactic Doll mutation come from? Who invented it? Why?"

Nelson said, "About twenty years ago, GMed had a team of geneticists working on the project called Galactic Doll. The specs came from higher up, but no one knows for sure who developed them. Years were spent experimenting on prostitutes, because they desired such body enhancements, especially if the alterations were free. Yes, packaging the current Galactic Doll genetic mutation was the pinnacle of our genetic achievements, though the healing silver nanoparticles are a close second."

Janet smiled. "We received our awards for this. If only our hands weren't all crippled up, we could continue our invaluable research."

Nelson added, "And now nearly every adult woman on

Earth is a vision of beauty, a Galactic Doll. Incredible. You have to admit, Molly, your body is quite shapely and a vision of beauty, except for the arms, that is."

Anger seethed in Molly. "Do you know that some women loathe being a Galactic Doll? They hate what it's done to their bodies."

"They must be imbeciles," Nelson replied. "Look, it's a healthy modification, too. Overweight people will lose all those extra pounds. Anorexic women will put on proper weight during the mutation. That mutation makes all women's bodies as close to ideal health parameters as possible. You'll never see an obese woman on Earth again." He puffed up.

Molly couldn't argue against the health aspects. "What about their babies? Their babies inherit the Galactic Doll mutation. That's what I heard."

Janet said, "Too soon to tell for sure. Give it time. See how your baby fares. It would be wonderful if all baby girls were born as Galactic Dolls, too. We may be generating a bright future for all women."

Only if you want to look like a whore, Molly thought but decided against saying it.

Nelson said, "Look, Molly. You did an incredible job exposing and bringing those guilty GD men to justice, making our world a better place to live. Janet and I have done the same thing, helping all women to live healthier, better lives."

Having listened to this exchange, Eve was satisfied she'd made the right decision in crippling their hands.

Randi finished the pre-flight checkout and was ready to lift off when a group of men rushed up to the Cartwright Airliner. The control tower ordered her to let the men talk to Molly. She led Molly to the rear where a non-descript man entered alone, leaving four GPan security men outside the Airliner.

"I'm Doctor Kane. GPan wants Molly and Ted to have another chance to get their arms regrown. I've arranged to have it done today. If Molly will come with me, we'll meet Ted at the Med Center. He should be there by now."

Suspecting Molly didn't trust the man, Randi called Ted using Molly's phone.

"Molly, hey. Great news. We're getting another chance to get our arms back. Have you heard yet?"

"Er, yeah. A Dr. Kane just found me. Are you at the Med Center?"

"Yes, we're waiting for you to get here. I'm elated. Bye."

"Best news in a long time," Randi said.

She hugged Molly and promised to relay the unexpected good news to everyone. Molly left with the men.

Soon, she watched the doctors inject Ted and then herself. She watched a nurse moving an infrared wand over her body. As she slipped into another genetic mutation coma, she felt confident they would awake to a true miracle.

***

When the group landed on the atoll, they found the facility had been abandoned, which wasn't unexpected. Following Nelson's directions, Eve got the EMAC generator running, powering up the facility. The missile attack had caused no damage to the lab. While Eve and the Padella doctors set to work, Randi checked on food and living accommodations.

An hour later, Randi joined the three in the lab and noticed how grim the three faces looked.

"What's up?" she asked.

Eve turned away from her work. "It's wild. In simple terms, everyone's blood including that of the Padellas is filled with two very different gold nano dot genetic mutation particles. Neither is active. However, our blood—yours and mine—show only traces of both these particles. The samples from Ted and Celeste also show the same high concentration as does Molly's blood. You and I have just returned from Brussels, Tau Ceti. Conclusion: we've only been partially exposed to these particles. We don't know yet how they are being transmitted.

"What's even stranger, they're inert, awaiting activation. Normally, they're activated by irradiating the body with infrared radiation to which these gold dots are sensitive. But these do not respond to IR radiation. We're still exploring what will activate them."

Janet interrupted her. "Tell them about one of the particles or I will."

404

"Okay. One of the two particles in everyone's blood is nearly identical to the Padellas' Galactic Doll genetic mutation sequence. The second gold nanoparticle is similar too, but with significant differences, and we don't know what those changes will do."

Nelson interjected, "We have determined they are sex related. The nearly identical Galactic Doll genetic mutation appears to attach to X-chromosomes, while the different one attaches to Y-chromosomes. So whatever these things are, we think each sex will experience different mutations."

"What kind of mutations?" Randi asked. Her stomach knotted, and she felt weak in her knees. This could harm every person on Earth. Had they missed something about the Sixth Invaders? Were they real and not just robots?

"They used our work," Janet said. "Our ID markers are still there in those bits of unused DNA sequences. But the mutations—the changes—aren't ours."

"What do they do?" Randi persisted.

"We won't know until we can get them activated," Eve answered. "Once that happens, the full sequence will open, and we can tell. Back to work, doctors."

A few days later, Eve and the Padella doctors discovered the trigger.

"Randi, we've done it!" Eve said. "It's activated by a signal in the Very Far Infrared region, far beyond normal zones. A special laser light is required. We've got the sequences opened. Soon, we can tell what they are doing."

Around noon the next day, they gathered for lunch, compliments of Randi. The Padella doctors looked ghastly pale.

Eve said, "This isn't good. The sequence that latches onto a male body is likely to genetically mutate them into a form of male Galactic Doll but with additional and unknown changes. It's a derivative of the usual Galactic Doll mutation with major alterations. The one that hooks onto a female body will make a Galactic Doll, but we think it's the normal version. Anyway, we've done all we can do here. Best head back after we eat."

***

May Day 2352 came, and Leslie took Bev and Gail to visit Molly and Ted. Bev's return to Chicago had been delayed over a week. Many other cities around the world wanted her to join their local parades welcoming their soldiers home.

Leslie explained, "This time, they like were only in a coma a few days. Their arms are like regrowing, but they're awake. What's weird is like this Dr. Kane fellow doesn't exist, but we're not complaining since their arms are like regrowing."

Bev frowned. "Hi, Cool Head. I'm back. Got delayed by all the parades."

Bev still wore her fancy uniform. She looked at Molly and Ted lying on the twin beds. Their new arms looked more like a baby's arms, rather incongruous with their adult body sizes.

"Hi, yourself. I missed you. Now you're a famous general. Coolest, Bev."

"I think I was a figurehead. They've more or less abandoned the First Division, by letting everyone go home on an infinite furlough. They said, 'Don't expect to be called back unless there's another ground attack on the Sol Empire.'"

"Great. I'm glad you're back. I can use your help with my PI business."

"Hey, you did good, kid. What with all the GD CEO stuff. It was in the news on Brussels. So what's up?"

Molly outlined what was new.

Bev said, "Well, I've good news for you, too." She put an arm around the blonde woman. "Remember my aide, Gail Jackson, here? Well, we got married on Brussels."

"Wow, congratulations, Bev. Wonderful news. Hi, Gail. Saw you on GEnt's video, too. I wish I could hug you both. Doctors think I can do that in about a month. We have your new apartment fixed up for you. Number five, right Leslie?"

"Right. I like brought them here from New O'Hare to see you two first."

"After we move in, we'll find jobs," Bev added. "It's incredible that you both are getting fixed up. I see they've got armed guards on this room."

Ted chuckled. "Yeah. Deanna's doing. She's not going to

let anything happen to us this time."

Leslie's phone rang, and she answered it. "Weird, Molly, just plain weird. Delivery men like came by and dropped off one of those new hair and nail machines, what they call a dressing/undressing robot machine, and a humanoid looking maid robot—one for each apartment. Janine like took delivery for all five apartments. What is like weird is that there's like no charge or cost to us."

Ted said, "I told you we missed something big. You don't get something for nothing, not in this world."

"Well, we'll like check them out when we get back and give you two a report. Oh, and Randi and Eve are like returning late tonight. So I expect I'll like have lots of news for you tomorrow."

***

Commander R'Ina said, "Ted Billings has discovered too much about Galactic Robotics' secret robot projects. Also, that we've infected Earth humans with the dual genetic mutation particles has somehow come to Molly's attention. We need those two taken out of the equation for a time, not killed mind you. We don't want to attract more attention."

"It's taken care of, Commander," G'Karn said. He saluted his leader, but with little enthusiasm. "I have them getting their arms regrown, an action that will hospitalize them for over a month."

G'Karn knew the Sixth Invaders Recon Force 125's tour of duty ended in another six Earth months. He looked forward to returning to Home World and a quiet, peaceful life, not this deceptive, devious role Commander R'Ina had forced them into after their arrival on Earth so many years ago. Covert affairs held no interest for him. Worse, he felt some of the things they were doing to these humans were unethical.

"Excellent, G'Karn," Commander R'Ina said. "Now then, how are the activation sequences progressing? I see from your last report the biological agents have been inserted into most humans within the greater Chicago area. So how goes the activation process? The Very Far Infrared beam? The recordings for their comm centers? When can we proceed? And how long will it take to infect this entire world with the bio agents? We only have six months left."

He sighed. "The EMAC ship with the Very Far Infrared beam will be ready to go later this week. My calculations show that the bio agents within the greater Chicago area can be activated in one long night. My assistants are programming the flight path now. It's automated, so there's no chance for error or mis-coverage. Already distribution of the many utility robotic devices here in Chicago has begun. The last estimates I've seen shows all deliveries and installations will be completed by May 14. I'd recommend that to be the night of bio agent activation, Commander."

"Less than two weeks. Okay, I can deal with that. And the world?" she barked.

"A year." He saw her jaws clenching and a deep frown appearing. "No rushing science. I have to prepare the dual bio agents. We have to distribute them over the areas, coordinating well so we don't miss a section of the Earth. So far, we only have the central section of this country infected with the dual agents, and that's rushing it. Mistakes happen when things are rushed, and I'm rushed. Plus, the Earth companies have finite manufacturing capacities. We've many millions of robot devices to prepare in advance."

"Six months. Speed it up, G'Karn. I want this entire project completed by the time we're replaced, and that's six months away. Make it happen."

"Aye, sir." He saluted again, barely raising his left hand. From his point of view, this whole recon situation in the Sol Empire had gone wrong, very wrong.

Chapter 30 Disaster Strikes

"Oh, I can get used to this," Holly Ann said.

It was early morning on May 15, 2352. She and Kyle had just gotten up, and their long hair was rather tangled. She stood on the base of the machine and pressed a lever switch with her knee. Overhead, the machine electrostatically charged every hair, while the fan facing her chest blew each individual strand upwards its full length. After cycling through, the machine turned off, but the decelerating fan blades blew her falling hair to the back of her head, leaving it brushed out, as well as neutralizing its electrostatic charge. Her scalp felt invigorated.

"Can I do it again?"

"No, dear. It's my turn," teased Kyle. "Then, you gotta see how the dressing machine works. When you weren't here, I used it to get the back zipper pulled up. Clumsily, though. Oh, and I've got the maid programmed to vacuum the place and cook our meals. That's something, I suppose. Only none of us can figure out why GR is putting these machines in every home and even in public restrooms."

Eve and Randi knocked and entered. They and Celeste were staying in Molly and Ted's apartment while the two were at the Med Center getting their arms regrown.

Eve said, "Morning. Holly Ann, have you figured out how to make that robot thing make breakfast? If not, we're making something now. Have you noticed it's strangely quiet outside?"

Frantic pounding on their door interrupted them.

"Guess not anymore," Holly Ann teased.

Leslie called out, "Randi, Eve, help. Something's like wrong with Felix. He's sick or something. Help."

Randi opened the door.

"Leslie, what's wrong?"

"Felix. He's unresponsive. I think he's like ill. Come see." She tugged on Randi's arm.

"Okay. Coming." They found Felix unconscious. "May

I?" Randi asked. Leslie nodded and pulled the covers off his body. "Damn."

"What?" Leslie asked. Worry lined her face.

"What?" Eve asked, who had just entered and joined them. Celeste was right behind her, followed by Kyle and Holly Ann.

"Is that what I think it is?" asked Celeste.

"Looks like it," Eve said. "Genetic mutation coma. See, his breasts are already enlarging. We best check on everyone else. How are you feeling, Leslie?"

She patted her arms, bosom, and hips.

"I'm like fine, I think. Nothing's like any different that I can tell. We best like check on Hank and Janine."

Leslie covered Felix back up and led the way next door where they found Janine and Hank just sitting down to breakfast.

Hank said, "No, I feel fine. Perfect as long as my looking like a Galactic Doll doesn't count."

The group checked on Bev and Gail, who were also fine. Then, they headed into Molly and Ted's apartment, where Celeste had breakfast waiting.

As they ate, Hank said, "Have you noticed how quiet it is? Mornings, it's rather noisy, what with people going to work."

Janine's phone rang. Everyone watched her face lose its color. "We'll be there soon. Bye. That was Deanna. She's at the Cartwright Skyscraper. Russell's unconscious and so is Jana."

"Oh crap," said Holly Ann. "We best check on Carl. He's still sleeping."

She and Kyle left to do so. A minute later, she shrieked. Kyle rejoined them, his face pale.

"Carl is in a coma too. We best stay with him."

"Right. Bev, Gail, you watch over these apartments. Randi, Eve, and I'll go over to check on Deanna," Celeste said.

"We'll come too," Hank volunteered.

When the five reached the MTES, Hank said, "Where is everyone? It's deserted."

"I've never seen it this deserted," said Janine. "Something's wrong—citywide. Where are all the EMACs and shuttle crafts? There's not even rocket noise from New O'Hare. Creepy. Is Chicago sleeping?" Janine asked.

"I have a bad feeling someone has activated those nanoparticles," said Eve. "Randi, Bev, Gail, and I won't be affected since there are almost none of those particles in our systems."

When they reached the living floor of the skyscraper, they found Deanna wiping the brows of Jana and Russell. She had them lying on the same bed, but both were in comas, verified by Eve. Further, two security guards at the front desk were in comas.

"Dear god. What will happen to them? We stayed here in town last night." Her face was pale.

Eve sighed. "We don't know. I can speculate that the men are being mutated into male Galactic Dolls. Perhaps, that's what's happening to Jana."

Randi suggested, "Why don't we go up to the roof and have a look down at Chicago? Deanna, it's as though the city is deserted. From up there, we can get a better picture of central Chicago. Maybe this isn't as widespread as we think. Ted said GR made millions of their robots, not billions. Maybe it's isolated and not worldwide."

When they arrived at the main doors leading to the roof deck, the night security guards were slumped over their guard stations. "Comas," Eve pronounced.

"Fricken scary," said Celeste. She shivered. "I have a bad feeling."

"It's like a graveyard," said Randi.

They gazed over central Chicago. Over two centuries ago, Chicago had grown—though some might say it had gobbled up smaller towns—until around the turn of the last century when the mass migrations to the new worlds began.

"Hey, look there," Randi said. "Far off."

In the extreme distance, they could see a few EMACs and some small shuttle crafts flying about.

"So the whole world isn't affected, just central Chicago," said Eve. "That's a lot better. Let's get back to the others."

"Wait. What's that?" asked Randi. "It sounds like those dog whistle things that Bev ran into."

High in the sky, they saw a drone EMAC hovering. The sounds came from it, radiating downward in a cone of coverage. "Oh no!" said Randi.

***

The sound had already swept past the audible range, reaching that incredible aesthetic wavelength or frequency. They stood stunned, unable to react in any way. Words floated into their minds. Hearing seemed so disconnected from the world of this beautiful energy.

"Women, you must always help the men around you. Women, you can do anything you want. Men, you now have different ways to do things, but you must practice a lot. Both men and women are to use the new robot helpers."

The message repeated a dozen times before the white energy dissipated. Time passed before the three shook themselves awake.

***

"Wow. Oh, I have to help you, Hank," said Janine. She scratched her head and rubbed her forehead.

"We men have different ways to do things. What am I saying? Of course, you four can do anything you want," said Hank, rubbing his forehead.

"I know. But we need to use those new robot machines," Janine added.

"Men must practice a lot," said Hank. "What's the matter with me?"

"Brainwashed!" said Eve. "We've been brainwashed, just like Bev and the other women. There must be Sixth Invaders around after all. Still, I have to help you men. Do you need anything, Hank?"

"Get us home," said Hank.

"Look, that EMAC. It's moving further south, and the dog whistle machine must be on it," said Randi. "Come on. Let's get home. The wind's mussed up my hair so I have to use that new robot helper machine. Why did I say that? Let's get back fast."

When the trio returned to Deanna, Deanna asked, "Hank, do you need anything? Women are supposed to help men. Oh, we have the new robot machines in that room. We're supposed to use them. What am I saying?" She rubbed her head.

Randi said, "I think we've been brainwashed, like Bev, but first, I have to use the new hair robot machine."

After they all used the new hair machine, the five departed and returned to their apartment complex. They checked on Felix and Carl and found everyone gathered around Felix's bed. Carl was now lying beside Felix.

"It happened again. The dog whistle thing. Of course, men have different ways to do things. We can do anything we want, right, Gail?" said Bev.

"Right, Kick Ass."

"Hey, come watch the broadcast. It's saying all stations are playing the same thing over and over," Randi said. "Eve, when it's over, let's give each other a quick therapy session and erase this implanted crap."

Everyone gathered around the cramped living room. The comm center was on. GEnt cameras showed two gray humanoids standing behind the CEO of GPan, Mr. Armstrong, who looked glassy-eyed and didn't speak.

Aliens! Compared to the sitting Mr. Armstrong, they estimated the aliens were between six and seven feet tall. They were thin, and what skin was visible was a light gray color. The one on the right spoke; the voice sounded female-ish. She, if the pronoun applied, wore a black top, pants, and boots. The other wore a light yellow dress. Both aliens' hair was thick and black, like coarse horsehair. Their busts appeared to be similar in size to Galactic Dolls. The speaker's hair was short, rather like a man's haircut, but the alien in the dress had long hair. The camera cut off at their knees.

"Pay attention, people of Earth. We're the Sixth Invaders Recon Force. I'm Commander R'Ina; this is my Chief Science Officer G'Karn. As many of you are aware, the population of central Chicago is in a coma, a genetic mutation coma. We have already introduced the genetic mutation nanoparticles into everyone on this world. However, we have only activated those nanoparticles here in Chicago. If anyone tries to attack us, we will activate the particles in every human body on this entire world.

"The mutations are gender specific. On the left of your screen, you can see what a typical male of your species will look like after the process finishes in eight days. Your world calls them male Galactic Dolls. Yes, they will have no arms.

"On the right of your screen, you can see how a typical female, who has not yet undergone the change, will appear once the mutation is finished, a usual Galactic Doll. We've implanted everyone to help men, but also that women can do anything. Men will have different ways to do things.

"Additionally, everyone is implanted to make use of the new robot helpers. These include the hair and nail machine, the dressing/undressing robot, and the maid robot, which handles cooking and cleaning duties. In eight days, Channel Nine will run continuous holographic video clips of how men can do things using their feet, compliments of the Padella doctors.

"The helper machines have been distributed to each household in the central Chicago area. These household occupants are now in their mutation comas. Thus, when they wake up, they will have the machines and robots on which their lives now depend. So again, I warn you: if anyone tries to attack us, the nanoparticles, which are now in everyone's bodies throughout this world, will be activated, but in that case, we will not provide these life-dependent machines and robots.

"Why Chicago? The Sol Empire's governing corporations are here. Nothing can stop the mutation process that will leave all your male leaders looking much like this sample image—a perfect toy for your women to use. The Sixth Invaders have taken control of Earth and, by proxy, the Sol Empire. Soon, our main battle fleet will arrive. Further resistance by other systems in your empire will be futile. Again, if Earth resists us, we will not hesitate to activate the nanoparticles in every human body on this planet and let you deal with the aftermath.

"This recorded message will replay continuously until we replace it with the many how-to-do-it videos needed by your males."

A blank screen appeared, before the video repeated.

What surprised the viewers were the two sample images being shown, those of Ted Billings and Helen Hugo. Most Chicagoans were familiar with his image from Molly's stint as temporary CEO of GD.

Eve turned it off. "Guess there really are Sixth Invaders."

"Ted said there were only a million of those machine-robot things," said Bev. "Bet anything they'll be doing this to the rest of the world, city by city, whether we attack them or not. My hair's a mess. Mind if I use your hair machine, Leslie?" Her face twisted. "Damn, I said that didn't I?"

She found it difficult not to get up and use the machine.

Eve said, "If millions of Chicago men wake up in eight days and find themselves like Molly and Ted were, that will be an incredible disaster. Remember Mary? She wanted to commit suicide rather than living as Molly is. In addition, men won't like becoming Galactic Dolls either. We could be looking at a controlled, but slow, mass extinction of the human race as we know it. We have to stop them."

"Well, that broadcast like came from Galactic Expansion's skyscraper," said Leslie. "I like recognized it from other news clips. Top floor. I suppose I best like use the hair machine. The Windy City's like mussed up my hair, too."

She grimaced, but not about her hair.

Kyle said, "We best do something. In eight days, there will be millions of desperate, frantic, and terrified men. Some men will probably kill themselves. It's humiliating to suddenly be a male Galactic Doll. But an armless one..."

Eve said, "Say, we better check on Molly and Ted. The Med Center might be in major trouble. So many of the doctors and staff are men."

"Gail and I are coming too," said Bev.

"I best like stay here with them," Leslie said. "Poor Felix. He's still like in a coma. He'll be like devastated when he wakes up. So will Carl and Russell. But like why isn't Kyle or Hank affected? Call me if Ted's like losing his arms again."

Eve said, "Astute question, Leslie. Why aren't Kyle and Hank affected? Perhaps it's because they're already Galactic Dolls. Still, I would have expected they'd lose their arms."

"Hey, my arms seem just fine," Hank said. His eyes opened wide as his facial muscles tightened.

"Mine too," added Kyle. His skin paled. To Holly Ann, he said, "I'll stay with Carl so you can go check on Molly. Maybe they botched their mutations. Even so, there weren't very many of us male Galactic Dolls before."

Eve pressed her lips together before replying. "You might be onto something. Perhaps something we've done has forced these Sixth Invaders to bump up their timetable. Often mistakes are made when people are rushed. Come on. Let's see how Molly and Ted are doing. Best use the hair machine first." She slapped her face for having said that.

The small group arrived at the Med Center, which was understaffed. They saw no males. Everyone was relieved to find Molly and Ted still alive and their arms still present.

Then, Deanna phoned Eve. "Have you seen the aliens on the news? This is a disaster. Molly and Ted are amazing, determined, and fearless. Me? I can't imagine living without my arms. Russell will be devastated. My stomach's in one big knot right now. Soon, I need to use the new hair machine."

Eve said, "If their genetic change is like ours, we think it'll be eight days. But Deanna, we have to do something. Today, they're doing this to maybe a million people. Central Chicago. We saw that from your skyscraper's rooftop. They have an EMAC flying over the city with one of those dog whistle machines. They've implanted us, but we don't know what they said. Randi and I are working on it. Yes, I need to use ours soon too. My hair is all messed up."

"What can we do? They said they'd do this to everyone on Earth if we bother them."

"They'll eventually do it to everyone anyway," Eve said. Her jaw tightened as an idea formed.

Bev interrupted. "I can see why they disbanded the First Division. Now GD hasn't got an army to counter them. We're scattered all over this world and several others."

Molly smiled. "That's only mostly true. Look, you and Gail aren't affected much at all. Probably the other members of your division aren't either."

"Yeah, but they're scattered."

"We saw only two of these aliens. We don't need an army, just a few good soldiers with big guns."

Bev and Gail grinned, and Bev said, "She's got a point. I reckon several dozen soldiers from the First Division are here in the Chicago area. Come on, Gail. It's time we contacted them. We'll need blasters."

Gail said, "Arsenal's in Joliet. We'll need a plan."

Bev said, "Leave that to me. I'll case out the GPan building. Find us a way inside."

Gail added, "Let's kick alien ass."

***

One by one, Eve and Randi pulled the others aside to give them enough therapy to desensitize this new, albeit minor, implant. Most had a good chuckle when they spotted the precise words spoken when they were "zapped" by the aesthetic energy. Unspoken by all was what could have happened if the message had said "Kill yourself," or "Kill your neighbors," or "Kill your leaders."

Late afternoon, Bev and Gail stood two blocks from the hundred-story GPan skyscraper.

Bev said, "I can't believe how many women stopped us. It's as if every woman in Chicago has zillions of questions. 'What are we to do?' How do we answer that? Hell, I don't know. Not yet."

"I don't think many men are going to be able to adapt to this dramatic change to their body. Well, Kyle did okay, but he had exigent circumstances," Gail said.

Bev laughed. "What's exigent mean? Sometimes you 'educated' people use big words."

Gail laughed. "Pressing, really demanding, urgent. Kyle was wanted dead or alive, and Holly Ann was about to be turned into a Galactic Doll. They had to do something and fast. And Hank's accepted his situation well, too. After all, being a male Galactic Doll is preferable to not having an arm and leg."

"Makes sense. Look at what the mutation did to women. The multitude of body shapes, proportions, and looks all changed into the one more or less common Galactic Doll form."

"That's the whole point of a genetic mutation," Gail

417

said. "It mutates what *is* into what is desired by the designers of the mutation. Men will lose their strength, masculinity, and robust muscles if they have them. What I found interesting—have to remember to talk with Eve about this—is those two aliens. Could it be that this whole Galactic Doll mutation thing was their idea?"

"I thought that, too. I bet they had a hand in it. Hold on!"

"Aren't those the robots Ted talked about? They're all around the entire GPan block!"

"Damn! They have guns, too."

The two had seen women on the streets and MTES. Now as they neared the GPan skyscraper, a dozen women approached the skyscraper and these new robot policemen. To Bev, it appeared as though they wanted to ask the aliens questions.

With alarming speed, six of the robots nearest the women drew their guns and opened fire. From their training, Gail and Bev identified they fired fifty-caliber shells, total overkill. Her own 9mm Glock was more than enough to kill a person, ignoring the even deadlier blasters and laser guns. Stunned, the two watched three of the women's torsos shredded.

Almost in slow motion, she saw the big guns pivoting their way as the robots continued their automatic fire.

"Dive!" Bev screamed.

She and Gail dove out of the way, but another woman didn't. She, too, was murdered. Bev and Gail rolled until they had the corner of a building separating them from the deadly fire. Only then did they get to their feet, cursing and swearing. The pungent odor of cordite assaulted their nostrils.

They split. Gail headed off to round up what other First Division soldiers were around Chicago while Bev returned to the Med Center.

After explaining what had happened, Bev asked, "Molly, I need your help. We need another way inside that Galactic Expansion building. We can't defeat so many robot soldiers."

"Okay, I'm on it, but I'm stuck in this bed for weeks yet. Let me think, Bev."

"Thanks. I best head home. I'll check with you in the morning. We're going to kick alien butt."

That evening, Molly couldn't sleep. Bev had asked her to find a way into GPan. Bev's vivid description convinced her that one couldn't just walk into the building or even get within a block of it. As she lay in her Med Center bed, she forced herself to ponder Bev's request. When her idea finally gelled, she fell asleep.

***

After supper, a case of nerves struck most of the women. Leslie said, "I'm a little afraid to like go to sleep. Will I like wake up and find my arms gone, too?"

"It's damned scary," Janine said. "No offense, but I don't think I could live like Molly's been forced to live. Mary Trout couldn't." Her face flushed, and she stared at the floor.

Bev changed the topic. "Gail found a dozen men from the First Division. They're joining us tomorrow morning. Molly is thinking about an alternative way inside GPan."

Chapter 31 The End

Molly awoke. She felt terrified, but couldn't put her finger on why. The comm center display continued to play whatever was being broadcast on Channel Nine by the alien Sixth Invaders. Commander R'Ina was talking. Off to the alien's right side, the images of Ted and Helen stood as a reminder of the outcome only days away.

"Today," she began.

Just then, gunfire erupted. Bev's small force charged into the studio, large guns firing. A disintegrator shot produced a three-inch hole in the commander's forehead. She dropped like a rock. The Chief Science Officer, G'Karn, hiding under a desk, raised his hands, surrendering.

Surreal, thought Molly. *How did they get inside the GPan building?*

Bev, Gail, and some soldiers appeared in the camera's field of view.

Bev said, "Okay, GPan skyscraper is secured. All the Sixth Invaders in the building are eliminated except this one, their science officer person. He wants to say something." Turning to G'Karn, she said, "Okay, we're interrogating you now. What the hell have you done to us all?"

G'Karn said, "I'm so sorry. Commander R'Ina made me do this. But I've good news. She rushed me. You can't rush science. I made errors. I botched the male mutation. Men won't be losing their arms entirely. For a while, they will be weak, but in time they should strengthen. The commander almost shot me because I messed up. She had me working on a correction formula, which I have nearly finished. It should have been released on central Chicago tonight."

Molly doped off, similar to what happens when reading a book late at night. She awoke to find other images playing on the large display. She struggled to make sense of what she was seeing. To her, it seemed as though she was looking at a movie of another woman's life. Fragments formed the following story in her mind. *How can I be seeing this?*

Last year, Terri Torelli worked at Segway Research Laboratories in Chicago, a company devoted to finding a fetal genetic nanoparticle cure for inherited birth defects. Her husband of one year was Private Ernest Torelli, who was off fighting the Sixth Invaders on Brussels, Tau Ceti. Terri watched the GEnt coverage of what these invaders did to the soldiers they captured via the dog whistle machine.

In horror, she saw her husband being placed into the giant machine and coming out having lost an arm and leg, barely able to crutch himself away from the machine. She watched as he turned and used his remaining arm to pound the armor-encased invader with his crutch. She screamed when he was forcibly put back into the machine, this time reappearing as only a head and torso. Terri vomited, cursed, and screamed at her comm set. Then, she saw these inhuman invaders toss him into the pit along with severed hands and feet. She saw him buried alive.

Somehow, months flicked by in a haze. Molly saw Terri watching Molly's own news conference and realized that Terri had learned the truth of GD's involvement, that these invaders were really robots, that the whole thing had been fabricated by GD as a nightmarish test or plot.

She heard Terri shrieking, but her mind struggled with just how she could hear Terri.

"They're insane. All of them. Insane. Beasts. I hate them. All CEOs. All those execs. All deserve what Ernest got. They do. All of them."

Her curses echoed off her apartment walls, past the baby bed she'd purchased in hopes of soon having a child, a child who died in that hideous pit with him. She laughed. Not a normal, humorous laugh, but one filled with glee, a sickening laugh. Terri's mind cracked.

Yet, she was educated, a competent geneticist. She went along with the current push to have women appearing as beautiful Galactic Dolls. That was fine because Terri had a plan. She saw GPan had recently hired many geneticists. She applied and was hired. After signing a non-disclosure agreement, the most stringent she'd ever seen, she met the disguised alien scientist and began working for him.

After a week, she knew what they were designing and how it worked, but because of the contract she'd signed, she dared not say anything to anyone. The penalty was immediate termination. Considering what they were making, she understood why such a harsh penalty was invoked. Yet, in her mind, this was the *answer* she sought, and she often cackled to herself each evening before she fell asleep.

Terri was there when Commander R'Ina chastised Chief Science Officer G'Karn for having made such an awful blunder with the male version. When the commander ordered him to remedy his mistake, she was pleased. Vengeance was still hers to obtain. She stayed unobtrusively in the background helping him repair his errors.

He altered the sequence that defined arms. Now, instead of merely becoming thinner and weaker, they would be absorbed by the body, removing them from their physical forms. From her earlier work, she knew the two forms of the genetic mutation gold nanoparticles only differed in the sequences that resulted in arm absorption. Thus, if the new version was injected into either a man or woman, the result would be the same—a Galactic Doll who lacked arms.

When G'Karn announced he'd corrected his errors, Terri cackled and laughed in glee. Following the commander's orders, they'd created enough of the new mutation particles to redo central Chicago. The rest of the central continent would have to wait a bit longer. All that remained was to bind the new genetic agents to the proper sex controlling particles, one for males, and one for females.

Terri watched General Bev and her soldiers killing the aliens and taking control of the GPan skyscraper. That night, she sneaked back into the lab, long after everyone else had vacated the building. She bound the corrected arm loss agent to the male particles, a process that took her hours to complete.

Unlike G'Karn's method of delivery, she pre-charged the particles. That meant they didn't need to be irradiated to cause them to activate. Once inhaled, lungs would transfer the nanoparticles into the bloodstream, triggering the genetic mutation process.

She lugged the containers out to the drone EMAC spreading ship, the one that had been used to disperse the original particles into the air over Chicago and then the rest of the Midwest. At three in the morning, Terri lifted off. The spread pattern for Chicago was still in the flight controller's memory. All she had to do was select it from the menu; she pressed Execute. Terri chortled hysterically for hours until just before dawn the EMAC landed on top of the tall GPan building, its run finished.

Now, Molly realized just what Terri had done and the horrible damage this would cause. She tried to stop the insane woman, but like a nightmare, she was unable to change anything. All she could do was watch what was happening.

Terri Torelli returned home as the sun rose reddish against stratus clouds. She collapsed onto her bed, smiling at her empty baby bed. "T'is done!" She whispered to it and to the memory of Ernest, his head and torso, her only remaining memories of him. All others had long ago vanished, replaced by this nightmare image.

Images swirled. Confused, Molly gasped and looked over at Ted, who was sleeping. His regrowing arms vanished as she looked at him. They were still in the Med Center, but her arms were now those that she'd had when she was six. She doped off again.

Molly awoke. She found herself home in her apartment, along with Ted, now an armless Galactic Doll again. Everything seemed strange to her.

"Well, we've done it, dear," he said. "It's Halloween, and your plan to have us train men and boys in how to use our feet and toes as hands and feet is done. We've salvaged a good many lives—three hundred men and boys each day for months. Well done."

Her attention drifted to the comm center display. GPan executives from Moscow published some statistics. Nearly one in ten adult males or around fifty thousand found a way to commit suicide, unwilling to continue living. Most of those had been corporate executives. Another ten percent had body swapped with their wives so they could continue to earn a living, though many had new jobs and new corporate sponsors, usually with a lower subsidy. Around a half million of the males were eighteen or younger, and these had little choice but to adapt to their new body forms.

Other images appeared—fashions this time. The introduction of Leslie's new line of male Galactic Doll apparel helped raise morale. Shirts with snaps instead of buttons were tailor-fitted around their enormous busts. Their pants with Velcro fastening belts fit their new forms. Suit coats and jackets rounded out the line. Heels were problematical. A black leather heel with rounded toes became the standard for men, complete with the necessary tall heel. They didn't look at all like those worn by women. Thus, many men regained a measure of self-respect. As far as hairstyles, most men and boys kept their hair long, because the hair and nail machines automatically handled the trims for them, as well as keeping toenails trimmed.

Confused, Molly rubbed her eyes. Now, she saw news reports indicating that the various Moscow galactic corporations had taken over as the Sol Empire leaders. Here in Chicago, women had been appointed to run the many local galactic corporations, since those in Moscow declared the armless men weren't capable of running them. She yawned and doped off.

She awoke to her crying baby son. She lifted his armless body out of his crib, just as Ted made his way into the room.

"My turn to nurse him," he said. "It's a damn shame all male babies are now being born without arms."

Molly, who just knew that she was the CEO of the local GD corporation, said, "It's worse than that. All female babies born to a Chicago Galactic Doll are inheriting her genes, becoming Galactic Dolls themselves. What's troubling is that all women who were exposed here in central Chicago are also giving birth to armless boys, even though some of those women have married men from other places and those men were never infected."

Ted said, "Yes, that's what we're told. This male mutation is dominant. Galactic Robotics is gearing up to produce millions more of our helper machines and robots. Already, there are a hundred thousand new armless babies in

Chicago."

Molly's mental images drifted again, further confusing her. Now, Petr Leonovich, the CEO of Earth GPan, appeared on the display. His face looked grim.

"At this time, I have had to make the hardest decision of my life. All men and women of central Chicago are being terminated as I speak. As everyone knows, the genetic mutations of the Sixth Invaders turned those men into nearly helpless cripples, armless Galactic Dolls. Initially, many of these handicapped men found ways to kill themselves. Those who adapted, thanks to the robots and machines, and all the women who were also infected have become a global catastrophe, sucking the life out of everyone else who has to support them. Male babies are born armless, continuously adding to the gigantic problem of nearly helpless men. Today, ten years after the infection, over a million boys have been added to the problem. Their numbers are growing exponentially.

"Thus, to save the rest of Earth's population, I have to take this drastic action. Those who have moved from central Chicago will be located and terminated as well. We must put an end to this hideous mutation before the only men left on Earth will be as helpless as these Chicago men."

Molly smelled a bitter almond odor. Her mind finally made the connection: cyanide. She coughed, slumping to the floor. Turning her head, she saw her son and Ted also lying on the floor, gasping. Then darkness replaced the awful images.

Chapter 32 Attack

First thing in the morning, the group checked on each other. No more people were affected, but the three men's arms were shrinking, much to everyone's dismay. That firmed Bev and Gail's resolve to attack the aliens.

"You aren't eating anything that mechanical thing is cooking," Gail said to Bev. "I'm incredible in a kitchen."

Her mate smiled and headed into their small kitchen. Soon, Eve, Randi, and Celeste joined them. Over bacon, eggs, toast, and coffee, Bev explained what she and Gail had accomplished yesterday.

"So, we've rounded up twelve men and one woman from the First Division in the Chicago area. They're reporting here around ten this morning. You three be on the lookout for them. Now, we need a plan. A frontal assault is out. I'm hoping Molly has an idea."

An hour later, Eve, Randi, Celeste, Bev, and Gail sat beside Molly and Ted in the Med Center.

"We got weapons and men," Bev explained to Molly, "but we need a way inside."

Molly's face was ghastly pale, and she exhaled before speaking. "I'm not dead! I've just had the worst nightmare ever. So weird. So vivid. Cyanide. They killed all of us who survived this alien attack."

"Huh? What are you talking about?" Bev said.

"Must have been just a weird dream," Molly said.

"Hey, tell us about it," Eve said. "This could be important."

Molly described her awful nightmare. "It was so vivid, so real, but so disjointed."

Eve said, "There have been rare individuals who have the knack for glimpsing the future. Perhaps, Molly's done just that."

"Well, I sure don't want that future," said Molly.

Bev changed the topic. "Well, the first thing we gotta do is get inside that skyscraper. We can't go up against a hundred robot fighters."

Molly smiled and relaxed. It felt good to have told the others about her freaky nightmare. Plus, she had the answer Bev needed.

"Yes, the streets are out. I know another way. It's a sneaky way into the building—something we PIs know about. The sewer system. The turn of the century Sewer Rebuild Project here in the Loop area put in tunnels eight feet tall, all dumping into the giant recycling basin next to the lake. All the Loop building basements also drain into it. It's late spring, and it hasn't rained for several days. My idea would be to sneak into GPan from their basement sewer line."

"Molly, you *are* brilliant," Bev said. She nodded to Gail. "Great plan. Where do we get access to it? How do we find the right basement?"

"The Cartwright building's basement connects to it. It's about ten blocks to GPan. The tunnels are marked. Frank and I sneaked down there when we were in high school. I'm coming with you to show you the way."

Gail gave Bev a sharp, questioning glance.

Bev said, "Molly, you've got all these tubes stuck in you. Your arms are regrowing. No way are you going down in those tunnels. You'll have to give me directions."

Molly sighed, but Ted chuckled. He said, "Told you so, dear."

She gave him a dirty look.

Gail said, "Look, Molly, we can hook up a wireless video comm feed from us to you. Then, you can direct us from here."

"Okay. Otherwise, you're likely to get lost down there. You'll need helmets with lights on them—like miners wear."

Bev and Gail left to make necessary arrangements.

***

An army truck pulled up the back alley by Leslie's apartment complex. Bev and Gail greeted them. "Hey, brought you proper fatigues and boots, Kick Ass," one man yelled, tossing them a duffle bag. "Go change while we drink our coffee."

"Thanks," Bev said. "Guess you fellows won't get to gape at your Galactic Doll soldiers this time." Several soldiers laughed.

Wearing heavy-duty fatigues, a flak jacket that would stop a fifty-caliber slug, and heavy boots—though with heels, Gail and Bev marched out to the truck. Bev said, "Okay, check your weapons and miner's hats. We'll set up the video comm system so Molly can direct us. We're sneaking in via the storm drain tunnels."

An hour later, Molly said, "Comm check. Are you hearing me okay?"

Gail had set up a receiving unit in Molly's Med Center room, complete with headset so she could talk to them down the tunnels and see what was happening. Also, Molly was recording it.

"Hear you loud and clear," Gail replied.

Bev nodded and took the lead. Following Bev and Gail, soldiers with miner's lamps on their helmets, several types of weapons, and full backpacks marched into the Cartwright Skyscraper past the comatose guards.

"Bring up the torch. Cut this lock off the grate," General Kick Ass ordered.

A soldier went down the iron rung ladder first. He gave an all clear hand signal, and the other followed him down.

Gail brought up the rear. "It smells!"

The water level was only a few inches, but the odor was pungent, worse than rotting fish on the lake shore.

"Okay, gang. See those markings on the domed ceiling?" Molly said. "They parallel the streets above us."

She gave them precise directions, leading them junction by junction towards GPan.

Justice. Millions of men would demand justice in six more days. If nothing else, Molly wanted to give them that.

A half-hour later, the group moved up to the ladder leading up into GPan's basement. Bev flashed silent hand signs. Two men with the cutting torch moved up and cut through the lock. After more signs, men climbed up the ladder, fanning out, blasters at the ready. Gail stepped out onto the concrete floor, bringing up the rear. She moved to Bev's side, taking up her usual protective stance. Hand signals flashed, and men scattered, checking out this deep underground basement.

Without warning, Molly heard popping sounds, as though someone was making loud noises with their chewing gum. Bev moved towards the sounds, and Molly realized she had heard blasters firing. She stared in disbelief at the video coming from Bev.

Two of the gray aliens lay dead on the floor. Each had the same giant bosoms she'd seen on the broadcast, but these must be males, since they wore dresses, as had the science officer in the broadcast. What shocked her was the giant bank of electronics they had been working with. An empty cot lay nearby. Molly spotted two sets of metal head harnesses with many wires attached and connected to a machine. She suspected body swapping. But who swapped into whose body?

She had Bev pan past the instrument panels, but the symbols looked like hieroglyphics to her.

She whispered, "Holly Ann might figure this stuff out." Then, she chuckled. "Why am I whispering?"

Gail's camera pointed towards Bev, who gave Molly a grin. Bev panned over the wall of equipment; many lights suggested the equipment was in operation. She whispered to Molly via Gail's camera. "These machines might be controlling the robot soldiers. If we turned them off, the other aliens will discover it and realize they're under attack."

"Ben, stay here and see if you can figure out how to turn these things off, but wait until I signal you. We don't want to alert other aliens."

"Aye, aye, Kick Ass."

Bev led the others to the stairs. There were two stairwells in opposite corners. The main elevator occupied another corner while a large freight elevator marked the remaining corner. Considering how huge the basement was and how many smaller rooms had been cleared, Bev assigned two soldiers to basement duty. Tim and Fred took up positions from which they could watch two entrances each, leaving Ben free to study the machines. Bev split her soldiers up, sending half up each stairs, eschewing the elevators, for their unexpected use could also raise the alarm.

Sure enough, on the first floor, they spotted two more aliens guarding the main entrance doors. A hail of faint popping sounds followed; the alien women, wearing the familiar black apparel, dropped to the floor, bodies oozing a reddish blood, not dissimilar to humans. Bev's right hand poked the air above her head; Gail smiled. These aliens could be killed just like any other human or beast. After a thorough search of the floor, Bev signaled them to the stairs once more.

Outside, a dozen robot soldiers marched back and forth past the main entrance doors.

An hour passed. Bev had to search a hundred floors, each as large as the basement. But couldn't it go faster?

After finding the second and third floors vacant, though filled with uncountable offices, Bev suspected they'd not find many more aliens until they reached the hundredth floor. Still, she insisted on thoroughness. She didn't want to be confronting the alien leaders and have an unknown alien they'd missed shooting them in the back.

As they finished clearing the ninety-ninth floor, she could sense the excitement rising. This was it. The final assault against these aliens. She gave the silent signal and up her group went. Just outside the doors, over her comm, she whispered, "Go."

Gail opened her door, and Bev's group entered, fanning out, guns covering all directions. At the other end of the building, simultaneously, Sam and his half did the same thing. Each group faced a choice. Hallways led off in both directions from the stairs. Bev hand-signaled, sending half her group in one direction led by Gail, while she took the remaining men and headed the opposite way.

Gail's group of four rounded a hallway corner and looked into a huge room. She recognized it from the comm center images—the CEO's office. Mr. Armstrong's comatose body lay off to one side. Commander R'Ina stood behind the huge desk. She held a large, foreign-looking weapon. She must have been alerted to trouble. Science Officer G'Karn dove for cover beneath the desk. He was unarmed.

Gunfire blazed. Commander R'Ina fired a split second before the others. A large slug slammed into Gail's vest and exploded; her fingers clenched. The jerk caused her automatic fire to surge upwards, shattering the giant windows behind the desk. Her fellow soldiers returned fire. Commander R'Ina took several shots to her head and several to her chest before she dropped her gun. One blaster drilled a three-inch hole through the center of her head, after which her body slumped to the ground.

Molly whispered to Eve, "That's just like what I dreamed!"

Just then, the others came running up. Bev was in time to catch Gail as she slumped to the floor. "Did we get it?" Gail whispered and then struggled with her vest, frantically trying to rip it off. It smoked.

Someone yelled, "Commander's dead."

"Bev, get me out of this!" Gail said.

Bev helped her remove the vest that now had a huge hole in it. Already a giant bruise formed on her chest. Her breathing was jagged.

"Think something's broke."

"Thank heavens for the vests," Bev said. "Stay put while we check this out." Bev moved over to the fallen commander and drained her blaster into the alien's body, shredding it, nearly cutting it in half. "That's for shooting my Gail."

Meanwhile, someone alerted the basement group.

Ben relayed, "Killing the power to these machines now."

Bev saw the alien man shaking beneath the desk.

"You, alien, get up. We're not killing you. Tie him to that chair. We'll interrogate him. Find out where the rest of the aliens are. See if anyone can get that comm center going so we can broadcast this to the world."

"I got it," Gail said. "I think it only broke some ribs."

"Oh, let an engineer at it, boys," another female soldier barked. She leaned her gun against the wall and examined the electronics in the room.

Also, after Ben shut down the electronics in the basement, Bev noticed the robots just outside the skyscraper became inert. "Ben, you three go out there and destroy all the robots you can find." She turned to the alien.

"Don't kill me, please, please." Chief Science Officer G'Karn pleaded. His body twitched.

Glancing at the shredded body of the commander, Bev

realized why the man was so scared. She said, "As long as you answer our questions truthfully, we won't harm you. You've just seen why I'm called Kick Ass." She nodded towards the dead body.

"What do you want to know? I'm just a science officer."

Molly saw Bev was in no condition to question him. So she took the lead. Via Gail's comm set, she posed the questions.

"Something's gone wrong with your genetic mutations. Right?" Bev relayed the question to him.

"The men were supposed to lose their arms—according to her plan, but because of Ted and Molly's discoveries and actions, she ordered me to speed up the development. You can't rush science, but she wouldn't listen. No, it looks like none of them will lose their arms. Commander R'Ina was upset over that. She ordered me to fix that error."

"Okay. How many more of you aliens are here on Earth?"

"Just us in this building. We're just a reconnoitering squad. Twenty female soldiers and ten of us domestics and science men. Commander R'Ina thought we could capture this world or at least subdue it, preparing it for conquering by our fleet."

Molly said, "Okay. Thirty of you. Bev, how many have you found?"

"Thirteen. Fourteen counting this one. That leaves sixteen more aliens around. Where are they, science man?"

"I don't know. The soldiers know that. Wait, two are still out with the EMAC implanting your people so they know what to do when they wake from their comas, but I'm not sure."

"All right. So these nano things. How many people have been infected? How do these things get into their bloodstreams?"

"I've no idea. They were released into your atmosphere last week. Rush job. Can't be triggered until far IR beams are used. We've exposed the central part of this continent so far. The commander wanted the whole world done, but I told her that would take at least another year."

Molly asked, "So those two in the EMAC—when are they due back? Do we want them implanting more people? How do we get them back here?"

"I can call them. Not sure if they will obey me. I'm just a science officer. Wouldn't the implanted ideas be invaluable to the men when they wake up? I was against doing this mutation thing, but I've no power."

Bev rubbed her face. "Yes, perhaps we should let them finish. It's going to be a disaster. When do you expect them to return?"

"They won't when they hear what's happened to the commander."

"We're live now, General," Gail called out.

Bev swivelled around to face the camera. "Hello, everyone. This is General Kick Ass Blythe and members of your First Division. We've just terminated the commander of these alien Sixth Invaders. I think we've got the robot army disabled too. We've terminated all the aliens in the building except their science officer here. Two others are flying around Chicago in their EMAC.

"I have positive news to share. Molly and Ted Billings discovered too much of what was going on, which forced the aliens to rush their genetic mutations. Take heart. They botched it. Men aren't going to lose their arms after all. At least, we think this is so. But the men in central Chicago will be mutated into male Galactic Dolls. That much is certain.

"From what I've discovered so far, the aliens used a body swapping machine, putting their people into our CEOs, like Mr. Armstrong, using him to pull off their nefarious schemes. I suggest we appoint Molly Parkinson PI, recent CEO of GD, to be the temporary CEO of GPan. Let her uncover all the sordid details."

Molly shook her head no and told Gail, but Bev ignored them. She was on a roll.

"They built all those robot policemen or soldiers to protect themselves from us. They furloughed the entire First Division, taking our ground forces out of the picture. Yesterday, those robots gunned down unarmed women who walked too close to this building.

"Our Sol Empire leaders are in comas. You high-ranking corporate executives, get here as soon as possible. Do what you can to keep the corporations running. I don't believe the aliens will attack us anytime soon. But for at least another six days, we're defenseless. I don't know how soon I'll be able to stop the remaining aliens who may be here. There's likely another sixteen around Earth. So I can't guarantee anyone's safety. We'll try to get this recording broadcast on an endless loop so others can be informed. Expect regular press conferences soon."

While her engineer worked on setting up the replay loop, Bev had her soldiers drag the dead down to the basement.

G'Karn said, "My office is around the corner. I have a medical experimental lab down on the floor below this one."

"Are you a doctor?" Molly asked via Bev.

"Yes, that's part of my duties as Chief Science Officer. Commander R'Ina was angry that the male formulation contained the error, so she insisted I find my mistakes. Too late for the planned aerosol spray over central Chicago, but I made a new batch. She was planning another round of exposure, but you've stopped her."

Bev said, "Good god! Well, I'm glad we did. Show me your lab. Let's destroy that batch."

"Wow, Eve. This is just like I dreamed it," said Molly. "I've got a bad feeling about this." The hideous nightmare loomed large in her mind.

He led the way. "I had no choice, not really. Your society is so backward compared to ours. Males on our world stay home, caring for and raising our young; we're domestics. On your world, your men perform the work that our women do. I think that's what so confused her—roles being backward. Ah, here's my lab."

Bev entered a huge room, brilliantly illuminated by hundreds of overhead lights, institutional white and with a sterile smell. Complex medical machinery lined one side while many supply cabinets and other equipment lined the opposite side. At one end, a gigantic cooler held countless vials, bottles, and canisters. Even to Bev's untrained eye, it looked and smelled like a medical laboratory.

"My repaired nanoparticles—here they are. All these vials here contain my further researches."

"You mean the thingies that make men lose their arms?"

"Yes, the gold nanoparticles carrying the genetic mutation sequences. They're right here, but I've not yet finished them. Today, if this was injected into anyone, male or female, they'd lose their arms. She wanted your corrupt men eliminated from running the corporations so women could take control."

"How much—I mean how many people could it effect?"

"Central Chicago. I made just that much, not like the original batches, which she used to spread over the central part of this continent."

"Who else has access to your lab, this room? I noticed it isn't locked, and those refrigerators aren't secured either."

"Oh, anyone, but only my human lab assistants are ever in here, and they've not been here since we finished making this repaired batch. Terri has been helping me with that. I only finished repairing my errors yesterday, but she has already launched the irradiation process."

As she watched the streaming video, Molly realized Terri hadn't yet stolen the repaired biological agent. "Eve, it's not come true yet—my vision thing. If I really was seeing the future, this Terri woman will steal this stuff tonight and spread it over Chicago while we sleep."

"Okay, Bev. Humor us," Eve said into Molly's microphone. "Have your people remove all his genetic materials from this building. Store it some place that's safe and a place others don't know about. Then, have someone hiding in the lab. If Molly's right, this crazy woman will try to steal the stuff tonight."

"Damn scary," said Bev. "Okay, will do."

That night, Lieutenant Betsy, Bev's engineer, locked the alien up in one of the private rooms and locked down the skyscraper. She armed the automated system that would rouse her if intruders came, though anyone with a proper ID card and clearance could enter. She hid out in the lab as Eve asked

435

and dozed.

A shriek awoke Betsy. She saw a young woman standing before the empty shelves. Terri Torelli smashed beakers and vials, cursing all the while. Betsy fired her Taser and secured the woman. She locked her in a side room until morning came and General Bev could interrogate her.

***

"Bev. Gail. Wake up. Something has like happened to my feet," said Leslie. She continued to bang on their door.

Janine stepped out of her apartment. "Leslie, look at my feet." Neither women wore any shoes, but their feet rested flat on the ground. "I swear my legs and feet have un-mutated if such a thing is possible."

"Me too. Oh, my."

A sleepy-eyed Bev opened the door, staring at Leslie and Janine. She'd just risen and had wrapped a robe around her. "What's up?"

Leslie giggled. "We're lucky again."

"What's happening?" asked Gail. She joined Bev by the door.

"Like look at your feet," Leslie said.

"Hey, our feet are back to normal," said Bev.

"They like un-mutated," said Leslie.

Hank joined them, followed by Kyle. Both had taken the time to dress and wore their usual tall heels. Hank said, "That's not fair. My feet are still messed up."

"Same here. No change in mine," Kyle said.

"All right," said Bev. "Now we *are* getting somewhere."

As the group ate breakfast together, Bev said, "I'm sure glad I insisted my soldiers head home yesterday. They'll be back soon. I didn't want to gamble with the aliens. They could do something awful to us while we sleep."

***

Bev and her soldiers visited GPan once more. The bodies of the women murdered by the robots were still lying outside the building. City services were non-existent. Few ventured out of their homes, and those few women who did were scared, a fact not lost on Bev or Molly.

Molly and Ted watched from their Med Center room via

436

streaming video; Eve, Celeste, and Randi joined them.

At the skyscraper, they found the science officer making breakfast for Bev's engineer, Betsy. She'd stayed behind guarding both the alien and the skyscraper, though no one thought anyone would attack the place.

"Hey, you were right," said Betsy. "That Terri woman tried to break in here last night. She's off her rocker. Got her locked in a closet. What should we do with her?"

"Take her to a Med Center," Bev said.

When they unlocked the door and let Terri out, she cackled. "Execs will pay. Pay. Pay. No baby for me. Now they pay like Ernest paid. Give me the bio agent, please, please, please. Make them pay."

She launched into another round of insane laughter.

Bev asked, "Eve, can your therapy help her?"

"No. I've no idea how to even reach someone who is insane. Once more, technology has outstripped our humanity."

One soldier carried her out of the building, still shrieking and protesting.

Molly asked via the comm set, "Can you ask G'Karn about our feet? Will the men's feet be un-mutated too?"

"Yes, yes," G'Karn replied. "It's part of my goof. She rushed me, and I made mistakes. This is one of them. I got it right on the male version. I suppose you women could visit Med Centers and get injected with their usual Galactic Doll agent so you can get your legs and feet mutated back again. Oh, I do so love your bacon and eggs for breakfast. Such a taste treat. We have nothing like that on our world. The commander rarely let me out of this building. People used to live in some of these fancy suites, but she kicked them out during the night hours so we could do our work."

While Bev and her crew got the video system ready for more broadcasts, Celeste chatted with Molly and the others.

She asked, "Have you given any thought to all these men who will wake up in a few days? How are they going to react? Survive?"

Ted said, "Well, I thought I was a freak. Still do, but Molly doesn't. Hank doesn't because he has his arm and leg back. Kyle's fine too. But what about all the men and boys who wake up mutated?"

"I see what you mean," said Molly. "They'll need guidance and encouragement."

"Precisely. I've been wondering something, something that no one is talking about. Us—men and women—these are genetic mutations we've had. If we have babies, won't these mutations manifest themselves in our children?"

"Damn. I see your point," said Molly. "There will be a million men who potentially could have more children. Have to ask Eve about this. I'm ignorant of such things. I'm ignorant of so many things. I only made it through high school. I trained to be a good PI; that's all I used to want to be."

"And now you're not so sure?" asked Celeste.

"Yeah, I can see just how ignorant I really am." After a pause, she said, "I feel horrible. I must have missed all kinds of things when I was at GD. And now people are being hurt and threatened because of that. Maybe I'm just kidding myself about being a competent investigator. Maybe I am a pathetic loser."

Ted said, "Dear, you did a brilliant job. Honestly, I never dreamed there could be so much corruption within one corporation. Besides, the Sixth Invaders had body swapped with the GPan CEO, so there was no way they were going to let us get more discovered."

"But I still feel sick. I shouldn't have let them hide so much from us."

"My god, do you realize in those few months, you uncovered and exposed two hundred six crimes? Had over two hundred arrested? You averaged two crimes discovered and exposed each day. In my book, Cool Head, that's fabulous."

"Hum," Molly bit her lip, "when you put it that way, we were incredibly busy. Two a day? Wow. I hadn't looked at it like that, only what we must have missed."

Celeste smiled. "You're bright, Molly. I can't see Leslie going after more education or Janine either. But you have potential."

Molly chuckled. "Don't know 'bout that. Celeste, Randi, Eve, Deanna, Ted..." She paused, fighting her wetting eyes for a moment. "You have the brains. Not me. I just want to help people. That's all. Mr. Armstrong—or the alien leader—offered me a job with the Galaxy Detective Squad. I turned him down. I know Chicago, not the galaxy."

"You don't have to specialize in something, not like Eve or I have. Why don't you consider taking general education courses at the University of Illinois, Chicago campus? They have an incredible library and resources. You can take all your courses online, too."

Molly laughed. "You can see why I feel so dumb."

Eve said, "Molly, you aren't dumb. Look what you've done. You glimpsed the disastrous future for us, saw what Terri planned to do, and got us to stop her. You've changed the future for millions of Chicagoans. That's remarkable, incredibly helpful if you ask me. To answer your question, we'll have to study these new mutations before we can answer what will be transmitted to our children."

She continued, "As far as Terri goes, I understand why she cracked and wanted to do it. The average person has no way to get any form of justice in our corporate-controlled world."

A phone call interrupted them. Molly received a conference call from Petr Leonovich, the CEO of Earth GPan, and Gregor Mantovo, CEO of Earth GD, both in Moscow.

Petr said, "We've ordered men to stay well away from Chicago for the moment. We can't have more becoming infected. All attempts to replace key corporate personnel are on hold." He hung up.

"That was expected," Molly joked. "Not helpful at all."

Gail asked, "What's going to happen in four days when maybe a million men wake up to discover their bodies are Galactic Dolls? How will Chicago even function without them?"

Molly said, "They need clothing that sets them apart from us women. In my visions, Leslie created a male line of clothing for the armless men. Maybe she can still do that. Someone, call Leslie for me."

While Molly chatted with Leslie about clothes designs, Celeste continued speculating.

"I suspect many men won't be able to adapt. Just a wild

guess, but I suspect at least half the men who find they are male Galactic Dolls will find a way to succumb. Children and teens will probably do okay, but not the older men—the workers and corporate men. Many services will be adversely affected. Who will handle the deliveries, like our grocery orders? No one is picking up the dead bodies outside GPan. Women will have to step up and take over running Chicago if that's even possible."

Ted said, "Say, what about implanting the men with something like this: Men, you have to survive. You must learn new ways to do things. Stop and think how. Or have patience. Don't give up. You can do it. You know, use those mental implants for something good."

Bev overheard them and said over the comm system, "I like that. Implant them so they don't kill themselves. Implants can be a good thing, right?" She looked into the camera.

"You're knocking them unconscious and giving them an enforced behavior pattern that must be obeyed. An implant isn't a good thing. It's downright nasty," Celeste answered. "But I see your point. We'll have perhaps a million men and boys waking up in four days quite terrified. So in this case, maybe we should consider adding to their mental trauma. Let me discuss this with Eve and Randi."

Meanwhile, G'Karn sent Betsy up to the roof landing dock. Betsy reported that during the night, the EMAC with the implant machine attached had been returned by the aliens and was parked up there, but the two alien soldiers had vanished.

Later, they decided not to use the alien implant technology. Eve said, "Let's not add to this world's inhumanity."

***

That afternoon, Bev, Celeste, Gail, and Betsy transported GEnt equipment to the Med Center so Molly could hold the first of her press conferences. They brought G'Karn with them. Betsy ran the recording equipment.

"Welcome, everyone. Today, we will learn some shocking truths about what's been happening in the Sol Empire over the last twenty years. The alien with me is called G'Karn. He is part of the Sixth Invaders Recon Force, a small

440

squad of thirty, and he is their Chief Science Officer. They arrived in the Sol Empire two decades ago. Their purpose: study humans and make recommendations on how to conquer us.

"Commander R'Ina led the squad. The Sixth Invaders brought with them powerful electronic devices we call dog whistles and body swapping machines. To that, we can add mental implanting machines. Yes, they used their implant technology on all in central Chicago. That's why you say silly things like my hair is mussed up so I need to use the hair machine right now. We've all been implanted, but unlike the captured female soldiers of First Division who were given an insanity implant, this implant is more or less benevolent.

"What I failed to discover when I was temporary GD CEO was the involvement of GPan. The aliens carefully hid their and GPan's involvement from everyone. I've convinced Chief Science Officer G'Karn to explain what they did in his own words. G'Karn."

The camera zoomed in on the gray alien. "When we came here, we disguised ourselves and observed. We have devices that make our bodies indistinguishable from yours. With our body swapping machine, as you call it, our commander switched places with Mr. Armstrong of Galactic Exploration. Posing as him, she did many things. I think all that power went to her head. Unlike me, she believed we could conquer your world. How?

"We almost did it in central Chicago. In our species, males and females each have large mammary glands, because we usually have twins and our children have voracious appetites. We discovered your society has reversed the roles of males and females. On our home world, we males handle the domestic duties and raise our children. Our females run everything, much like your males do here on Earth.

"Commander R'Ina's plan was simple. First, convert Earth's women into fashionable Galactic Dolls, that resemble our females. She ordered me to help your geneticists to develop the mutation process, so I dropped key hints here and there. A husband and wife doctor team made good use of that, inventing the Galactic Doll mutation. That phase went without a hitch, though it took many years.

"She moved on to the second phase of her plan. Her recorded message outlined what it was supposed to be. All men would be mutated into what your people call armless male Galactic Dolls. She believed Earth women would then be forced to take over and control everything.

"Molly and her group discovered too many of our secret plans, forcing us to speed up our timetable. As I keep saying, science cannot be rushed. My attempts to genetically modify human males the way R'Ina wanted failed.

"A week ago, our forces released my latest formulations into the air. They took seven days to disperse the agent throughout the Midwest. Today, both types of nanoparticles are in everyone's bloodstream. I designed the particles to need a special frequency to activate them, so they can't be accidentally triggered. Humans who are not in comas now are safe from the mutations.

"Her plan of dependency also involved putting special robot machines in every home. In secret, millions of these were built by Galactic Robotics, who believed they were just following GPan's predictions of what helpful home devices were desired by people. Also, she used the war on Brussels, Tau Ceti, as a testing ground for the more advanced robots. Getting the glitches out, as we say. With their perfection, she ordered thousands. She used them as soldiers to protect our squad. General Blythe has already turned off their control circuits, so they won't be a threat to you. With the First Division furloughed, these soldier robots would have control of Chicago.

"Her plan might have worked if we hadn't been rushed. With all males on the planet turned into armless Galactic Dolls and with those few robots, she could have taken complete control of Earth.

"Finally, I'd like to add that I am pleased her plan has failed. Who are we to inflict such pain and hardship on your species? It's one thing to fight a battle and win a war fought honestly, but this—this was inhuman, to use your own term. Sorry.

"She ordered me to repair my mistake. I did so,

completing it a couple days ago. Molly discovered this, and General Blythe confiscated the agents before they could be used. So the males will not be losing their arms though they will be weakened for a time. Also, I made an error with the female mutation agent. Already some women have seen the changes. Your feet and legs are normal again." He turned to look at Molly.

Molly said, "These summaries of what's been happening will be made available to our men when they wake from their comas. I've invited several men from these corporations outside of Chicago to take temporary control here, but they're afraid to come to Chicago because sixteen of these aliens are still at large and could well cause more problems. So it's up to us who live here to keep our city functioning. I call on all women to step up and lend us a hand."

Chapter 33 Recovery

The next day, several things happened. First, Leslie called Molly. "I don't like know what's happening. A robot just like showed up at our door. It's human-like—arms and legs—and it talks."

"What's it saying?"

"It said, 'I'm here to assist Felix.' Then, it like walked into our bedroom and went inert. Plus, another one is like standing over Hank, and there's one for Ted. Celeste let it inside, but it went like dormant. She thinks it's like waiting for Ted to come home. I called Deanna. A robot is like standing beside Russell too. Oh, wait. Celeste says to turn on the comm center. A new alien message is like coming through."

Molly switched it on, but was startled to see the gray face of the deceased Commander R'Ina.

"Earthlings of Chicago. This is Commander R'Ina again. By now, you've discovered when your men and boys wake from their mutation comas, they will be armless. You've seen how well the hair and nail machines work, how adept the dressing/undressing machines are, and how the maid robot handles domestic chores.

"I'm here today to tell you that we Sixth Invaders are not inhumane. Beginning this morning, each adult male will have their own personal assistant robot, programmed to assist them with eating and personal grooming. These robots are being distributed as I speak, all automatically. Further, beginning tomorrow, three hundred thousand delivery robots will go online, serving all major stores. They will deliver your groceries, apparel orders, and so on. These delivery robots will temporarily replace those deliverymen who are no longer capable of such work. We Sixth Invaders do not want you humans to starve to death while you make the transition to a female-controlled society.

"Females, you should take control of your city, your corporations, and your companies today. A month from now, all men on the North American continent will be armless

444

Galactic Dolls for your pleasure. Two months from now, Europe will be handled. Within six months, all males on Earth will be armless Galactic Dolls. So be wise. Start taking control of your world today.

"Remember, continuous holographic videos will begin playing on Channel Sixteen showing males how to use their feet and toes, though the personal assistant robots will help them with some actions. Females of Earth, get started today. Six months from now, we will move outward to your colonies on other planets and moons of the Sol Empire. That is all for now."

The video ended. A notice scrolled saying this recording would replay in ten minutes.

Leslie, who was still on the phone, said, "Well, I guess that like explains the robots. Oh, Bev wants to talk to you. Bye."

"Molly, Bev, here. Shit's hitting the fan this morning. Moscow GD has reactivated the First Division. My soldiers are pouring into Chicago as we talk. They're terrified of being attacked by the mutation agent. So GD is ordering my male soldiers to wear biological containment suits when they enter central Chicago. They're amassing just outside the affected zone, down by the Joliet burb."

"Wow. So what is Moscow GD ordering you to do?"

"Search and destroy the remaining Sixth Invaders. Gregor Mantovo, GD Earth, is supposed to be here by noon. He said he'll get the info we need out of our captured Science Officer. I think he means to torture G'Karn."

"Crap! Okay, keep G'Karn safe for now. I'll get unhooked from these tubes and join you at GPan as fast as I can get there."

"Molly, don't you need to stay hooked up? You can't jeopardize your arm regrowth."

"This is more important, but I'll check with someone first. I figured there would be a mad dash to see who takes over controlling the empire corporations."

Bev laughed. "Sure won't be women like Commander R'Ina wanted. Say, wasn't that freaky—seeing her on the comm sets this morning?"

"She had it set up on automatic, I wager. Oops. Got a nurse here now. Call you back. Bye," said Molly.

An hour later, a harried doctor and another woman entered Molly's room. "Morning, Molly. Nurse said you wanted to leave before the process is finished? I'd advise against it," she said. "I brought along one of Galactic Medicine's geneticists, who wants to talk to you. This is Marge. As far as your arms go, they are the equivalent of an eight-year old's arms. That's how we've decided to describe the regrowth process. They are still growing, so your body requires the proper nourishment, which the IVs are providing you."

Marge said, "I work in genetics. Our problem has always been that genetic modification experimentation on humans is illegal. If we have a bright idea, we spend years testing it on mice. If there are no complications with mice, then we're allowed a very limited test on lifer criminals on Mercury. We are allowed a limited test on sample humans only if those tests go well. What I'm trying to say is that if tomorrow we think we have a way to regrow men's arms, we won't have the okay to do it for likely a decade. I wanted you to know that. But there are two other things you should know."

She sighed and continued. "I did preliminary tests on mice. This new strain that makes male Galactic Dolls is dominant over the ordinary Galactic Doll agent."

Molly frowned and said, "Huh? Simple words, please." *I hate how dumb I am.*

"It means my idea of injecting Ted here with the original Galactic Doll mutation agent to have his body regrow arms again wouldn't work. Thank heavens that's not needed, because this new mutation is dominant over the older one. What I'm saying is that right now, we don't have a way to regrow the men's arms—not like we did before with you and Ted. This new strain that's infected Chicago is untested. We know little about it. We'll need years of testing to know if these new strains can be used to regrow missing appendages."

Molly cursed, but Marge wasn't done.

"There's one more thing. I'm not sure if this is good or bad. It's the Padella doctors. Yes, Dr. Nelson Padella is in the mutation coma just like all the men are, but this new strain is repairing both his and Dr. Janet Padella's hands."

Molly's jaws clenched, but the strange look on Marge's face suggested she had more to say.

The geneticist said, "Molly, Dr. Janet Padella looks as though she's maybe twenty-five years old. Dr. Nelson already looks years younger, even though his body is in the middle of the mutation coma. In fact, when I visited their assisted living complex, all the women appear to be in their mid-twenties, not their sixties. All the men, while mutating, also look decades younger, though it's hard to tell with the men. So our older people are growing younger if that's the right term.

"And that's not all. It seems to cure their dementia, at least with the women. No one ever thought of subjecting those who had lost a limb to the Galactic Doll mutation agent until that accident with you and Ted. Same with our older people."

Molly decided not to correct her—that it wasn't an accident.

"If you recall, we got permission to run that one controlled test on Hank West. Now, the Galactic Doll mutation is the answer to regrowing lost appendages—until this new biological agent, that is.

"We've petitioned Moscow Galactic Medicine to run some controlled experiments on our older people. I hope the older Galactic Doll mutation agent will rejuvenate them, but we'll see. Anyway, I would like to obtain samples of these new agents that the alien man made and used to infect us. It may hold the clue to longevity if not a cure for dementia."

"Okay, I'll see what I can do to get you a sample. Only General Bev knows where the agent is being kept. She'll be on camera here shortly. Why not stick around and watch with us? You can tell her what you want."

On the display, they saw a dozen soldiers wearing yellow biological containment suits and carrying large blaster rifles patrolling the perimeter of the skyscraper. Then, Betsy activated the chest streaming video systems, and Molly saw Gail, Bev, and Betsy in the CEO's office on the top floor, along with G'Karn. Also, both Petr Leonovich, the CEO of Earth GPan, and Gregor Mantovo, CEO of Earth GD, were there along with six other guards, but all eight wore the yellow biological containment suits. These men were taking every precaution to avoid being exposed.

His voice muffled by the thick spacesuit-like containment suit, Petr of GPan said, "Molly, we've discussed what our response must be to this attack and disaster. Most of those who worked for your local corporation offices and those who worked for the empire-wide corporations will be transgendered Galactic Dolls. Having them in control of the corporations is a precedent that we're most uncomfortable with. Look, this whole Sixth Invader thing happened on their watch. We feel that in some way, it's the fault of those who worked for these central Chicago corporations. Thus, we're going to replace them all."

Molly couldn't believe what she was hearing. This meant that Deanna's husband, VP Russell Godwyn, was out of a job. All the contacts she had in the corporate world would be gone. Not good.

He went on, "We recognize there are many more non-corporate men who have been mutated. Our estimates suggest around twenty-three hundred corporation men are in comas, while closer to a million other men and boys are too. So, I agree with you. We need to consider how these affected men will be sponsored when they wake up. Obviously, they cannot continue on as though nothing happened."

Molly interrupted, her face taut. "Some men can continue with their old jobs, just using different ways and means and given enough time to learn to adapt. Teachers will still be able to teach. They'll just look and dress differently."

"True. There are so many men to consider. All right. I'll propose that men who wish to resume their former work may do so as long as they can prove they can still do the work. That should handle your teachers. Via video-conferences, Earth's corporate executives have discussed this at length. We wish to replace these freaky-looking corporation men, but we're open to allowing a few more Galactic Doll women to have higher positions within the corporate hierarchy. That's our best compromise."

He continued. "These transgendered men will have to find other employment, other sponsors, doing jobs more suited to women since they mostly are that. We won't abandon them, but we will investigate this Chicago mess, and those found guilty of crimes against the Sol Empire will be terminated.

"Women who are already working and sponsored can continue as normal. Yet, some women who were not working when this happened might prefer to go to work or return to a job they once had. The corporations are willing to renew or extend such contracts so that these women can support their freak men."

Molly changed the topic. "Has any thought been given to the long-term effects of these genetic modifications? Will all our children be Galactic Dolls?"

"The geneticists we've talked to are divided on this topic. More studies must be done. For now, we're confident the two child rule will suffice. If it becomes a problem, such families might be limited to one child, just as families have been for centuries.

"Molly, we'd like you to be here when we make this announcement this afternoon, so we will send a camera crew to your Med Center room."

"Okay, but Marge and I would like to talk with Science Officer G'Karn."

"Say, we've been trying to get him to divulge critical information, such as where the remaining Sixth Invaders are located, but he refuses to talk to us. Maybe you can pry the information out of him. Mind you, we'll soon have cruisers, heavy cruisers, and battleships hovering over Chicago. We're ready to blast these diabolical aliens to smithereens."

Marge went first, with Petr and Molly listening. She explained what she'd discovered about this new mutation agent of his and asked her key questions.

G'Karn said, "Yes, it rejuvenates your older men and women. I couldn't believe that your society killed off everyone when they reached sixty years of age."

General Bev told them where they could find the remaining samples and his research that she'd confiscated yesterday. Soldiers and Marge headed off to secure them for GMed.

With a sad look, G'Karn said, "Molly, your leaders keep asking me questions I don't know the answers to. Write these numbers down. It's the coordinates where decades ago we parked our spaceship. Captain L'Grina is in charge; she hates humans, so do be careful."

Before resuming his interrogation of G'Karn, Petr relayed the coordinates. Just then, one of Petr's guards cursed. "Traitor!" He fired his blaster at the Chief Science Officer, drilling a three-inch hole through his chest.

The guard laughed cynically. "Now, we will wipe out every male on this world."

Blam. General Bev fired her own gun, killing the soldier.

She said, "I bet Captain L'Grina swapped bodies with your guard so she could get close to G'Karn. Damn, didn't see that one coming."

"General, you and your sister here are in charge of Chicago for now. Men, let's get the hell out of here before they get to us!" Petr yelled.

Their heavy suits made a hasty exit quite clumsy, and Bev couldn't keep from chuckling.

Molly said, "We should give G'Karn a proper burial. He was a gentle alien who tried to do right by us."

Bev nodded her agreement. "Hell, Molly, no one has yet learned just where these aliens come from or even the name of their race and planet."

With little else she could do, Molly laid back and dozed.

***

Chicagoans called the eighth day the Shell Shock Day. More than a million males awoke from their genetic mutation coma to find their bodies altered. The automated procedures of Commander R'Ina had already provided one set of clothing to each male, along with all the machines. Thus, upon awaking, they had something to wear.

The five households rushed from apartment to apartment, when Felix awoke with a terrific scream, followed by Carl.

Leslie helped Felix dress while Holly Ann handled her baby. Then, everyone watched the special broadcasts that

450

General Bev arranged, via the talents of Betsy and Gail. The lengthy series of repeated recordings educated the terrified males of Chicago.

"Leslie," Felix said, "I'm scared. I've never known how Ted or Hank or Kyle could handle this. How are we going to survive? Pay the bills? Because I don't think I can continue as a security guard."

"Molly like gave me a good idea. We're like going to design a new line of apparel for you men, so you don't look like women. That should help. We're like going to make Costumes R Us a big company. You like should try the hair and nail machine. It works well."

Hank's phone rang, and he put Molly on speaker phone.

"Look, fellows. I've checked with Kyle's school. They've lost half of their teachers. Kyle, they want you back. Also, Hank, if you want to teach history, Kyle's high school will hire you today. Every school in central Chicago is struggling to find enough teachers to reopen school this fall. You have the summer months to work out the details. Kyle can help you."

Kyle looked at Holly Ann. "I love teaching, but those boys—she's right. They need role models. It's got to be terrifying for those young men. Hank, I think you should teach, too."

"I'd love to teach history," Hank said. "We look weird, but I've never complained because I have a whole body. Maybe we'll be able to help them. Count me in, Kyle."

Molly said, "We understand, guys. Okay then, that's settled."

Leslie asked, "So like tell me again what you saw in your vision for male clothing. Felix, you pay attention."

She grabbed a pad and took notes while Molly did her best to describe what she'd seen.

"Brilliant, Molly," said Leslie. "Come on, Felix. That like has to be our first action. We like need to design male clothes."

Hank said, "Suits would be great. We'd feel more comfortable in them than wearing women's dress gowns."

Over Molly's shoulder, Ted yelled, "He's right."

***

What of the remaining aliens? When dozens of warships

arrived at the location where the Sixth Invaders had landed their ship decades ago, they found the ship gone, but the bare ground suggested they'd recently moved the ship. As far as anyone could tell, the aliens had departed or were deep undercover. For months, Petr kept the entire world and Sol Empire under tight security, anticipating another attack that never came.

By Halloween, GPan executives published some statistics. One in ten adult males or around fifty thousand committed suicide, unwilling to continue living as transgendered men. Many of these had been corporate executives. Another ten percent of adult males had to take new jobs with new corporate sponsors, usually with a lower subsidy. Around a half million of the males were eighteen or younger, and these had little choice but to adapt and continue their educations.

The introduction of a line of male Galactic Doll apparel helped raise their morale. Shirts with snaps instead of buttons were tailor-fitted. Their pants fit their new forms. Suit coats and jackets rounded out the line. Heels were problematical. A black leather shoe with rounded toes became the standard for men, complete with the tall heel. They didn't look like those worn by women, many of whom ceased wearing such heels.

Thus, many men regained a measure of self-respect, for they looked a little more like normal men.

***

During June, Molly, Leslie, Janine, and Deanna became pregnant. Their due dates scattered around February 2353, but Molly's date was Valentine's Day. She thought it would be terrific if it happened on that day.

By July, Petr and the other world corporation leaders had replaced the twenty-three hundred men who had previously run the Sol Empire, by moving the empire-wide offices from Chicago to Moscow, but Petr allowed women to staff the local Chicago corporate offices. Many women believed this was an equitable beginning. Helen Hugo became the CEO of the local Chicago Galactic Defense.

Ted resumed work at Galactic Robotics as head of Chicago's Research and Development Department. He reported that ten of the latest robot models had vanished during the late May fiasco. Five had Prime Directives programmed into their software, but five hadn't been programmed yet. For now, everyone forgot about the ten human-like robots.

After Ted returned to work, Molly confided in Deanna, "Being a PI used to be all I desired."

"And now?" Deanna asked.

"It's not enough. When I tried to sort out the corruption in GD, I was helping. That vision I had and that we acted upon saved millions of lives. Of course, that's assuming what I saw would have happened if I'd not gotten Bev to take actions to change it. Deanna, I need to do more than just be a PI. To do that, I have to know more. Be smarter. It's just I don't know what I want to learn or could learn. In many ways, I'd like to learn genetics so I could develop cures for these mutations. On the other hand, Celeste and Eve's therapy is powerful and vital. It's salvaged my life and Ted's too. What do you think?"

Deanna smiled and then chuckled. "Nope. It's your life and your decision, Molly. But I will say this. The world has plenty of geneticists. I heard even the Padellas' are back in operation. I agree with your evaluation. Their therapy has worked miracles in my life too."

Molly laughed. "I can take a hint. We aren't just bodies with minds. Someone's got to help us, the beings, the spirits. Celeste needs a hand, and right now, I seem to have hands again." Both laughed.

The End.

A Favor to Other Readers

How about helping other readers? Many readers rely on reviews to make the decision whether to buy a book. You can help them make their decision by leaving your opinions and viewpoint in a short review of the positive things of this book. Writing the review and expressing your opinion only takes a few minutes, and other readers will appreciate your efforts.

Click this link: Sol Empire Volume 1 For the Want of Humanity https://www.amazon.com/dp/B07CCYFY6K/ scroll down to Customer Reviews; click on Write a Review, and enter your review. Thank you.

Author Information

Visit My Amazon.com Author Page
Vic Broquard Author Page

Follow My Blog
Vic Broquard's Blog

Follow Me on Social Media
Facebook
Google+
LinkedIn
YouTube

Other Books by Vic Broquard

Without Warning (fantasy)

The Trident Series: (fantasy)
   Volume 1 The Trident and the Book
   Volume 2 The Trident and the Scepter
   Volume 3 The Trident and the Resurrection

The Adventures of Elizabeth Stanton Series: (science fiction)
   Volume 1 The Evolution of the Path
   Volume 2 The Great Messiah
   Volume 3 Of Kings and Queens and Troubadours
   Volume 4 Chaos in the Aftermath
   Volume 5 Power Plays
   Volume 6 Age of Exploration
   Volume 7 Abducted
   Volume 8 The Emperor and Empress
   Volume 9 A Job Worth Doing
   Volume 10 Degradation
   Volume 11 The Second Crusade
   Volume 12 When Worlds Collide
   Volume 13 Dark Ages

The Lindsey Barron Series: (fantasy)
   Volume 1 The Rod of the Apocalypse
   Volume 2 The Board of Governors
   Volume 3 The Crown of Moses
   Volume 4 Dominus for President
   Volume 5 The National Health Care Program
   Volume 6 States Justice
   Volume 7 Cross and Double-cross
   Volume 8 Down the Dragon Hole

Zoran Chronicles Series: (fantasy)
   Volume 1 A Dragon in Our Town
   Volume 2 Dragons, Power, Courts, and War

Planet of the Orange-red Sun Series: (science fiction)

455

Volume 1 When Kingdoms Fall
Volume 2 Dark Ages
Volume 3 Age of the Towers
Volume 4 Difficillis Exitus
Volume 5 Age of the Lords
Volume 6 The Renegade Tower
Volume 7 Rebellions
Volume 8 The Aliens Return
Volume 9 Power Struggles
Volume 10 Guilds, Genetics, and Gods
Volume 11 Magi, Witches, Swords, and Superstitions
Volume 12 The Voyage of the Eagle's Seed
Volume 13 Eagle's Seed and Origins
Volume 14 Justifications
Volume 15 Responsibilities

The Return of the Wizards: Twelve Companions – The Making of Wizards (fantasy)

Slow Comes the Dark Series: (science fiction)
Volume 1 Creeping Darkness
Volume 2 Serendipity
Volume 3 Darkness Descends
Volume 4 Perversion Incarnate
Volume 5 Extermination Wars

Reclamation Series (science fiction)
Volume 1 For the Want of a Pill
Volume 2 Organ Donors

Dragons, Magic, and Me (fantasy)
Volume 1 The Box

The Sol Empire (science fiction)
Volume 1 For the Want of Humanity
Volume 2 Fear
Volume 3 Greed
Volume 4 Power Moves